The Undesired

Also by Yrsa Sigurdardóttir

Last Rituals
My Soul to Take
Ashes to Dust
The Day is Dark
I Remember You
Someone to Watch Over Me
The Silence of the Sea

About the Author

Yrsa Sigurdardóttir works as a civil engineer and lives in Reykjavik. All her adult novels have been European bestsellers.

About the Translator

Victoria Cribb studied and worked in Iceland for many years. She has translated numerous novels from the Icelandic, including works by Arnaldur Indriðason and Sjón.

The Undesired

Yrsa Sigurdardóttir

Translated from the Icelandic by Victoria Cribb

HODDER &
STOUGHTON

First published in Great Britain in 2015 by Hodder & Stoughton
An Hachette UK company

1

First published with the title *Kuldi* in 2013
by Veröld Publishing Reykjavik

A CIP catalogue record for this title is available from the British Library

Hardback ISBN 978 1 473 60549 7
Trade paperback ISBN 978 1 444 77828 1
eBook ISBN 978 1 444 77829 8

Typeset in Sabon MT by Palimpsest Book Production Limited, Falkirk, Stirlingshire

Printed and bound by Clays Ltd, St Ives plc

Hodder & Stoughton policy is to use papers that are natural, renewable
and recyclable products and made from wood grown in sustainable
forests. The logging and manufacturing processes are expected to conform to
the environmental regulations of the country of origin.

Hodder & Stoughton Ltd
Carmelite House
50 Victoria Embankment
London EC4Y ODZ

www.hodder.co.uk

This book is for my little sister,
Ýr Sigurdardóttir – a great doctor and
wonderful mother of eight

Pronunciation guide for character names
(Nicknames in brackets)

Ódinn – Oh-thin

Rún – Roon

Lára – Lowh-rra

Heimir – Hame-irr

Róberta – Roh-berta

Krókur care home – Kroke-ur

Diljá – Dilly-oh

Thorbjörn (Tobbi) – Thor-byern (Tobbee)

Einar – Ay-nar

Lilja – Lili-yuh

Veigar – Vay-guh

Hákon – How-cun

Baldur – Bal-duh

Sigga – Sick-a

Eyjalín – Aya-leen

Nanna – Nunnah

Keli – Keh-lli

Logi – Loi-yee

Kalli – Kal-ee

Helena – Heh-lena

Halla – Had-lah

Kolfinnur (Pytti) – Kohl-finnur (Tehtti)

The End

Ódinn was jolted awake by a cough. How long had he been asleep? Perhaps he'd only nodded off for a moment. He chuckled to himself and was puzzled by how breathless he sounded, though he didn't feel it. Sensing the drowsiness returning, he struggled against it. Where was he, again? An attempt to smile resulted in such a pathetic twitch of his lips that another laugh escaped him. Then there was silence – but no, he could hear the throbbing of an engine. The noise lulled him and his eyelids drooped again. He heard more coughing and half opened his eyes, looking round with some effort. He was still in the driver's seat. Beside him sat his daughter Rún, head slumped forward, black hair hanging down and masking her delicate features. He started laughing as if it were the funniest thing he had ever seen. Something was wrong. Was he drunk? No, that wasn't it: he was happy.

Rún coughed again, her head jerking up each time. Her fine hair swung gently to and fro as if in a breeze, and Ódinn almost burst out laughing again, yet beneath his weird elation he was aware that there was nothing funny about any of this.

They were in the car. Inside a garage. Ódinn's chin had sunk onto his chest. Infinitely slowly he raised his head, as if it were made of glass. Whose garage was it? He ought to know but couldn't remember. What are we doing here? Why do I feel so strange? He could sense the answers echoing at the back of his mind but they kept eluding him. It frustrated him because he knew they were desperately important.

Ódinn breathed feebly through his nose. When he blinked, his vision cleared for a moment, but with each blink it felt as if his eyes were closing for the last time. Overwhelmed now with hilarity, he managed a wide grin. He felt amazing. By a great effort of will he took hold of his daughter's little hand, which was quite limp. His inexplicable mirth died down and he squeezed her damp palm. Rún didn't stir, just hung there in her seatbelt.

A ray of rational thought pierced his haze of contentment. Something was very wrong. Why were they sitting in the car in this familiar-looking garage? He ought to know and made another effort to remember how they'd ended up here. But just as the clouds in his head seemed to be parting, the thought evaporated. Lára. Lára. Lára. His ex-wife – Rún's mother. How did she come into this? She was long dead. He chuckled again.

Now it was his turn to cough until his chest ached. When he recovered he realised how odd the air tasted. Sour. Poisonous. Still smiling, he groped for the button to turn up the blower to full blast but his arm slumped heavily onto the gearstick. It should have hurt but the pain was so dull he didn't even wince. It was as if he were wearing a thickly padded ski-suit. Glancing down, he saw that he was dressed in his ordinary clothes. Not his parka, though. That was odd. Wasn't it freezing outside? It was winter, wasn't it? Ódinn was unsure. Not that it mattered. Something – or someone? – was telling him everything was going to be all right. Perhaps it was Lára; it sounded like her voice.

God, it was depressing to see Rún hanging there beside him like that. It was spoiling his buzz. He looked away, infinitely slowly, his head still as fragile as glass. His chin touched his left shoulder and he drew back his lips in another grin. That was much better: now he could see that the window on the driver's side was open. His heart missed a beat. Outside the car the air appeared grey and misty. Why did this jog his memory? Exhaust fumes. The engine's poisonous exhalations. He knew about this, didn't he? It was connected somehow to his work. Ódinn tried holding his breath and his head seemed to clear a little. His mirth gave way to despair as he remembered having heard or read that those who die of oxygen deprivation experience a rush of euphoria just before the end. The brain grants the unlucky victim one final mercy: to die happy.

Who had done this to them? Who? Ódinn could hear himself giggling but there were tears sliding down his cheeks. He must be able to remember. Where had they been? He thought he could taste burger, and dimly recalled getting a takeaway. With Rún. But where were they now? The fog descended again, only penetrated by the realisation that he had wasted precious energy thinking about something that no longer mattered, when he should have been trying to get himself and his daughter out of the car. Darling Rún, only eleven years old. He summoned the strength to turn and look at her again. He wanted to scream but didn't have the energy. His daughter was dying before his very eyes, and he couldn't even reach out to her.

Ódinn giggled, the tears pouring down his face. He hated this. Who wants to feel hilariously drunk at the moment of their death? Let alone their child's. A rattle, half-cough, half-laughter, burst from his throat. This was the end; it was too late to change anything. He had failed his daughter. Other fathers might have succeeded in opening the door, dragging themselves along the floor to the passenger side and saving their child. All he need do to save their lives was open the garage door the merest crack. Or to save hers, at least. He didn't care about himself, as long as she survived.

Laugh one more time, his brain commanded. Ódinn obeyed, guffawing helplessly, at the limits of his endurance. Then broke off when his befuddled thoughts suddenly crystallised. He remembered where they were, though not how they had got there. Remembered why Lára mattered, although she was dead. Remembered the two boys who had died in exactly the same way, long ago. And what was more, he knew now who was responsible for their current predicament. Anger stirred feebly but grief had taken hold now, displacing even the intoxicating merriment.

Ódinn couldn't hold his breath any longer. This was the end. He opened his mouth and drank in the poisoned air.

Chapter 1

Ódinn Hafsteinsson missed the heft of a hammer in his hand, missed taking aim, raining down blows on a four-inch galvanised nail. As a student he'd never sat a minute longer over his studies than necessary, and after graduating he had quickly given up on his first position at an engineering firm because it had condemned him to spending his days hunched in front of a computer screen. Instead, he'd found his vocation preparing quotes for his brother's contracting company. This too should have been an indoor job but he managed to wangle it so that he got his hands dirty on as many site visits as possible. It had been a dream job. Yet now here he was, a desk jockey once more, pale, bored and lethargic after three months' incarceration in an office. And today was one of the bad ones: a gale raging outside, all the windows closed and a heaviness in his head that only intensified when he was summoned to see his boss.

As always, Heimir Tryggvason's lazy eye was pointing off to one side, and Ódinn experienced the usual urge to follow it to see what it was looking at. 'Come to me if there's any problem,' said Heimir. 'I'm not too clued up on the background but I might be able to help.'

Ódinn just nodded, having already thanked him twice for the same offer.

'The priority is to try and get a sense of the scale – find

out whether we're dealing with a ticking time-bomb here. I hope not, of course, but if we are we could at least get in ahead of the media – and the inevitable outpouring of public sympathy. It would make a nice change.' Heimir's lips stretched in a humourless smile, his lazy eye swivelling so far to the side that only half the pupil was visible.

'Is that everything, then? I think I'm fairly clear about what's expected of me – I'm to pick up where Róberta left off and complete the report.'

Heimir's smile vanished. 'To be honest, I'm not sure how much use her work will be to us. She was in a worse state than anyone realised.'

Ódinn opened his mouth to speak, then thought better of it. No one could have failed to notice that Róberta had been in very poor health. She had sighed at every step, and was constantly clutching at her left arm and shoulder, her face twisted with pain. Though no one said as much, few were surprised when it was announced that she had died of a heart attack. Neither had they been particularly startled to hear that it had happened at the office, after hours; she was often the last to leave. Even so, it was horrible to think that their colleague had spent a whole night dead in their work-place. And depressing that no one had missed her when she failed to make it home. It had been a nasty shock for the first employees to arrive that morning, and Ódinn was profoundly grateful not to have been among them. Róberta had been found sprawled in her chair, arms trailing at her sides, head craned back, mouth gaping and features contorted with suffering.

Why Heimir had seen fit to assign her one of the office's very few genuinely demanding projects was anybody's guess.

He was certainly no judge of character. Perhaps he'd used the same criterion he was now applying in transferring the case to Ódinn: as an engineer, Ódinn could be trusted to take a rational approach and remain emotionally detached when dealing with sensitive issues.

'I'll start by checking how far she got. She may have achieved more than we think.'

'Well, don't get your hopes up.' Heimir shot him a look intended to convey sympathy.

Ódinn rose to his feet, feeling a tingle of anticipation. At last he had been entrusted with a job he could really get his teeth into, and would no longer have to struggle to fill his days. This was a serious case, a report on the Krókur care home, which had operated as a residential home for delinquent boys in the 1970s. He was to find out whether the boys had suffered any lasting ill effects as a result of mistreatment or abuse and, if so, whether they had a right to demand damages. The home was unusually shrouded in silence; no former residents had come forward to ask for compensation or pour their hearts out in the media – with any luck because there was nothing to tell.

'You'll find Róberta's files in her cubicle.'

Even a lowly entity like the State Supervisory Agency had its unofficial pecking order. All employees were allocated the same bland office furniture, but some got to sit by a window, while others faced a white, Artexed wall. Ódinn belonged to the latter group, yet considered himself a rung above Róberta, who had been stuck in a corner as far from the action as you could get. The only visitors she had were those who had specific business with her. But at least she'd had peace and quiet to work in, and, whereas others had been ordered to remove all personal touches, no one had made a fuss about the pictures that adorned her cubicle. Possibly no one had even noticed them. Now, faced with her wall, Ódinn could make no sense of the collage; it was like an intricate picture puzzle with no discernible connection between any two images.

'Kind of crazy, don't you think?' Diljá Davídsdóttir, who occupied the neighbouring cubicle, was peering over the partition, glad of the distraction.

'I don't know. Better than a blank wall.' Ódinn bent to examine one of the pictures, which, unlike the rest, was an original photograph rather than a printout. Judging by the clothes and faded colours, it was fairly old. A few more years and all that would remain would be a shiny white rectangle. 'Are these relatives of hers?' The photo was of two teenage boys in a grassy hollow, wearing jeans with turn-ups and rather grubby, threadbare jumpers. At first there seemed something vaguely familiar about the older boy, but, on second glance, this impression faded. He probably just had one of those standard-issue Icelandic faces. Also, Ódinn now realised, the boys looked so different that they could hardly be from the same family.

'Search me. She wouldn't answer my questions and I wasn't about to beg. I just left her to her cutting and pasting.'

Ódinn straightened up. It was pointless trying to work out the rationale behind the collage when the only person who knew it was lying in her coffin in Grafarvogur Cemetery. He decided to start with the paperwork. Out of the corner of his eye he noticed that Diljá was still watching. 'Did she have some sort of filing system?'

'God, yes. She was about the most organised person I know.

8

Though whether it'll make sense is anyone's guess.' She regarded Ódinn with wide blue eyes. 'I bet it's insanely complicated.'

'I hope not.'

'Why are you interested, anyway? Have you got to go through all her stuff?' She grinned broadly. 'Yay! I was sure I'd be lumbered with that.'

'Don't celebrate too soon.' Ódinn opened a file and flicked through it. 'I'm only supposed to focus on material relating to the Krókur care home. Presumably someone else'll have to deal with the rest. You, maybe?'

That wiped the smile off Diljá's face. Her red lips thinned into a straight line and her jaw clenched. 'I wouldn't touch that job, and if I were you I'd find a way to get out of it.'

The file he was holding did appear to relate to Krókur, so he put it on the desk and grabbed the next one. 'Well, I'm not exactly drowning in exciting projects.' Over the years the office had found itself increasingly sidelined. Others had proved perfectly capable of solving the cases that had once fallen within its domain, and all that remained were crumbs from the tables of more powerful government offices, or assignments that Heimir managed to cadge at his monthly meetings with the representatives of other agencies and ministries.

'Still, you wouldn't catch me investigating a load of juvenile delinquents,' she replied. 'Even if they were abused. It's all water under the bridge, and it's not like they were innocent victims like the kids at the other homes.'

'Calling them juvenile delinquents is a bit harsh.' Ódinn replaced the second file, which turned out to have no connection to Krókur, and took out a third. 'From what I can gather their offences were pretty minor. After all, they were only in their early teens.'

Diljá snorted. 'Like that means anything. Children are perfectly capable of committing crimes. The other day I saw a discussion on Kidsnet about a boy up north who's supposed to have murdered two children. He wasn't even a teenager. For all you know, there may have been one of those at Krókur. I'd pass.'

'There weren't any murderers there. It would have been mentioned.'

Diljá's eyes strayed to Róberta's desk. 'She used to talk to herself all the time. Róberta, I mean.' She hesitated, then continued: 'Sometimes it was just muttering to herself. But now and then I couldn't help hearing every word. And, I'm telling you, it was *really* weird shit.'

'So?' Ódinn said absently, his attention on the files. Diljá's dark hints held no interest for him. They hardly knew each other but he'd never been impressed by the endless stream of gossip she produced over the coffee machine, about people he'd never heard of or politicians who pissed her off. Not for the first time he thanked his lucky stars that he hadn't gone home with her from a work party two months ago. The offer had definitely been there, and at the time spending the night with her had seemed like an excellent idea. But he'd had to pay a visit to the gents and by the time he got back she'd turned her attention to the office's only other single man. For the next few days the atmosphere between Diljá and this man had been so tense that it was a relief to everyone when one of them was absent. If Ódinn ever found himself a girlfriend, it wouldn't be at work. Not that it was likely to happen anywhere else either. A single parent with an eleven-year-old daughter, not particularly handsome and far from loaded – a man like that was hardly going to be the hottest bachelor in town. But he couldn't complain. Casually mentioning his daughter was often all it took to persuade a one-night stand to leave before breakfast.

'You know what I think? I think that case was the death of her. There's something creepy about it and I'd think twice before taking it on.'

'I've *already* taken it on.' Ódinn had no interest in prolonging the conversation by pointing out that Róberta's illness had long predated her investigation into the fates of the boys at Krókur, though whether a demanding case had proved the final straw was another matter.

Personally, he was confident that it wouldn't get to him; he had no intention of becoming emotionally involved with other people's suffering as he had enough of his own. Unlike the wretched boys at Krókur, however, he had been responsible for his own fate. At twenty-four he'd met Lára, the future mother of his child, who had been two years older. They had moved in together, got married, and a year later had a daughter. Her arrival had finally brought home to him what should have been obvious long before: that he and Lára were hopelessly unsuited. When he walked out on Lára and their newly christened daughter, his wife hadn't seemed unduly upset. They'd both adapted to the change and life had carried on as normal, though doubtless it had been much tougher for Lára than for him.

Then, less than six months ago, disaster had struck. Lára had fallen out of the window of her flat and his life had undergone a transformation. Ódinn the weekend dad was a thing of the past; fatherhood no longer consisted of a film and a visit to the Hamburger Factory every other weekend. He had changed jobs in order to be able to take proper care of his daughter, and his uncomplicated, cushy existence was history. Though still not used to the change, he was gradually finding his feet.

'I'm not kidding. I often used to hear her groaning as if the stress were killing her.' Seeing that Ódinn was unimpressed, Diljá added, with slightly less vehemence: 'Sometimes it sounded like she was talking to someone. Though not to me, that's for sure.'

'I expect she was talking to herself or muttering under her breath. It's not that unusual, especially when someone's ill.' As far as Ódinn was aware heart disease didn't usually manifest itself in delirium or bipolar episodes, but what did he know? He regretted letting himself be drawn into gossiping: if he'd resisted, Diljá might have given up and left him to get on.

When she spoke again there was no trace of the little-girl voice she adopted to appeal to men; she sounded like an adult, albeit an indignant one. It was a distinct improvement. 'I know what I'm talking about after listening to her for nearly two years. She wasn't like that until recently. The change had something to do with that case. It's up to you whether you believe me or not. Just don't say I didn't warn you.' She sat down again without waiting for his response. Although she'd be able to hear him over the flimsy partition, he decided not to answer. When it came to women, he had a tendency to put his foot in it. He went back to examining the files.

It was too late to resurrect the conversation when he finally came across a second folder of documents relating to Krókur. Oddly enough, he found himself missing Diljá's chatter; it would have provided a comforting backdrop to what he now read. The first page was a photocopy of the picture on the wall of the cubicle that had caught his attention. Underneath, Róberta had written two names and placed a cross after each:

Thorbjörn (Tobbi) Jónasson †
Einar Allen †

Only now did Ódinn notice the cold draught blowing on him from the air-conditioning vent above his head. Goose bumps crept over his scalp and he snapped the folder shut. His own cubicle wasn't as chilly; he would take a closer look at it there. But the clumsily drawn crosses hung vividly before his mind's eye. Shaking off a feeling of unease, Ódinn quickly left the cubicle. He didn't care for the way the boys in the photo were watching him. Maybe it was the knowledge that they must have looked on equally impassively during Róberta's death throes. Perhaps they had welcomed her on the other side, finally able to tell someone what had happened at Krókur.

Chapter 2

January 1974

One of the washing-up gloves was leaking. Aldís gritted her teeth and carried on; it wasn't worth changing the scummy water for the few things left to wash. Besides, she couldn't face another lecture on extravagance and waste. She hadn't a clue what washing-up liquid cost but from the fuss they made here you'd have thought it was liquid gold. She had to use it so sparingly that the bubbles disappeared as soon as she put the dirty dishes in the sink. And it wasn't as if she was washing up for small numbers, either: seven boys for dinner, thank you very much, plus staff, not including herself. If the couple in charge had been in their right minds they'd have invested in a dishwasher long ago. But no, she'd be lucky if she got a new pair of gloves.

'Why are you always so bloody slow?' It was as if the mere thought of Lilja and Veigar had drawn the woman to her. She had crept up behind Aldís and was now breathing down her neck. 'You know we've got a new boy arriving later and you've still got to make up his bed.'

'No, I haven't.' Aldís was well aware this would be misunderstood; it was almost as if she wanted the woman to have a go at her.

'For goodness' sake, we've been over this a hundred times.

14

How could you forget? It's not as if you're required to use your brain much here.' From her tone it was clear that Lilja relished this excuse to nag.

Aldís met her own eyes reflected in the window over the sink. It was pitch black outside as the snow had thawed in the unusually mild weather and none had fallen since. 'I meant I haven't got to make up his bed. I did it earlier.' Her words were met with silence and she sensed that Lilja was casting around in vain for a put-down. 'I knew I wouldn't have time this evening, so I thought I'd better do it while the boys were out.' The new boy had been allocated the top bunk in a twin room. No one had slept in it since his predecessor had left a month ago; a boy so quiet that although he had only been gone a short while, Aldís couldn't for the life of her remember what he looked like. Perhaps it explained his success as a shoplifter before he came to Krókur: in that line of business invisibility was a definite plus.

'So you actually showed some initiative for once.' Lilja was incapable of praise. On the rare occasions she was pleased, it sounded no different from her scolding. For the first few weeks after Aldís had started her job, six months ago, she'd had no problem with the woman, but for the last two months Lilja had gone around looking like a thundercloud. It was hardly surprising under the circumstances. And she was especially bad when Veigar was away, as he was now, though fortunately this didn't happen often. Absurd as it seemed, Aldís got the feeling Lilja didn't trust her husband, though all he was doing was collecting the new boy. They were made for each other, really: she bitter and twisted; he in a perpetual bad mood. How could a woman fall for a man like that? Aldís couldn't understand why Lilja would worry about him cheating on her; it must be due to her recent ordeal. Perhaps Veigar had lost interest in her after what happened. It occurred to Aldís that he might be confronted with the same image she was whenever Lilja appeared – a vision of horror that it was impossible to erase from one's memory.

Aldís resumed the washing up. She didn't want to think about that now; enough was enough. She banged the crockery to block out the woman's heavy breathing behind her. There was no point suggesting Lilja go somewhere else; although the others were still working, she never stood over the male employees. They probably made her nervous.

Aldís felt uncomfortably aware of the clammy rubber glove as it occurred to her that Veigar might have started giving her the eye and that this was the explanation for Lilja's behaviour. The thought was unbearable. The boys were bad enough. Their eyes followed every step she took, until at times she felt like a hen forced to walk past a pack of wolves. She wasn't really afraid anything would happen but the sensation of being watched made her uneasy. They ranged in age from thirteen to sixteen and she was almost twenty-two, but the age gap didn't bother them; it was enough that she was female. However hard she tried to disguise her figure under baggy clothes or neglect her appearance – hair scraped back into a ponytail, face bare of make-up – the boys' eyes continued to track her every movement. And their number was about to increase.

To complete her discomfort, a deafening silence always fell when they started staring, as if they were waiting expectantly, though for what she neither knew nor wished to know. In the middle of the night she often started up from a recurring dream in which seven boys were gazing at her, wordless and unblinking. Although she could never remember the rest, when she tried to recall the dream the next morning her heart would start racing and all she could see were those lightless black eyes. Her half-hearted attempts to convince herself that her dream reflected the boys' yearning for kindness and warmth were in vain, and eventually she'd learnt that it was best to dismiss it from her mind once she was awake. Just turn over and concentrate on something else. Like when would be a good time to hand in her notice and get out of here. Mentally calculate how much money she had managed to put aside each month and how much she had accumulated in savings stamps. If she wasn't mistaken, she'd be able to move to Reykjavík before long, having saved enough to cover the rent of a room and her upkeep while she was looking for a job. A proper job. And she'd never set foot here again. Never in a million years. She wouldn't miss a thing.

With the last plate finally in the rack, Aldís ripped off the gloves, releasing a foul smell of rubber. 'We need new gloves. These are leaking.' Lilja was still in the kitchen, no longer breathing down Aldís's neck but inspecting the glasses in the cupboard for smears. She pretended not to hear. Rather than repeat herself, Aldís put down the gloves and said goodnight. It was probably just as well; if Lilja was ignoring her, she wouldn't be able to come up with further chores for her to do. Aldís left the kitchen, fetched her anorak and went outside.

Her room was in a small bunkhouse, a stone's throw from the main house. The farm consisted of three residential buildings, a cowshed and two smaller tumbledown sheds. The previous tenants had scraped a living from a handful of livestock, but when Veigar and Lilja took over they'd been faced with two choices: either throw in the towel or diversify. The upshot was a home for young offenders, with a little animal husbandry on the side. Not that the location in the remote south-west of the Reykjanes peninsula was particularly suited to farming, with its small pastures and barren, windswept terrain. Perhaps those who built the houses had planned to clear away the lava-field and sow grass for hay, but little had come of it. And it was too far from the sea to provide additional income from fishing. Maybe the original tenant had been after peace and quiet. There was certainly no shortage of either.

It was around half an hour's drive to the nearest settlement, Keflavík, and over an hour to Reykjavík. To begin with, Aldís had planned to go into town as often as possible but in the event she was seldom offered a lift. She had no car herself and her requests to ride in with Lilja and Veigar had been greeted with a marked lack of enthusiasm. Either the car was full or they were unsure when they'd be coming back, and so on. As it was hardly the end of the world, she didn't insist; it merely meant she spent less money and so would be able to leave all the sooner.

With every step she felt a lessening of the numbness that had slowly and inexorably taken up residence in her soul during the day. She started looking around for the poor bird that had been stranded here last autumn, left behind when the other migrants headed south. Perhaps it had realised when the others took to the air that it was too old for the journey, or perhaps it was injured in some way. Pitying the lonely, defenceless creature, Aldís had taken to slipping it crumbs and other leftovers from the kitchen, which had probably kept it alive, for now. Who knew what its future held?

The bird was nowhere to be seen but Aldís placed a dried crust in the usual place by the end wall of the main building. The spot was sheltered from the worst of the storms and as long as it didn't start snowing heavily, the bird would be able to feed on it later. She quickened her pace, though it wasn't as if she had anything to look forward to; she usually sat in bed and read after work, or listened to the evening radio serial before going to sleep. The story was seldom to Aldís's taste, but she preferred it to the snores of the workmen who shared the bunkhouse.

There was a faint smell of smoke and the orange glow of a cigarette lit up Hákon's face. The three men who boarded with her all chain-smoked. Usually they stank out the house, but from time to time even they would be driven out by the choking fug to sit on the steps instead. Hákon was staring into space and didn't turn, though he must have been aware of her presence. He was a man of few words and, despite having slept under the same roof as him for six months, she knew little about him. The same was true of Malli and Steini who also had rooms in the dump that went by the grand title of 'staff accommodation'. Among themselves they simply referred to it as 'the little house'. There was a communal sitting room that none of them used much: the television was broken and there were two cards missing from the pack on the coffee table. It was better to sit in one's room and daydream.

'Only just knocking off?' The words were accompanied by puffs of smoke that Hákon couldn't be bothered to exhale.

'Yes. The boys took ages over the fencing and came in late for supper.' The boys were expected to perform general chores around the farm, unpaid. Occasionally, they were lent out to other farms, and were allowed to keep the wages they earned from that, as well as for the odd bit of casual labour at one of the fish factories in the Sudurnes district. Yet for the amount of work they did, the poor creatures were paid a pittance. Like her.

'There's a new boy arriving later.'

'Yes.' There was little to talk about at Krókur and on a normal day Hákon would have made do with nodding at her and maybe saying goodnight. He was quite a bit older than her and, if Lilja was to be believed, had a criminal record as long as your arm for minor offences, such as forging cheques and committing burglaries to finance the unbridled drinking that he had, by his own admission, finally managed to get under control. Yet his eyes were still evasive and his hands couldn't keep still. 'Do you know anything about him?' Aldís added, so as not to seem curt. Not that she had the slightest interest in the boy. They turned up, full of anger, creating all kinds of scenes, but their cockiness was quick to wear off. Even the most highly strung and violent were crushed in the end by the futility of the place. They received no visits and no letters. And nor did she.

'He's from Reykjavík, I think. Messed up big time, so the system kicked in. Seems he's not one of the usual trouble-makers who've burnt all their bridges.'

'Oh? What exactly did he do?' Aldís watched as the cigarette smoke vanished into the darkness, only to be lit up by the headlights that now appeared at the bottom of the drive.

'Something bad. Really bad, by the sound of it.' Hákon took a final drag. He rolled his own cigarettes and Aldís had often admired the way he could smoke them right down to his fingertips.

They lapsed into silence and watched the car, a large, battered American model, make its slow way up to the farmyard. The headlights were switched off and all was dark again until the car door opened and a light went on inside. They couldn't see much but knew one of the figures must be Veigar. The other was slimmer and looked younger from the way it moved. When the doors closed, they appeared as silhouettes, making their way towards the main building, the boy's progress hampered by a large suitcase that twisted his body as if he were crippled. But he must have been strong, since he kept pace with Veigar, who didn't bother to lend him a hand. Perhaps the boy had declined his help.

'Something tells me this is going to be interesting. To put it mildly.' Hakón rose stiffly to his feet and flicked the butt into the darkness.

Aldís looked at the door that had closed behind Veigar and the boy. 'He'll be no different from any of the others. A pain in the arse at first, but he'll learn to toe the line. They all knuckle down in the end.'

'Maybe.'

'You don't agree?'

'There are always exceptions. Sure, most of the poor buggers end up like sleepwalkers, as you say. But not all of them.' Hákon spat on the gravel, then wiped his mouth with the back of his hand. 'Some start out bad and end up worse. I've worked here long enough to see that. You're lucky you haven't had to witness it. I'd watch myself if I were you.' He said goodnight, leaving Aldís on her own. She mulled over his words, unsure whether to dread or look forward to what was to come. She told herself any variety would make a nice change, but deep down she knew this wasn't true.

That night she dreamt the familiar dream, but this time she woke up, sweating in terror. Something had changed; the staring eyes were more menacing than before and the circle the boys had formed round her was tighter. She gazed up at the ceiling, vainly trying to recapture the feeling of security that sleep had deprived her of. Closing her eyes tight again, she forced herself to think about something else. About Reykjavík and how she would decorate the room she was going to rent; the stereo she'd buy; the records she'd listen to. It almost worked but then she felt the bad thoughts coming back. She struggled to hold onto the image of the stereo by murmuring the names of the bands who would have a place in her record collection, but it was no good; instead she saw again the blood-spattered floor of Lilja and Veigar's bedroom, the dark-red pools on the white sheets. Aldís wanted to scream. Why couldn't she forget this, like she had forgotten so much that actually mattered? Like what year the Treaty of Kópavogur was signed, which had led to her failing her history test in the sixth form, though she'd done her best to memorise the date. Perhaps she should have tried to forget it. That way it might have stuck.

She rolled onto her right side, then back onto the left. Neither position felt comfortable, so she tried lying on her back. But that's how Lilja had lain, screaming and bellowing in childbirth, so she hastily turned onto her stomach. If only the woman had kept her voice down, Aldís wouldn't have been eavesdropping outside their house when Veigar appeared with the bundle in his arms, his face as white as the only part of the sheet that wasn't soaked in blood and mucus. She had known at once that something was seriously wrong: towards the end Lilja's cries had suggested not physical pain but a very different emotion, and people didn't usually cover newborns with a sheet the way Veigar had done. Invisible in its wrappings, the baby was uncannily still and made no sound.

Aldís sat up. They had ordered her to clean the room and change the bed, and she could still smell the iron reek of blood. The smell alone would hardly have haunted her like this; she might have felt a little queasy at the memory for a few days afterwards, before forgetting all about it. But Veigar had tripped as he staggered away from the house and the sheet had slipped. Aldís expelled a breath and rubbed her eyes. If only she hadn't seen that deformed, grey head. At first she had taken it for a plastic doll whose head had been bashed in. Then she had realised that it was a baby, covered in some kind of white grease. The head appeared to stop short just above the eyes, yet there was no sign of any injury. Fine black tendrils of hair were plastered to the skin and the skull appeared to have been squashed flat by natural causes. The eyes were closed but, as she gaped in horror, they opened, seeming to meet her gaze. Staring, black eyes, like those of the boys in her dream. Either she was mistaken or the eyelids had flipped open when Veigar tripped. Neither theory seemed plausible for more than a moment, but they were at least bearable, unlike the third possibility – that the child had not in fact been born dead.

Aldís pulled the pillow over her head and lay face down on the mattress, humming a tune her mother used to sing when she was absorbed in her knitting. Aldís didn't want to think about her mother either, but even she was preferable to a deformed, dead baby. Thinking about her mother stirred up only hurt resentment, not horror.

23

As she was dropping off again, she was disturbed by a rustling outside the window. It wasn't the noise itself that made her strain her ears but the thought that there might be someone out there. Was the window open or shut? The curtain didn't appear to be moving, which was a good sign, but then the evening had been airless and still.

Aldís listened to the sound of her own breathing, prey to unsettling thoughts. No one knew what Veigar had done with the baby. He hadn't left the farm for days after the birth and, as far as anyone was aware, no priest or doctor had taken the child away for burial. If Hákon was to be believed, Lilja and Veigar were too God-fearing to consider burying an unbaptised child in consecrated ground. He reckoned the infant had been shoved in a hole somewhere on the property or quite simply thrown in the dustbin. Aldís refused to believe that anyone could be so heartless as to treat the body of their own child like rubbish, so in the following days she had searched the area for any trace of a small grave. In the end she concluded that if the child had been buried on the farm it wasn't anywhere obvious, as there was no sign that the soil had been disturbed. She had no idea what had become of the poor little mite.

The quiet scratching started up again and Aldís squashed the pillow over her ears. Hard as she tried, she couldn't remember if she had closed the window. And absolutely nothing would induce her to get up and check.

Chapter 3

There were so many things Ódinn wished he had done differently in life; so many decisions he'd made that had seemed unimportant at the time but were to have far-reaching consequences. One was the impulse to stay in town that fateful night instead of heading home with his friends once the fun had begun to wear thin. It wasn't the first or the last time, and as a rule it didn't matter; he'd just wake up a bit more hungover than usual, having run his card through the machine once too often, but on this particular night his loitering downtown had cost him more than a sick headache.

He'd got chatting to a young woman in the taxi queue. Her name was Lára and she'd been as unsteady on her legs as he was. He couldn't for the life of him recall what they had talked about but she had evidently fallen for his slurring, drunken chat-up lines, since they had ended up back at his place. The sex on that occasion had also failed to leave any impression on his memory, though if it had been anything like it became later on, that was no great loss. Unless the first time had been different. In any case, he had rung her a fortnight later after the woman at the dry cleaner's had handed him a crumpled note with Lára's phone number on it, which had turned up in his trouser pocket. Never before or since had a dry cleaner returned to him so much as an old credit-card receipt.

But it had happened and there was no going back. Ódinn had smoothed out the note and called to invite Lára out to dinner, setting in motion a chain of events that still showed no signs of ending, though her part in it was over. He'd had countless opportunities to extricate himself after that first proper date but instead they had moved in together and finally got married, despite all the evidence that they were unsuited. There were moments when Ódinn had been on the point of suggesting they go their separate ways, but each time she'd done something to charm the pants off him, and he'd abandoned the idea. Not until after the wedding did they realise the truth, and when the subject of divorce came up, they found themselves, almost for the first time, in agreement. But to their mutual surprise, Lára discovered she was pregnant, so nothing had come of it.

The arrival of their daughter had only made matters worse. She was a difficult baby from day one, constantly colicky and always crying, and although Ódinn adored the little creature, his love faded in inverse proportion to the growing bags under his eyes. Shortly after their wedding, he and Lára had purchased a small attic flat in the town centre, and this had gradually come to seem like a prison to him. It didn't help that Lára suffered from postnatal depression, and even when awake was reluctant to talk. After four months he could take no more. When he walked out he left the flat to Lára, taking it for granted that she would take custody of their daughter, or he wouldn't have left. To his mind, Lára had got by far the worse end of the bargain, so he didn't like to demand back his half of their small deposit. She kept the child and the roof over their heads; he got his freedom.

What a shit he had been. He could see that now that

everything had fallen apart in his hands. After moving out, he'd only needed to look after his daughter every other weekend or when things were difficult for Lára. Not that he'd even kept to this part of the deal. The more time passed after their divorce, the less often she turned to him for help, and ashamed as he was of the fact now, he'd justified it to himself at the time on the grounds that his job was so hectic, he needed to rest on his days off, et cetera. Lára had always got her child maintenance regularly, at the beginning of every month, which was surely what mattered most. Actually, the state had taken care of that before sending him the bill, but still . . . One thing was certain: he wasn't proud of his conduct now.

He was sitting in his car outside the sports hall, waiting for Rún. Feeling a sudden icy chill, he reached out to turn up the heater, only to discover that it was on full. He pushed the blower up as high as it would go but nothing happened. Irritably he blew on his hands, consoling himself with the thought that the car had never gone wrong before. Perhaps it was a temporary glitch. But it would be impossible to drive with a broken heater in this freezing weather, so he tried banging the dashboard. Nothing happened. He raised his fist again, only to stiffen at a sudden creaking noise from the back seat. There was nothing inherently menacing in the sound, yet his heart began to pound. A series of news items about drug addicts and drunks attacking taxi drivers late at night ran through his mind, and implausible though it was, it occurred to Ódinn that a criminal might have hidden in his car. There was a rustling noise from the shopping bag he had chucked in the back earlier. Perhaps some undesirable had been lurking in the supermarket car park. But of course that was impossible because the car had been empty when he put the shopping in. Resisting the impulse to open the door and jump out, he forced himself to snatch a glance over his shoulder. The back seat was as empty as it had been when he got behind the wheel. It must have been the contents of the bag settling. He heaved a sigh of relief, grateful that no one had witnessed his foolish panic.

It was probably his conscience pricking him because he had been thinking about Lára. He'd never admit it, even to himself, but for a split second he'd had the feeling she was sitting there behind him, horribly mangled from her fall, gloating over his regrets. Absurd. Nevertheless, he switched on the radio to drown out any further sounds from the back.

A few minutes later he spotted Rún's small figure emerging from the sports hall, and switched off the radio. Her name struck him now as rather an adolescent choice, but then he and Lára hadn't been very old when they'd pored over the baby books in search of the perfect, unique name, after the ultrasound had revealed their child's sex. She was eleven now, but had little in common with her age group. She walked out alone, head down, while the other girls had already left the car park in a chattering, giggling bunch. This didn't necessarily mean there had been an incident; Rún was unsociable and subdued by nature. When she caught sight of the car, however, she smiled, waved and speeded up.

Considering his shortcomings as a father, it was amazing how she had always idolised him. At the end of her daddy weekends she had invariably asked why she couldn't live with him instead, and, coward that he was, he had always told her that her mother wouldn't allow it. He had done other things he was more ashamed of, but it stung to recall it now. Still, a white lie was better than admitting that he didn't feel up to taking her on, or, if he was being honest, couldn't be bothered. Well, that was no longer an option. She lived with him now and would do so until she left home.

'Hi, sweetheart.' Ódinn squeezed her thin shoulder and the shiny orange fabric of her anorak crackled. 'How did it go?'

'All right.' Rún smiled thinly, not showing her teeth. 'I want to give up handball.'

Ódinn bit back a comment. They'd had this discussion three times a week for months – after every single session, in other words. But he was adamant: she had promised to keep it up all winter, and she was to stick to her word. She hadn't made any friends yet at her new school, and he'd hoped that handball practice would help bring her out of her shell. Not that he had a clue how little girls made friends. When he was her age they'd barely existed for him; sure, there were girls in his class, but he and the other boys hadn't associated with them. What he did remember, though, was that the handball girls used to hang around together. 'Give it time. Soon you'll be furious with me if you have to miss a session.' He squeezed her shoulder tighter as if by doing this he could toughen her up a little. 'Remember the deal. You stick it out and we'll go somewhere nice this summer.'

Rún chewed her upper lip and stared out of the window. Her eyes were filled with an inexpressible pain that Ódinn had no idea how to address. He felt guilty for not having sought professional grief-counselling for her, as their GP had urged. Instead he had trusted his gut instinct, which didn't seem to have turned out particularly well. Suddenly, she turned to him, no longer looking sad. 'Let's go home. I'm hungry.' She didn't mention their deal, and neither did Ódinn. What was the point? She was going to the next handball session and they both knew it.

They didn't speak much on the way home, but that wasn't unusual. Neither was chatty by nature. They were alike in this, though so different in appearance. She was uncommonly petite and delicate, whereas he was big and burly; she had dark hair and eyes, and strikingly pale skin that never seemed to tan; he was fair and blue-eyed, and caught the sun the moment he set foot out of doors. Chalk and cheese.

Ódinn drove straight home. His brother Baldur, who had built their block of flats, liked to refer to it as a condominium, but even that wasn't enough to shift the apartments. Apart from the old lady on the ground floor, and him and Rún on the second, the building was empty. Baldur had sold Ódinn the flat for a knockdown price when Rún unexpectedly came to live with him and he'd been forced to say goodbye to his bachelor pad in Hlídar. At the same time Ódinn had quit his demanding job with his brother's firm and started at his current workplace. New flat, new job, new life.

He smiled as he drove up to their block. The advantage of their new home was that there was never any shortage of parking spaces. He generally used the ones outside because there was something so depressing about the empty underground garage. As the old lady didn't own a car, the garage resembled the set of a disaster movie in which he and Rún were the sole survivors. He ignored the real reason for his reluctance: the vague fear that someone was lying in wait for them, lurking behind the rough grey concrete pillars. Ridiculous, of course.

They stepped over the pile of junk mail in the entrance

hall and climbed up to the second floor. From the old lady's flat came the faint sound of a radio; otherwise all was quiet. The lift had never worked, but father and daughter didn't mind the stairs since the shopping bag was light, containing nothing but flat-cakes, butter and cheese for Rún's packed lunch. Ódinn hadn't yet got the hang of organising the food shopping for the week, so was forever having to pop out for small purchases and then again for things he had forgotten. He'd learn eventually, as he would in all the other areas of their life that required improvement.

Involuntarily he hesitated before turning the key in the lock. Rún looked at him in surprise. 'Why don't you open the door?' She put down her sports bag as if prepared for a lengthy wait.

'I don't know.' Ódinn gave her a foolish smile. 'Just being silly.' Silly was the word. He'd had a premonition that he shouldn't open it, though he didn't know why. Perhaps his nerves were still on edge after what he had imagined earlier in the car. But he sensed that something had changed. Not necessarily inside the house, but something was different or was about to overturn all his certainties. A year or so ago he would have laughed at this but now he knew better, for he had experienced the same sort of premonition the day Lára died. He had been lying in bed with a truly epic hang-over when his phone lit up with an unknown number on the screen. And he hadn't wanted to answer.

Don't answer. Your life will never be the same. Don't answer.

Only at the third call from the same number had he given in and picked up. *Bye-bye, Weekend Daddy.*

But this time the message wasn't as clear, as if it didn't really matter whether he opened the door or not. So perhaps the premonition didn't relate to what awaited them inside; at least, there was no incessant voice echoing in his head: *Don't open!* He must still be jumpy from the bag rustling like that in the car. Ódinn shook off his feeling of trepidation and smiled at Rún. It *was* silly. And, come to think of it, the premonition about the phone call had been wrong. Though his life had undeniably become more complicated and restricted since Rún entered it, he had no desire to turn the clock back. He had been offered a chance to mend his ways and for that he was grateful. He turned the key in the lock.

They were met by a fresh breeze and Rún frowned. At first Ódinn didn't understand her reaction, then he twigged.

'Who opened a window?' Her voice was even higher than usual and she looked terrified. It was an unspoken rule with them that no window should be opened unless for a specific reason. Once he was sure she was asleep, Ódinn would open his bedroom window a crack, but he was always careful to close it before waking her in the morning. It didn't take a psychologist to guess what lay behind this phobia; her mother had died falling out of a window. The attic flat Ódinn had handed over to Lára had eventually cost her her life. To Rún, open windows were death traps, and Ódinn hadn't even tried to explain the difference between the narrow gap of a slightly open sash window and a large, wide open dormer window like the one her mother had fallen from. Plenty of time for that later. Nor did he try to explain that her mother had not been irresistibly pulled to the open window by ungovernable forces. She had been perched smoking, as was her habit, half in and half out of the window. In the gutter at the bottom of the steep roof they had found a small flower pot and the household broom. The assumption was that Lára had knocked over the pot, which rolled down into the gutter, and in trying to fish for it with the broom she had lost her balance.

'I must have forgotten to close the window in my room, sweetheart. I was boiling last night and opened it a teeny-tiny crack. A fly would have had difficulty squeezing through it.' Ódinn tried to make light of the situation, concealing from Rún that this couldn't possibly be the explanation. He distinctly remembered shutting the window, though he could conceivably be confusing this with another day. The faint whiff of cigarette smoke did nothing to help. He didn't smoke, and Rún certainly didn't. Had the old lady downstairs started sneaking the odd fag?

Rún sniffed the air, her face even more anxious. 'I don't want to go in.'

'OK.' Ódinn impressed himself with his new-found skill at handling their relationship. 'I'll go in and close the window. When I've done that and made sure everything's absolutely fine, you're to come in. You can't stay out on the landing forever. I'm not lugging your bed out here. Remember what a job we had forcing it through the door in the first place?'

Her smile was not amused. 'It smells of cigarettes inside. Like at Mummy's.'

There was a time for truth and a time for white lies. 'I know. Baldur mentioned that there were some workmen round today, doing something down in the basement. He warned me there might be a smell of smoke in the building.' There must be a natural explanation but Ódinn didn't think now was the right time to run through the possibilities, all or none of which might have been correct. Rún needed a single concrete reason, even if it meant having to pretend he had spoken to his brother. 'Maybe they had to go into our flat, and opened a window while they were there.' He regretted adding this last bit. Now there were two possible reasons for the open window instead of the simple explanation that he'd forgotten to close it. Rún looked even more dismayed. 'Wait here while I close it.'

Ódinn walked straight into his bedroom and swept back the curtain. The window was shut, as he'd remembered. Spinning on his heel, he went into the kitchen, not even bothering to glance into the sitting room. Deep down he had known all along where the draught and smell of smoke were coming from.

The kitchen window stood wide open. The latch was unfastened and the large casement window was flung wide. In spite of the breeze, there was no mistaking the smell of smoke, as if someone had just stubbed out a cigarette. Ignoring the numbness creeping up his legs, Ódinn slammed it shut. Instantly, the reek of smoke evaporated and everything was restored to normal. He leant against the sink and stared out of the window. This must be due to fatigue and stress. Under great strain, people could experience all kinds of hallucinations. So why not a bad smell?

Then he remembered what his daughter had said when he woke her that morning. She had raised her head and stared at him bemused, as if still asleep, though her eyes were wide. Then she had asked in a husky, drowsy voice if Mummy was still angry. Ódinn had exclaimed that nobody was angry in heaven. But instead of accepting this and climbing out of bed, Rún had added, eyes fixed on him, that Mummy wasn't in heaven – she was too angry for that. Ódinn had dismissed this as nonsense, but omitted to ask whom her mother was supposed to be angry with, since he believed he already knew. No doubt Lára had hated him all those times he had repeatedly let her down. He richly deserved it. But that it should reach beyond the grave – that was absurd. To do Lára justice, she seemed to have tried to conceal her resentment from Rún; at least his daughter had never mentioned it. And if she could control herself when alive, surely she must be able to do so after death? It was just some nonsensical idea of Rún's, the result of her nightmare.

Yet Ódinn couldn't shake off his sense of unease. The ball had started rolling. He had a hunch that it was linked somehow to Krókur and the two boys whose death seemed to have been greeted with general indifference. Perhaps the day of reckoning had come.

Chapter 4

January 1974

Aldís was itching to find out what the new boy had done wrong. As a rule, the boys were only guilty of minor offences but, especially given what Hákon had said, she was convinced that it was a different story with this one, Einar. He was self-possessed and seemingly well brought up, quite different from the other boys. He seemed far more mature, too, as if he'd made better use of every year of his life. The other boys, in contrast, were constantly fidgeting, as if driven by small engines fuelled by all that was forbidden. In fact, the new boy seemed so out of place that she thought the system must have got the wrong person; it should have been a completely different Einar.

She had tried asking about his past but got nowhere. Veigar and Lilja had told her to mind her own business, and the workmen knew no more than she did. All she knew for sure was that his crime must have been serious enough to take him out of circulation. But what had he done? Veigar was permanently on edge in Einar's presence, his eyes constantly seeking out the boy, as if he needed to know his whereabouts at all times. She had witnessed similar behaviour before: her uncle owned a large dog that had once bitten his wife, and the woman used to behave exactly the same around the beast.

Aldís had begun to fear the dog herself, though it had never done her any harm. But Veigar's darting glances had completely the opposite effect on her: instead of being afraid of Einar, she became intrigued. A sneaking, malicious voice in her subconscious whispered that her interest was simply due to his appearance, but Aldís immediately rejected the idea, annoyed by the notion that she should be attracted to someone so much younger. None of the boys at the home were yet adults – they were all under seventeen. But there was no getting away from the fact that Einar stood out. Rather than being pinched and covered in acne, his face was strong-jawed, almost like that of an adult, and was out of keeping with his slim frame. He was taller than most of the others, too, though he still looked as if he needed a little more air pumped into him. And his eyes betrayed a tanta-lising sorrow, but that could have been her imagination, or even astigmatism.

'You can call the boys in to dinner.' Lilja stuck her head into the dining room where Aldís was finishing laying the table. She always did her best to make it look nice for them but never really succeeded. The cloths were stained and the plates and cutlery didn't match. Yet she tried to arrange everything neatly, mindful of what her mother used to tell her about always showing respect for food. Having enough to eat shouldn't be taken for granted: the world outside Iceland was full of people who went to bed hungry.

Aldís had never actually left the country herself but thought her mother must have been exaggerating. The few people she knew who had been abroad hadn't mentioned anything about poor people. Personally she'd be prepared to put up with a bit of hunger if only she could travel. She straightened a knife beside a chipped plate, cross with herself for letting her thoughts stray to her mother. She had to keep reminding herself of the grudge she had against her, keep fuelling the anger that had a tendency to mellow. Her right cheek burned at the memory of the slap that had turned her life upside down; the crack as her mother's work-worn hand had made contact with her face.

Aldís sniffed loudly. She had always known that things would change when a man came into her mother's life. When it finally happened, Aldís had been so happy for her, so pleased her mother would no longer have to struggle on as a single parent, that she'd gone out of her way to be friendly to the man. But she hadn't been on her guard. Had ignored the glances, the tendency to brush against her, until the disgusting creep had come up behind her, reeking of spirits, squeezed her breasts and whispered that he'd seen the way she looked at him and now they could finally . . . They had been alone at home. Aldís had violently shoved him away, stammering that she didn't want him to touch her. Ever. He had called her obscene names that she couldn't bear to recall, then stormed out. When her mother came home from her Women's Association meeting, Aldís had blurted the whole thing out, assuming that she would take her side and send the man packing. But the woman who had cradled her in her arms, and worked her fingers to the bone to make a decent home for her, had stared at her with cold eyes, trembling slightly, then slapped her face, snarling that she was jealous and didn't want her own mother to find love. Then she had clasped a veined hand over her mouth and collapsed in tears. Instead of comforting her and suggesting they throw the man's stuff out together, Aldís had been filled with a self-righteous fury and packed her own bags. Before she knew it she was standing on the walkway outside the badly painted block of flats, looking up at the window of her room for the last time. She had neither seen nor heard from her mother since.

Aldís sniffed again, then pulled herself together. There was no point brooding over the past; the future was what mattered. She put the last glass on the table and despondently surveyed the result. Anyone would have thought she hadn't made an effort, but it couldn't be helped. She hurried out to fetch the boys, almost breaking into a run since it was boiled haddock for supper and if it sat too long in the pan it would start to congeal. The poor wretches had been working their guts out all afternoon and deserved better than that. Though she wouldn't exactly describe them as friends, and she found them intimidating at times, that didn't mean she was heartless. You couldn't help feeling sorry for them, stuck in this limbo. No one left here a better person, for all the supposedly edifying sermons and back-breaking toil.

The boys' dormitory was in an annex to the main building where the dining room and kitchen were located. There was no connecting door and the annex was locked in the evenings. To make it even more homely, bars had been fixed over the windows to prevent the occupants from running away under cover of night. Shortly after starting work here, Aldís had thoughtlessly asked Veigar if he wasn't afraid the boys would be trapped inside if there was a fire. He had answered curtly that they weren't stupid and were perfectly capable of calling for help. She was thankful that the same rules didn't apply to the little house where she slept.

As Aldís approached the dormitory, she stifled a yawn. For the past few nights she had been repeatedly disturbed by a noise outside her window, yet could hear nothing once she was properly awake. On one occasion the curtain had moved and, half asleep, she had thought someone was forcing their way inside. But of course that was impossible since her room was upstairs, and, besides, there was nobody out there. But she'd had to pull her pillow over her ears before she could drop off again.

The uproar hit her as she opened the annex door, and she was suddenly aware of how tired she was. Too tired to ignore this racket. She hesitated in the doorway, wondering if it was safe to go in. The boys were all yelling at once, apparently either urging someone on or shouting at him to stop. Clearly this wasn't the usual boisterousness, so Aldís marched in to see what was happening. If she went to Veigar and Lilja for help, all hell would break loose and the resulting crackdown on discipline would make life difficult for the staff as well as the boys.

The annex was not large, consisting of four bedrooms, a sitting room, and a bathroom with shower facilities and sinks. Aldís shoved aside two of the youngest boys, who were hanging back in the sitting-room doorway as if alarmed at what was happening inside. They jumped when they saw her but looked relieved, as if the Saviour himself had arrived to drive out the evil spirits. 'What the hell's going on?' She had to bellow at the top of her voice to make herself heard. Apart from the two youngest in the doorway, Aldís counted four boys, and was surprised at what a din so few of them could make. They had their backs to her, eyes trained on the floor beside the battered three-seater sofa.

Aldís's words had an astonishing effect. All four boys turned as one and stared at her uncomprehendingly. She didn't know what to do. Their eyes were ablaze with excitement, their mouths still open after breaking off mid-yell. She couldn't see what they were looking at but could hear a scuffle or sounds of movement behind them. 'What's the matter with you?'

No one spoke; they simply stared at her.

'What on earth's going on? Move back.' Her voice conveyed a confidence she didn't feel, but luckily they obeyed and stepped aside. She wasn't sure what she'd have done if they'd turned on her.

Two boys were grappling on the floor. The sight wasn't uncommon; Aldís had seen more than enough fights since she'd begun working at Krókur. But this was different from the usual kind of scrap in which two boys started punching each other and ended up in a hate-filled embrace, hammering at each other's backs.

What was happening on the floor in front of her was no embrace.

It was the new boy, Einar, and Keli, one of the bigger boys, who had been at the home longer than most. The younger boys feared him even more than they feared Veigar. He was extraordinarily adept at picking on their weak spots and seemed to take pleasure in tormenting those who weren't as strong as he was. For once, however, Keli was getting the worst of it, and, now she came to think of it, Aldís never remembered seeing him in a fight before. His victims usually had the sense not to stand up for themselves, so things never went that far. Of course, that explained the noise. All the boys present had wrongs to avenge. Aldís considered her options. She wasn't strong enough to drag Einar off Keli, but even if she'd had the strength of a man she wasn't sure she'd have intervened. Einar's face, usually so sad or dreamy, now appeared almost demented, his teeth bared like a dog or wild beast about to devour its prey. His eyes were filled with such violent hatred that you'd have thought they belonged to an older man.

Keli's features, on the other hand, were contorted with terror. Einar had him by the throat and he was turning redder and redder. Aldís swallowed. 'Pack it in, you two. It's suppertime.' The words came out automatically, her voice sounded almost casual. Turning on her heel, she swept out. One of the little boys in the doorway whispered confidingly as she passed: 'He said his girlfriend was a slag. A disgusting slag.'

Aldís might as well not have bothered to take all that trouble over laying the table. The boys bolted down their food as if it were a race and left the table looking as if a troop of monkeys had been at work. The cutlery lay strewn all over the place, several dirty glasses had been overturned and the cloths were spattered with grease. Yet Aldís felt no resentment; that's how it was. They ate so as not to starve and had no time for manners. Today, however, they had been untypically quiet over their food; most sat staring blankly at their fish and spoke little to their companions. Perhaps they were still recovering from all the shouting. Aldís had helped with the serving, and every time she walked into the dining room the boys had exchanged glances, as if wondering whether to give her the cold shoulder or welcome her. Was she friend or foe?

'Thanks for not telling,' she heard a voice say behind her.

She almost dropped the plate she was holding but managed to disguise her shock. She'd been so preoccupied that she hadn't noticed Einar. 'Can I help you clear away? It'd take no time with two of us.'

'No. No, thanks.' He was standing far too close.

'I'll help anyway. I owe you one. You could've got me into real trouble.'

'You're in big enough trouble already. You're here, aren't you?' Aldís turned away and carried on stacking dishes. 'I'm not sure I'll keep my mouth shut next time I find you half murdering one of the other boys. You were lucky. And maybe Keli deserved it.' She stole a glance at him and saw that he had moved over to the other table and was gathering up the dirty plates. It had never occurred to any of the other boys to help and, against her will, she found herself feeling well disposed towards him, forgetting for a moment how frightening he had looked as he tightened his grip round Keli's throat. 'You'd better watch out. He's bound to try and get even.'

'He can't touch me.' He put on a show of bravado. 'But of course I don't want any trouble – I want to go home. He didn't report me earlier, though, so perhaps he'll leave me alone. I hope so, anyway. I've got to get out of here as soon as possible.' He had finished stacking the plates.

The pile he held was crooked: instead of scraping the leftovers onto the top plate, he'd stacked them any old how. She blushed, suddenly conscious what a mess she must look in her old clothes, grubby from the day's chores. He was fresh from town where her old clothes had long gone out of fashion. Her hair was scraped back in a ponytail, which she hadn't touched since that morning, and her face must be red and shiny with sweat. As a rule she paid no attention to how she looked; the worse, the better, really. 'Leave them. I'll deal with them.' All friendliness had left her voice, but only because she wanted to be alone. Alone with the washing up, like any other evening.

'Don't be daft. I'll carry them through for you. Have you got to wash up? I'm good at drying.' His smile was thin and did not betray any happiness.

'Why are you here? What have you done?' The words were out before she could stop them.

Einar put down the plates and averted his eyes. Now it was his turn to flush, but Aldís couldn't tell if he was angry or ashamed. 'Nothing. I've done nothing.'

'Yeah, right.' She watched him leave the dining room without saying goodbye, his fists clenched. She shuddered at herself. Why did she have to behave like that? It wasn't as if she often had company when clearing away after meals. She heard the front door slam and was suddenly unpleasantly aware of how alone she was. Lilja had gone for the evening and wouldn't be back, so there would be no one to break the silence. If she listened hard she could hear a tap dripping. The kitchen door swung slightly and Aldís felt her blood run cold as she listened to the drops plinking on the scuffed steel of the sink. The thought lanced into her mind that someone was standing there, counting the drops, waiting for her. *When's Aldís coming? One, two, three* . . . She gulped and looked away from the door. Between the old, faded curtains she could see black glass and beyond it the night. She hurried over to the window to close the curtains. Instinctively she felt that if she looked out, the face she saw in the glass would not be her own.

She no longer wanted to know what Einar had on his conscience. Nor did she want to know what had happened to the deformed child. All she wanted was to jump into bed and pull the covers over her head.

Chapter 5

The windowless meeting room was full of a stuffy, chemical fug, a blend of all the perfumes and aftershaves those present had applied that morning. Ódinn's nose itched; he felt as if a hole were being drilled between his eyes. To make matters worse, his feet were soaking and at the slightest movement his right shoe emitted a low squeak. Both discomforts could be blamed on office cuts. There wasn't enough money to lay a few metres of ducts and purchase a pump to air-condition the windowless room, or to provide staff parking by entering into an agreement with the owner of a nearby underground garage. For those who drove to work, the office was in the worst possible location in the town centre. By the time Ódinn had dropped Rún off at school, the students from Reykjavík Sixth-Form College had, as usual, hogged all the free parking spaces in the vicinity, forcing him to squelch for what felt like miles through the slush.

'How are you getting on with your case?' From the silence that followed Heimir's question, Ódinn realised it must have been addressed to him. His mind had wandered during the tedium of a typical Monday meeting to plan the week ahead, preoccupied with thoughts of Old Spice, wet feet and parking spaces. Originally, the idea had been that everyone should stand during these meetings, to keep them short and sweet, but before long they had all taken to sitting down and people were permitted to drone on for as long as they liked, since none of them had anything urgent waiting at their desks.

'Slowly.' Ódinn considered leaving it at that so the meeting would end sooner, but Heimir was always encouraging them to describe their cases in detail, so he decided to play along. 'I think I've got a fairly good overview of what Róberta was doing, so the plan now is to pick up where she left off. There's a ton of paperwork – as well as the photocopies she organised in files, there are around six cardboard boxes of original documents, most of which I've gone through. They include invoices, lists of residents, a few photos, and so on. She seems to have been on top of everything and already separated out the essentials. Actually, it's a bit unsettling to see how tidily she left it all – as if she had a premonition that she wouldn't be able to finish it herself and that someone else would have to take over.' Embarrassed, Ódinn's colleagues lowered their eyes or studied the faded landscape photographs on the walls.

Diljá appeared to be the only person unmoved by the mention of Róberta. She sat absent-mindedly picking imaginary fluff from her red nail polish. 'If she'd known her time was up, I reckon she'd have chosen somewhere else to pop her clogs. It's kind of sad to die at your desk.' She didn't seem to notice that her words only deepened her colleagues' discomfort. Even Ódinn felt a pang. He wondered if the first people on the scene had assumed Róberta was asleep, perhaps even prodded her, only to discover that she was unnaturally stiff. There was a pop as Diljá blew a bubble in her chewing gum. 'So, in other words, her work wasn't completely useless?'

Ódinn pushed away the mental image of the dead woman, lying back with her eyes fixed on the Artexed ceiling panel

47

and fluorescent lights. 'Yes. There's nothing wrong with what she did so far.' He tried in vain to meet his boss's eye. 'As well as sifting through the documents, she made a list of all the boys ever admitted to the home and drew up a table for their details. I'm not sure Data Protection would approve, but what do you think, Heimir? Can I carry on filling it in?'

Heimir's attempt to look as if he'd thought long and hard about this issue didn't deceive his subordinates for a minute. 'I'd need to consult my notes but as far as I remember we went into it very thoroughly at the time and decided there was nothing illegal about it.'

'If you went into it at the time, there's no need to look up your notes. You must have okayed it or Róberta wouldn't have adopted that approach. She'd never have gone against orders. So I'm assuming I can carry on gathering the information?' Ódinn tried to look nonchalant. Heimir was too slow-witted to work out how he could veto this approach without revealing his complete ignorance of the matter.

'What kind of information are we talking about here?' Diljá folded her arms under her breasts, causing them to jut out even further than her Maker – or bra designer – had intended. Ódinn's neighbour drew in a sharp breath as if he'd been punched in the stomach. Diljá's lips twitched as she observed the reaction of her former one-night stand. She went on: 'You know – is it sensitive stuff about the inmates or just the sort of info you could look up in the telephone directory?'

'Bit of both.' Ódinn noticed that the woman minuting the meeting had nodded off. He couldn't blame her: no one read the minutes and in her place he'd have been tempted to add all kinds of rubbish just to prove the point. 'There's a list of all the boys' names, as I said, with their date and place of birth, the reason they were sent to the home, current address and occupation, and, where relevant, date of death. The table also contains a column for their family circumstances, but that's blank. The question is whether Róberta intended to fill it in with the situation at the time or as it is today. The only columns she's fully completed are the names and dates of birth. There are still gaps in the other columns, though the amount of information missing varies.'

'How do you know there's no one missing?' Evidently Diljá had not forgiven him for being so cool with her last week. 'I mean, she might have had another hundred names to add. You can't be sure the list's complete,' She smiled mockingly at him. There was a glimpse of white teeth between the lips she'd painted scarlet to match her nails. She reminded him of an extra in a vampire movie. His neighbour was still squirming in his chair, just waiting for an opportunity to escape.

'I compared it to the records and the number's consistent. I also did spot checks on the names and they match, like all the other information I've tested.' Ódinn's wet feet itched and he longed to go to the gents and remove his socks.

Ódinn was feeling quite pleased with his day's work. He'd filled in a large number of boxes in the table and the remaining blanks mostly related to boys who had moved abroad as adults. Until it was clear whether further action would be necessary, there was no point searching for their original addresses. Why waste time on that if everything turned out to have been above board? He hadn't yet uncovered anything suspicious. Admittedly, he still had to go over the documents

49

in detail, but so far he'd found no indication that the state would be liable to pay compensation. No doubt the poor boys had found life there pretty tough, but the home didn't appear to have been nearly as bad as similar institutions that had already been investigated.

The Krókur boys, unlike their counterparts at other institutions, hadn't been sent to the home because of difficult family circumstances but because they had all committed some minor offence. The rationale had been that it would be good for them to cool their heels at the residential home, which was intended to be, as one document of the time put it, 'a detention centre for adolescent boys who have gone off the rails'.

Other homes had taken in children whose families were judged incapable of caring for them; children who had done nothing wrong but were simply the victims of circumstance. It seemed rather perverse that the system should have meted out gentler treatment to young offenders. But his view of how humanely Krókur had been run might change. He hadn't yet spoken to any former inmates; the paperwork represented the points of view of everyone except those on the receiving end of the care. Nevertheless, he thought it unlikely that anything much would emerge from the interviews that he intended to conduct at random. When the committee set up two years ago to investigate care homes had advertised for former inmates of state institutions between 1945 and 1978 to come forward and testify, none of Krókur's old boys had taken advantage of the opportunity. Yet Krókur's operations had fallen within this period, and the inquiry had been widely publicised. The assumption was, therefore, that none of them were burning with a long-held sense of injustice.

He could afford to be optimistic. What's more, ugly stories had long been circulating about the other homes, without the need for any public inquiry to expose them. But Krókur was different; few were even aware of its existence, though that could be because the home had only operated for a relatively short time, and the residents had been older, more hardened and therefore less likely to complain of bad treatment after it closed down.

In other words, he couldn't rule out the possibility that the place had been badly mismanaged, despite the lack of rumours. He had yet to obtain information, for example, on the two boys who had allegedly died in an accident. According to what he had uncovered so far, they had suffocated in a car belonging to the home. The engine had been left running and they'd failed to notice that the exhaust pipe was blocked by a snowdrift. Óðinn hadn't been able to find much information on this. He'd trawled the internet for old news reports but 1970s journalism had been sketchy compared to what he was used to nowadays. The articles were so circumspect, so careful to show consideration for the next of kin, that they revealed next to nothing. Doubtless it had been considered a disgrace that the boys were at a home for delinquents, so the incident was glossed over. After a brief press release about the tragic accident, the story was dropped. There weren't even any obituaries. All he had was a copy of a letter from the local magistrate that had been buried in one of Róberta's files. In it, the magistrate stated that the investigation had concluded that the boys' death was an accident which could not be attributed to neglect by the managers of the home or any other individual responsible for them. Their presence in the back seat of the car was unforeseen, and it would have been unreasonable to expect the managers to monitor every single boy in the place twenty-four hours a day. Nor was it possible to predict what boys like that might get up to. They had enjoyed a certain degree of freedom on the property and in this case had used it for a foolish prank that had cost them their lives.

It was hard to tell how much credence should be given to official statements of this type from the period, yet Ódinn could see no reason to doubt its veracity. Admittedly, the tragedy was described in rather unfeeling language, but perhaps that had been the official tone in the seventies. After all, what motive could a magistrate have had for covering up for the couple who ran the place? Then again, one never knew what might go on in a small community, so he resolved to track down the police files on the accident, if they still existed.

If the official reports had been lost or destroyed, it was always possible that relatives of the deceased might still have copies. So far this was the only untoward incident he had dug up on Krókur, so it was vital to get hold of the paperwork. Otherwise his report wouldn't be fit for purpose. His task was to assess whether the state was liable to pay the former residents compensation for lasting damage. It was hard to imagine more lasting damage than death.

Although he agreed with the magistrate's view that the home was never intended to be a high-security prison, it nevertheless bothered Ódinn that the place had been closed down shortly after the accident. It occurred to him that the two events might be linked, though he had no evidence. And without evidence, his conjectures were no better than fantasy, so tomorrow's task would be to get hold of the police files and comb through the press coverage – if any more could be found.

He still had the police reports on Lára's death hidden away in a cupboard. Lára's mother had obtained them with the help of a lawyer and, after reading them herself, had passed them on to him. At the time he hadn't wanted to know what they contained, but he had hung onto them anyway. He couldn't understand why the woman had gone to the trouble, though later he saw the sense in it. He would have to force himself to read through the files eventually, but he was mainly keeping them for when Rún grew up and wanted to know more about her mother's death. That reminded him that he had intended to take the shirt box containing the papers down to the storeroom where Rún was less likely to stumble across it. She was still far too young for its contents. At present the box was sitting on one of the top shelves in his wardrobe and, although he very much doubted she'd go rummaging around in there, he couldn't be sure what she might get up to. It wasn't that she was a naughty child, but he didn't yet know her well enough to judge whether his shirts and suits might prove of interest to her.

If he got round to moving the files, who knows, he might even take a glance at the contents himself. But he would have to go through them when there was no risk of being interrupted by Rún and having to shove them hurriedly under a chair. The real reason for his reluctance, though, was not concern about where he read the reports but what they might contain. He was afraid that once he had acquainted himself with the details of Lára's death, he wouldn't be able to get them out of his head. Perhaps the boys' next of kin had felt the same when they received the reports of their deaths: they

might still be gathering dust on the top shelves of two separate wardrobes. He hadn't yet found out whether their parents
– they would all be in their eighties by now – were still alive,
but it was perfectly possible.

Ódinn picked up the half-empty coffee cup, switched off
his monitor, went along to the staff kitchen and put the cup
on top of all the others in the sink. His shoes were chafing
his bare feet and he wanted to go home. And yet he didn't. It
was hard to deceive himself: ever since they'd been met by the
smell of smoke and the open window, he had been assailed
by an increasing sense of apprehension in the flat. The most
innocuous background noise or slightest movement could be
enough to make him jump. It was all very silly and he'd never
mention it to anyone, but he couldn't rid himself of the feeling
that he, Rún and the old lady were not alone in the building.
He knew this was absurd but that did nothing to diminish his
fears. He'd even refused when his brother Baldur offered to
have Rún for a sleepover at the weekend, though previously
he would have jumped at the chance. It would have allowed
him to hit the town with some mates or have them round to
watch the footie, but equally it would have meant spending
two nights alone in the flat. When they were both home he
could attribute any unexpected noises to his daughter; he didn't
want to hear the same noises when he was alone.

Ódinn retraced the steps he had taken that morning through
the slush. The temperature had dropped sharply and a frost
was forming. His feet were freezing and without his socks
he was intensely aware of the hard pavement and wet snow
underfoot. His irritation was so excessive that he wondered
if it was a sign that his anger was finally finding an outlet.
The grief counsellor he'd been encouraged to see had warned

him that Lára's death and the changes to his own circum-stances might have this effect. Unable to concentrate on what the man was saying, Ódinn had felt he was wasting his time. When the counsellor suggested he make further appointments, he had left, promising to think about it. How could a complete stranger advise him on coping with the upheaval in his life? Life was constantly changing. And everyone adapted to new situations in their own way. He thought once again of how that same counsellor had strongly advised him to send Rún to a child psychologist, and of how he had been even less receptive to that idea. She was his child and he was perfectly capable of looking after her. She wasn't mentally ill, she was just grieving for her mother, and there were other cures for that besides specialist help.

No, that definitely hadn't been a very intelligent decision. Either for himself or Rún. So much was unresolved: his daughter was seething with repressed anger and insecurity, and he himself was still in shock although the accident had been six months ago. Perhaps they would both have made better progress if he'd accepted help; perhaps Rún wouldn't keep asking him what would happen to her if he died; perhaps everything would be clearer if he'd followed the counsellor's advice. The last few months had passed as if he were in a fog and he suspected that the same was true for Rún. He had inadvertently deprived her of closure, refusing to speak about her mother's death, changing the subject, trying to stop her even thinking about it. Of course it had been doomed to failure. As a result they were both neurotic and emotion-ally numb. That was probably why she dreamt about her mother so often, and why those dreams were becoming ever more bizarre and frightening.

He couldn't undo the past. The question now was whether he was going to continue to ignore the obvious or pull himself together. He owed it to his daughter and her late mother to try at least to put their lives in order, in the hope that Rún's nightmares would cease and he himself would stop imagining that something was lurking in every dark corner of their flat.

Ódinn reached the car and fumbled with numb fingers for his keys. He got in and closed the door. As he sat there breathing out clouds of steam in the icy interior, he decided that this evening, after Rún had gone to sleep, he would begin his campaign of self-improvement by reading the reports on Lára's death. It would be a start. Then he would search for the card of the child psychologist he had been recommended and make an appointment. Together they would work their way through this.

He smiled and started the car, never suspecting what awaited him in the unread police files in his shirt box.

Chapter 6

The block of flats stood on the edge of the development, exposed to the elements. Beyond it lay nothing but barren moors and gravel flats. Ódinn had settled himself on the sofa with the curtains drawn. They stirred in the gusts of wind that buffeted the windows, as if someone were standing behind them, pushing them out. The gale had been raging for over an hour and showed no signs of abating. At this time of year it was as if the weather forecasters were paid extra for storm warnings; no sooner had one gale passed than they were warning of another, even worse. The wind usually got on Ódinn's nerves, but in the circumstances it seemed eerily appropriate.

Although the sheaf of papers on the sofa looked modest enough, the thought of leafing through it was daunting. He had intended to read the whole thing carefully, starting at the top, but after the first paragraph of the post-mortem report he couldn't face any more. Judging by this brief summary, the full report of the injuries to Lára's body would make gruesome reading. The detail about the broken bones protruding through the skin of both her arms was almost more than he could bear, but even worse was the information that the fractures indicated she'd tried to shield herself as she fell. Obviously, she couldn't have died before she hit the ground, but he'd never stopped to think exactly how her death had come about. She fell. She died. Determined as he was to confront the facts, he hadn't been prepared for this. As a respite from the report, he calculated on his phone how long the fall would have lasted, using a simple equation for a free fall that he remembered from sixth form: one and a half seconds, if Lára had fallen in a vacuum, which unfortunately did not apply in this case. He guessed at two. Two seconds was a long time if death was waiting at the end of them.

The document lay patiently beside him, waiting for him to steel himself to read on. Phone in hand, he stared distractedly at the TV. He had the volume on mute so as not to disturb Rún, so whatever problems the grim-faced actors had meant nothing to him. Ódinn lowered his gaze from the screen back to the innocent black letters on the white paper. He ran his fingers lightly over the page but couldn't feel any palpable imprint. Yet they had scoured his soul. Why couldn't the report simply have said that she died instantly, or even on the way down? As a child he'd been told that people who fell from high-rise buildings perished before they hit the ground, unable to breathe due to the speed of their fall. Of course, a three-storey, corrugated-iron-clad house didn't really count as a high-rise, but perhaps it was the memory of this explanation that had stopped him from giving any thought to Lára's death until now. The last thing he wanted was to imagine how she must have felt as she fell. It was easier and less painful to believe that her end had been mercifully quick.

He lifted his eyes to the television again. Now one of the actors was crying and the other seemed at a loss as to how to stem the flow. The scene was so corny that it galvanised Ódinn to pull the shirt box towards him. He'd find the courage to read the post-mortem report eventually, but in the meantime surely the rest couldn't be as harrowing. He found a

police report compiled two days after the accident and decided
he had to read it; he mustn't be a wimp like the cry-baby
on screen. It was all in the past, nothing could be changed
now, and he couldn't be too much of a coward to face up
to the investigation report. Nothing could be worse than
what Lára had been confronted with on her descent. Not
even the post-mortem report. One thing at least was certain
– if he could force himself to go through this he would be
in a better position to help Rún deal with her loss. Well, he
hoped so, anyway. If he kept ignoring the past he could
hardly expect his daughter to work through it, as she so
desperately needed to. Now his eyes had been opened he
could see with sudden clarity much that he had overlooked.
Clichéd as it sounded, it was like a revelation.

The report consisted of police interviews conducted with
Lára's neighbours. The house contained four flats in addition
to Lára's attic rooms, but Ódinn only knew the old man in
the basement. The other names meant nothing to him. People
seldom stayed long in the building; they tended to buy their
first flat there, under the impression that it only needed a
fresh coat of paint, then, as the truth gradually dawned on
them, they started plotting their getaway. Ódinn began with
the man in the basement, but his statement was of no value;
he had been out when Lára fell and seemed to have had next
to no contact with the mother and daughter. He didn't even
know the little girl's name, though they'd lived under the
same roof ever since Rún was born. Ódinn had always found
the man a bit odd: a secretive recluse, living down there,
half underground, with no apparent interest in other people.

Rather more had been gleaned from the other occupants.
A young couple with a small child, who lived on the ground

floor, had revealed the little they knew about Lára. That she was a single parent, worked as a bookkeeper and had a mother living in the same street, two doors down. They'd been awake at the time but hadn't noticed anything out of the ordinary. The husband had gone out jogging an hour before the accident. Everything had appeared normal when he left and again when he returned some forty minutes later. He hadn't observed anyone in the stairwell or garden. Nothing unusual had occurred until they sat down to breakfast at their kitchen table and Lára fell past the window. Their child, who was facing the window, had in its innocence laughed aloud over its porridge – a macabre detail that made for uncomfortable reading. All the evidence indicated that the accident had come out of the blue, which was consistent with the facts as Ódinn knew them.

The occupants of the first floor had been sound asleep, so they could be quickly dispensed with. But when Ódinn read the witness statement of the neighbours on the floor below Lára's, the plot thickened. Their version of events did not tally with the young couple's. They were sisters from the east of the country, who had moved to Reykjavík to study at the university. They'd been renting the flat, which was for sale, for six months. Reading between the lines, Ódinn got the impression that they were down-to-earth young women, but he could have been wrong. Though he regarded himself as a fairly good judge of character, it was one thing to read someone's testimony, but quite another to meet them face to face. Nevertheless, he had no reason to doubt what they said, so their statement pulled the rug out from under his feet.

The sisters claimed to have heard people moving about in

the flat upstairs shortly before Lára's scream rang out. There was the sound of something breaking and voices, though of course it could have been the radio. They couldn't be more specific about the gender of the voices or whether they'd been arguing. Later, both retracted their statements, no longer sure they'd remembered right. The sounds had probably come from the street. One sister also thought she'd heard the door opening upstairs, though she added that she couldn't be a hundred per cent certain. Naturally, she hadn't been paying attention to background noises, since she had no reason to think that morning would be different from any other. What caused her to doubt she'd heard the door creaking was that the bell hadn't been rung. She could be sure about that because the racket it made drove her up the wall; she'd been fed up anyway about having to wake up early to study, so she'd definitely have noticed the noise of the bell. For what it was worth, neither had heard anyone leaving the flat or hurrying downstairs after Lára fell, but that may have been because they had dashed over to the other side of the flat to see what was happening.

Ódinn put down the report and ran his fingers through his hair. No one had breathed a word to him about the possibility that it hadn't been an accident. Either the information that Lára might not have been alone had gone no further than the police and the sisters, or they hadn't wanted to tell him. The media, at any rate, had been silent on that score. And so had Lára's mother. He felt a surge of anger. What was wrong with the woman? Hadn't it occurred to her that this might have been important to him?

To be fair, though, he'd been sitting on the files for months, so he could perfectly well have found this out for himself.

Perhaps she'd been waiting for him to bring up the subject. Or she'd read in his eyes that he had enough on his plate coping with himself and Rún. He calmed down a little. Since the police hadn't treated the case as murder, with the inevitable press furore, they must have had other information.

Hearing mumbling from the bedroom, he automatically shoved a cushion over the shirt box. Ears pricked, he waited until he was sure Rún hadn't woken up before he uncovered the box again. Luckily, she was a deep sleeper, which must have spared her from an even greater shock at the time of Lára's death. It was one thing to wake up to the news that your mother had died in an accident, but something else altogether actually to witness her fall – it didn't take a genius to work that out. And she might have tried to see what had happened to her mother, leant too far out of the window, and it was anyone's guess how that might have ended.

Ódinn didn't envy Rún's grandmother, whose task it had been to break the news to her. The young woman from the ground floor had rushed round to fetch her, because the door to the flat upstairs was locked and she hadn't wanted to risk waking Rún, if she was home, by shouting and banging. The news would come better from a family member. Since Lára's mother lived practically next door, she had reached the flat before the ambulance. Ódinn shuddered at the thought. Had she caught a glimpse of her daughter's body as she ran to the front door, but forced herself to go on for fear that something might happen to her grandchild as well? He tried to imagine how he would feel if early one Sunday morning he had to race to the scene of an accident in a panic. It was hardly surprising that Rún's grandmother had been a bit strange ever since. She'd always treated Ódinn with chilly reserve but on the rare occasions they'd met since Lára's death she had cut him dead, refusing to look at or speak to him, even to say hello.

He'd had little contact with her for years, so for all he knew she might already have been suffering from depression, but it seemed unlikely. It must have been her daughter's death that changed her from an aloof person into something like a ghost. Lately, however, she had thawed a little and they could now speak about Rún on the phone, though their conversations never got beyond the superficial. The woman probably held him responsible for the fact that Rún didn't want to go and stay with her, indeed could hardly be persuaded to visit her. But that was far from the truth; it was entirely Rún's decision. He sympathised with his daughter: her grandmother was eaten up with bitterness, so he almost never put pressure on her to go round. As a result, Rún had only seen her grandmother a handful of times since her mother's death. Hopefully it would be possible in time to increase the number of visits, but as long as she returned home miserable and out of sorts from her grandmother's house, it was better to keep their contact to a minimum. The woman was bound to pull herself together eventually.

He heard Rún tossing and turning in bed, then all was quiet again. She must be dreaming. Although she hadn't woken up, Óðinn was not entirely easy. He peered into the hallway leading to the bedrooms, as if expecting to see movement. He didn't know why but he had the uncomfortable feeling that Rún was watching him from the shadows, aware that he was trying to get to the bottom of her mother's fate, and unhappy that he wasn't including her. But that was ridiculous; she was fast asleep, lost in those strange dreams or nightmares about her mother that seemed to afflict her every night. Which was exactly why he was sitting here now, re-opening old wounds. Their life had to change. At any rate, he had no desire to end up like the melodrama he was watching unfold on the TV screen. The actors were now engaged in a screaming match, involving great histrionics, which looked as if it could only end badly. Ódinn reached for the remote control and switched it off.

He resumed his reading but the material no longer exerted the same hold on him. He was briefly taken aback to come across a photograph of the kitchen after the accident. His dismay had nothing to do with blood or signs of violence but with the open kitchen window. Everything else was disconcertingly similar to how it had been before he walked out on his wife and daughter, as if time had stood still for Lára, while for him it had moved on. Dirty dishes were stacked by the sink and there was the same clutter of knick-knacks on the shelf. Ódinn couldn't help looking around and comparing it to his own flat, which was so obviously a bachelor pad that it was almost embarrassing. He'd spent his money on a music system and other gadgets. A good sofa and a coffee table sufficed for furniture. There were no vases or ornaments to cheer the place up, apart from the pottery bowl Rún had made at school, which sat on the TV cabinet. From the outside it looked quite good and was nicely painted, but on the inside it was covered in tiny cracks. Like his daughter, he thought, and immediately felt ashamed.

He continued reading. It didn't take long to discover why the investigation hadn't focused on an uninvited guest. The police believed that Lára had gone down to the basement to put on a wash in the communal laundry. She had offered to wash some tablecloths for her mother, and these were still in the machine when the police checked. His former mother-in-law had confirmed this: her own machine was broken and she hadn't been able to afford to get it mended because of a cashflow problem. Apparently she had asked for the cloths to be destroyed afterwards.

The police concluded that the person the sister from downstairs had heard opening the door was no burglar or assailant but Lára herself. She had nipped down to the laundry and naturally hadn't rung the doorbell when she went back upstairs. The police were of the opinion that she had gone straight to the window for a smoke, with tragic consequences. There was a brief note about a minor discrepancy between the time given by one of the sisters and the time the police believed the accident had occurred. The sister thought she'd heard the scream very shortly after the footsteps had entered the flat, but that was inconsistent with the time required for Lára to take up position, light a cigarette, knock over the flower pot, fetch the broom, clamber onto the windowsill again and try to retrieve the pot, before falling out herself. When the police conducted a second interview with the sister, she had retracted her statement, saying she couldn't be sure how much time had passed between the door opening and the scream. There had been no sign of a visitor in the kitchen but the radio had been on, so that was probably the source of the voices the sisters had heard. A broken glass bowl had been found on the floor but the pieces had been swept into a pile. Since no unidentified fingerprints were found on the broom handle, it was assumed that Lára must have broken the bowl, perhaps when she knocked the flower pot out of the window, and swept up most of the fragments before attempting to rescue the pot. A half-smoked cigarette had been found under her body. It all pointed to the same conclusion: an accident. Ódinn wasn't quite sure if this was a relief or not. Which was better, death by misadventure or murder? Did one feel better knowing that there had been an accident or that a loved one had been murdered, and, either way, why? The consequences were the same. He had no answer to this. But whatever had happened, it appeared that he had not been kept in the dark about any mysterious details.

Towards the end of the same report, however, a fact emerged that was not in doubt. Shortly before her death, Lára had broken up with a man she had been seeing for two years and had even lived with for several months, and their decision to part had not been particularly amicable, according to police sources. Ódinn was completely wrong-footed. He'd had no idea. Lára had been in a serious relationship with a man for all that time and hadn't said a word about it to him. Neither had Rún. Of course, Lára had been under no obligation to tell him about her private life, but Rún was another matter; he had been entitled to know about such a major change in his daughter's circumstances. Why hadn't Rún herself said anything? She must have realised that the man her mother was always meeting was her boyfriend; she was quite old enough to be aware of that. Even if they'd kept their relationship secret to begin with, she must have put two and two together when he moved his stuff in. She could hardly have thought the man sharing her mother's bed was a lodger.

He restrained the urge to charge into Rún's room and start interrogating her. It would only drive her further into her shell. And now he came to think of it, Lára *had* said something ages ago about a new boyfriend, but he'd asked no questions. The thought of her with another man – and any discussion of the subject – had made him uncomfortable. Since she hadn't referred to it again, he'd assumed the relationship was over; these things happened, as he knew from personal experience. Actually, he might even have seen the man, without realising, when he went to pick up Rún. He'd very rarely gone up to the flat; she generally waited for him on the pavement outside and the man might well have been standing nearby. His name, Logi Árnason, rang no bells.

Glancing at the clock, Ódinn saw it was not yet midnight. He grabbed the phone and called Kalli, who'd kept in touch with Lára after she and Ódinn split up, not because he was especially considerate but because his wife Helena was Lára's cousin. Their old circle of friends had been torn apart by the divorce. The men with wives or girlfriends had stuck with Lára; the few who were single had remained loyal to Ódinn. After Lára died, some of those who had almost disappeared from his life had got in touch again, but it was all rather awkward and he didn't know if it would last. Still, he was grateful for the fact now because it meant he could ring Kalli without his call coming entirely out of the blue.

'Why didn't you tell me Lára was living with someone?' Ódinn launched straight in with no time for polite chit-chat or apologies for ringing so late. He merely announced himself and got straight to the point. Then, realising how bad this sounded, especially since he had to keep his voice down because of Rún, he added belatedly: 'Sorry. Did I wake you?'

'No.' Kalli didn't exactly sound pleased. 'But if you'd rung ten minutes later I'd have been asleep. Are you out of your mind? Because that's what it sounds like. Anyway, what on earth was I supposed to tell you?'

Ódinn couldn't be bothered to keep apologising. 'I don't know – inform me that my daughter was sharing a roof with a strange man? You didn't say a word.'

He thought he heard a sigh at the other end. 'Are you kidding?'

'No, I'm asking: why didn't you say anything? Any of you? I can't believe you were the only one who knew.' This was grossly unfair but he didn't care. When he met up with his friends, they had talked about anything but Lára.

'Look, Ódinn, I wasn't the only one in the know. And if you think digging up the past will make you feel better about yourself and your daughter, I'm afraid I can't help you. The guy was no one special. His name was Logi or Láki . . .'

'Logi Árnason.'

'Right. Logi. He's an artist or something – not my kind of guy. I met him a couple of times but Lára gave up inviting us to dinner with him when she realised we didn't hit it off.' Kalli took a deep breath, perhaps to stop himself badmouthing Logi any further. 'Anyway. When they moved in together it was only Helena who went round; I was allowed to stay home, thank God. Then after they broke up I heard from Helena that the guy had been a total shit. I just said yes and no in the right places – mainly yes, or I'd have been in the firing line myself. You know what it's like when women go on about their exes.'

Ódinn didn't know, but he could imagine how Lára and Helena must have talked about him back in the day. With Kalli nodding along. But he wasn't going to ask about that. 'Was he violent? Did he knock her about?'

Kalli laughed. 'No, I'd definitely have heard if he had. I expect he was just an ordinary bloke – a bit more of a tosser than usual, but ordinary enough. Lára did get mixed up with one idiot after the divorce and she'd never have put up with that again. She sent that guy packing after the first slap. She was no fool, you know.'

'So Logi wasn't the first?' The moment the words were out of his mouth he realised how crass they sounded. Lára was a young woman with the same needs as him. Just because she'd been left alone with Rún didn't mean she had to live like a nun. He hadn't exactly behaved like a monk himself. But the difference was that since the divorce he hadn't managed to form another relationship that progressed as far as living together.

'Uh, there were a few. Not many. You almost certainly got more action than her, if that makes you feel better.'

'No. I don't care. I'm glad she had boyfriends.' Ódinn felt the need to explain himself to Kalli; he couldn't afford to lose his friendship or give him the impression that he was cracking up. 'It's just that I've been looking through the police reports and thought at first there was a chance Lára might have been pushed, though there turned out to be no evidence for that. But when I read that she'd recently gone through a bad break-up with some bloke, it occurred to me that it might not have been that simple. He could have been involved. I'm probably talking bullshit, though. I'm not in a very good place at the moment.'

'No problem, Ódinn. Ring whenever you like. As often as you like. Just not so late next time.'

Ordinarily, Ódinn would have been embarrassed at having made a fool of himself, but right now he felt that one awkward phone call made no difference.

Outside the gale raged over the barren landscape, buffeting

the windows with increasing ferocity, and Ódinn felt the throbbing in his ears adjust to keep time with the gusts. It didn't help matters when the curtains billowed out, then fell back against the windows. But not quite flat. It looked as if there were a figure standing behind them. A small figure. Lára's height.

Nothing could have made him lower his gaze to the floor in front of the curtains. He found himself expecting to see a pair of gruesomely bruised and shattered legs. Of course it was just his overactive imagination but even so he gathered up the papers in a panic, switched off the lights and vacated the sitting room. You could never be too sure.

Chapter 7

January 1974

Of all her chores, cleaning Veigar's office was Aldís's least favourite. It wasn't because of the size since it was hardly more than a broom cupboard, with barely room for a desk, three bookshelves and an extra chair, squeezed in so tightly that any visitor with long legs would be impossibly cramped. Some of the boys were real beanpoles and no doubt this added to their woes when they were called into the office to be reprimanded. It was certainly hard to clean in such a tight space and Aldís spent her time trying not to knock over the teetering piles of papers on the desk. She often wondered what they contained and why Veigar didn't file them away. Once or twice she'd run her eyes over the top pages but seen nothing of interest, and she'd never been tempted to dig further into the pile in case her employer caught her at it. He had a habit of materialising when she was cleaning, as if to check she wasn't slacking.

Aldís almost had a heart attack when the phone on the desk starting ringing, causing the piles of paper to tremble. She'd been sweeping dust out of the corner and straightened up so suddenly that she banged her shoulder on the heavy bookcase. Putting down the broom, she rubbed her sore shoulder and stared at the black telephone. It fell silent. She was about to resume her sweeping when it began to shrill again, with renewed vigour. After the ninth ring, peace was restored. Aldís stared at the phone, realising that it had never rung before while she was in there. She stood as if hypnotised, convinced that it was waiting for her to turn back to her housework before shattering the silence again.

The moment she picked up the broom, it started. At every jangling ring she grew more agitated, feeling somehow that the call must be connected to her. Perhaps it was her mother, calling to tell Veigar how pathetic and useless she was; that the police had been informed about the money Aldís had stolen from her bag the evening she ran away. Far-fetched as it sounded, you never knew. Since her mother hadn't made the slightest attempt to get in touch, she must still be angry with her. She could have picked up the phone or written; it wasn't as if she didn't know where Aldís was. The friend who'd put her up for the first few nights had told her mother about the job advertisement that Aldís had responded to: *Young girl required to clean and assist in the kitchen at a residential care home in the capital area, pay as per collective wage agreements for public sector workers, etc.* She wasn't to know that the advertisement had been rather free with the facts; Krókur may have been closer to Reykjavík than, say, Akureyri, but 'in the capital area' was pushing it. Not that it would have made any difference; she had been desperate to get away at once.

Perhaps it was her friend calling? Aldís used to ring her from a payphone on the rare occasions when she went into town, but they seemed to be growing further apart every time they spoke, so much so that Aldís thought she probably wouldn't bother to call her next time she got the chance.

Perhaps their friendship would have lasted if she'd stolen in to use the office phone from time to time, but they'd only really become friends in the first place because they'd both been left out of the groups that formed when they started school. After Aldís left town, the girl had presumably found herself other company; during their last phone call she'd talked a great deal about a girl called Halla who worked with her at the fish shop. No doubt she had taken Aldís's place.

The ringing stopped, only to start up again immediately. By now Aldís was convinced that the call was in some ominous way connected to her. She gnawed at her cheek, trying to decide what to do. But before she could make up her mind, her hand had picked up the receiver, almost of its own accord. She flushed as she raised it to her ear. It was weeks since she'd last spoken on the phone and she had never answered another person's call before. She hadn't the faintest idea what to say, but some part of her was glad she had done it. If she'd carried on cleaning and left it to ring, she would have spent all day, perhaps all week, worrying that something bad was going to happen; that her mother would ring again, for instance, and this time Veigar would answer. 'Hello.'

The woman at the other end was so astonished to receive an answer that she was too flustered to introduce herself properly or explain who she was calling about. 'Oh, er, hello. I just wanted to talk to someone who could give me news of my son – I'd rather talk directly to him but I'm told it's not allowed.' Aldís couldn't speak, so the woman floundered on. It was obvious from her voice that she'd been nervous about making the call. 'I've tried so often that I was about to give up. I'm on my break at work and got permission to use the phone but usually I can only call in the evenings and then nobody answers. I'd started to think I'd got the wrong number.'

'I'm just the cleaner. I can't help you.' It sounded harsh but it was the truth.

'Could you maybe fetch the person in charge? I wouldn't take up much of his time.' The woman couldn't hide her desperation. 'I've got to get back to work so I definitely wouldn't keep him long.'

Her voice was imploring, as if Aldís were in possession of some drug that could save her life. But her hands were tied. 'They have very strict rules about parents. The boys are forbidden to talk to them on the phone and I know Veigar doesn't want any direct contact with them himself.' The hesitation on the other end suggested the woman had no idea who Veigar was. 'He's the manager here and he's in charge of everything.'

'I see. But do you think he'd be willing to have a very quick word? I'm so terribly worried and just wanted news. It's awful not knowing anything.'

Aldís wanted to tell the woman to try again later; she couldn't help her, but the pain in her voice was too much. 'What's your son's name?'

'Einar. Einar Allen. Do you know him?'

Aldís stared down at her scuffed slippers. Originally tartan, they had been splashed so often while she was scrubbing the floors that the pattern had worn off the toes. 'Yes, I know who he is.'

'Could you tell me how he's doing? Please.' No doubt she had her pride but her question betrayed abject helplessness.

'He's fine.' Aldís couldn't bring herself to say anything

more. The woman's son, like all the others, was being driven mad by the futility of life at Krókur. And his frustration would grow worse with every day that passed, or so Aldís believed. She was dying to ask what Einar had done wrong but didn't dare. 'He's reconciled to being here.'

The woman was no fool. 'I don't suppose you'd tell me if he wasn't.'

'Maybe not.' Aldís thought she heard a noise out in the corridor. 'I've got to go. I really shouldn't be talking to you. I'll be in trouble if I'm caught.' She glanced at the door as if she expected it to be thrown open any minute, but, hearing nothing else, she relaxed slightly.

'One more thing before you go. Give him my love. Tell him I think about him constantly.' She broke off once she'd got this off her chest, then added in a rush: 'And tell him to remember it was the right decision. The alternatives would have been much worse. It's really important.'

Aldís wasn't sure if it was really important she pass on this last bit or if it was really important for Einar to remember. Maybe it was both. She didn't know if she'd pass on any of it but agreed in order to cut the conversation short. She felt rather guilty about not being honest with the mother, so to make up for it she blurted out that she generally cleaned the office at this time on Tuesdays and Thursdays, in case the woman wanted to ring again. Then she hung up, cursing herself for having agreed to take a message. She had enough troubles of her own without becoming a go-between for this strange boy and his mother. Yet part of her wanted to be involved in the secret, as if she were part of a loving family again. She might learn something useful for when she had her own children.

*   *   *

'Like me to leave while you're doing that?' Einar stood awkwardly in the doorway of the room he shared with another boy. His expression had been ugly when he opened the door, but softened when he saw who it was. 'The others are out. They've got an extra lesson but I was let off.' Lilja was responsible for the teaching at the home, which was mostly for the sake of appearances.

'You needn't leave. I'm only going to give it a quick sweep.' Aldís had known he'd be in his room; Lilja had been complaining about having to give the boys extra tuition after the coffee break, and let slip that Einar and a couple of the others had a free period. Aldís had mentioned casually to Veigar that she was going to clean the floor in the boys' dormitory, but he was too engrossed in the bills that had arrived with the milk van to give her alternative orders. For the same reason he had failed to notice that she was unusually smart, wearing her neatly combed hair loose and dressed in her least shabby clothes.

Einar opened his door wide to let her in, but didn't move, so they touched briefly as she slipped past. She hoped he wouldn't notice her blush. 'I won't be a minute.' If she was honest, she'd have to admit to herself that a spark of attraction had been kindled inside her, which she really shouldn't fuel. She shouldn't have come here. The sensible thing would be to avoid this boy. His attraction probably stemmed from the fact that he was superior to all the other males in the place, which wasn't saying much. He seemed mature, without being old and worn out like the workmen. A straight-A student among a class of slow kids. But it was too late to be sensible now that she was standing in his room, and if she was going to give him the message, this would probably be her only chance. She might not be able to catch him alone again any time soon.

'Your job's pretty boring, right?' Einar threw himself down on the bottom bunk, which she knew belonged to his room-mate.

Aldís shrugged, her colour deepening. What was the matter with her? She was much older than him; it should be the other way round: he should be shy in her presence. Why should she be ashamed of her job when her situation was a sight better than his? She wasn't the one locked up in a juvenile detention centre. 'Well, it's not the most exciting job in the world. The moment I've saved enough money I'm out of here.'

'What'll you do then?' He rested his cheek on his hand and gazed at her, almost unblinkingly. His gaze was challenging, his dark eyes hard to read.

'I'm going to get a job in a fashion boutique. Or become an air hostess.' It was impossible to turn any redder. Aldís had never told anyone her plans before, but then, thinking back, she realised no one had ever asked.

'Do you speak English?'

Aldís was relieved he hadn't laughed at her dreams or said that a frump like her could never become an air hostess or work in a fashion boutique; that she should stick to scrubbing floors. 'A little. I've got a textbook that I'm studying.'

Einar continued to gaze at her. 'I used to want to be a pilot. My dad was in the air force.'

Given his foreign surname, Aldís wasn't surprised. 'I bet he was pleased. Proud, I mean.' Who knew, maybe one day they might work on the same plane?

'He doesn't have any contact with me. He and my mum

were never in a relationship. He's got a new family somewhere in America.'

Aldís leant on her broom. 'At least you have a nice mother.
Mine's a real cow. I hope I never see her again.' She straightened up, a little annoyed with herself. It wasn't a fair description of her mother, who'd been good to her until her recent
betrayal. But Aldís hardened her heart, smothering any feelings of sentimentality or regret. She didn't want to forgive
her mother. She didn't deserve it. 'Actually, that's why I'm
here. I've got a message from your mother.'

There was a creak from the thin wooden base of the bed
as Einar abruptly sat up and swung his feet over the side.
For a split second, remembering his ferocious temper, Aldís
thought he was going to attack her. If he went for her like
he had Keli the other day, she'd be completely defenceless.
But it turned out that wasn't what he had in mind. 'Where
did you see her?'

'I answered the phone in Veigar's office – don't know what
came over me – but your mother was terribly grateful. He'd
never have spoken to her.' As Einar didn't reply, she asked
warily if she'd done the right thing by letting him know; if
he really wanted to hear his mother's message.

'What did she say?'

'She asked me to tell you that she thinks of you constantly.
Or you're constantly on her mind. I forget which. Not that
it matters. She sounded like she was missing you.'

Einar nodded carefully. 'Thanks. Did she say anything
else?'

Aldís was about to say no when she remembered what the
woman had added. The important bit. 'Yes, she said the
decision had been for the best. No, sorry, she said to remember

you made the best choice. Or something like that. And that it was important.'

Again Einar's dark head moved up and down, more emphatically this time. Aldís couldn't tell how he was taking the news. 'Do you understand what she meant?'

'Yes. No. I don't know.' He didn't seem to want to discuss it, so Aldís didn't press him. How was it possible to understand and yet not understand?

'If she rings again, should I pass on a message?' Careful not to meet his eye, Aldís started sweeping. The floor was fairly clean; there was no dust under the bunk, only a single, inside-out sock. Bending down, she picked it up and put it on the bed. When she first started work at the home she'd been revolted by having to touch dirty socks or hair in the plughole, but she'd long since got over her squeamishness.

'Tell her I'm looking forward to going home.' Einar lifted his feet off the floor so Aldís could sweep under the bed. 'There's nothing else to say, really. What would you want to hear if you were her?'

'Me?' Aldís smiled, then saw he was serious. 'I don't know. Maybe that you're doing OK, in spite of everything. It's not like it'll do any good to tell her you're having a lousy time – if you are. It'll only make her feel bad too. Better just to lie.'

'I'm neither happy nor unhappy, so you can tell her that without having to lie. Being here's like being shut in a box, like being snatched out of your life and put in storage. Everyone here's like that, like they're just waiting for this to end. Every day that passes, you're one day closer to going home and picking up your life again.' He grabbed the broom handle. Aldís was taken aback: he was much stronger than he looked. 'But you're different somehow. Your life's not on hold.'

She wondered if that was good or bad. If he was right, it must be because she had nowhere else to go. He had friends – and a mother. But there was no one waiting for her. It looked as if she'd even lost her schoolfriend. Her eyes dropped to his hand on the broom handle. 'I've got to get on. It'll be suppertime soon and I'll have to go and help.'

Einar released his grip and drew his feet onto the bunk again. He was silent and Aldís didn't dare continue the conversation. There was so much she wanted to know about him but she was afraid of saying something stupid. Instead, she concentrated on finishing the floor, stooping so she could reach right under the bed. Towards the back the broom encountered an obstacle that was heavy, yet strangely yielding, unlike anything she'd found under the boys' beds before. Clothes were softer; magazines, books and shoes more solid. She stole a quick glance at Einar but his face was unreadable. Neither of them spoke, though it must have been clear from her expression that something was wrong.

Perhaps it was the oppressive silence, but Aldís was suddenly gripped by a strong reluctance to look under the bed or drag the object out into the open. Rather than stand there, open-mouthed and rooted to the spot, she forced herself to bend down, only to get a shock. There was nothing there: only a peculiar odour, like damp moss or earth. After a moment, she looked under the bunk again. It was dark over by the wall, but she could see nothing that could have obstructed the broom. The odour was stronger, but now it reeked of decay, like fish that had been sitting too long by the kitchen sink.

Instead of asking Einar to check if he could smell it, Aldís decided to keep quiet; she had an intuition that this experience was intended for her alone. Hastily, she swept up the last bits without bothering to push the broom under the bunk again. She mumbled something as she closed the door, and he mumbled back. On the way to the kitchen all she could think about was what the broom might have encountered. Her mind presented her with the image of Lilja's dead baby, the blood that coated it now turned black, the glistening eyes open and covered in a grey film of mould. Aldís pulled her sleeves over her fingers in an attempt to combat the chill that seized her. What on earth had become of the child?

Chapter 8

You could have heard a pin drop. Ódinn, who had always prided himself on being able to work under any conditions, found the silence oppressive. He even missed his colleagues' chattering. He had persuaded himself that by coming into the office on a Saturday he could finish everything he'd neglected during the week, but this was just a pretext. There was nothing urgent awaiting his attention.

To be honest, he was sitting here to avoid being alone at home while Rún was at her grandmother's. He couldn't relax in the flat; he was constantly on edge, the hairs rising on the backs of his arms at the slightest noise or movement. What exactly he feared, he didn't know. Hanging around at work was the lesser of two evils. He'd have preferred to spend the afternoon with his daughter, watching a film, going for an ice-cream, doing something she enjoyed, maybe even visiting the Family Zoo. But he hadn't been able to get out of sending her to her grandmother's or it would have been the fourth weekend in a row that they'd fobbed her off with feeble excuses. As usual, Rún had protested but given way in the end and now they were both sitting in their separate places, respectively checking the clock to see if the hands would go round any faster. Perhaps the day would have seemed shorter if he'd had a deadline to meet.

As if to underline how little reason he had to be in at the

weekend, the coffee machine was refusing to work. The grounds had got inside the mechanism and the blockage wouldn't shift, whatever tricks Ódinn tried. The instant coffee tasted as if the jar had been sitting there ever since the builders left, as if even the joiners who'd installed the office furniture had turned up their noses at it. Still, the noxious brew managed to perk him up slightly and went some way towards combatting the soporific humming of the computers that no one had bothered to switch off when they left on Friday. The gloom outside contributed to the soporific atmosphere; the grey, overcast sky blending in with the dirty snow that blanketed everything; no hint of blue anywhere. It was as if heaven and earth had merged into one. Yet another storm was forecast and the clouds were just waiting for their chance to dump another load of snow on the city. He hoped it wouldn't arrive just yet. Rún's grandmother lived in the town centre and he had no desire to negotiate the narrow one-way streets on his bald tyres. If it suddenly started coming down heavily, he would dash out and collect Rún early, regardless of their prior arrangement. Being late was out of the question. Rún's grandmother wouldn't mind if she stayed a bit longer, but his daughter's well-being was paramount. Still, with any luck the snow would hold off and they could stick to the agreed time. Or his former mother-in-law would probably blame the blizzard on him too. You couldn't please everyone. But then pleasing people had never been his forte.

When they were growing up, his brother Baldur had generally been the favourite. And Ódinn had never been the popular one in his group of friends; he was well enough liked but had always been in someone else's shadow. Perhaps that was why he clung so tightly to Rún; it felt nice to be somebody's number one.

Presumably the teenagers at Krókur weren't exactly the apples of their parents' eyes either. The documents Ódinn was currently looking at were accompanied by several photographs, showing boys who had clearly seen a thing or two, and none of it pretty. Instead of looking out at life with cheerful anticipation, their faces were those of people who expect the worst: clenched jaws, knitted brows. Ódinn doubted this was entirely down to Krókur. Although their stint there was unlikely to have been a particularly pleasant experience, it would have taken more than a few months to convert tender youths into such hardened cases, and few of these boys had been there more than a year.

In the seventies, places like Krókur had been regarded as a good method of preventing boys from going off the rails, but the outcome had proved disappointing. At any rate, the home had closed down and there was no evidence that the former residents had emerged as model citizens. Inquiries into other care homes, where even younger children of both sexes had been placed, had exposed appalling cruelty and mistreatment, to which people seemed to have turned a blind eye at the time. Like so many other attempts to solve social problems, the idea of removing children from their families and the environment they knew had proved disastrous – in hindsight. But the saddest part was that something equally wrong-headed was almost certainly common practice now, though no one would notice for decades, by which time it would be too late.

Ódinn felt depressed by such thoughts. His feelings of sluggishness didn't help either. All he had achieved in the last two hours was to draw up a table of contents for the report. He decided to stand up, stretch his limbs and wander over to Róberta's cubicle to go through her files again, in case he had missed something.

He sneezed as Diljá's cloyingly sweet perfume tickled his nose, and the noise echoed through the deserted office. After it had died away, he could hear nothing but the humming of computers. Ódinn listened hard; it sounded as if Róberta's computer was switched on. He thought of checking if she'd kept any files on her own hard drive instead of saving them onto the office server. She wouldn't have been the only one; constant repairs and updates to the computer system had caused countless delays, which led to people ignoring office protocol. As he sat down it occurred to him that this was probably a breach of internal regulations, perhaps even illegal. But there was no harm in trying. If he could get into her computer, he'd go ahead. When he started work he'd been allocated a password and told to change it, but he hadn't bothered. If Róberta hadn't changed hers either, it could be interpreted as a sign that she didn't mind other people accessing her files. He entered her first name and the numbers 789.

The computer welcomed Róberta Gunnarsdóttir. After a moment's hesitation, Ódinn got down to business. He would only open work-related files; if he came across anything personal he'd close it at once. Perhaps it was a bit unethical but never mind.

There were no files on the desktop. This struck Ódinn as odd, since it was contrary to his own practice. At the bottom of the screen he noticed two open Word files but when he clicked on them he discovered to his surprise that both were blank. The files bore the names of the two boys who had died in the accident at Krókur: einar.docx and tobbi.docx.

He tried clicking 'undo' several times in each, in case any text had been deleted, but nothing happened. There was no way of knowing what information Róberta had intended to collate in the documents, but it was unlikely to have been part of the report. The intention had never been to discuss the boys on a case-by-case basis, even if they had died at the home. The preliminary investigation was only supposed to establish whether any staff action might have made the state liable for compensation.

This must be a sign that Róberta had been suffering from a mental block about work, perhaps as a result of her poor health. The drafting of the report had obviously been too much for her – not necessarily the primary cause of her illness, as Diljá had implied, but more than she could cope with in the circumstances. Perhaps she'd become trapped in a vicious circle of feeling too ill to concentrate, resulting in stress that made her even more unwell, further hindering her progress on the case, and so on.

After looking through the folders on the computer Ódinn was fairly sure there was nothing relevant to Krókur apart from the two empty files. He wondered if he should risk checking her e-mail, as he was bound to encounter sensitive personal material. On the other hand, there had been no e-mails to or from Róberta about Krókur on the server, so if they existed it stood to reason that she must have saved them onto her own computer. Either he could act now or he could seek formal permission, which might take months. And by then he would long since have submitted his report. Ódinn opened her e-mail program.

A window sprang up containing all kinds of reminders: invitations to two internal meetings; an appointment to have the oil changed in her little car; a wedding and a hairdresser's appointment earlier the same day. Ódinn wondered if the hairdresser had been notified that Róberta couldn't come on account of her own death, or if she'd turned up to work and waited impatiently for the customer to show up. Ódinn deleted one reminder after another until the window vanished, then began to go through the calendar in case anything was hidden there, such as meetings with former Krókur residents. Apparently not.

The inbox contained only a hundred or so e-mails, of which sixteen were unopened. Ódinn scanned the subject lines of the most recent messages and saw that they were mostly advertisements or notifications from her bank about payments that Ódinn had no wish to pry into. He carried on down the list until he found a message that seemed promising. It had been sent from a Gmail account and was labelled 'Krókur – urgent'. To further underline its importance, it was marked with a red exclamation mark. Ódinn opened the message expectantly. His failure to find anything so far had made him feel like a nosy fool, but all that would change if he stumbled on some information that might actually matter.

He blinked and reread the text to make sure he had understood it right. The sender had used capital letters for impact.

BLOODY NOSY BITCH.
LEAVE WELL ALONE.
OR YOU'LL REGRET IT.

Hastily reordering the messages by sender, Ódinn ascertained that Róberta had received seven similar communications, all from the same uninformative address: krokurcarehome@

gmail.com. Why hadn't she reported this? Or perhaps she had, and no one had told Ódinn? None of the messages appeared to have been forwarded or replied to, so she'd probably kept quiet about their threatening contents. Ódinn decided to read them in order.

They began politely enough. The first e-mail asked Róberta please not to go raking up stuff about Krókur. It would do no one any good, least of all those who had been residents there. They wouldn't care anyway, almost forty years after the event. Róberta had sent an official-sounding reply, refusing to abort the inquiry and informing the recipient that he or she was welcome to submit an appeal. It was like adding fuel to the flames. The sender's rage had escalated with each communication; the fate with which Róberta was threatened if she continued her investigation became increasingly nasty. Ódinn hastily forwarded the e-mails to himself. He wasn't particularly keen to sit brooding over them in the deserted office.

All of a sudden he felt no better here than at home. He was acutely aware of his solitude and when he stood up and looked over the partition he thought he saw the shadows swiftly retreating under the furniture. As if they had crept out to smother the already gloomy light, then fled back into hiding so he wouldn't see. Ódinn regretted now that he'd switched on only the light above his own desk. When he thought he heard something moving over by the coffee area, he turned off his monitor and hurriedly left. Just before the door slammed behind him he was convinced he heard the scraping of a chair. Not until he was sitting in the convenience store near Rún's grandmother's place did he feel himself again. They didn't sell coffee, which is what he craved, so he made do with a Coke and a paper. He read it from cover to cover, including the small ads, then called it a day and went to pick up Rún. Who cared if he was twenty minutes early? Rún would be glad.

When his former mother-in-law opened the door to Ódinn, Rún came running out and jumped into his arms. The old woman was less pleased. 'You're early.' The words were crabby, to match her expression.

'Yes. They're forecasting a storm and I didn't want to risk getting stuck. I'm not in a four-wheel drive.'

'When aren't we expecting a storm?'

'Perhaps the weather'll be better next time.'

'And when will "next time" be? I hope you won't leave it another month between visits.'

'No. Let's hope not.' Ódinn tried to send Rún a mental message to hurry up and put her shoes on. He smiled awkwardly at his ex mother-in-law who was standing there with her arms folded, looking worryingly thin and more haggard than he'd ever seen her. He realised there were so many things he wanted to ask her but couldn't in front of Rún. He remembered how close she and Lára had been, since there had only been the two of them. After the divorce Lára must have turned to her mother for help, so the woman would know more than anyone about her situation before the accident. No doubt she could give a blow-by-blow account of her daughter's relationship with Logi and judge whether there was the slightest chance that he could have pushed her out of the window in a fit of rage.

But with Rún present there was no way to bring up the subject and Ódinn couldn't picture the two of them arranging to discuss the matter in private. As well as information on

Logi, he wanted to know more about the scene of the accident, hear firsthand how Rún had reacted, whether it was
conceivable that his daughter might have seen or heard something but was reluctant to tell, perhaps for fear of meeting
the same fate as her mother. He also wanted to know if the
woman had brought the laundry to Lára that morning and
seen anything out of the ordinary – such as Logi. As far as
he could remember, the police hadn't asked about that, which
he found odd. Or perhaps they had and the answers had
satisfied them, so they had seen no need to include them in
the report.

'Bye, Rún dear. Come back soon.' The woman stooped
and kissed her granddaughter's head with dry lips. Rún made
no attempt to avoid the caress, but he could see her look of
distaste. He wanted to ask if Rún had always been so cool
towards her or if it was connected to the trauma she'd experienced. Her grandmother had broken the news to her and
perhaps in her childish way she couldn't forgive the messenger.

Once they were sitting in the car and Rún had fastened
her seatbelt, he laid his hand lightly on her shoulder. 'That
was nice of you, Rún. Your granny loves you and she'd be
sad if she never got to see you. We often have to do things
we don't enjoy, especially where our nearest and dearest are
concerned. Later you'll be glad you kept in touch.'

'What do you mean, "concerned"?' Rún stared straight in
front of her, her face expressionless.

'All I mean is that you've made an old woman, who loves
you more than anything else in the world, happy. She has no
one left but you.' He smiled at her but she didn't appear to
notice, just continued to stare straight ahead. He added:
'She's not too fond of me, though.'

'She's mean.' Rún clamped her lips shut and Ódinn guessed he would get no more out of her for the moment. He started the car and they drove in silence down the one-way street, past their old house. Rún kept her eyes firmly lowered, but Ódinn's gaze wandered up the corrugated-iron cladding, with its flaking paint, to the window Lára had fallen out of. The flat had still not been sold and the darkened window told him nothing. A memory stirred at the back of his mind but for some reason he didn't care to examine it, and felt relieved once they had driven past.

Chapter 9

January 1974

The grey ribbon of smoke rose vertically from Hákon's glowing cigarette, before wandering in zigzags above his head. It was as if the smoke knew it must avoid his eyes, or the cigarette wouldn't be allowed to dangle a moment longer in the corner of his mouth. Aldís sat patiently on a stool, watching him repair the washing machine, glad of the excuse to idle. 'Why are you working here?' She didn't know why she had come out with the question now. After all, she'd lived under the same roof as him, Malli and Steini for months without ever bringing up the subject. None of the men talked much, except for the odd comment about the weather. It wasn't that they were shy around her, since they hardly spoke to each other either.

Hákon turned slowly, looking surprised. Aldís couldn't tell whether he was affronted by her curiosity or had been longing for a chance to talk about himself. 'Why am I working here?' The question required him to think, which he didn't seem particularly pleased about. 'Well, I don't really know. Blokes like me can't pick and choose where they work or what they do.'

'Why not?' Again the words escaped her before she could decide if they were a good idea.

They were both startled when his adjustable spanner clanged against a pipe on the wall; Aldís especially. 'I've got to keep off the bloody booze. And this place is pretty good for that. No temptations, you see. None at all.'

This time Aldís stopped to think before she spoke. Lilja had been right, then. Not that it came as a surprise. Hákon certainly looked as if he'd drunk more than was good for him: the lines etched on his face, his coarse reddened skin, his hair as thin as that of an old doll. Bad teeth, too; though they were still hanging in there, the gaps between them were suspiciously wide and Aldís always had the feeling that if he took a bite out of an apple, he'd leave a tooth or two behind. 'You're not planning on staying here forever? Just because there's no booze?'

Hákon shrugged his bony shoulders. 'Might as well. Got nowhere better to go. At least I get my meals and a roof over my head.' He took a drag without raising his hand to the cigarette. It perked up as he inhaled, then drooped again.

'But there's loads of other places to live. I'm going to rent a room when I leave. In town.'

Hákon pushed his tongue into his cheek. The action smoothed out his wrinkles. If he put on a bit of weight he might not be bad-looking. 'They may be willing to rent you a room in Reykjavík but that's not to say I'd be so lucky. You're young and pretty and have your whole life ahead of you.' He took another drag, an unusually short one this time; smoke in, smoke out. 'Just use your opportunities wisely. You don't want to end up like me.'

An involuntary expression of dismay crossed Aldís's face. Hákon gave a hoarse laugh, but clearly he was hurt. She couldn't think how to retrieve the situation, so sat there in silence, watching him work. He sucked on his cigarette one last time, then stubbed it out on the painted concrete floor. It left a black streak that Aldís would have to clean up and it occurred to her that he might have done it on purpose. A tiny act of revenge because she'd offended him. He finished repairing the machine without uttering another word. But when he'd gathered together his battered tools, he paused in the doorway, mulling something over, then turned and fixed his colourless eyes on Aldís. 'If I were you I'd quit right now. No reason to hang about. This is no place for a young girl, Aldís. You don't belong here.' He hesitated, seeing her mulish expression, then added: 'Get involved with anyone here and you're asking for trouble. In your shoes I'd get out. Believe me, there's no future in any of these boys.' He disappeared, leaving her scarlet in the face. Was her crush on Einar so blindingly obvious? Was everyone talking about them? The thought made her dizzy. If there was one thing she couldn't stand it was whispering and giggling behind her back. She'd had enough of that at school.

She started throwing dirty sheets from the large pile into the washing machine as if flinging her enemies into the fires of hell, angry with everything and everyone, though mainly with herself. The sight of the bedlinen revolving in the machine soothed her slightly. It didn't matter; there was little she could do to change other people's opinions. But Hákon had got to her. He was right; there was no reason to hang about. She'd saved up enough to support herself for several months, if she was careful, while looking for a new job. Too bad inflation was so high: in the time since she'd started work here and begun paying into a savings account, prices had shot up. The rooms for rent were far more expensive than when she'd begun looking, and there were fewer advertised every day. She needed to get a move on, the sooner the better. Her earlier plan of waiting until spring, then looking for work in the good weather seemed foolish now. What did it matter if it was cold or hot? The earlier she left, the earlier she'd end up where she wanted to be. Not here, and not in her home town.

Outside in the dark, her resolve weakened slightly. It was only just 8 p.m. but she couldn't see the hand in front of her face. She heard a low chirrup from the bird overhead; it was probably letting her know that it was time to top up its food. Well, it would just have to wait until morning. Or perhaps it was simply reminding her it was there. If she moved to town, the poor creature wouldn't stand a chance. No one else at Krókur would bother to look after it. Perhaps, after all, it would make more sense to stick to her original plan and wait until spring. It wasn't only the thought of the bird: she didn't like the winter darkness; it was so desolate somehow, and wouldn't be any more bearable if she was living on her own in Reykjavík. Though at least they had street lighting there: here the only light came from a few windows where people were still up and about. Once everyone had gone to bed it would be like the dark side of the moon.

The damp cold pierced her to the bone. She'd pulled on a cardigan to pop out to the laundry, which was on the ground floor of Lilja and Veigar's house, but now she regretted not having taken the time to put on her anorak. Sleet began drumming on the corrugated iron and she broke into a run. Halfway to the little house, she saw that the door to the main building was open. It swung gently to and fro in the wind, but all was dark inside. Aldís slowed her pace, wondering if she should pretend not to have noticed, but the thought of the soaking floor and the mess that would await her in the morning if she didn't close it made the detour worthwhile. She was wet anyway. She ran over, ducking to shield her face from the wind and sleet. Not until she was under the eaves did she look up and shake the flakes from her hair. The front door swung back and forth, and now she could hear the low squeaking of the hinges that were long overdue an oiling. Only as she was reaching for the doorknob did it occur to her that she'd been the last to leave that evening. And she had closed the door behind her. Definitely.

'Hello? Is there anybody there?' Aldís withdrew her hand. There was no answer. If she listened hard she could hear the ticking of the grandfather clock just inside the entrance. She wanted to run over to the little house and fetch Hákon, who must have gone back to his room after finishing the repair job. He could come with her to check that everything was all right. After supper no one had any business in the dining room: Veigar and Lilja had a private kitchen, and the bunkhouse Aldís shared with the workmen had its own small facilities with a kettle. One of the boys must have sneaked inside. Or maybe more than one. Glancing over, she saw that a light was still burning in their dormitory. On the other hand, Hákon wouldn't be too pleased at being dragged out in the cold and wet. She tried calling again. 'If anybody's in there you'd better come out right now. I'm about to lock the door. It won't be funny when Lilja opens up tomorrow morning.' She didn't in fact have a key since the door was never locked, but the boys weren't to know that. Still no one answered, and there was no sound. Perhaps the door had been left on the latch. She stood there, rigid, staring into the gloom.

There appeared to be wet footprints on the floor. Aldís edged closer to make sure. Yes, there was no doubt. Someone had walked inside – and not long ago, either, since the floor had been dry when she'd gone over to the laundry after finishing the washing up. It was impossible to tell if the prints belonged to a member of staff or one of the boys, several of whom had large feet. But the tracks were clear enough to show that they were pointing inwards. Whoever it was had not come back out. 'Hello?' Aldís's voice sounded shrill and timid, not strong and fearless as she would have liked. The person hiding inside would know now that there was nothing to fear. The door swung inwards again and Aldís pushed it further open, revealing the hall and empty corridor. Having made sure that there was no one lurking just inside, she entered cautiously and reached for the light switch.

The yellowish glare of the dirty ceiling light briefly dazzled her. 'I know you're in here.' The brightness had boosted her courage, lending conviction to her voice. 'Come out or I'm coming in to get you.' She had gone too far. She wasn't at all sure she wanted to search for this uninvited guest alone. From inside the house she heard a noise but couldn't work out what it was. It was too faint to tell if it was speech or just mumbling or moaning, but she'd heard enough to realise that it wasn't in the least frightening. It was far too pathetic for that. Aldís inched her way inside to hear better. Perhaps it was an animal, a feral cat or dog that had sought shelter in the dining room.

But animals didn't open doors or wear shoes.

A whining outside warned that the wind was picking up. As if to confirm it, the door banged into Aldís, and, while she was still rubbing her sore arm, it slammed shut behind her. She bit her cheek. This was silly: there wasn't any danger; she was just working herself up into a tizzy. The person inside wished her no harm; all she had to do was find him and chase him out. It couldn't be simpler. The footprints belonged to one person, so there was no reason to fear encountering a whole gang of boys – unless they were in their socks. Hard as she tried, she couldn't remember if she'd seen any shoes in the porch. Having the advantage of age, she might be able to take on one of the boys, but never two or more together. Conscious of this, she walked down the corridor and turned on another light. Her steps, short and hesitant, gave the lie to her supposedly restored confidence.

'Where are you?' No reply. Aldís wondered where to begin her search, then realised it was obvious. The wet footprints led along the corridor. They faded the further in they went, but nevertheless it was clear that they led to the dining room. What was the attraction there? It contained nothing but tables and chairs, and a sideboard for storing threadbare tablecloths and the like. If it was a thief in search of silver he'd chosen the wrong house: there were no valuables here.

Aldís found that she was tiptoeing as she approached the dining-room door. At least she would have a small head start if she took the person by surprise. If it turned out to be one of the older boys up to no good, she'd probably have time to whirl round and run for it before he caught her. Five steps, four steps, three. The lights dimmed but didn't go out. Aldís emitted a loud gasp and all her plans of a stealthy approach were ruined. Anyone waiting inside must have heard her, but then he couldn't have failed to notice when she turned on the light. She paused, waiting for her heartbeat to slow, and at last heard a sound from the owner of the footprints. It was the same strange throaty noise she had heard before, but now she was closer and could hear more clearly. It sounded like one of the boys, but his voice was so strangely hoarse that she didn't recognise it. Perhaps he'd hurt himself, banged his head and wandered in here in his confusion. But there was no sign of any blood on the floor.

The noise came again and this time Aldís could make out words. She thought she heard the boy pleading: '*Go away, go away.*' Did he mean her, or could he conceivably be talking in his sleep? No one had mentioned that any of the boys were sleepwalkers, but then so much was kept secret from her. The words were repeated and this time there was no mistaking them: '*Go away, go away.*' The boy had raised his voice; he sounded terrified. Was there someone else in there with him? None of the boys were exactly in awe of her and, since she had called out several times, there could be no doubt who she was.

The lights flickered again. Aldís steeled herself to take the two remaining steps to the door. She had no wish to stand there in the dark, not knowing who was behind it. The light switch in the dining room was nowhere near the doorway, so Aldís wouldn't be able to turn it on when she looked inside. The light spilling in from the corridor would have to do. Though weak, it was sufficient to show Aldís a boy sitting in the gloom at the furthest table. He had his back to her, so she couldn't see who it was, but she could tell that he was one of the youngest. A chill ran down her spine when he spoke again, without turning, as if he had eyes in the back of his head. 'Go away. Leave me alone.'

'Come on. You shouldn't be here.' Aldís spoke gently,

fairly sure now that the boy must be delirious. Confused, rather than dangerous.

He turned, slowly and deliberately, and she glimpsed black eyes in a pale face. 'I wasn't talking to you.'

The instant he had spoken, Aldís realised they were not alone. The lights in the passage dimmed and a moment later everything went black.

Chapter 10

'If you compare how you feel now to how you felt before you started looking after your daughter, what comes to mind? Do you feel happier, more anxious, more irritable – anything like that? Sometimes people experience all of these emotions at once.' The therapist, whose name was Nanna, gazed into Ódinn's eyes, as if his answer really mattered to her. Either she was a consummate actor or possessed of extraordinary empathy. Her business card said *Child Psychologist*, but she seemed to know a thing or two about adults as well. When Ódinn rang her, she had been keen to take on Rún's case but insisted on meeting him first. She said she needed some background information, but he found her questions pretty similar to those the grief counsellor had asked him six months ago. He decided to put up with her probing of the tender places in his psyche, though he'd rather they were left undisturbed. You had to hand it to the woman: she was very clever at disguising the interrogation as a conversation between equals. And it was a definite plus that Nanna was young and attractive. He really couldn't complain about spending an hour in her company. Ideally, he would have liked more time to prepare his answers, but she'd had a free slot the day he rang.

'I think I've calmed down, generally. But I haven't really thought about it.' Fearing this sounded rather brusque, Ódinn tried to elaborate. 'I'm not anxious about anything specific, except perhaps what I'll do when Rún's a teenager and starts bringing boys home. Apart from that, I reckon we'll be OK. But it's hard to tell right now whether I'm happier or sadder because you could say we're both still going through a process of adjustment.'

'Were you happier before, in general?'

'I just felt different; I had nothing to worry about but work and my own backside. It's not hard to please yourself in that situation. Actually, I was under far more pressure at work then than I am now. But I had no problem coping. Perhaps because I only had myself to think about.'

'This has been a huge upheaval for you both. Your daughter's whole world's been turned upside down, while in your case it's a new job, changed home life, bereavement.' For the first time Nanna didn't end with a question. She gave him a friendly smile, tucking her curly hair behind her ears. Ódinn noticed that she had a deep dimple in one cheek when she smiled, while the other remained perfectly smooth. As if one side of her was not as amused as the other.

'It sounds worse than it was. I think. To be honest, it all happened so quickly that my memory's a bit patchy. I haven't been able to talk about it properly with Rún, so I can only guess what it was like for her. I have tried, but with limited success. It's my fault; I'm always relieved when she changes the subject, and I never pressurise her to go into detail about what happened. Wouldn't know how, and I'm afraid it'll only make her more confused.'

'There's no need for you to try and guess how she feels, or felt. I'll find out from her. But tell me, did you sleep badly while all this was going on?'

'Yes, quite badly.' Although it wasn't long ago, the memory

was hazy. 'I haven't thought much about that time but recently I came across some sleeping tablets I was prescribed and remembered the problem I had with insomnia after Rún moved in. I never used them, though. Don't like taking pills. I just put up with sleeping badly. Maybe it was a mistake.' He didn't say so aloud, but it suddenly occurred to him that all that sleep deprivation might have damaged some nerve centre in his brain, leaving him with an overactive imagination. He might be stuck with hallucinations for the rest of his life. He swallowed and felt his Adam's apple move up and down.

'No, not at all. It was very sensible of you.' She smiled and he felt as if this was an interview and he had just been told he'd got the job. 'The body uses sleep to fix information in the memory – to file it away, if you like, so you can retrieve it later. That's why it's so important to sleep after revising for an exam; if you study all night your brain doesn't have a chance to process the information. It's stored somewhere in the memory but you don't know where. It's a bit like absent-mindedly laying down some papers instead of filing them in the correct place, then not being able to find them when you need them. By lying awake like that, you've prevented the memories of that period from remaining clear.' Again Nanna smiled and again he felt as if he were a model client. Perhaps everyone who saw her felt like that. 'Am I right? Do you have a clear memory of that period?'

Ódinn stopped to think before answering. Hitherto he'd made no attempt to recall that time in any detail. He'd never seen the point of dwelling on things that went wrong or were difficult. Brooding on the past, worrying about the future – it didn't achieve anything. Not in his experience.

'No, I can't say I remember it well – the main events, obviously, but not exactly what I was thinking or feeling.'

Ódinn was aware of how feeble this sounded but it was the best he could do. He looked away and stared out of the window at the traffic. He didn't really want to say more in case her questions strayed into territory he was keen to avoid. She might ask him how he'd felt on learning of Lára's death, and he didn't want to go into that.

When Lára smashed onto the rock-hard ground, he had just got back from a bender, so tired and off his face that he couldn't even recall how he'd got home or where he'd spent the previous few hours. Though he did have a vague memory of engaging in a heated discussion with a young man on his stag do, who had been as drunk as he was. As Lára raised her arms in a vain attempt to break her fall, he had been snoring off his drunkenness in bed. He tried not to betray his disgust at his own behaviour; he didn't want to rouse Nanna's curiosity. If he admitted what he had been doing, her lovely smile would turn sour, and he didn't want her to despise him. Besides, he wasn't like that any more. 'If I've managed to mislay the bad memories, is there any point raking them up and filing them away in the right place?'

The young woman's smile grew rather fixed, but she carried on smoothly. 'Well, maybe not. I'm just trying to get a picture of what happened. That way I'll be in a better position to help your daughter. And perhaps you as well. You mentioned that you're suffering from strange sensory perceptions that you believe may be connected to your ex-wife's accident. That's quite unusual, so I'm trying to get a sense of the circumstances. What you describe suggests that you're still struggling to assimilate what's happened and that it's manifesting itself in this way. Just because you're not always conscious of things doesn't mean they're not there in the background. I strongly advise you to seek help for yourself while Rún's coming to me. The therapist you saw originally is very highly thought of.'

Ódinn hadn't expected that. He stole a glance at the huge minimalist clock on the wall. 'Excuse me, but what could he do to stop these delusions? I'm fed up with them, to put it mildly, so I'd be extremely grateful if you could just give me some advice now.'

'It's not that simple, I'm afraid. I don't have any magic solutions. If you're adamant that you won't see a therapist, I could ask your GP to prescribe tranquillisers. That class of drug has proved effective for people suffering from the sorts of fears you describe. The point is that we manage to shut out all kinds of noises and movements in our environment because we'd go mad if we responded to all these stimuli. It's part of the defence mechanism that we humans developed after we started living in communities, such as the towns and cities we live in today. We stopped registering the noises around us. What I believe is happening in your case is simply that you're suffering from a mental disturbance that results in anxiety and a state of constant alertness. You're picking up sights and sounds you never noticed before. Tranquillisers would mitigate the effects. But a talking cure could provide the same relief.'

'Thanks, but no thanks.' Ódinn wasn't in such a bad way that he was prepared to start knocking back the happy pills or seeing a shrink. He couldn't face turning up regularly to sit in a minimalist room and rabbit on about himself. Though

he didn't know a lot about it, he was convinced that tranquillisers came with a whole raft of side effects, quite apart
from being addictive. 'I thought there might be some other
way. Hypnosis, or whatever. Something you could offer here
and now.'

Nanna laughed sharply. 'I'm qualified to use a variety of
methods but I only treat children. Treatment in your case
would require more than one conversation. This meeting is
about Rún, not you. There's no question of your walking
out of here completely cured and everything going back to
normal. Though I can understand if that's what you were
hoping for.'

Ódinn didn't bother to deny it: the desire to find a quick
fix for his troubles was nothing to be ashamed of, though
clearly he wasn't going to be so lucky. 'Do you think I'm
cracking up?'

'No, I don't think so. Though note that I only said *think*.
I know too little about you to be a competent judge. People
crack up, as you put it, in all kinds of different ways. And
you can rarely tell by looking at them. But I wouldn't worry
too much.'

This wasn't the answer Ódinn had been hoping for. He
had asked in order to hear an unequivocal *no*. 'I'm not really
too worried about myself. I'll survive, even if I have to put
up with this crap a bit longer. I'm more concerned about
Rún, as you know. She doesn't talk much about how she's
feeling but she has a lot of nightmares about her mother,
and I suspect she's going through the same process as me. I
doubt I'm giving her enough support, though I'm doing my
best.' He straightened his shoulders, so as not to come across
as a complete wimp. 'But I'm prepared to do whatever's

necessary to help her get over it.' Except see a psychoanalyst. Or take tablets.

'Did it start at the same time for both of you?' For the first time in the conversation Nanna appeared to be taking him very seriously. A bad sign, surely? 'It's quite unusual for two people to experience the same hallucinations, especially if they began at the same time.'

'Rún's been in a bad way ever since she came to live with me. Understandably – she's lost her mother. But it's been different lately. She used to sleep at nights and didn't seem as frightened as she does now, just sort of stunned.' He thought for a moment. 'Yes, it did start around the same time.'

'Did it coincide with any other changes in your life? At the time or shortly beforehand?' Nanna dropped her eyes. 'A new woman in your life, for example?'

'No. Nothing like that.'

'What about work? Have you been under increased pressure?'

Ódinn couldn't help smiling. 'Not really, but it's not exactly overwhelming. I finally got a decent project, but actually things have been a bit slow for my liking. In other words, the situation has changed slightly – but for the better.'

'Is it possible that the pressure's greater than you want to admit – that it's upsetting your daughter without your realising? Do you take work home with you, for example?'

'No, nothing like that. There was no pressure at all before, but now I've got a project I have to finish by a certain date. That's all there is to it. I was even allowed to set my own deadline, so you get the picture. Nothing to affect Rún.'

Nanna didn't appear convinced.

* * *

When he got back to work and they began their meeting, Heimir, unable to hide his curiosity, asked Ódinn where he had been.

'I was at the doctor's.' Ódinn wasn't about to admit that he'd been seeing a therapist.

'Nothing serious, I hope?' Heimir's gaze was avid. He was clearly dying for Ódinn to spill the beans.

'Oh, no, not serious.'

'That's a relief. It's a bit of a worry when young men like you start having doctor's appointments. But if you say it's nothing, there's no call for alarm.'

'I didn't say it was nothing; I said it wasn't serious.' Ódinn didn't know why he wanted to confuse Heimir. Why would he want to nettle this harmless man? It wasn't his fault that Ódinn's life was a mess. On the contrary, Heimir had given him a job. God alone knew what sort of state he and Rún would be in now if he had still been working for his brother, with all the endless absences from home that would have entailed. 'By the way, I wanted to let you know that I'm thinking of talking to some of the old boys from Krókur. If they're willing to speak to me, that is. But I wanted to get the green light from you first. I don't want to do anything that might be unpopular.'

'Why should it be unpopular?' Heimir looked a little apprehensive and his lazy eye darted to one side. He ran his palms over his shiny, empty desktop, as if wiping away invisible dust. As usual he was wearing slightly too smart a suit and tie, prepared, as ever, for that rare eventuality, a meeting at one of the ministries.

'Suppose one of the people I interview wakes up to what it means and talks to the press afterwards. Up to now there hasn't been a peep out of any of the old boys, so maybe it's a bad idea to rock the boat. But the report won't be worth the paper it's written on if I don't mention the residents' experience. The documents I have at present only give the official line, and, let's be frank, the state proved blind to what was going on at other care homes. Official papers only ever tell half the story.'

While Ódinn was waiting for an answer he found himself tuning into the faint sounds that reached them through the closed door. He heard the secretary tapping on her keyboard, the whistle of the kettle, the irritating ringtone of a mobile phone that it seemed no one was ever going to answer. He was so relieved that he had to fight back a grin. The therapist had been right; he'd become over-sensitive to his surroundings. All the things he'd taken as a sign that he was either crazy or haunted had been nothing but normal background noises and movements that he didn't usually register. But the longer he listened, the more uneasy he felt, until the urge to smile vanished. He wished Heimir would make up his mind. The tapping on the keyboard now sounded as if something horrible were being typed – as if the dreams of some wretched underdog were being crushed; the phone call seemed to forebode bad news: a premature death or cancer diagnosis.

Ódinn coughed to drown out the sounds, if only for a moment. At that, Heimir finally seemed to wake up. 'Now you come to mention it, I hadn't considered the press angle.' He paused, waiting for Ódinn to continue.

'Well, the thing is, the press are bound to hunt out the old boys once the report's published, and if it gets out that we've compiled it without investigating their side of the story, the shit will really hit the fan.'

'So you want to conduct some interviews?'

'It's not a question of what I want. Their testimony is an essential part of the report – if only to confirm that the management of the home was exemplary. But, of course, it's also possible that the public image bears no relation to what really went on at Krókur.'

The lazy eye that had slid away was now fixed, as if it had found the answer beyond the line of sight.

'Yes, I suppose it would be a good idea to talk to them. But didn't Róberta already do that? I have a feeling she did, and I'm wondering if it'll look bad if we go back and interview the same people.'

'I haven't found any evidence that she did, but there's nothing to say she didn't either.'

'Have you checked her timesheets?'

'No, I didn't realise I could access them. To be honest, it hadn't occurred to me.'

'She always filled them in conscientiously, from what I remember. Provided a detailed description of the day's tasks.' Heimir gave Ódinn a look as if to say it wouldn't hurt him to follow her example. 'I'll have them printed out for you. You can't access them yourself. With any luck, she'll have included any interviews she did – perhaps even with the names of her interviewees. That might help you track down her notes.'

It sounded reasonable. Ódinn prepared to wrap up their meeting. 'One more question. Did Róberta ever complain about receiving threats?'

'Threats?' Heimir was obviously taken aback. 'Why on earth would you ask that?'

'Oh, no reason. Let's discuss it another time.' Ódinn half

regretted raising the subject, unwilling to own up to having read her e-mails. 'By the way, who outside this office would have been aware that Róberta was compiling the report?'

Heimir frowned, his eye slipping back into place. 'Just a minute . . . are you implying that someone from the Ministry of the Interior or Child Protection Agency was threatening Róberta? Why would they?' He huffed indignantly. 'It's out of the question. For one thing, we've never discussed who in our office was handling the assignment, either when she was dealing with it or since you took over. People aren't exactly waiting with bated breath for the findings, you know.'

Ódinn nodded and took his leave before Heimir could prolong the meeting. If no one within the system knew that Róberta was writing the report, the e-mails were unlikely to have originated from an insider. Which left only her interviewees. And, it stood to reason, they could only have been old boys or staff from Krókur.

Róberta had described her tasks briefly but succinctly in her timesheets. Ódinn had received a printout of the last six months because Heimir couldn't recall precisely when she had told him about the interviews. Halfway through reading them, he was brought up short. One entry said: *Read and checked letters*. That had taken two and a half hours. The following day had the same entry: this time Róberta had spent an hour on the task. What letters were these? He hadn't come across any letters among her documents. He made a mark against these two entries and continued reading. Shortly afterwards he encountered another entry that made even less sense. It said: *Read up on anencephaly*. He entered the word into the search engine and discovered that it referred to a birth defect or disease. He opted to view images with the results and seldom if ever had he laid eyes on anything so disturbing. They showed babies which at first sight seemed to have eyes at the top of their foreheads but, on closer inspection, it turned out that their eyes were correctly placed, it was the top of their heads that was missing. He clicked on 'back' and read an article on the condition, which explained that it was a birth defect that caused the foetus to develop without a brain. As a result, the cranial bones developed abnormally in the womb, flattening out directly above the eyes instead of forming a dome over the non-existent brain. What possible relevance could this have for the case or for Róberta? Ódinn wasn't sure he wanted to know. Hastily he closed the browser.

He went to the nearest window and stuck his head out for a breath of fresh air. Perhaps he wasn't the right man for this, after all. But his doubts were quick to pass and, returning to his desk, he began poring over the timesheets again. What a nightmare.

Chapter 11

January 1974

Nobody believed her – except perhaps Tobbi, but that didn't count because he'd been there at the time. The others stared at her blankly and either said she must have imagined it or told her not to talk nonsense. The latter group included Veigar and Lilja, who were also angry with her for frightening the boys like that. She was hysterical, they said, and had better keep quiet until she calmed down. They had gone on and on at her last night and again this morning. Even the bird, perched on the roof of the main building, turned its back on her as she walked across the yard.

Aldís swung her legs back and forth as she sat on the rickety wooden bench behind the little house, waiting for her rage to subside. The bench had seen better days, as the three hollows worn by past backsides showed. Her plimsolls appeared from under the seat and disappeared again, appeared and disappeared, and each time they reappeared her resentment grew. Now there was a hole in one of the grubby toes. Her first task after she moved to town would be to buy herself a pair of smart new shoes. No one would offer her a decent job in these scruffy things. Air hostesses wore high heels, not flat-soled plimsolls that were falling to bits. She took a drag on the cigarette her housemate Steini had rolled for her when he saw how she was feeling. He was a man of few words and this was his way of showing Aldís that he was on her side, though he knew she wasn't really a smoker. She exhaled a cloud of smoke that the wind instantly snatched away as if it were a plaything.

'Got one for me?' In her agitation over Veigar and Lilja's stubborn refusal to listen she hadn't noticed Einar approaching. But then he padded around so quietly, unlike the noisy blundering of the other boys. The quality seemed innate in him rather than studied, reminding Aldís of a documentary she'd seen about big cats.

She suppressed a cough. 'No, only this one.' She held out the half-smoked, drooping cigarette and picked a flake of tobacco from her lip. She hadn't got the knack of smoking roll-ups and the end that had been in her mouth was wet and limp. 'Want a puff?'

Einar sat down beside her and inhaled greedily. 'God, I've missed this.'

'It's sugar I miss. I dream of big bottles of Coke and liquorice sticks.' Aldís waved the cigarette away when Einar tried to pass it back. 'I don't really smoke. You can keep it.'

He smiled and took a deep drag, the end flaring red. 'This is fantastic. Sorry I can't pay you back in sweets. Why are you smoking, if you don't normally?'

'I'm just so pissed off that I thought I might as well. I was hoping it would calm me down.' Aldís didn't know if it was the nicotine or his presence but all at once her anger subsided, leaving behind a dull torpor, like a dirty mark on her soul.

'Is it because of what happened last night? Tobbi told me. He was shaking like a leaf when he finally got back to the house.'

The wind changed direction, blowing the smoke over Aldís. She raised a hand to wave it away, then let it drop. She didn't want Einar to think she was uncool. It was bad enough being caught wearing these shoes. She tucked her feet under the bench. 'He deserved it. If he'd backed me up I wouldn't have got such a bollocking.' She licked her lips; they tasted of the cigarette. 'He's a total idiot. That's the only explanation for his reaction. I'd like to belt him.'

'It's not worth it. He's sorry enough anyway, without you giving him a beating. I've hardly been able to get any sense out of the poor little sod.' The cigarette had burnt down to Einar's fingers and he flicked the butt away. It landed in a flowerbed adorned with dirty snow and a few bare stalks left over from the previous summer. 'What actually happened? Everyone's talking about it but no one seems to know a thing. The story gets weirder and weirder the more the others try to fill in the gaps.'

'I doubt they can make it any weirder than it really was.' Aldís wished she'd accepted another of Steini's roll-ups; that way she could have kept Einar beside her a little longer. He didn't look as if he was going anywhere, but, like everything enjoyable, this was bound to be over far too quickly.

'You needn't tell me unless you want to. But if you'd like to offload, please, feel free.'

Einar was unlike anyone else she'd ever met: he was actually interested in what she had to say, and when they talked, she felt as if she mattered. Usually she found people only spoke to her because they wanted an audience. 'Yes, I'd like to. I'm just surprised anyone can be bothered to listen. Veigar and Lilja wouldn't even let me finish before they started having a go at me.'

The couple seemed to grow more uptight by the day. Aldís could hardly remember what they'd been like at the beginning. True, they'd never been exactly lively or fun, but at least they'd been fair. Now they were just perverse. Aldís had noticed that their treatment of the boys had become colder and harsher too. The loss of their baby and the money troubles she'd heard the workmen muttering about must be putting a strain on them; perhaps they faced losing the property that they'd only recently acquired. What would become of the boys then? And the workmen? She didn't really mind on her own account; she'd simply leave as planned.

'They're such bloody hypocrites. They make me sick every time they open their mouths. They're either preaching Christian homilies or coming out with something that's the complete opposite. I'm not sure the Jesus Christ they worship would be particularly flattered to have them on his team.' Einar glanced at her, obviously waiting for her to begin, then said: 'I promise to let you talk if you want to. And I'm not religious, by the way.'

Now that she had a sympathetic audience, the story seemed terribly lame to her and she was afraid he would think so too. She was embarrassed; her fingers fidgeted in her lap and she began to swing her legs again. 'It sounds so silly. But it didn't feel like a joke at the time. Tobbi didn't think so either, though he claims not to remember now. There was someone in there, someone who'd followed him or gone with him into the dining room. Anyway, I haven't a clue how they wound up in there, or what would have happened if I hadn't walked in on them.'

'So you don't know if it was a man or a woman?' There

was a hint of doubt in Einar's voice, as if he found the idea rather far-fetched.

'No. There was a power cut and I couldn't see.'

'Is it possible that there was nobody else there? Apart from Tobbi, of course.'

Aldís shuddered. 'There was somebody there, all right. I know it. Tobbi does too. He wasn't alone when I came in – he told me so himself. I think he'd been talking to the person when I barged in, and whoever it was fled. Perhaps it was one of the other boys, but I don't think so.' She longed to mention the horrible stench of blood that had filled the air the instant everything went black, but stopped herself for fear he wouldn't believe her. The same applied to the whispering that, disorientated by the darkness, she'd been unable to pinpoint the source of. She inadvertently ground her teeth as she remembered the pathetic whimper Tobbi had made, though he was normally pretty tough for his age. Aldís had had her share of frights but she'd never experienced anything like that before. Blinded by the darkness, all she had known was that somewhere nearby was a presence that wished her harm. It was just so difficult to find the words to describe it. People didn't want to listen to anything unsettling or hard to understand. The incident with her mother had taught her that and it still hurt. And if her mother had been capable of betraying Aldís, there was no reason to think others would behave any better – however nice and sympathetic Einar might seem.

'So you didn't actually see anyone?' Einar's voice conveyed neither mockery nor doubt. His question sounded genuine.

'No. But I heard footsteps and breathing and mumbling that sounded like gibberish. Almost like growling.' At first, when everything went black, it had crossed her mind that it might be a wild animal. Ridiculous though it seemed now, the noises and stench had suggested as much. 'And there was a disgusting smell of blood.' Aldís decided she might as well say it, even if he laughed.

But he didn't; he frowned and looked at her seriously. 'Blood?'

'Yes. The smell. Not actual blood. Just the smell of it. Foul. Stinking.' The wind had blown a strand of hair over her face; she tucked it behind her ear. 'When the power came back on and Steini, Hákon and Veigar arrived, we searched everywhere but there wasn't a drop to see. Neither Tobbi nor I were bleeding, so the smell must have come from the burglar or whoever it was. Because it vanished at the same time as the intruder did.'

'Do you think he was wounded?'

'I don't know. There wasn't a single drop of blood on the floor or anywhere else in the building. Perhaps the smell came from bandages or dressings.'

'Are you positive it was the smell of blood? Could it have been something else?'

'No.' Hearing how sharp she sounded, Aldís stopped herself. When she spoke again her voice was much softer. 'I work in a kitchen. I know what blood smells like.' She didn't want to admit that it had reminded her of the reek after Lilja gave birth; the reek of the poor, malformed little baby and of the room she had been made to clean.

'Of course.' Einar grimaced slightly as if he could see into her mind and glimpse the white skin of the deformed newborn, wrapped in its sheet. 'Did they find any footprints? Or had the snow drifted over them?'

Aldís shook her head. 'There were no tracks visible but that doesn't mean anything. Lilja and Veigar took it as proof that I was talking rubbish, but it was sleeting and even my footprints had disappeared.' She looked resentfully skywards, as if the heavens were to blame. 'If that stupid little jerk Tobbi had told the truth it wouldn't have mattered. But he wouldn't speak and just shook his head when they tried to interrogate him. Now everyone thinks I'm nuts.' She looked at him. 'But I'm not.'

'I believe you. If that helps.'

It helped a great deal: one person was all she needed. 'Thanks.' She didn't like to say any more for fear of sounding sentimental.

Einar turned his gaze to the flowerbed where the cigarette butt had landed. 'God, I'd kill for another fag.'

Aldís was silent as there wasn't much she could do about that. He'd probably only said it to change the subject. She was relieved in a way, as there was not much more to tell. She'd told him the facts; the rest was speculation, which would add nothing to the story. 'There are some cigarettes in a box in Lilja and Veigar's sitting room. I clean it every other week. I could pinch one next time.' Of course it was unwise, but she didn't care. They'd never notice that one was missing; neither of them smoked, and as far as Aldís knew they never had any visitors. The cigarettes were bound to be dry and past their best anyway. She could probably get away with stealing several.

'Don't. Not on my account. But I'd be grateful for a packet if you're going into town any time soon.' He fished a worn leather wallet out of his back pocket. 'I've got money. Enough for one, anyway.'

'Are you allowed to have a wallet?' According to the regulations, the boys had to hand over all their belongings on arrival. Battered suitcases were unceremoniously confiscated and the couple went through their clothes, books and whatever else they or their parents had deemed necessary for their stay. Aldís had often witnessed this and seen how painful it was for the boys to relinquish the only thing that connected them to home and their old life. But the rules were understandable when you considered that the boys were perfectly capable of smuggling in booze, porn mags and anything else they wouldn't have access to at Krókur. She was fairly certain that Lilja and Veigar didn't allow them to keep any money they'd brought with them. Not that they had the opportunity to buy anything here, but they might sneak to a call box to ring a cab and run away. Or pay one of the others to do something forbidden, like stealing from the storeroom. She was aware that Veigar held back the meagre wages they earned for casual labour at the fish factories and didn't hand them over until they left.

'I didn't tell them. Just lied when the old man asked if I had anything on me.'

'How do you know I won't report you?'

Einar stiffened in the act of opening his wallet. 'I just know.' He tried to catch her eye but all her attention was fixed on the photograph in the plastic pocket of his wallet.

'Who's that in the picture?' she asked, peering at it.

Einar snapped his wallet shut. 'No one.' He seemed annoyed, but she must have been mistaken because the next moment he looked at her and smiled. 'My mum. Bit corny, really.'

'No, not at all.' Though it was. They both studied the

brown wallet in his palm until he stuck it back in his pocket and folded his arms.

'So you'd like me to buy you cigarettes?' Aldís asked warily.

'No, not now. Later, maybe.' He didn't explain why he'd changed his mind and their conversation was suddenly stilted and awkward, though Aldís couldn't work out what had changed. He said goodbye and left her sitting there, feeling even worse than before. The wind whipped the hair from behind her ears, whirling the strands up around her head as if they were trying to break free. She struggled to hold them down but eventually gave up and sat for a while with a writhing mass of locks flying in all directions.

Rage and misery struggled for dominance inside her and she wondered if it wouldn't be best if she simply died of exposure here on the bench. It was cold enough. The world would be indifferent to her death, but those who had treated her badly would be sorry and regret not having made up with her. Like her mother, for example. She'd deserve it. But Aldís wasn't born yesterday and realised that life wasn't like that. Most people would merely shake their heads and tut that it was typical of her; she'd always been a silly girl. Lilja and Veigar would unquestionably take that attitude.

In the end, she grew fed up with being fed up. Why was she letting other people upset her? She had been in the dining room yesterday evening, not the people who thought they knew better about what had happened there. It was ridiculous to let their stupidity get to her. She needn't doubt herself. Feeling more cheerful, she pulled her hood up and her wild hair was instantly calmed and returned to its place as if nothing had happened. With her vision restored, she spotted Einar's brown wallet under the bench as soon as she stood up.

Aldís picked it up, turned it over in her hands and dusted some snowflakes off the back. She stood contemplating it, wondering whether to run after Einar and return it to him or seize the opportunity to take a peek at the picture he hadn't wanted her to see. Having checked there was no one in sight, she opened the wallet. There was the photo behind the scratched, matt plastic. It was not of his mother. The picture showed Einar with a young girl who was beaming at the camera and had her arms wrapped round his neck. She was arrestingly beautiful: wide eyes fringed with thick lashes, high cheekbones, and full lips parted to reveal large white teeth. She looked more like a model from a fashion magazine than anyone Aldís had ever met, and her radiance seemed to have infected Einar, who appeared even more handsome in the picture than in person. Yet it was at his girlfriend that Aldís found herself staring. Her beauty nettled Aldís, foolish though that was. It was none of her business if Einar had a girlfriend; she should have been pleased that she was gorgeous and not some minger. And yet . . . She longed to know the girl's name, who she was and if they were still together. His reaction when Keli had called her a slag certainly suggested they were. Surely no one would fight for the honour of an ex.

Before she knew what she was doing, Aldís had begun to go through his wallet. One of the first things she pulled out was his ID card. The copper stud which fastened the plastic pocket had worn a groove in the leather and dented the ID card. She resolved to put it back in exactly the same place. But the thought evaporated when she saw the last two digits of his year of birth, printed in red in the top right-hand corner.

No wonder Einar appeared more mature than the other boys. He was eighteen, closer in age to her than to the youngest boys. Aldís held the card up to the watery winter sun to check whether the year had been tampered with – it wasn't uncommon for underage kids to flaunt forged ID cards to get into nightclubs – but it hadn't. The forgeries rarely stood up to daylight, though they were good enough to get their owners past the doormen in dark clubs. She lowered the card, convinced it was genuine.

So Einar was eighteen, going on nineteen, nearly three years older than he should have been, according to the rules. This place was intended for troublesome boys who were too young to be treated like adult criminals. A boy who was eighteen when he committed an offence should have been sent to prison.

Aldís pushed the ID card back into its place with trembling hands and closed the wallet. Then she replaced it carefully under the bench. She didn't want him to know she had picked it up or he'd immediately guess that she'd looked inside. No, it was better like this. He would discover that he didn't have his wallet, come back and find it lying there, without suspecting her for a minute. She breathed easier. He must never know she had looked in his wallet.

Chapter 12

The old lady could hardly manage her bags as she struggled to open the door that the wind was equally determined to hold shut. Leaping out of the car, Ódinn ran over, grabbed the heavy door and held it for her so she could squeeze past him inside. 'What a gale!' Without waiting for an answer he shouted to Rún to hurry up. She picked her way gingerly from the car, only staying on her feet with the greatest of difficulty. It was hardly surprising since she had insisted on wearing her summer shoes that morning. Ódinn had long since given up trying to influence what she wore, having come to the conclusion that she would eventually learn from her mistakes. Or at least he hoped so, though he knew full well that tomorrow morning they would be faced with the same dilemma and by then the previous day's mistake would be forgotten.

'How's your little girl? Isn't it lonely for her here, with no other children in the area? Hardly any adults either, for that matter.' The old lady watched as Rún let go of the concrete bollard and began to battle her way across the last few slippery metres to warmth and shelter.

'She's fine, thanks.' Ódinn waved encouragingly at Rún. Of course he could have gone and helped her but he felt it would convey the wrong message. She had chosen those shoes in spite of his warnings and now she'd have to pay the price. 'I'm not sure it'd suit her any better to be surrounded

124

by kids all day. Not while she's still coming to terms with her loss. It might be a problem later on, but by then hopefully more people will have moved into the area – into the building, too.'

'Yes, I suppose so.' The old lady didn't sound convinced. But she seemed glad of a chance to catch her breath and have a bit of a chat, since she showed no sign of moving. Perhaps she was hoping for help with her bags. 'Tell me, Ódinn, are you having work done at the moment?'

Ódinn turned his gaze from Rún, who had only a few steps left. 'Me? No. Why did you think that?' The memory of the open window and whiff of cigarette smoke came back to him and his heart began to pound.

'I heard tramping on the staircase this morning after you'd left, and knocking on the pipes. Or that's what it sounded like. But when I looked out onto the landing I couldn't see anyone and no one answered when I called. I thought you'd probably got some tradesmen in. Up to now there's always been a note in the mailbox when your brother's got people coming round. Perhaps he forgot this time.' The woman's watery blue eyes met his. Age had merged the colour of her iris with the whites. 'That's likely to be it, don't you think? It can hardly be tramps. We're far too out of the way, and anyway there's nothing to steal.'

'I'd be very surprised if it was.' Ódinn tried to smile. 'I'll ring Baldur and ask. I expect he just forgot to let us know.'

Rún took a leap that almost ended badly, and hurtled in through the door. Without a word, she brushed the snow from her shoulders, shook the flakes out of her hair, then stamped her feet. By the time she had finished a small puddle had formed on the floor.

'Dear me.' The old lady smiled at Rún, who didn't look up. 'Don't you have any winter shoes, dear? Aren't those a bit slippery?' This would hardly encourage Rún to join in the conversation. Ódinn intervened.

'We have to suffer to be beautiful.' He took the old lady's bags, which weren't as heavy as they'd looked when she was struggling with the door. 'I'll pop these inside for you.' He turned down a cup of coffee, claiming weariness after a long day.

'Perhaps you'd let me know what your brother says,' the old lady added before they parted, the anxiety plain in her voice.

'I'll do that.'

'I'm thinking of calling the police if it carries on like this. It's very uncomfortable being alone in the building with strangers thundering around.'

On the way upstairs Rún asked what the woman had been talking about. Ódinn tried to hide the effect their only neighbour's words had had on him. 'Oh, apparently there were some workmen here today – probably finishing the other flats. She was a bit upset by the noise.'

'Have they got hammers?' Rún was several steps ahead of him as usual. She was lighter of foot and generally in more of a hurry. 'I haven't heard any hammering.'

'Apparently they were mainly thundering up and down the stairs. Anyway, you wouldn't have noticed since you weren't home at the time.'

'Maybe I'll hear them tomorrow.'

'Oh?' Ódinn wished she'd stop prattling while they climbed the stairs. He was out of condition after sitting behind a desk for months, and although he hadn't put on weight, he didn't have the breath to race upstairs and talk at the same time.

'There's a staff training day at school.' She slowed her pace and looked down at him. 'Don't you remember? I gave you a note last week.'

'Yes. Of course, of course. I'd forgotten.' He remembered putting down the note without reading it. 'Damn, we should have dropped by the shop. I'm not sure there's much for you to eat tomorrow. Perhaps I'll only do a half-day and bring you home something for lunch. How does that sound?'

'All right.' Ódinn couldn't tell whether she liked the suggestion – perhaps she'd been looking forward to spending the day alone at home. At her age he'd have preferred to be left to laze around in peace rather than have his father constantly in his hair, looking for ways to amuse him.

'It's up to you. I'll do whatever you like. As ever.' It was no lie.

Rún snorted as she sprinted up the last few steps. Ódinn didn't ask how he was supposed to interpret that. Her mother would probably have known but he did his utmost to avoid any comparisons with her; he knew perfectly well what the outcome would be. Rún wasn't a bit out of breath as she waited on the landing, nor did she seem to be giving any thought to her father's offer. She pulled off her coat, dropped it on the floor and went into her room without a word. As usual. One day he'd have to sit her down to talk about her untidiness, but right now other aspects of her upbringing were more important.

The flat was dark, cold and uninviting. Ódinn hastily switched on the lights and the television, although he wasn't intending to watch anything. Then he fetched the phone and rang Baldur's number, afraid he'd forget to call him as he'd promised the old lady. It rang for a long time and Ódinn stood patiently at the sitting-room window, gazing out at the bleak landscape.

When his brother answered the noise on the phone was deafening and it was hard to hear over the screeching static. 'What's up? I'm a bit busy.'

'I'll be quick. Dísa on the ground floor heard some people in the building. She asked me to check if you'd had men in doing some work.'

Baldur laughed. 'No, mate. We're racing to finish a warehouse and we're already into danger time. If any of my boys had been round at yours instead of pulling their weight here I'd sack him on the spot.'

'I see. Perhaps it was an estate agent showing people round?'

'Unlikely. They don't have keys to the building.' The high-frequency whistling intensified and Ódinn had to hold the phone away from his ear until the worst had passed.

'What a bloody racket. Aren't you going deaf?' Unable to think of any other plausible reason for the noise in the building, Ódinn was unwilling to involve his brother further. He didn't want Baldur, who knew him better than anyone, to sense that something was wrong. Not so long ago Dísa's words would have had no effect on him. The last thing he wanted was to let on to Baldur that he was suffering from mental exhaustion and seeing a shrink.

'What?'

'I said, aren't you going deaf?' bellowed Ódinn.

'Hey, take it easy, I was joking.' Baldur called out an order to someone behind him, then added: 'I've got to get on, but listen, why don't you and Rún come to supper on Friday? I know Sigga'd be delighted; she's a bit pissed off with me these days because I'm so rarely home. Maybe Rún'd like to come for a sleepover? She'd be company for Sigga if I have to pop in to work. It's good for her to be around women sometimes. They can go to the mall at Kringlan, or whatever it is girls like doing.'

Ódinn smiled to himself. Rún had little interest in shopping trips. But maybe she'd enjoy them more without him. 'Sounds good. Let's do that.' They said goodbye and Ódinn hung up. He continued to stare out of the window at the weather: it wasn't every day you could literally see the wind. The whirling snow clothed the gale in white, giving form to an enemy that was usually invisible. Between squalls, he could dimly make out the distant landscape before it was obliterated again.

Ódinn's thoughts wandered to the two boys who had died in the car all those years ago, presumably in weather like this. Why hadn't they got out when they realised the air was filling with poisonous exhaust fumes? Perhaps the weather had been so wild they'd preferred to huddle in the warmth in spite of the fumes, or perhaps they hadn't even been aware of the danger. He had scoured the newspaper archives, but found nothing except the original reports of the accident. Nor had he managed to get hold of any documents relating to the inquest; they'd probably been destroyed or lost long ago. Tobbi's parents were dead and so was Einar's mother. Ódinn hadn't even tried to track down his father, an American serviceman who had returned home after his tour of duty in Iceland, leaving no forwarding address.

All Ódinn knew for sure was that exhaust fumes were dangerous to people sitting in a car with a blocked exhaust pipe. While reading up on the subject, he'd come across a tragic story about a baby in Canada. Unaware of the risk, the father had started the engine so his child wouldn't get cold in its seat while he was digging out the car and scraping the windscreen. By the time he got in himself, it was too late. Ódinn had also read that in some cases people experienced a sense of euphoria before they began suffering from cramps and lost consciousness. Perhaps the boys had died happy.

A noisy ad break distracted Ódinn's attention from the window. In his current bad mood he couldn't bear the jaunty jingle exhorting the audience to buy, buy, buy some junk that anyone could live without. It dawned on him how much he missed his old job; the racket going on behind his brother on the phone had reminded him how he used to love working in that high-energy environment. An environment where things were built, the results of your work were visible and tangible from day to day. And there was never any mention of grief or death.

'What's for supper?' Rún emerged yawning from her room.

'Hot dogs. How does that sound?'

'Great. I like everything you cook.'

Although you couldn't really dignify his efforts in the kitchen as 'cooking', he felt a warm glow inside. Rún followed him to the kitchen. 'What did Baldur say? Are there builders working here?'

His happiness gave way to a familiar sense of dread. Rún would be alone at home tomorrow and it was quite possible she would hear the same noises as Dísa – assuming, of course, that the old lady hadn't been mistaken. 'He wasn't sure. Maybe. But you know what? He invited us to dinner on

Friday and asked if you'd like to stay over. Go to the shops with Sigga or something fun like that.'

She made a face at the mention of a shopping trip. 'I'm up for that. I think. But I don't want to go to Kringlan. I've already got enough of everything.'

Ódinn was touched. His daughter certainly wasn't greedy. Her wardrobe resembled a hotel closet in which the contents of one small suitcase had been hung up. Nor did she have a huge pile of toys like those in the few other children's rooms he'd seen. She had no more possessions now than when she'd first moved in. Several times he'd offered to take her to the toy shop but she'd always declined, with a genuine lack of interest. When left to her own devices she mostly amused herself with her little games console or read books. Afterwards they watched television together or played Snakes and Ladders – a great favourite. He put up with the game, unbelievably boring though he found it, because her pleasure was all that mattered. 'It's up to you, sweetheart. If you don't want to go shopping, nobody's going to force you.'

'I know.' Rún wrinkled her nose as she entered the kitchen and Ódinn didn't blame her: there was a rotting smell from the bin that he'd forgotten to empty in the morning rush. He tied up the over-full bag and took it out onto the landing. Amongst all the modern minimalism, the refuse chute was glaringly old-fashioned, but it did its job. Opening it, he was met by a cold blast, redolent of stale rubbish. He pushed the bin bag into the hole and was about to give it a shove when he thought he heard the echo of voices in the chute. He recoiled instinctively, then moved closer, ignoring the stench, to listen. Perhaps he'd misheard; perhaps the sound had been caused by the vacuum that formed when he opened the door. But no, there was the unmistakable sound of voices. Ódinn couldn't make out the words: it was almost like whispering; probably a bunch of stupid kids who'd sneaked in to smoke or get up to some other mischief. Couldn't they have found a better place? What were they thinking of, trekking all the way up this desolate cul-de-sac to hide in the bin store? There were plenty of weatherproof construction sites in the area that would be a lot more inviting.

Ódinn dropped the bag and yelled after it: 'Hey, you! Get the fuck out of there!' There was a thud as the bag fell into the dustbin at the bottom, followed by a sudden hush. Ódinn wasn't entirely satisfied; he would rather have heard the slamming of a door below or some sort of kerfuffle. 'Get lost!' he shouted. 'Or I'll call the police. This is private property.' How dreadfully middle-aged and pompous he sounded. If he'd been a teenager on the receiving end, he'd have bust a gut laughing.

But nobody laughed. There was no sound but a low sucking noise from the chute. 'Right, I'm going to call them.'

'Why are you shouting, Daddy? What's the matter?' Rún was standing in the doorway, regarding him anxiously.

'It's nothing, love. Just some kids down in the bin store. I was chasing them out. They're not supposed to be in there.'

'What are they doing there?' Her worried expression had not entirely disappeared.

'Teenagers can be a bit daft.' Ódinn was about to add more when he was thrown by the whispering starting up again. He couldn't stop himself from putting his ear to the chute, though he could see his daughter's eyes widening and her expression growing even more dismayed. He couldn't distinguish any words but every now and then there was a giggle. Suddenly he felt certain it was only one person. Whisper, whisper, giggle, giggle. He couldn't be sure but he thought he heard the voice say: *Just you wait*, like the threat of a small child, though there had been nothing childish about the way it was uttered. Without waiting to hear more, he slammed the door of the chute, pushed Rún inside the flat and locked the door behind them. The giggling had conveyed no amusement, no: 'Hee hee, that stupid man's still there.' Instead, Ódinn had the impression that the words and suppressed laughter were full of malice, and he didn't want his daughter to hear. He'd been frightened enough himself.

Half an hour later he said goodbye to the two policemen. They'd asked if he had by any chance been drinking or smoking or if he was on medication, because the snow in front of the door to the bin store showed beyond a doubt that no one had set foot there. The noises had been purely imaginary. Ódinn wished he could fetch Rún from her room to back up his story, but had no intention of letting her hear about the trackless snow.

'Did the police make the teenagers go home?' Rún had emerged.

'They'd run away by the time the police finally showed up. Perhaps they heard the sirens.'

'There weren't any sirens. I saw the car arrive.'

'Well, I warned them I was going to call the police, so they must have done a runner.'

Rún clearly didn't believe this, which was hardly surprising given that he didn't believe it himself. He tried to console himself with the thought that at least whoever had been in the bin store had gone now. But the consolation was short-lived. They were bound to come back. Perhaps it was the same

person or people that Dísa had heard. Ódinn eyed the in-
adequate lock that was all that separated them from the
communal area. Tomorrow he would buy a bolt for the door.
And while he was about it he had better call in sick, because
there was no way he was leaving Rún alone at home.

Chapter 13

Ódinn knew he ought to focus on the visit, but his thoughts kept straying back to the office where Rún was being looked after by Diljá. When it came to it, he hadn't liked to call in sick, so he had taken his daughter with him to work. And, of course, he hadn't exactly relished the prospect of spending the day in the flat himself.

Everything had gone smoothly; Rún had behaved like an angel, playing on the computer at an empty desk nearby. None of his colleagues had remarked on this or asked why his daughter had come to work with him, since they were all familiar with his circumstances. Detecting pity in their faces, he felt annoyed. There was no need to feel sorry for him and Rún; they'd manage, whatever happened.

Every now and then he looked up from his work and, as if he'd spoken, she looked up too and they exchanged conspiratorial smiles. Sometimes it was as if they were sharing the same thought: *It'll be all right*. But when midday came and he had to go out briefly, the false sense of security quickly evaporated and he wanted more than anything to take Rún along. There was no question of cancelling the interview now that he'd finally managed to arrange it. The man was the first person who'd agreed to discuss his time at Krókur, and Ódinn didn't want him to change his mind. So far all the others had refused, and although the list was far from exhausted, it wasn't a promising start.

Ódinn was expecting the visit to be over quickly, so Rún could theoretically have waited out in the car. But it was such a cold day, he would have had to leave the engine running, and it would have been impossible to relax, thinking of her alone in the car in the drifting snow, worrying that it might block the exhaust. It was the lesser of two evils to leave her in Diljá's company.

Trying to push these thoughts aside, Ódinn knocked on the weathered door. There was plastic tape stuck over the bell to show it was broken. The wood was so solid that Ódinn might have been knocking on stone. He rapped again, so hard that his cold knuckles ached.

The door was opened by a woman of indeterminate age. Her rough, colourless hair looked as if it had been hacked short with nail scissors. She was wearing a baggy, frayed man's jumper that had once sported a brightly patterned yoke. Her grey-tinged face was cross-hatched with deep wrinkles, apart from the smooth skin round her mouth, which suggested that life had seldom given her reason to smile. Looking at her lips, Ódinn expected the worst, but his fear proved unjustified; her teeth were unusually fine and white.

'Are you Ódinn?' Her voice was predictably gruff and hoarse.

'Yes, hello.' He felt the calluses on her palm during the firm handshake. 'Are you Kegga?' There was no way of guessing the woman's real name. Social Services, who had assisted him in arranging the interview, had only supplied her nickname. 'I assume you know why I'm here?'

The woman nodded indifferently. Only those who had

reached the end of the road sought refuge here, so as warden of the halfway house, she must have received plenty of visits odder than this one. 'He's in his room and awake. You did want to see Pytti, didn't you?'

'Er, I only know his full name, Kolfinnur Jónsson. Is that Pytti?'

'Yes.' The woman opened the door. The house stood on Snorrabraut and from the outside there was nothing to indicate that it didn't contain ordinary flats. Inside, however, he was met by that unmistakable institutional smell, a combination of industrial cleaning fluid, stewed coffee and the wet anoraks hanging from the sagging coat-rail in the small lobby. 'No need to take off your shoes unless you want to.'

Ódinn decided to keep them on but took care to wipe his feet thoroughly. In spite of the smell of cleaning fluid, the floor looked decidedly grimy. 'How many people live here?' Judging by the anoraks, there must be around eight residents.

'Five at the moment. There's quite a quick turnover. Not everyone lasts the course. It's hard for them to keep to the house rules, and breaking them leads to immediate expulsion.' The three remaining anoraks must have been left behind when their owners were shown the door. He hoped it had been summer at the time. It was hard to imagine how anyone could survive on the streets in the depths of the Icelandic winter without a coat. Even in warm weather, it seemed a bit heartless to throw out the homeless. The woman apparently read his mind. 'You can't run a place like this if people are allowed to behave as if they're still on the streets or in some crack house. It's not fair on those who are genuinely trying to turn over a new leaf.' She showed Ódinn into an open-plan seating area off the lobby. 'It doesn't take much to make someone lose heart in the early stages of recovery. As I know to my cost.'

Ódinn had no idea how to respond. Surely the woman didn't expect him to start questioning her about her battle with addiction? 'Has Kolfinnur . . . I mean, Pytti, been here long?'

'No. About three months. He came here from the Hladgerdarkot treatment centre. He'd been there for seven or eight months, I think.' The woman opened a door into the bedroom wing. 'Agga from the ministry told me about your inquiry.' No one connected to this place seemed to go by their given name and Ódinn toyed with the idea of introducing himself as Oggi when he met Pytti.

'I won't force him if he doesn't want to talk to me. I gathered he was willing, but I understand that raking up the past can be difficult.'

'He's quite laid-back about it.' She stopped and turned. 'It doesn't matter what I think but I'll say it anyway.'

'Sure.' Ódinn took an involuntary step backwards as the woman was suddenly standing uncomfortably close. 'Are you unhappy about me talking to him?'

'I'm not sure. What bothers me is the risk that you'll put two ideas in his head that could have a negative effect on his sobriety.' With sudden vehemence she held up her index finger and said: 'Blame.' Then raised a second finger and added: 'The prospect of money.' She held her fingers in the air, so close she could have pinched Ódinn's nose.

'What do you mean by blame?'

The woman lowered her hand. 'One of the most important things for a recovering addict is to take responsibility for his own life. Not to be eaten up with self-pity and constantly brooding over who or what's to blame. Do you follow?'

'I'm not sure.' It would have been easy to pretend he did, but Ódinn was afraid she'd question him and expose him as a fraud. 'If someone's suffered an injustice, surely he has a right to compensation? Regardless of the path he's chosen in life. At least, that's my opinion.'

Her nostrils flared as she drew a sharp breath. 'I'm not denying that. What I mean is that when addicts are trying to get their act together, they need to look to the future and into their own hearts. Everyone's got a sob story. There's always someone worse off than us. As you can imagine, not in our wildest dreams do we want to end up like this. But if you start looking for excuses for your problem, you'll find either that you were born an addict or that life's been cruel to you from the word go. Or both. Then you'll be so depressed by the injustice of it all that you'll end up wallowing in self-pity. You have every right to, I'm not denying that, but it won't change anything. You'll be just as fucked as ever.'

'I'm not intending to encourage that sort of reaction. Not deliberately, anyway.' Ódinn wondered if he himself could achieve the level of stoicism she advocated. Probably not. 'Nothing's emerged so far to suggest that the boys were badly treated at Krókur. I'm actually hoping Pytti'll confirm that. I'm planning to talk to other old boys too, but the number will rather depend on what they say.'

The woman emitted a sharp rattle, apparently of laughter. 'Not badly treated, you say. You're optimistic.'

'You mean Breidavík and places like that? I'm hoping they were the exception, not the rule.'

'Hope away. It doesn't alter the fact that if you want to look after children properly you have to love them. And people seem incapable of that when it comes to other people's kids. Especially if they're naughty or difficult or unusually vulnerable. You might manage it with young children, but older kids and teenagers never have and never will have a chance with strangers. It's as simple as that.'

He didn't like to remind her of the countless adoptions that had brought happiness to children all over the world, since she was no doubt referring to cases where children were placed with non-family members for shorter periods. Besides, she had a point. Behaviour that you can put up with from your own offspring can be hard to tolerate from other people's. If Rún had been a guest in his home he'd almost certainly have lost his temper with her at times over her frequent mood swings and terrible untidiness.

The woman turned on her heel, stomped down the corridor and knocked, quite loudly, on a door. The reply was indistinct but apparently intelligible to Kegga, who opened the door. 'There you go. I'll be out front if you need me.' She left without introducing the two men or putting her head round the door to check if Pytti was in a fit state to receive visitors.

'Come in.' It was a male version of Kegga's rasp. A man was sitting on a narrow divan which looked as if it had been bought at the bargain bed warehouse. The rose-patterned pillowcase clashed with the striped duvet and pink sheet, and the rest of the furniture was a similarly mismatched assortment from the Good Shepherd charity shop: dressing table, chair, small desk and a fitted cupboard hardly large enough to accommodate an ordinary person's socks and underwear but probably more than adequate for the few rags that were all the room's occupant owned. On the cupboard door hung a small picture of Salome receiving the head of John the Baptist on a golden dish. The message was clear: 'And you think *your* life's shit'.

The man gestured Ódinn towards the rickety chair and he sat down, hoping it would support his weight. It creaked but didn't collapse. Ódinn introduced himself and received the man's nickname in return. 'I was told you were willing to talk to me. I hope that wasn't a misunderstanding. I won't bother you for long, I promise.'

The man laughed and Ódinn saw that he hadn't been as lucky as Kegga in the dental department. Every other tooth appeared to be missing and those that remained were brown or discoloured. His nose had obviously been broken more than once without the benefit of medical attention and even his ears seemed to have received their share of abuse. 'Bother me? My dear boy! I've nothing better to do today; or any other day, for that matter.'

Ódinn noticed that the room contained no form of diversion: no television, computer or radio, not even a book. 'You never know.'

'I've got to go to a meeting at suppertime but apart from that I'm free. Free as a bird.' The man roared with laughter, which quickly deteriorated into a hacking cough.

'A meeting?' At first Ódinn thought the man was joking, then realised he must be referring to an AA meeting. 'All right if I begin?' He was in a hurry to get the interview over with, uncomfortable at finding himself in such close quarters with a human tragedy that it was too late to reverse. All this man could look forward to now was palliative care.

'I'm all ears.' Pytti seemed tickled by his own sarcasm.

'Right.' Ódinn drew his notes from his jacket pocket. 'I'm conducting a preliminary inquiry into the treatment of the children at Krókur. Checking that it wasn't anything like what went on at some of the other residential care homes for children and teenagers.'

'Funny you should say children. I didn't feel like a child when I was there. But now, looking back, I realise I was of course.'

Ódinn glanced at his notes, calculated Pytti's age and was disconcerted to discover that he was only fifty-two years old. 'You were fourteen. Is that right? There for just under a year?'

'Something like that, yes.'

'Do you remember that time?' Ódinn studied the battered face in the hope of being able to determine the truth of his answers.

'Yes. Not the day to day, but I reckon I remember it all right. The early years of my life are quite clear in my mind, but after that whole decades are more or less a blur. Maybe the old memories have lasted so well because they weren't replaced by any new ones. Blackouts don't leave much behind.'

'How would you describe your time there? I mean, the way you were looked after. And anything else you happen to remember. Were you ever mistreated by the staff or would you say you had nothing to complain about? Apart from your loss of freedom, obviously.'

'That's a big question.' The man returned his stare intently. Perhaps he was trying to gauge Ódinn's sincerity. 'It was no better or worse than the years before or afterwards. But you have to take into account that I had a miserable life both before I arrived and after I left. So it didn't make much difference.'

'I'm sorry to hear that.' Ódinn would have to tread carefully. He wasn't here to write a report on the man's life, only the eleven months he had spent at Krókur. Most of the boys who wound up there had lived in wretched conditions. Not in every case, but from the reports he'd read Ódinn was struck by how many of them had come from alcoholic families. Or, if they weren't alcoholics, their parents had been struggling with poverty or other problems. In the end it was their sons who suffered, who vented their frustration at the injustice of the world through vandalism or petty theft, for which they paid with their freedom. Pytti belonged to the former group: his parents had been serious alcoholics who had subjected him to appalling neglect. It wasn't a good sign if conditions at Krókur had been no better than those at his childhood home. 'What was the reason for your unhappiness at Krókur? Was it anything specific or were you just unhappy in general?'

The man leant back on the bed and raised his gnarled hand thoughtfully to his chin. His tremors were so bad it looked as if his fingers were playing an invisible piano. 'It was miserable and just . . . pointless somehow. I was there for a ridiculous reason – I broke a window at school in a fit of rage. Who'd spend a year locked up for that nowadays?'

'No one.' Ódinn said no more. He wasn't here to stand trial for or defend the past conduct of the child protection authorities. If that were the case, what on earth would he say to vindicate the other care homes where innocent children had been incarcerated?

The man seemed satisfied with Ódinn's reply. 'We should have been at school during the day and chasing skirt in the evenings. Not stuck in the arse end of nowhere, counting down the days till our release.'

'Weren't you given any lessons?'

'Lord, no.' Pytti thought for a moment. 'Well, they did try to knock something into our heads but we spent most of our time doing chores around the farm.' He coughed again. 'I wasn't bad with the books as a kid. But I got no support at home so in the end I gave up and started messing around.' He fixed his gaze on the wall behind Ódinn's head. Perhaps he was reflecting on what his life might have been like if he'd received a normal upbringing. Ódinn couldn't help wondering about it himself, at any rate. But when Pytti began talking again it was on a different subject. 'Between trying to teach us and making us slave away on the farm, they forced us to listen to a load of Christian bollocks. Not that the couple preaching were exactly models of charity. But we were supposed to see the light. Mend our sinful ways, as they used to say.' This was followed by more phlegmy laughter. 'Got a fag, by any chance?'

'Sorry, no.' At that moment Ódinn regretted that he didn't smoke; he'd have liked to have been able to treat this man to some tobacco. 'There were between five and ten of you in residence at any given time. Presumably there were misdemeanours that had to be dealt with. How were they punished?'

'The usual. You were taken aside and preached at. Sometimes you were locked in a room and made to read the Bible. Or went without supper. Had to muck out the cowshed. There were various punishments.'

'Did they include corporal punishment?'

'The odd slap. Got one of my teeth knocked loose, if I remember right.'

Ódinn noted this down. 'Who hit you?'

'Veigar. The manager. The old sod. Mind you, he was probably younger than I am now.'

'He was under forty at the time.' Ódinn put down his pen. 'Was he free with his fists?'

'Oh, I don't know. He used to lose his rag. But nothing serious, really. It didn't bother boys like me, who were used to getting a smack with our orders, but others didn't take it so well. The old lady was far worse, though she never belted us. I'd have taken an old-fashioned beating any day over a dirty look from her.'

'A look?'

'Yes. She was off her rocker. Used to glare at you like she could drill a hole through your head. Gave me the willies. Said all kinds of ugly stuff too that had you shaking in your shoes.'

'Oh? Like what?'

'God, don't know if I want to remember.' He licked his lips; the tongue that darted out of his mouth appearing startlingly red against his grey skin. 'Bible quotations and nasty stuff about what pathetic little shits we were. How we'd end up on the scrap heap. That was about the worst thing that could happen to you; that you'd never amount to anything. I reckon that hit me the hardest. It wasn't like you didn't already know, but sometimes you managed to forget for a bit and it wasn't much fun being reminded.'

Ódinn drew a breath and wished he were somewhere else. At his computer, where he could check on Rún. It was hard to see what a report about the injustices experienced by boys so many years ago would achieve. No amount of compensation could undo the damage they had suffered. And what exactly had caused the damage? Would this man's life have been different if he had never been sent to Krókur? Of course it was impossible for Ódinn to judge, and anyway it made no odds. An injustice was an injustice, regardless of what came before or after. 'It emerged during the inquiry into other care homes that sometimes it was the kids themselves who made the other kids' life a misery. The staff left them to it and bullying and beatings by the older kids were rife. Was that the case at Krókur?'

'Not that I recall. Sure, there were fights, but don't forget we were a tough bunch. It would've been a miracle if we hadn't got into scraps. There was a lot of teasing, too, but not enough to hurt. Or not for long, anyway.'

Evidently Pytti hadn't been bullied himself or he wouldn't have made so light of the teasing. But others might have a very different story to tell. Ódinn felt overwhelmed with gloom at the thought of having to interview other old boys. 'Is there anything else you'd like to mention, anything I haven't asked about?' Ódinn had the feeling he'd overlooked some important aspect, but the longing to get out of here, to get back to Rún, was becoming unbearable.

'Only that it was a horrible place. The place itself, I mean. The farm and its surroundings. It wasn't like proper country-side. I don't know what the hell it was. Just the arse end of nowhere. It was crazy trying to farm there. There was some-thing wrong with the whole thing. Nothing to do with the people.'

'I don't quite follow. What do you mean?'

'I can't explain it, but I wasn't the only one who was creeped out by the place. We all were. It was a bad place. Some of the others claimed the old man had buried their child on the farm and that was why there was this spooky atmosphere.'

'Their child?' Ódinn hadn't seen a word about the couple having a child.

'Child, or foetus, or whatever. I don't know what it was. But the woman had a baby that was stillborn or died at birth. Anyhow, there was no chance to baptise it, and because they were so Christian they didn't like to give it a decent burial in a churchyard or put it in a coffin with someone else. So they just shoved it in a hole in the ground.' Pytti's gaze grew shifty as he read the disbelief on Ódinn's face. 'You don't believe me but that's what happened. And two of the boys paid the price.'

'Hang on a minute. How do you mean?'

'They died. Two of them. Did you really think it was an accident?'

Chapter 14

January 1974

Aldís's face was puffy and hollow-eyed after her sleepless night. A splash of icy water helped, but only for a moment. No sooner had the colour faded from her cheeks than she looked as tired and wretched as before. She felt like hanging a towel over the mirror while she brushed her teeth. A shower would have been a godsend but there was only a bathtub which took too long to fill. Besides, there was a risk she'd drop off if she lay in the hot water, and drowning in this place was not a tempting prospect.

She spat out the toothpaste and rinsed her mouth. She wished she could do the same to her brain, rinse out the churning thoughts that had kept her awake. They had revolved around what upset her most – her relationship with her mother, and also all the mystery surrounding Einar. As she tossed and turned in the darkness her problems had appeared ever more insurmountable. The pain in her stomach intensified and nothing worked to distract her mind. She had an oppressive sense that everything was going wrong, and, what was more, nothing could be done to prevent it. She'd tried her best to come up with different ways of sorting out her life, but to no avail. Each time, her fatalistic side told her she had no control over her future. Even her dreams, when they finally came, were bad. When her alarm clock went off she was snatched out of a world that she preferred not to recall. All that remained was a dim memory of a hole she couldn't climb out of, which was slowly but inexorably filling with mud that oozed down the sides. She didn't want to remember, especially not the vague feeling that there was something unpleasant down there with her. Still, on the bright side, at least it meant she must have drifted off for a while, though she had no idea for how long. Probably longer than she thought. It was always the way.

She turned on the hot tap to wash her hands and, while it was warming up, plucked up the courage to look in the mirror. Through the mist that crept up the glass it looked as if she had a red mark on one cheek, where her mother had slapped her. She didn't wipe away the condensation as she didn't want to see it any more clearly, but her cheek felt hot and tender to the touch.

There was a peremptory knock on the bathroom door. 'You're not the only one who needs the toilet.' Hastily, she tidied away her wash things and opened the door. Malli was leaning against the wall with a goading look that made her want to answer back, but she stopped herself. It wasn't his fault she was feeling like this. And she had no wish to get into a stupid quarrel first thing in the morning. Back in her room, once she'd tied her shoelaces and drawn her hair back into a neat ponytail, she felt slightly better and slapped her knees as if to remind her legs that it was time to go. She'd be in a right state later. But she'd have to stick it out, and the best way was to keep reminding herself how many hours she'd put behind her and how many were left. As she knew from experience, she'd feel better when the day's work was half done and the end was in sight. Mind you, she'd have to conserve her energy since it was her day off tomorrow and she was damn well going to treat herself to a trip to town, even if she had to walk there. She was running out of various things, and, who knows, buying something pretty might help to soothe her inner turmoil.

Cheered by the prospect of a shopping trip, she hurried out, only to come face to face with Tobbi whose nose was almost pressed to the door when she opened it. Though he wasn't exactly an alarming figure, Aldís was startled. 'What are you doing here, silly? Can't you knock?' She spoke more sharply than she usually did to the younger boys but she couldn't help herself. Her heart was hammering and her body needed an outlet for the adrenaline that was pumping through her veins. Besides, she was still pissed off with him for not telling the truth about what had happened in the dining room.

'Sorry. I was going to knock but you opened the door.' The boy lowered his head, shamefaced, and stared at his feet. His hair had grown out and the black fringe flopped limply over his forehead and eyes. Lilja was supposed to cut the boys' hair but recently she'd neglected her duty and some of them were looking distinctly shaggy.

'Come to apologise, have you? You needn't think you'll get off that lightly. I couldn't give a shit about your excuses. If you want to make it up to me you can bloody well go and tell Lilja and Veigar what really happened.' She suppressed an impulse to grab him and force him to look her in the eye.

'That's not why I'm here.' He was mumbling as if he had a mouthful of chewing gum, which might well be the case. His grandmother regularly sent him little parcels of sweets and since it was Tobbi's job to fetch the post, he was able to squirrel them away. Not a bad reward for his efforts, though he had to walk all the way down the slip-road to collect the mail from the old milk-churn platform that stood by the turn-off. Otherwise Veigar and Lilja confiscated all treats, saying they had no place at the home. Aldís had seen Lilja feeding the pigs with sweets that had arrived in the post and, as far as she knew, the boys weren't even told they'd received a package. Aldís didn't know which was worse: withholding their parcels or keeping quiet about the fact they'd been sent a gift from home and letting them believe they'd been abandoned. She had often considered exposing the couple's behaviour to the boys but always stopped herself. She was afraid of the consequences, not just for herself but in case she provoked a mutiny. Any such behaviour would be harshly suppressed and the boys would be worse off than before. Once, she'd plucked up the courage to mention it to Lilja, who had replied that it was best this way since some of the boys never received any post, and the others' good fortune would only lead to unhappiness or envy. In other words, everyone ought to feel equally bad. Aldís hadn't had the nerve to respond.

'I've brought you something.' Tobbi reached into his back pocket and held out an envelope, folded but not crumpled.

The wind went out of Aldís's sails. She stared, speechless, at the folded envelope. Never had it occurred to her that she might be in the same boat as the boys. Before taking it, she asked in a low voice: 'Have Veigar and Lilja confiscated other letters to me?' The boy nodded and Aldís thought she detected a hint of shame in his expression. She glanced briefly at the address and instantly recognised the handwriting. 'These letters to me, did they all have the same writing on them?'

'I think so. I'm not sure.' Tobbi shuffled his feet. He still hadn't met her eye.

Aldís snatched the envelope from him. It was heavier than she'd expected but not enough to suggest it contained anything other than paper. With a lump in her throat, she took a step backwards and shut the door in Tobbi's face. She neither thanked him nor harangued him to tell the truth about the incident in the dining room. She was too tired, angry and upset.

She knew the elegantly formed letters of her name as well as her own writing. The envelope burned her fingers and she wanted to hurl it into the corner. It couldn't have come at a worse time, catching her when she was so down after a night of fretting. About how her mother had failed her, among other things. It felt like fate; the same fate that had whispered mockingly to her last night that she had no control over what was to come.

Aldís stuffed the envelope into her pocket and left her room, roughly drying her eyes. She would read the letter later.

Anger can be useful at times. Aldís was filled with a resolve that she'd forgotten she possessed. Those around her seemed to sense that something was up and for once Lilja avoided speaking to her or ordering her about. She even bit her tongue when she caught Aldís stuffing two pieces of bread in her pocket for the bird, though up to now Aldís had stolen crusts for it when no one was looking. Now she couldn't give a damn about Lilja's reaction. In fact, she was sure she'd explode if Lilja so much as breathed heavily in her direction. Getting it out of her system like that might feel wonderful, but living with the consequences wouldn't be much fun, especially since

Lilja had started harbouring grudges. Aldís was also scared that she'd blurt out exactly what she thought about their stealing her post, and on no account did she want to do that. Not until she had mentally rehearsed her speech, tweaking it until it was perfect.

Every time she moved, Aldís could feel the envelope in her back pocket and it was enough to keep her rage smouldering all day. It was unbelievable that they should have the temerity to confiscate her letters. They were bound to have read the contents as well. The thought made the fury and hatred blaze up inside her as never before. They had no right to pry into her private affairs, perhaps even sneer at what her mother wrote, which was surely an attempt at an apology. In between trying to come up with a plan for getting her own back on Lilja and Veigar, she wondered what was in the letter, always coming to the same conclusion: her mother was begging her to take pity on her. To get in touch or come home. What else could it be? She would hardly be writing to say that Aldís was a bloody liar who couldn't bear for her to find love, though of course it couldn't be ruled out. Perhaps her mother wanted her money back, though it had only been a small amount. It was these fears that stopped Aldís from shutting herself in a room during the coffee break and tearing open the envelope. Better wait until she'd finished work.

'Are you angry with me?' Einar loomed over her as she was crouching with the dustpan in the room where the Christian meetings were held. When she first started work at the home, Aldís had attended the gatherings, not out of a desire to hear the word of God but for a bit of variety in her monotonous life. Veigar and Lilja's faces had lit up when they saw her taking a seat behind the boys but their pleasure

153

had been short-lived because she had only attended three meetings. She couldn't bear the repetitions and Bible quotations that the couple thundered at the boys by turns, or the sanctimonious looks on their faces. Now she only ventured into the room once a week to clean it.

'No.' Aldís stood up. 'Why should I be angry with you?' She hadn't the energy to discuss the matters that concerned him, let alone the business of the letters. Another time.

'You were so strange at lunchtime.'

'I'm just not in a good mood. It has nothing to do with you.'

Einar reached out as if to touch her face, then changed his mind. He put his hands in his pockets instead and rocked on his heels. 'Tobbi told me about this morning. I just wanted to let you know. And to say that Veigar and Lilja are bastards. Total bastards.'

Aldís couldn't agree more but didn't say so. She couldn't decide whether to ask him to leave her alone or welcome his company. 'Why did he tell you?'

'I saw him nip over to your house this morning after he'd gone out at the crack of dawn. He was supposed to go for the post yesterday but they never got round to sending him. I didn't know if it was you he went to see or the other guys who live there, so I interrogated him. I can get him to talk pretty easily.'

Of course he could. Tobbi was thirteen; Einar nearly nineteen, almost an adult. But Aldís couldn't say as much without revealing that she'd stolen a look in his wallet. And she had no intention of doing that. Not yet. 'Did you ask if he'd seen any letters to you?'

Einar's face took on an odd expression, though it seemed

a normal enough question to Aldís. 'No. I didn't ask.' He was a bad liar. As if to head off any further questions, he added quickly: 'I'm going to slip out this evening if the weather's good. Maybe go for a walk, enjoy a bit of freedom. I was wondering if you'd like to join me. If I get into trouble, I promise not to let on that you were there too.'

'How will you get out?' Aldís asked, to defer having to answer. Breaking out of the boys' dormitory was child's play, as she well knew.

'I'll find a way.' His smile didn't reach his eyes. 'What do you say? Are you coming? It'll do you good. We'll go far enough away that you can scream yourself hoarse if you want to. It can help to let off steam.' He seemed to be talking from experience.

Aldís fiddled with the handle of the dustpan as she considered her answer. If they were found out, she could get into serious trouble, even lose her job. But so what if she did? It would hardly be the end of the world if she didn't get a reference from Veigar and Lilja. Though she tried to do her work conscientiously, she wasn't sure what sort of recommendation they'd give her anyway. If the worst happened, she could simply go to Reykjavík sooner than intended. 'I'll come. Where shall I meet you and what time?'

Einar's face lit up. Once they had agreed on a time and place, he hurried out, turning in the doorway to wink. He had gone by the time she managed to wink back.

Before leaving the room, she gave in to the urge to empty the dustpan under the carpet by Lilja and Veigar's lectern.

Aldís had her anorak on and was ready to go out and meet Einar before she finally opened the letter. She had been sitting on her bed for ages, contemplating the innocent envelope, but now impulsively she grabbed it and ripped it open. She sat with the letter in her lap, eyes fixed unseeingly on the black writing that ran across the page in perfectly straight lines as if her mother had used a ruler to ensure that none of the words went astray. Then, taking a deep breath, she began reading.

My darling Aldis,

I hope you've read my earlier letters though I haven't heard back from you. I'm so afraid that you'll throw them away unopened when you see who they're from. But if you're reading this, I beg you again to get in touch, ring or write, even if it's only a few words.

As I've written before, Lárus has gone, so you needn't worry that he'll answer the phone or read what you write to me.

I miss you more than words can say and I'd give anything to be able to turn the clock back and react differently. But there's no point talking about it - I failed you and I'll just have to live with the fact and try to make up for it. Ever since you were born you've given my life meaning, been the one thing that's brought me happiness and joy. Without you, life's not worth living.

Please let me hear from you, my darling Aldis. Not knowing how you're getting on and how you're feeling is killing me. I love you and always will, and I beg you to overlook those few seconds when I doubted you, and remember instead all those years when my behaviour was guided by my real feelings for you.

Love,
Mum

Aldís put the letter down. She wanted to read it again but wouldn't let herself. Before she could decide how she felt, she had to get hold of the previous letters. When had her mother realised that she was telling the truth? Had she thrown the bastard out or had he walked out on her? Was it only then that her mother had really started regretting her behaviour? Rather than trying to order her thoughts, Aldís got up and left the room. It was still ten minutes until she was due to meet Einar but in the meantime she meant to pinch a bottle from the larder. She had never felt any desire for alcohol before: it tasted vile and she didn't enjoy feeling drunk and talking crap. Not as a rule. But at this moment it felt appropriate. Even if it led her to do something she'd regret. Though it was hard to imagine what could make her position here worse than it already was.

Chapter 15

'We were hoping to hang on to you a bit longer.' Diljá winked at Rún and smiled at Ódinn. Her lipstick had worn off while Ódinn was out, a sign that she'd looked after Rún diligently, not even popping to the loo to touch up her make-up. He felt torn between gratitude for her care and trepidation about her possible motives. What had Diljá been saying to his daughter while he was away?

'Oh, you want to get rid of me again, is that it?' Rún looked at her father, her expression unreadable. Afraid his attempt at a joke had misfired, Ódinn ruffled her hair gently, to show he didn't mean it. 'And there I was thinking I was indispensable.'

'Not entirely.' Diljá winked at Rún again. She picked up her bag and her shoulder sagged under its weight. Ódinn had often been puzzled by all the clobber some women carted around with them, especially as they could never find anything in those black holes when they needed to. 'Look after my chair, Rún,' Diljá added. 'I'm going to get a coffee; I won't be a mo. Can I get either of you anything?' They said no thank you, and Ódinn watched as she headed to the loo.

'What did you two talk about?' He turned to his daughter.

Rún shrugged. 'Nothing special. I was just drawing.' The desk in Róberta's cubicle was littered with coloured-in pictures. He had no idea where Diljá had dug up the crayons, since they were hardly standard office equipment. Perhaps they'd been lying at the bottom of one of Róberta's drawers. It was a good thing Diljá hadn't lent Rún a biro as she tended to press so hard that the pictures would have been engraved into the surface of the desk.

'Want to bring your drawings over to my desk? It's much nicer for me to have you within reach while I'm working. Here you're so far away you might as well be at home.' Ódinn had moved Rún over to Róberta's cubicle to be near Diljá while he was out. He hadn't stopped to think about it before he left, but now he regretted having left her at the dead woman's desk – worse, in the exact spot where she'd given up the ghost. 'Come on, sweetheart. Let's shift your stuff. I've got a bit of work to do, then we can go.' He'd promised to leave earlier than usual so she wouldn't have to spend all day at the office, and he meant to keep his word.

'Who are they?' Rún pointed at the photo of the two boys on the wall.

Ódinn swallowed. 'They're just two boys. From the olden days.'

'What are their names?'

'Einar and Thorbjörn.' Although Pytti's account of their deaths had been pretty far-fetched, he couldn't get it out of his mind. What was he supposed to do with the information? Gloss over it? If he repeated Pytti's story he'd probably find himself at the employment agency looking for a new job once the report was published. No one would want to read an official inquiry that contained gossip about the corpse of a baby buried somewhere on the property at Krókur, and he still didn't quite understand how it was linked to the story of the two boys. It had been difficult enough to follow Pytti's rambling story without the addition of a dead baby.

Eventually, however, Ódinn had got the gist: the exhaust hadn't been blocked by snow; the boys had died because someone had stuffed a rag into it. Pytti's theories about who might have wanted to dispose of them had been as vague as the rest of his tale: first it was the couple who ran the home, then the workmen, then one of the other boys. The motive for the crime was also obscure, and all Ódinn's attempts to find out what it was had met with a blank stare. As with all conspiracy theories, Pytti's story was vague, muddled and almost certainly fictitious. But something about that detail about the rag made it seem plausible.

'Why are they on the wall of your office?' Rún stared intently at the old photo.

'I don't know. It's not my desk. Maybe the woman who used to sit here liked the picture.'

'They watch you.' Rún frowned. 'Their eyes follow you.'

'That's just because they were looking into the camera.' Ódinn stepped to one side and the boys' eyes seemed to pursue him, as they had the first time he saw the photo. Foolish as it was, he felt as if they were waiting impatiently to see what he would do; if he would expose the truth about their fate. He wanted to lean over to the photo and tell them that one mysterious death was quite enough; he didn't need any more. But right now his priority was to get Rún out of the cubicle. 'Come on. There's juice in the kitchen.'

But Rún sat tight. 'Where's the woman who used to work here? Did she leave like the man who had the other desk?'

'Yes, she left.'

'Why didn't she take her stuff? He didn't leave anything behind.'

'She didn't have time. It'll be cleared out soon.' Ódinn

spun the chair round and had to restrain himself from snatching Rún out of it.

'That's not Róberta's chair, by the way.' Diljá was back at her desk, coffee cup in hand. She had reapplied her lipstick and Ódinn had to admit that she was looking particularly gorgeous. For an instant he envied Denni going home with her from the office party. But her next comment brought him back to earth. 'I swapped it with Denni's. He didn't dare complain, though I don't suppose he was exactly thrilled.' Diljá smirked and sipped her coffee. 'Serves him right.'

'Why?' Rún looked between the two of them. 'What did he do?'

'Nothing. That was the trouble.' Diljá hung her bag over her chair again, sat down and began to hammer away at her keyboard.

'What do you mean, nothing?' Rún looked up at her father. 'And what was wrong with the other chair?'

'There was nothing wrong with it. Diljá's only joking.' Maybe he should have called in sick today after all. The feeling intensified as he gathered up Rún's drawings. One was of a figure that appeared at first glance to be making a snow angel while another stood watching. Then it dawned on him that the first figure had its mouth open and was clearly a woman with flailing arms and legs, either falling or just landed. Only the back view of the other figure was visible but it appeared to be female too, going by the bare legs sticking out from under a garment resembling a coat. Unless it was a man in shorts. Another picture showed a gravestone with *Mummy* written on it. The grave was decorated with smiling flowers that were at odds with the headstone and its inscription. He would show them to Nanna at tomorrow's appointment. He was brought up short by the third drawing. It was of a boxy car with two screaming faces in the windows, their round mouths almost exactly like the mouth of the woman in the first picture. Ódinn's eyes darted to the photo on the wall. Obviously Diljá had told Rún how the boys died. What on earth had she been thinking? Christ, he really should have stayed at home.

'There was no need to tell my daughter about those boys dying in the car.' Ódinn folded his arms to stop himself losing his cool and wagging his finger in Diljá's face. He was trembling with rage, justifiably incensed that someone would upset his child. 'What possessed you? She's got enough on her plate without hearing something like that.' The child's phobia about open windows was bad enough; he didn't want her refusing to get in the car as well.

Diljá turned, making no attempt to hide the Facebook page open on her screen. 'What are you talking about?'

'Rún. You told her about the boys who suffocated in the car. The boys in the photo on Róberta's wall.' Ódinn took care to keep his voice down so Rún wouldn't be able to hear at the other end of the office.

'Are you out of your mind?' Diljá frowned. 'I didn't talk to her about those boys, let alone tell her how they died.' She made as if to stand up. 'Why would you think that?'

Ódinn's anger gave way to surprise, then blazed up again. 'Maybe because she drew a picture of them while she was in your care.' He pulled the folded drawing from his pocket and showed it to her. Diljá held out a hand but Ódinn snatched it back, folded it again and returned it to his pocket. 'You're hardly going to claim it's a coincidence?'

'I wouldn't know. I didn't say a word about it. Why would

I? You must have done it yourself. It's your case, not mine. I have zero interest in it. Zilch.'

'Me?' It took all Ódinn's self-control to stay calm. 'I wouldn't tell my daughter about that – for Christ's sake!'

'Don't get tetchy with me. I didn't do it. We were talking about something completely different.'

'Like what?'

'Like what an idiot you are.' Diljá glared at him defiantly. 'It's a wonder the kid turned out so well. She must take after her mother.'

Ódinn was flummoxed. He had no intention of engaging in childish bickering with Diljá, and anyway, he believed her. Why would she have told Rún? Because she'd run out of things to say? Hardly; Diljá had all the gossip in town on the tip of her tongue. 'If you didn't say anything and I didn't either, then how did she know what happened to the boys in the photo?' The anger had vanished from his voice; to his annoyance he now sounded whiny with fright.

'Search me. How should I know? I can't for the life of me imagine why she would draw that – perhaps it's just meant to be screaming kids on a rollercoaster.'

Although unlikely, the explanation wasn't wholly implausible. He would have to question Rún but didn't want to alarm her. That was why he hadn't asked her about the picture in the first place, though he'd noticed how closely she had been watching his reactions as he gathered up the drawings. Instead, he had pretended nothing was up. He felt exhausted by constantly walking on eggshells. 'Is there any chance she could have been digging around in Róberta's files and found some document mentioning how they died? You'd have heard the rustling, wouldn't you?'

Diljá blew a lock of hair from her forehead. 'Yes, probably. Though I can't be sure. Of course, sound carries between the cubicles. But Rún could have been turning pages and reading them without my noticing, if she'd done it stealthily enough. Though I can't imagine she would. Since when have kids been interested in files?'

Óđinn suddenly regretted being rude to Diljá. You had to hand it to her; in spite of her faults she was one of the few people worth talking to in the office. 'Tell me something. You said sound carries between the cubicles – were you ever aware of Róberta receiving threats? Did she ever mention it?'

Diljá shook her head. She was sitting back down now with her legs crossed, looking at him warily. 'Never.' Then she brightened up a little and added, pleased with herself: 'Actually, she did receive a pretty odd phone call once. She suddenly raised her voice and became very agitated. Said something about e-mails, asked if the caller had been sending her messages. I interrogated her the moment she hung up but she wouldn't talk about it. Just fobbed me off with some cryptic comment.'

'Do you remember what it was?'

'Not word for word; something about how certain people were a bit odd. That she should have known, she'd been warned this person wasn't right in the head. But it was all part of the job and she'd just have to put up with it.' Diljá swung one leg. 'Then she took a swipe at me, saying unlike some people she didn't spread gossip – the person in question may have behaved stupidly, but *she* knew how to react professionally. As if I didn't?'

This was neither the time nor the place to discuss Diljá's

discretion, so Ódinn faked mild indignation on her behalf. 'Did she happen to say if it was a man or a woman, or where their paths had crossed?'

'No. If she did, I've forgotten. She was careful not to give away the sex of the caller, and she didn't mention where she knew them from, but it was definitely work-related. I have a hunch it was a woman, though. Women her age react differently to men and women when they're angry, and this sounded like a quarrel between women.' Diljá's shapely leg ceased its swinging and her face grew serious, transforming her almost into a stranger. 'I told you not to take on this case. There's something very weird about it. Róberta got so creepy. Always staring at the photo of those boys, and doing all kinds of other crazy stuff. And now it's like you're losing the plot too.'

Ódinn didn't like the direction their conversation was taking. 'Did she interview anyone from the home, as far as you know?' There had been no indication of this on Róberta's timesheets, but given the calls and e-mails she had received, she must at least have discussed the case with someone from outside the office. Someone, what's more, who was very keen to block the inquiry. And Ódinn wanted to know why. He would rather a major issue didn't come to light after the report was published, but it was hard to imagine what could provoke such a dramatic reaction nearly four decades on apart from a serious crime like murder. 'Do you think she spoke to any of the former residents? The man I talked to earlier said no one had contacted him before, but perhaps she spoke to other old boys.'

'No.' Diljá seemed disappointed not to be able to carry on discussing the sinister side of the case. 'Almost certainly not. I'd have known – she usually told me where she was going when she went out. As if I cared.' She reached for her coffee cup and peered into it. 'Bloody thing must be leaking.' She looked back at him. 'But she definitely interviewed members of staff. One or two. Maybe more.'

'Any idea who? I can't find anything about staff in the files.'

Diljá shook her head. 'No. Not a clue. I just know she did. Wanted to start at the right end, as she put it. Probably thought the boys were beneath her – though they're old men now.'

'Or she was afraid of them. There's no telling what motivates people. Often it's quite different from what you think.'

He started to walk away, then turned. 'I forgot to say sorry. I behaved like a fool just now.'

'Well, I never. A man who can apologise.' Diljá tilted her head and Ódinn feared she was about to angle for a date. Feared, or hoped? He didn't know. But she didn't say anything else. Nodding a farewell, he walked away, but after he had gone a few steps she called after him, peering round the partition: 'Know why I swapped the chair?' He shook his head. 'Because it wouldn't stay still. Fobbing it off on Denni was just a bonus. I couldn't put up with it any longer. It kept creaking just like it did when Róberta was sitting on it, and it moved around the cubicle. I'm telling you, this case is seriously fucked up.' Her head disappeared back behind the partition.

Ódinn sighed. Back at his desk he found it difficult to concentrate and caught himself constantly glancing over at Denni, though he could see nothing odd about his chair. Finally, he switched off his computer and left the office with Rún, an hour earlier than intended.

Only when they were sitting in the town centre, with an ice-cream tub each, did he feel himself again. 'I think she fancies you.' Rún licked chocolate sauce off her spoon.

'Who?' Ódinn searched in vain for more chocolate chunks in the slush at the bottom of his tub, then pushed it away.

'That woman at your office. Diljá.'

'Oh, I don't think so.'

'Yes, she does. She asked loads of questions about you, like if you had a girlfriend. She does fancy you.' Rún pushed her ice-cream into the middle of the table; she'd had enough too. 'What'll happen to me if you marry her? I don't want a new mum. Could I move in with Uncle Baldur?'

Ódinn took Rún's hand. Her fingers were cold and a little sticky. 'I'm not going to marry Diljá, Rún. No way. Nobody's going to push you out of your home, so you can stop worrying about that right now.'

'What if you die? What then? Would I go to Uncle Baldur's? I don't want to live with Granny.'

'I'm not going to die. Not any time soon. Anyway, you'll be a grandmother yourself by then and I hope for your sake you won't still be living with me.' They both watched, distracted, as half a wafer sank slowly onto its side in her tub. Finally, it slid right down and vanished in the melting ice-cream. Their eyes met and in her face he read a sadness that revealed not fear but certainty.

'What was that picture of the car meant to show, Rún?' He phrased it as carefully as he could.

'Boys.' She stared down at the white tabletop. 'Boys dying in a car. Some people die like that. They can't breathe.'

'What made you think of that?'

'I don't know. I just drew Mummy falling and then those

boys. I can't draw happy pictures. I try, but nothing comes.' It was a good thing she had an appointment with the psychologist tomorrow. Pity it wasn't later today. Or right now. Ódinn couldn't tear his gaze from the small-featured face, the red cheeks and delicate lips that she pursed shut as if to ensure she wouldn't say anything to disappoint her father.

But she didn't need to say anything. Ódinn felt as if he had set off down a precipitous slope, unable to see what lay at the bottom; all he knew was that he was gaining momentum, would break into a run soon, and after that there would be no stopping until he reached the end of the road – an end he dreaded. He forced a smile and Rún smiled unhappily back. What on earth was going on inside that little head?

Chapter 16

January 1974

Aldís didn't know what had woken her, the chattering of her teeth or the drips plinking into the icy bathwater. Cautiously opening her eyes, she was relieved to discover that it was still dark. She had a splitting headache that eased slightly when she closed her eyes again. Another drop fell from the tap and the sound echoed for a long time in the silence. If she didn't get out she'd die of cold, naked in the bathtub. The thought of the humiliation was enough to stir her into action.

At first she made do with sitting up. Afraid she would faint if she tried to stand, she sat there, shaking like a leaf, half in icy water, half in freezing air. As if that wasn't bad enough, she felt sick and had a foul taste in her mouth. She gripped the slippery sides of the bath and slowly heaved herself out. The cold clutched at her body but she tried to concentrate on controlling her shivering so she wouldn't fall back in. At last she was out, but it was only when she was standing on the floor in a pool of water that she looked round for a towel and discovered there wasn't one.

As Aldís gathered up the clothes strewn across the floor, the events of the night slowly came back to her. She couldn't remember all the details, which was a blessing, really. It was enough to recall the most important parts. Such as how she had ended up in the bathtub. She was too cold to blush, and too tired and sick to feel ashamed. She managed to dry herself a little with her clothes. That warmed her up slightly and stopped her from shivering so violently. She wrapped her clothes around her: there was no way she could put them on, she was still too wet and weak. And her trousers were too tight. It was no coincidence that she had been wearing them; they were the only garment in her wardrobe that could by any stretch of the imagination be called smart, and she had wanted to look nice last night. The sales assistant at Karnabær had told her they should fit like a second skin and that she'd have to lie down to zip up the flies. If Aldís had known she was going to have to take them off twice before going to bed, she might have chosen a different outfit.

She and Einar had slept together. By that point she had drunk a great deal of the bottle she had pilfered from the larder. She couldn't really remember the sex, except for a hazy impression of his being considerate; in spite of his eagerness he had given her the chance to enjoy herself as well, unlike the boys she had been with before, who had just pumped away on top of her as if paid by the minute. One hadn't even bothered to do more than push his jeans just below his buttocks before getting down to work – she remembered squeezing her eyes shut and trying to think of something else. It hadn't occurred to her to do that last night. She could recall that much, though the details were patchy. She hadn't minded that her earlier sexual encounters were a bit of a blur, but this time she regretted having drunk so much. Then again, she'd never have done it sober. Would have flatly refused. If only because she wasn't on the pill and he, naturally, didn't have a condom. She remembered that much at least, which was why she'd ended up in the bath. Despite being pissed out of her mind, she had followed the advice of a friend who'd once told her that a hot bath after sex prevented conception. It had better be true.

After satisfying herself that there was no sound from the landing, she peered out. She had no idea what time it was – the darkness told her nothing as it didn't get properly light until nearly midday at this time of year – so the workmen might well be rising. The last thing she wanted was to bump into them, half-naked. She made a frantic dash to her room. Not until she had shut the door, flung down her clothes and climbed under the duvet did her shivering abate and her breathing slow to normal. She was still terribly cold, still queasy, still had a crippling headache and a ton of self-loathing. What had she been thinking?

Aldís put her head under the duvet, closed her eyes tight and clasped her hands over her ears. But however hard she tried, she couldn't shut out the memory of all the rubbish she'd poured out to Einar in her woozy state. Those slurred words could never be unsaid; her only hope was that he had been just as drunk. The evening's theme had alternated between whining about the unfairness of the world and making grandiose declarations about her huge potential and her future plans, and unfortunately she had the impression that he'd mainly listened and kept quiet about himself. She had asked him why he'd been sent to Krókur but received no answer, and, incredible as it seemed, had been too caught up in talking about herself to challenge him about his age or the girl in the photo. She had the feeling she'd aired all her dirty laundry. Bloody booze – she was never drinking again.

Aldís opened her eyes wide. What had they done with the

bottle? For most of the time they had been holed up in the little coffee room adjoining the cowshed, of all places, though admittedly there hadn't been much choice in terms of where they could hang out. Lilja, Veigar or the workmen were bound to be keeping an eye on movements around the main building after the incident with Tobbi, and they couldn't use her room with her housemates next door, or the boys' dormitory, for obvious reasons. There had been no question of staying out in the cold, either, so as a last resort they had plumped for the cowshed. The bottle would probably be sitting right there when Veigar or the workmen turned up in the morning, on the dirty, wobbly little table. Determined as she was to hand in her notice, she would rather not leave Krókur under a cloud, which is what would happen if the couple discovered that she'd stolen their drink and gone on a bender with one of the boys. But if she managed to dispose of the bottle, no one would be any the wiser. After all, it had stood untouched behind a stack of tins ever since Aldís had arrived at Krókur.

Stretching a trembling hand out from under the duvet, she fumbled for the alarm clock on the bedside table. To her relief, it was still about an hour before anybody would be up. There was nothing for it but to force herself out of bed. She'd have to dash over to the cowshed and remove the bottle and any other signs of the night's debauchery. Her headache reminded her of its existence and her stomach joined in. She almost wished it were too late, so there would be no point dragging herself out of bed.

Aldís had been dreading going outside in the cold but the wind was actually exhilarating. Although her headache didn't disappear entirely, it did at least recede enough for her to move. She drank in the bracing air as if she were drowning, but the ends of her wet hair froze and when they brushed against her bare neck she felt as if she were still lying in the icy bath. She zipped up her anorak as far as it would go but didn't pull up the hood in case her headache made a come-back. Better to put up with frozen hair. It had been snowing and the tracks that had marked her meandering progress home that night were almost buried. The snow leaked into her summery plimsolls, clutching at her instep and forming lumps under her soles, making them ache. She regretted not having put on any socks. When she looked round she saw that she was leaving a clear trail. She would have to try and obliterate her footprints on the way back from the cowshed, so it wouldn't be obvious that someone had been there in the small hours.

She might just get away with it. She smiled at the thought as she walked quietly, hands in pockets, towards the shed. But her smile vanished as she remembered more of what had passed between her and Einar last night. Her stomach churned and she paused to fight the nausea so she wouldn't throw up on the pristine snow. It was as if her guts were rebelling against what had seemed such a clever idea last night. She couldn't remember which of them had started it – probably her. Aldís took several deep breaths, then carried on walking, feeling a little better. What a relief that she'd never worked out where the couple's child was buried. Had she known, she and Einar might have gone through with their plan last night to dig it up and lay it at the couple's door. Like a parcel from a mysterious benefactor. *From me to you, dear Mum and Dad*. Last night it had seemed to them a singularly appropriate punishment for the couple's theft of her letters and their abominable behaviour in general. Aldís shuddered and thanked God she only had to retrieve an empty bottle, not the corpse of a child.

By the time she reached the end wall of the boys' dormitory, her eyes had grown accustomed to the dark, but at that moment a half-moon emerged from behind the clouds and the white blanket of snow sparkled blue all around. Only the shadows cast by the naked bushes reminded Aldís that it was still night and that she should have been tucked up in bed, fast asleep, dreaming about what to do on her day off in town. That was looking unlikely now. She'd hardly have recovered in time to catch a ride with the postman, and she couldn't picture herself crouching by the road, trying to hitch a lift with strangers. Not in this condition. Her day off was ruined. Fed up, she shoved her hands deeper into her anorak pockets and quickened her pace. It wasn't as important to tread softly in the crunching snow here because the boys could be trusted not to give her away, if they woke. Yet she found herself scanning the windows in search of inquisitive faces. There was no one to be seen; even the bird had found itself shelter for the night. But she did spot faint tracks, presumably Einar's, leading behind the building. Aldís paused and peered round for some means of obliterating them. Veigar was sure to spot them when he woke the boys and it wouldn't take him long to work out that someone must have slipped out after curfew.

Seeing a shovel in the porch, she grabbed it and, after a few clumsy attempts, got the hang of scraping away the footprints. She might as well continue behind the dormitory too, though it would mean trampling on the area she had already smoothed over. It was better to be certain; footprints under a window were bound to goad Veigar into action.

The clouds closed ranks, darkness descended and the snow turned grey again. Aldís could still see dimly but felt increasingly jumpy, acutely aware of the empty landscape stretching away behind the house, over hills and lava-fields. It was pitch black out there now. Reluctant to turn her back on this eerie void, she tried to work fast, moving crabwise so she'd be able to see out of the corner of her eye in the unlikely event that someone was out there. Then she stopped and peered down, puzzled, before stooping for a closer look. Under the window where Einar had apparently entered, she saw not only his tracks but another set approaching from out of the darkness. Without pausing to wonder how he'd climbed through the bars, she concentrated on the deep, unidentified footprints. Then, slowly and deliberately, she turned in the direction they had come from and followed them with her eyes as far as she could see. Some unknown person had walked in from the dark wasteland. And these tracks were deeper and sharper, more recent than Einar's. Aldís straightened up cautiously and retreated from the window round the corner of the building. There she frantically swept snow over her and Einar's footprints, trying not to think about the unknown person who might be lurking nearby. Perhaps the same person as the unseen presence in the dining room. Aldís almost expected to smell again the pungent reek of blood. Suddenly her headache and queasiness ceased to matter.

Leaning the shovel against the wall, she looked over at the cowshed. What had seemed a short distance now appeared endless. The clouds showed no sign of relenting and allowing the moon to shine through again. Aldís dithered in the porch. She wasn't sure which was worse: the idea that the bottle would be discovered the following morning or the prospect of trying to make it safely to the cowshed and back. She swallowed and steeled herself to make a run for it. If anyone approached she would scream at the top of her voice. The cowshed was almost within reach when she remembered that on the way back she would have to pause at every step to wipe out her tracks with one foot. It would be impossible to move fast. But it was too late for regrets now. She took a flying leap over the final stretch to the door.

Inside it was warm and the cows looked up sleepily from their stalls, then lowered their heads indifferently. *Her again. Alone this time.* The stink of manure made her gorge rise. Holding her nose she hurried into the coffee room and groped for the light switch. The glow of the bulb was dazzling and she felt her headache intensify.

The source of her present predicament and suffering was lying on the floor behind one of the chairs, still corked but two thirds empty. If she topped it up with water and put it back in the larder, the theft wouldn't be discovered for ages, by which time she would be far away. Unfortunately suspicion would fall on the workmen but that was tough luck. *Sorry guys.*

Before turning off the light and leaving the coffee room, she checked there was no further evidence of the night's adventure. She picked up the dirty blanket from the floor, pushing away the memory of what had taken place on it. Unable to recall where they had got it from, she stuffed it in a box in the corner.

She switched off the light, waited for her eyes to adjust, then held her nose in readiness to open the cowshed door again. She was about to close it behind her when she caught a movement outside the small window of the coffee room. Aldís stopped breathing and her knees threatened to give way. Once again she had to summon up all her strength to keep calm, and, although her first reaction had been to close her eyes, she forced herself to open one and look over at the window. She didn't know why it seemed better to keep one eye shut.

There was nothing to be seen. Only the dirty windowpane and greyness beyond. But that didn't alter the fact that a moment ago someone or something had been moving out there. Until she knew who or what it was, she wasn't going outside. She'd rather Veigar or the workmen caught her red-handed tomorrow morning. And that time was fast approaching.

The thought of this more prosaic danger gave her the courage to inch over to the window. Perhaps she should peer out, or duck underneath it in case whoever or whatever was outside looked in. Which was worse, to look out and see some unspeakable horror, or risk its looking in and seeing her? Deciding that the latter would be far more terrifying, Aldís started carefully pushing the table towards the window, only to flinch when a floorboard groaned under one of the legs. She had no idea if the sound would carry outside. Heart racing, she stood stock-still, trying to control her breathing. Nothing happened. Could it possibly have been the bird? Chewing her lip, Aldís abandoned her plan to move the table and hide under it. If she was going to be an air hostess she would have to be brave in a crisis, not stand rooted to the spot. But the last time she'd acted on this impulse, in the dark dining room, it hadn't turned out particularly well. Just thinking about it almost brought back the smell of blood.

She tiptoed to the window and stationed herself beside it, her back pressed so hard against the wall that she could feel the timbers creaking in the breeze. Then she turned her head with infinite slowness until she could see out and quickly scan the surroundings. She jerked back when she caught sight of a dark figure standing by the lone tree in the farmyard. A low sound of singing carried in through the cracks in the window.

Chapter 17

The smaller meeting room was only ever used by people slipping in surreptitiously to make private phone calls. As the door was right next to the coffee area, their efforts to be inconspicuous could be amusing to watch. But Ódinn couldn't give a damn if he was spotted: what did it matter compared to the problems he was facing at the moment? Instead of pretending to fetch a coffee or peruse the notices on the corkboard by the door, he marched straight into the meeting room under his colleagues' noses. Once inside, however, he closed the door, since he had no wish to be overheard talking to Rún's psychologist.

He took up position by the window and fiddled with the tilt rod on the venetian blinds while selecting the number, having first double-checked that he was ringing at exactly the time Nanna had specified. He stared at the blinds as he opened and closed them in turn; one minute dull grey view, the next off-white plastic strips. Just as he had begun to think the therapist wasn't going to pick up, he heard her familiar, preternaturally calm voice at the other end. 'I'm glad you called. I wasn't sure you'd received my e-mail this morning.'

Ódinn realised he should have replied to her message requesting him to call, but then communications had never been his strong point. 'Yes, sure, I saw it.' This was a waste of time; of course he'd read the message or he wouldn't be ringing now. He carried on fiddling with the blinds as they talked, opening and shutting them until the alternating grey and off-white were reduced to a blur. 'How did it go with Rún? She seemed all right after the appointment.' Then he added hastily: 'That was what you wanted to talk about, wasn't it?' Was it possible that his credit card had been refused and Nanna was chasing up payment?

'Since you mention it, we'd better get one thing clear. I don't want Rún to know we're talking. She needs to be able to trust me. You should also be aware that I won't discuss anything that might jeopardise that trust. She's my patient, not you.' He heard her draw breath. 'I hope you understand. Parents are often under the impression that they need or deserve to know everything their child thinks, but it's not necessarily in their best interests.'

'I'm not asking for that.' Ódinn released the tilt rod. 'You wanted me to call, remember?'

'Quite right.' Again he heard Nanna take a deep breath, as if she was leaving gaps in the conversation for him to fill. But Ódinn wasn't in the mood. 'Firstly, I wanted to let you know that the session went well. Rún's quite reserved, but I sense I'll get through to her eventually. Few people open up completely at the beginning of therapy, but in time she'll learn to unburden herself. So it's important she comes to see me on a weekly basis. If cost is an issue, we'll have to see what we can do. The state might well cover part of it.'

'I can afford it.'

'Good. Secondly, I wanted to ask you a few questions to help me understand Rún better.'

Ódinn leant against the wall beside the window. Opposite

him was a whiteboard that hadn't been used since he started at the office; at any rate, it was still covered with the same scrawl as when he'd first seen it. 'Fire away. I'll do my best.' He wasn't sure he was capable of giving Nanna the information she was after. Although he'd known Rún since she was born, until recently he'd effectively been her father in name only.

'How does she get on with her grandmother?'

'Well, she sees her less often than her grandmother would like, but that's my fault really. I should put more pressure on her, but she's just not keen to go round.'

'It shouldn't be necessary to put pressure on her. You do realise that, don't you? If all's well, children of her age should be eager to spend time with their grandparents.' When Ódinn didn't reply, she continued: 'I was wondering if their relationship had always been difficult or if it's linked to her mother's death?'

'I don't see how it could be. It wasn't her grandmother's fault.' Ódinn deliberately avoided answering the part about their past relationship, for the simple reason that he had no idea.

'She needn't have been actively involved. Children like everything to be cut and dried. Rún's mother dies and she needs a scapegoat to take the blame. I'm not implying that she holds anyone responsible for the accident; it's enough for her to be able to point the finger at someone who could have prevented it. I'm guessing she's cast her grandmother in that role. She lived close by and Rún may have got it into her head that her grandmother should have been there to save her mother. Something like that.'

'Could you make any sense of the drawings I gave you?'

Ódinn suddenly remembered the one that showed Lára after the fall, with a woman looking on. Perhaps it was meant to represent Rún's grandmother.

'Unfortunately, they don't tell me much at this stage,' Nanna said dismissively. 'But back to her grandmother. I'm interested in working more on their relationship, as it's a useful introduction to the trickier issues that we'll have to tackle in due course. Why do you think Rún doesn't want to see her?'

'I have no idea. I've never asked her straight out. But of course I've noticed that she's not too fond of her. I haven't made much effort to get to the bottom of it, but it occurred to me that Rún might feel smothered by her. She's the old woman's only living descendant, so that may be a factor.'

'That could well be it. It's as good a theory as any other.'

'What do you advise, then? Should I take her to see her grandmother more often? Less often? Never?'

'Don't change anything for now. It's far too early to judge what's best for Rún. I've only met her once.'

This wasn't the reply Ódinn had been hoping for, but he had to remind himself that Nanna had got in touch not to give him advice but to seek information. It had been naive of him to assume there might have been a breakthrough to discuss. 'I realise that. The fact that I'm asking stupid questions like that should make it clear how out of my depth I am. Pity you can't give me a manual. Just ask me what you need to know and pretend you didn't hear the rest.' He sensed that she was smiling.

'Don't worry, I'm used to it. If it helps, I assure you that life'll gradually become easier for the two of you, so there's no need to be overly pessimistic. Rún's a good, conscientious little girl who's suffered a major trauma. But kids are resilient. Much more so than adults.'

Cheers to that. Ódinn studied the faint writing that no one had bothered to wipe off the whiteboard. Perhaps they'd left it too long and the ink had permanently marked the surface. It consisted of various dates, and he tilted his head as if to satisfy himself that he wasn't seeing things when he realised that they were familiar. They appeared to relate to Krókur; at least, he couldn't imagine the office had much other business concerned with the 1970s. Presumably Róberta had sat in here puzzling over some aspect of the case. 'Tell me something else,' Nanna was saying, and Ódinn turned away from the board to try and concentrate on her. There would be time later to wonder about the dates. 'Now, I don't know the details of her mother's death, but is there any reason to suppose it could have been anything other than an accident?'

'Why would you think that?' Ódinn's voice came out sounding colder than he'd intended. Nanna had his full attention now. He himself was still in two minds; one day he was convinced that Lára's death had been an accident, the next that she had been pushed. Some days he changed his mind repeatedly. He'd even taken the trouble to dig up information on Logi Árnason, his chief suspect, only to discover that he'd moved abroad just before Lára died. In spite of this, he felt convinced at times that it hadn't been an accident, though who could have been responsible was anyone's guess. These thoughts tended to plague him most after he'd been dreaming about Lára.

'I don't think anything, it just occurred to me to ask. It was the impression I got from various things Rún said, as if that's what she thought. It's not necessarily significant. Perhaps she invented it. As I said, people often find it hard to reconcile themselves to accidental deaths.'

'The police treated it as a tragic accident, and I gather they haven't changed their opinion.' Ódinn fumbled for the tilt rod again. He needed to hold on to something simple and tangible. 'I know you don't want to tell me what she confided in you, but would you be prepared to let me know if she has anyone specific in mind?'

'As far as I know, she doesn't, and she didn't actually say it in as many words.' Nanna paused and this time Ódinn couldn't detect any hint of a smile. 'Does Rún sleep badly? Does she often have nightmares?'

'Well, I don't know what you'd consider often. She seems very restless at night and sometimes suffers from nightmares, yes.' Again it struck him how little he knew about bringing up children. Perhaps it would have been best for everyone if Rún had been adopted by a couple who longed for a child and knew how to look after them. But of course that was ridiculous; a couple desperate for a child would presumably be childless themselves, and therefore know even less than he did.

'She implied that her mother would come back as a ghost to avenge herself on the person who'd done this to her. Of course, it sounds absurd but that doesn't change the fact that it's making her miserable. Fear of ghosts can make life very difficult for a child.' Nanna hesitated, then resumed again, in a much gentler voice: 'If I understood her right, she thought her mother was after you. Perhaps because of the divorce, as it can hardly be because of the accident.'

'No. Hardly.' Ódinn's mouth was dry.

The woman seemed to sense how shaken he was; at any rate, she changed tack slightly. 'Actually, the most likely explanation for all this is obvious. You yourself said you'd been seeing and hearing things that didn't exist. Is it possible that Rún's aware of this; that she's noticed you acting strangely or even heard you talk about it? If so, that could have planted the seed in her mind.'

'No, that's impossible. I've shielded her from all that.' He may be an inexperienced father but he was no fool. But no sooner had he spoken than he realised it wasn't that simple. Of course she must suspect – when he took her with him to work, for example, without being able to give an adequate explanation of why she couldn't stay at home alone. And it was entirely possible that she'd noticed his frightened reactions at times. 'God, I don't know what to say.'

'You needn't say anything. Not to me, anyway. Just do your utmost to make sure she doesn't sense your anxiety. I know you're perfectly aware that none of it's real, so you'll just have to ignore it, at least when she's near. For your own sake too.'

'It's stopped. Luckily, I don't have to worry about that sort of thing any more.'

As if to give the lie to this declaration, a reflection seemed to appear beside his own in the shiny surface of the whiteboard. A dark shape, suggesting a figure standing beside him, though he knew he was alone in the room. He couldn't tear his eyes from the board; nothing would induce him to look round. Only now was he certain of what it was he'd been hearing and seeing recently. It was Lára. Lára was after him.

Óðinn ended the phone call in a distracted state. He answered yes or no, depending on Nanna's tone of voice, eager to get out of the meeting room and surround himself with the living again. Was he cracking up? Was this how it felt? The moment the phone call was over, he hurried out, inadvertently slamming the door. All eyes followed him as he returned to his desk. There he sat down and stared into space, profoundly relieved that nothing could be reflected in the matt surface of his computer screen.

He was losing his mind. Wasn't he? But in the unlikely event that these manifestations were real, why would Lára want to haunt him? What had he done? Absolutely nothing. No, that wasn't the explanation. It was self-evident: he was going mad and he might as well accept it. The worst of it was that he couldn't bring himself to go back into the meeting room to take a closer look at the information on the board, although he was dying to know what it meant.

Chapter 18

January 1974

Aldís used to miss the daylight during winter, but now she was grateful for the gloom. Her curtains were too skimpy to pull right across the window and on a summer's day she would have woken with burning sunlight on her face, making it impossible to open her eyes. She had no need to touch them to feel how swollen they were, and from the tangle of locks that fell over her nose when she sat up, she guessed her hair must be a complete mess. It really wasn't fair to have to wake up to a crippling hangover twice in one day, and on her day off too, which she had been looking forward to all week. The grey light that filtered in through the gap in the curtains was barely enough to warm her cheek, though it was well past one in the afternoon. She wouldn't be going to town now. Aldís gave a low groan, blinked several times, then sat for a minute or two on the edge of the bed with her eyes closed. The swelling felt as if it was dispersing down her face, and although this relieved the pressure on her eyes, she was afraid it would make her jaw sag.

A trail of abandoned clothes led from the door to her bed, as if she had wanted to ensure she could find her way out again; a drunken Gretel who'd lost her Hansel. In the middle, beside a crumpled jumper, lay the bottle she had retrieved that morning. It seemed to rock slightly with Aldís's clumsy movements. The green glass reminded her of the night's binge and she felt sick again, but fortunately the nausea passed as quickly as it had come, like the remnants of a dream. Or a nightmare. She slid gingerly out of bed and winced as her bare feet encountered the cold floorboards. After taking a moment to grow accustomed to the chill, she picked her way, naked, to the chest of drawers under the window. She had no desire to get back into the clothes that littered the floor; they probably stank of booze, and sex too, and she couldn't bear the thought of either in her current state.

The squeaking of the drawer went right through her, making her goose bumps worse. She took out underwear, vest and socks, and quickly pulled them on before searching for clean trousers in the wardrobe. There were no hangers, so her clothes lay in a sad little heap in the cavernous interior. Once she had her torn jeans on, she felt a little better; no longer cold, and able to think more clearly. But although the warmth coursed through her veins, she couldn't get rid of her gooseflesh; not while the events of the night were still fresh in her mind.

It had long been apparent to Aldís that Lilja and Veigar were not like other people, but why had Lilja been singing hymns under a tree in the middle of the night – and squealing like a pig? Aldís had almost fainted with relief when she realised who it was. Relief had made her careless; she had given in to the temptation to peer out of the window again just to see the familiar back view of her employer's scruffy anorak. By the time Lilja finally left, Aldís had begun to fear the woman would stay there until dawn, leaving her no time to make herself scarce before Veigar turned up for the morning's chores.

She managed it, though, scrubbing out her footprints on her rapid retreat to the little house. She left Lilja's tracks untouched, since they ran behind the buildings, as if the woman didn't want anyone to know about her nightly wanderings. Two women up and about on the same night, equally eager to pass unseen. Aldís could make no sense of Lilja's movements. The tracks under the boys' window must have belonged to her. But what had she been doing there?

Aldís lifted the curtain. Outside, tiny grains of snow were falling from the sky like dust, as if someone were shaking out laundry on the roof. Three boys, Einar not among them, were walking towards the main building, laughing and jostling each other. Hákon was crossing the yard as well, his back to her, weighed down on one side by the heavy toolbox. Now and then a puff of smoke rose from the inevitable cigarette in the corner of his mouth. Just before he vanished round the corner, she dropped the curtain and moved away from the window. No one else was about. Aldís sighed as she surveyed her cheerless room. So much for her day off.

There was nobody on the landing, as one would expect in the middle of a working day. After rinsing away the taste of alcohol with sickly sweet, minty toothpaste, Aldís splashed her face with icy water. Afterwards she felt marginally better, and she could see a ruddy glow in her cheeks – for the moment at least. She had another day off in a fortnight and would make sure she didn't mess that one up. She met her own gaze in the mirror and said aloud: 'Never again.' Next time she'd get a lift to town and do everything she craved:

buy an ice-cream, stroll down Laugavegur looking in the shop windows, then retrace her steps and treat herself to whatever most took her fancy. And ring her mother. Or not. After staring at herself for a while she looked away, far from convinced that the person in the mirror could be relied on to keep these promises.

She winced as the hairbrush tore through her tangles. She'd been in such a state last night that she'd left her hair to dry naturally. Eventually, however, she managed to tease out the worst of the knots, and disguised the weird kinks in it by putting it up in a bun.

The rumbling of her stomach reminded her that she hadn't eaten since yesterday's supper. As usual there was nothing edible in the little house and she regretted not having saved some of the chocolate from her last trip to town. She had two alternatives: either stay here and starve or go over to the main building and help herself to some leftovers from lunch. The coffee break wasn't until half past three. Lilja would start preparing it half an hour earlier, so if she hurried over now, with luck she might miss her. Without pausing to think, she pulled on her anorak and went out.

The snow crunched underfoot and the fine grains fluttering down from the sky settled on her eyelashes, making everything glitter. When she blew them away, the world turned dull and flat again.

The kitchen was empty, as she'd anticipated. As a result, every small noise she made seemed to echo, and Aldís wished she'd waited for the bustle of coffee time. Her thoughts strayed to the evening the uninvited guest had been on the prowl, and it seemed imperative to quickly grab something to eat and get out of there. She didn't want to hear any mysterious sounds, so she made as much of a racket as she could, banging the breadbin shut after taking out a flat-cake, jerking open the fridge door in the hope the hinges would squeak, loudly gulping down milk straight from the carton. The cold liquid felt so wonderful as it ran down her throat that she thought she'd never be able to stop. Finally, having quenched the worst of her thirst, she wiped the white moustache from her upper lip and replaced the nearly empty carton. Jars clinked together as she rummaged for the butter on the packed shelves. Closing the fridge, she turned and jumped with fright, almost dropping the butter dish on the floor.

Einar was sitting at the small table by the door to the dining room. He must have come in while she was delving inside the fridge. Above his head hung one of Lilja's cross-stitch samplers, which read *Lamb of God*. Although Aldís had never understood what it meant, she was sure the text didn't refer to Einar. He was as far from a lamb as you could imagine. 'I saw you coming over here. Hope no one noticed me slip out. We're supposed to be studying.'

Aldís was feeling too grim to be embarrassed by her appearance. 'I just woke up.'

'How are you feeling?' Einar met her eyes and from his expression she thought he was asking something quite different – whether she was having regrets.

'Terrible. But I'll recover.'

Einar fished a sugar-lump out of the bowl in front of him and put it in his mouth. Aldís guessed he was trying to buy time while he cast around for the right words. 'I thought you went straight back to bed last night. After . . .' He smiled awkwardly. 'After we left the cowshed.'

'I did.' Aldís fetched a knife and began to spread butter

on the flat-cake. She couldn't be sure if it was true, but as far as she could recall she'd slunk straight back to the little house after saying goodbye to him by the dormitory. 'Why do you ask?'

'Someone knocked on the window after I climbed in. I was back in my room by then but I heard it anyway. I didn't dare get up to see if it was you in case the other boys woke up.'

'It wasn't me.' Aldís folded the flat-cake and took a bite. Lilja made them herself and they weren't bad when fresh, but several days old they were dry and unappetising. She swallowed. 'But I think I know who it was.'

'Oh? Did you see?'

Aldís contemplated the dark flat-cake and tried to recover her appetite. 'No. I went back out to fetch the bottle we left in the cowshed and saw tracks leading to the window that obviously weren't yours. Then shortly afterwards I saw Lilja. She was skulking around behind the house, so it must have been her.' Her appetite vanished altogether when it dawned on her what this might mean. 'Do you think she could have spotted you climbing in?'

'Unlikely. If she had, they'd have replaced the bars by now – I'd loosened them and they're just propped up for show. So it looks as if everything's OK. It must be. Don't you think?' He glanced at Aldís but she had no answer. 'Anyway, it can't have been her. I met her just now and she was her usual grumpy, miserable self, but not angry. Besides, why would she have banged on the window unless she realised what was going on? She has a key, after all.'

Aldís couldn't answer this. Einar must be right but that didn't alter the fact that someone had walked up to the window and rapped on it from outside. Unless he'd imagined the incident. It wasn't her, and if it wasn't Lilja either, the whole thing was pretty bizarre. 'It can't have been anyone else. Who else would have been wandering about last night?'

'I know. It does sound a bit weird.' The sugar-lump rattled faintly against Einar's teeth as he transferred it to his other cheek. 'Are you positive it wasn't you? We'd both had a hell of a lot to drink and you were a bit . . . you know.'

'It wasn't me.' Aldís raised the flat-cake to her mouth but the stale smell made her lower it again. Her appetite had gone for good. 'I woke up just before everybody else and only went out then.' She omitted to mention the bath and its purpose. She had no desire to discuss the fact they'd had sex – or anything else that had passed between them. If neither of them mentioned it, it would be almost as if nothing had happened. In time they'd both forget and the incident would no longer exist in anyone's mind. And that would be that. Or so she hoped. 'That's when I saw her. Out by the cowshed. Long after you went inside.'

'Which makes it even more unlikely it was Lilja at the window. The knocking came just after I climbed in. She can hardly have been hanging around outside for hours. What on earth was she doing when you saw her?'

'Singing. To a tree.' He looked perplexed. 'Can you come out to the cowshed with me? I'll show you.' When he didn't move, she added: 'There's no one there at this time of day. If we sneak behind the buildings you won't be seen.'

He stood up with feigned nonchalance, though no doubt he'd rather have gone back to his books before anyone discovered he was playing truant. 'I'll just say I had to go to the toilet.'

They both knew no one would believe this excuse. Einar would be reprimanded and subjected to whatever punishment Lilja and Veigar considered fitting. Nevertheless, they hastened wordlessly through the snow to the cowshed. Light flakes were still falling. If the wind picked up it would drift and tomorrow her day would be spent shovelling snow from the doorsteps while the workmen and the boys were made to clear the slip-road to the farm. The bird joined them, flapping overhead with plaintive chirrups as if to remind Aldís that she hadn't fed it yet, but soon gave up and turned back.

'She was standing there.' Aldís pointed to the tree, which stood a little way from the gable of the cowshed.

'Was she leaning against it? Singing hymns to God? Looking at the sky, maybe?'

'No. She was standing there looking straight ahead. At the tree.'

Einar asked no further questions but walked over the soft white carpet towards the tree. 'They're weirdos, of course. She's even worse than him.' He scuffed at the snow as if searching for traces of the night's events, perhaps trying to ascertain whether Aldís was telling the truth. Bending down, he brushed his hand over the cold ground where Lilja had supposedly stood.

'Don't you believe me?' Aldís hopped from foot to foot behind him; she was cold and wished she were back in bed. The day was a write-off, and would only get worse.

'Yes, I do.' He seemed distracted, more interested in the snow than her. 'Look.' Straightening up, he held out his hand. It was red with cold. In his palm lay a small piece of wood that had been whittled to resemble a heart. 'Think she dropped this?'

Aldís took it carefully as if it might crumble between her fingers. It felt strangely clammy and warm to the touch, and heavier than she would have expected. 'I don't know. Not that I noticed.'

'Then perhaps she put it there deliberately.' Their eyes met; no further words were necessary. They had found the child's grave. It was beneath their feet, on the edge of the farmyard. By the roots of the solitary tree that didn't belong there any more than the little bones did. Aldís blushed with shame to think that it had ever have crossed her mind to use the corpse for a prank. Some things were unforgivable, however drunk you were. *Never again.*

The temperature was dropping and Aldís realised she was shivering again, though not as badly as when she had climbed out of the bath. Hastily she laid the heart back in its place and scooped snow over it. 'I can't stay out here any longer. Come on.' She glanced at Einar, expecting him to be similarly anxious. Lilja and Veigar would be apoplectic with rage if they caught them here, and it would be only too obvious what Aldís and Einar had discovered. But his eyes were not flickering nervously; they were shining with excitement and glee. There was no hint of any shame over the night's unspeakable plans. Aldís was trembling now as badly as she had when she woke in the bath.

Chapter 19

The dark-red wine looked thick and oily, but slipped down smoothly enough. Óðinn tilted the long-stemmed, wide-bowled glass and watched the swirling liquid rise almost to the rim as he increased the speed. He put the glass down.

'Do you like it?' From the expression on his sister-in-law's face, she wasn't expecting him to say yes. Óðinn was straddling a barstool at the island in Sigga and Baldur's kitchen, watching her fry a large pan of mushrooms. The huge heap suggested they were expecting a crowd to dinner rather than just him and Rún, but then they tended to cater generously in this house. While Sigga was slicing the mushrooms, he'd wanted to point out that, like most kids, Rún didn't eat them, but he didn't want to rub her nose in her childlessness. He'd never spoken to her about the couple's problem conceiving, but from what his brother told him it weighed heavily on her. 'Baldur bought a couple of bottles when he was abroad last summer. He's been dying to try it.'

'It's very nice.' Óðinn took another sip to make it look convincing. The wine had a more pungent flavour than he was used to; it was probably too good for his uncultivated palate. He felt the familiar warmth stealing through his body, though he would have preferred a beer.

Sigga shrugged and returned to stirring the mushrooms. The butter sizzled and spots of fat beaded on the black stone worktop. 'To be honest, I prefer white.' The hot fat spat again and Sigga whipped back her hand, raised it to her mouth, then shook it hard. 'Damn!' Her sunburnt arm seemed out of place against the wintry backdrop of snow on the decking outside the French windows. Baldur was standing out in the cold, barbecuing, which didn't fit with the season either. It was as if they were conspiring to pretend it was summer. Beside him, Rún was watching intently as he fiddled with a giant, silver-coloured grill that must have cost an arm and a leg.

'Need a plaster?' Ódinn leant over the island to see. It was a stupid question but he couldn't come up with any better response.

Sigga held out her slender arm to show him. 'It's nothing. Just stings a bit.' She drew back her wrist with a jingling of decorative bangles, no doubt bought on the beach during her winter holiday. She and Baldur had been intending to go together but he'd been too busy. Ódinn understood why she longed for a child. In reality she was as alone as he had been before Rún came to live with him. Baldur was always working and Ódinn doubted he made any distinction between weekends and weekdays. Ódinn had been the same when he worked for his brother; after all, he'd had nothing much else to do. Baldur had different reasons for being a workaholic; he owned the company and couldn't afford to slacken the pace if he and Sigga were to go on enjoying the luxuries to which they had grown accustomed. When it came down to it, though, Ódinn wasn't sure Sigga would choose the trinkets and baubles of the high life over a normal home life and her husband's presence. Still, he was no judge. He didn't know her well enough, though she'd been part of the family for a decade.

'Did you enjoy your holiday?' He wished Rún and Baldur would come inside; it would be rude to sneak out to join them, but he'd run out of things to say.

'Oh, yes. It was fine, in the circumstances.' She had no need to specify the circumstances. 'A bit lonely. But relaxing. Good to get away from this shitty weather.' Ódinn secretly rejoiced that she'd mentioned the weather – that inexhaustible topic of conversation – but his joy was premature. 'I should have taken Rún along. It would have done her good to get away for a bit.'

'Maybe not quite yet.' Ódinn watched Rún stamping her feet to keep warm. She turned to Baldur, beaming at some comment he'd made. It was so long since Ódinn had seen her smile like that that he'd forgotten she was capable of it. But she was always happy in Baldur's company; everybody was. One couldn't help being infected by his exuberant optimism. 'She's still getting over it.' But perhaps Sigga was right; a carefree holiday might be just what the child needed. 'We're going to Spain together in the summer. So long as she keeps up her handball practice this winter.'

'Are you kidding? You're seriously going to cancel your holiday if she throws in the towel?' Sigga gaped at him incredulously. Her face was as brown as her arms; her blonde hair almost white in contrast. She hardly seemed to belong here; it was as if she'd been washed up on these shores from some far-off land of perpetual summer. He couldn't remember ever having seen her this brown before, which must mean the trip had been utterly uneventful. Wake up, lie beside the pool, back up to the room, sleep. Repeat fourteen times. He couldn't see Rún enjoying that. Their trip would be different. If they ever went.

'She'll stick at it, so it won't come to that.'

'Really? She told me she hates sport.' Sigga turned off the heat under the mushrooms. 'I sympathise. I was made to play handball when I was a kid and I loathed it. You never knew when you were going to get a rock-hard ball in your face or ribs. I've never been so happy as the day I was allowed to quit.'

Ódinn was about to disagree and start listing the advantages of sport when the door opened. The cold poured inside, accompanied by a delicious smell of grilled meat from the heaped platter in Baldur's hands. Rún was holding his wine glass, an incongruous sight with her childish orange anorak and colourful, knitted hat. 'Aren't you two half frozen?'

'No way. What do you think we are, a couple of wusses?' Baldur winked at Rún, laid the meat down on the kitchen table and took back his glass. He was wearing an anorak over an apron sporting the slogan: *Be nice to me or I'll poison the food* – a birthday present from his employees back when Ódinn was still working for him. 'How's the new job? Still a complete waste of time?'

Ódinn flushed slightly, though he didn't know why. There was no reason to be ashamed of the fact that his job wasn't as dynamic and exciting as his last one. 'No, far from it. I've been given an interesting assignment.'

'Oh? What's that? Counting the streetlights on the Reykjanes highway? Checking if one of them's missing?' Baldur took a mouthful of wine. 'God, that's good.' He smiled at Sigga who smiled back and took a sip too. She winked at Ódinn over the rim of her glass and he raised his in return.

'No, actually. It's to do with one of those old state-run care homes. Not like the others, though – this one was for older boys, kids who'd gone off the rails. Maybe it's not an appropriate topic of conversation in present company.' He nodded towards Rún, who was taking off her anorak.

'I went to the office with Daddy,' Rún told Baldur. 'It's not as cool as your job. Everyone just sits at computers.'

'My point precisely. Cheers to that.' Baldur toasted them all. Still grinning, he turned back to Ódinn. 'Why don't you just hand in your notice and come back to us? I've got plenty for you to do. Frankly, the guy I hired to replace you is a waste of space. Even you look good in comparison.'

Rún gazed at her father, waiting for him to rise to this. But Ódinn was in no mood for the inevitable banter that would follow; he knew his brother too well to think he'd ever be allowed the final word. 'Not now. Later, maybe. You'll have to put up with the waste of space for the time being.'

Sigga had transferred the mushrooms to a bowl, which she now carried into the dining room. Ódinn saw her nudge her husband as if to tell him to take it down a notch. Baldur, oblivious to such things, didn't seem to notice. 'God, I'm starving.' Belatedly taking off his anorak, he started loading the meat onto the dish Sigga had brought out. 'We'd better get a move on – aren't you going to be late?'

Ódinn shook his head. 'I'll go when I've eaten. It's not that kind of party.' He'd been invited to the birthday of one of their old circle of friends. He suspected the invitation had something to do with that phone call he'd made to Kalli – much too late at night and in a bit of a state. No doubt it had led to talk about what a hard time he was having, and made them feel guilty for neglecting him. Now Lára was gone, there was no reason not to invite him; everything would be like it was in the old days. Except that now they were almost a decade older and their circumstances were very different from when they used to meet every weekend to knock back booze and hit the town. They were all married family men; he was a single parent. Óðinn didn't really want to go but he'd accepted the invitation for fear even more exaggerated stories would circulate about him if he refused, and he hated people feeling sorry for him. Well, he'd show his face but wouldn't stay a minute longer than necessary. Afterwards, he was thinking of seizing the chance to go into town, since Rún was staying the night; let his hair down for a change and check out the talent. He longed to be with a woman, though only for a casual fling, if he were honest.

They barely made any impression on the pile of food. Rún didn't touch the mushrooms, as he'd predicted, but ate plenty of potatoes and meat. Óðinn leant back in his chair, sipped at his umpteenth glass of red wine and relished the sensation as the alcohol spread through his body. The wine might not be to his taste but you got used to it. Even the party now seemed an alluring prospect. 'Thanks. Excellent food.' He surveyed the table. 'I don't know what you're going to do with it all. Survive on leftovers till spring?'

'Rún'll polish it off tomorrow morning.' Baldur turned a serious face towards the girl, who sat staring, huge-eyed, at the mountain of food. 'She won't be allowed home until she's eaten it all up. Especially the mushrooms.'

Rún glanced at her father and Óðinn grinned to show it was a joke. She grinned back and he felt even happier. Perhaps they should move in here; there was no shortage of room, after all. The basement was bigger than their entire flat. Sigga would welcome them and no doubt Baldur would too, because it would stop her complaining that he was always at work.

The thought was the product of the red wine; of course he'd never suggest such an unorthodox solution to their problems. Yet it was difficult to shake off the idea; Rún seemed so happy and contented in Baldur's presence. No, the solution was not to insinuate themselves into other people's lives but to sort out their own, to make their home life as easy and unstrained as the atmosphere in this house. And it was up to him to achieve it.

A smooth bass beat throbbed through the hot, sweaty air of the bar, penetrating every dark corner. There was no escaping it, but then nobody came here in search of peace and quiet. Ódinn stood at the bar that had suddenly emptied. A minute or two before, a crowd of customers had been trampling over each other to be served, but the moment this song started playing there had been a mass exodus to the dance-floor. He accepted a beer glass, beaded with moisture, from the bartender, and felt his hair bouncing in time to the deafening music. He had no one to toast but the barman, who barely reacted. Most of the other customers were younger than Ódinn and he didn't know a soul. Worse still, the girls were all too young for him. It had been the same at the other two places he'd looked in on. During the six months he'd been absent from the scene, a transformation had taken place. His age group had clearly started partying at home – a pity, if the birthday he'd just left was typical.

The gathering had been achingly dull, but informative. Now he knew there was no reason to miss his former friends. They and their wives had been a bit awkward around him at first, but, once they'd downed a few drinks, his old mates had come over, one after the other, to confide in him that they'd been meaning to call but somehow never got round to it. They'd keep in touch from now on, though. At first, he'd found this excruciatingly embarrassing, and, unlike his brother's red wine, it didn't grow on him. By the end he felt like telling them to fuck off and find someone who gave a shit. But he put up with it until finally he'd had enough and left the party to the accompaniment of sidelong glances from the women and exhortations from his mates to stay a bit longer – the fun was just beginning. He felt like shouting for joy once he was sitting in the taxi outside the block of flats. Never, ever again. He'd stick with his other friends – the ones who'd stayed loyal to him after his marriage ended.

'Hey! If it isn't the divorced guy.' Ódinn wouldn't have realised this was addressed to him if the man hadn't grabbed his shoulder. 'How're you doing?' He was quite young, drunk, but not completely plastered. He smiled glassily and seemed disappointed when he saw that Ódinn couldn't place him. He took a step backwards. 'Don't you remember me? I was on my stag night?' He might as well have been whispering but if the music had suddenly stopped it would have been obvious that he was yelling.

The fog in Ódinn's head shifted slightly. He ought to recognise the man. 'My mind's a blank.'

'Don't you remember? You were telling me not to get married.' The man moved closer, leaning in confidingly.

'Should've listened to you.' Then he straightened up again and bellowed: 'Joke!'

Now Ódinn remembered him. This was the man he had struck up a conversation with in a bar the night Lára died. At the time the guy had been sporting a ballet tutu over his trousers, and his face had been orange from the fake tan his mates had smeared all over him. 'Right! Hey, how're you doing?' Ódinn greeted him like a long-lost friend. At last someone he recognised. 'You look different with your normal clothes on.' He had only a hazy recollection of their chat, though he could remember enough to recall that he had talked a load of crap to the poor guy.

'You were hysterical, man! Determined to tell me the truth about marriage. That it was hell.' The young man smiled and gave Ódinn a friendly nudge that almost knocked him sideways. 'Sorry, mate. But you deserve it. I'd hardly recovered in time for my wedding a week later. You kept me out far too late.'

'It wasn't that late.' Ódinn had to shout into the man's ear. He was so grateful to have someone to talk to that he didn't want to risk the guy abandoning him because he couldn't hear a word.

'God, yes, it was. It was nearly eight in the morning by the time I crawled home.' The man waved at the bartender and ordered another beer. Ódinn assumed he must have had a hard time hailing a taxi because of the way he'd been dressed. He was under the impression that he himself had gone home much earlier. 'Did you go round and see your ex?' the young man asked. 'How did it go in the end?'

'In the end?' Ódinn stared at him in surprise. 'I went home.'

'Lucky for you. You'd have been in for a right bollocking

if you'd gone to see her in that state. Jesus, she'd have gone mental, man.'

'She? Who are you talking about?' People were coming off the dancefloor and in no time the crush by the bar had reached its former density. So bad was the jostling that Ódinn had to be careful not to spill his drink over the man.

'Your ex-wife. What's her name again?'

'Lára.' Ódinn didn't correct his use of the present tense. He had no desire to inform the man that she had died that same morning. Especially since it appeared he had been badmouthing her, for no good reason.

'Yeah. Lára.' A third of the man's full glass slopped onto Ódinn's shoes. Oblivious, he carried on talking. 'You wanted me to go along too, said she agreed with you and would tell me to call the whole thing off. Don't you remember?' Ódinn nodded, untruthfully. 'Did you go?' the man asked.

'No.'

'Phew! I was sure you'd gone to see her. You should've accepted a lift with me after all.'

'A lift?' He had begun to sound like an echo.

'Yeah, I offered to share a taxi. I was afraid you'd pass out on the way. Jesus, I was wasted, man. And you. Wow. You were totally fucking brollied.'

Ódinn wasn't sure he'd heard right. Had the man said 'brollied' or 'trolleyed'? It made no difference. He *had* been totally wasted. 'Are you sure you got home at eight?' It didn't make sense. If this guy had gone home first, he himself must have been out until eight or even later. This was news to him; Ódinn had assumed he'd got home about six. But he had no evidence to back this up. Had he really been in town when Lára died? Maybe even in the area? All of a sudden he could hear, not music, but the wail of sirens connected to some memory he couldn't for the life of him retrieve. Why did he have to meet this bloke again? The smallness of Icelandic society could be a curse.

'Hey! I want to introduce you to my wife. Come on, she's in here somewhere.' The man turned and scanned the throng. Ódinn seized the opportunity and began worming his way through the crowd to the exit. Behind him he heard: 'Hey, man! Come on! You've gotta meet Didda.' But he didn't look round. He had to get home.

The taxi receipt was buried at the bottom of the large salad bowl that Sigga and Baldur had given him as a housewarming present. Not so much as a lettuce leaf had found its way in there as yet; instead, Ódinn used it to store his credit-card slips. He sat on the sofa surrounded by bits of paper, too drunk to go about the task systematically. He had pulled out the receipts one after the other, dropping them when they turned out not to be the one he was after. The one he had been looking for was right at the bottom, among those he had brought with him from his old flat and chucked in the bowl after the move. Relics of old times, of life pre-Rún.

Leaning back, he contemplated the white ceiling. It was better than looking at the Hreyfill receipt in his lap. It recorded the time he had climbed into the taxi and the place he had ordered it from. It seemed the stag-do bloke had been right: Ódinn had got into the taxi just after Lára fell out of the window. And – to make matters worse – in her street. Right outside her house, if the receipt was to be believed.

A low thud came from the hallway leading to the bedrooms and Ódinn knew there was no way he was setting foot in there until daylight. He detected a faint whiff of cigarette smoke and his heartbeat grew rapid and fluttery. He would sleep here on the sofa; he wasn't going into his bedroom for love nor money.

Chapter 20

The blizzard had been raging so long that the roaring of the wind and the creaking of the house seemed to merge into a ceaseless howl. Would it ever ease up? Aldís could hardly remember what silence sounded like, and even though it was warm indoors she couldn't shake off the chill. It didn't help that the windows were covered in snow. She worried about the bird, trying to imagine where it could have found shelter. For all she knew it might have been blown out into the barren wastes, never to be seen again. The thought saddened her, though she'd always known the poor creature might not make it. There were constant weather alerts on the radio, as if anyone could possibly have failed to notice the storm. These were the most severe conditions Aldís had experienced since coming to Krókur; it was the first time all the boys' work had been suspended. Veigar and Lilja had judged it unsafe for them to move between the buildings, so for once they were idling in their rooms.

She could probably have taken time off too, since there was nothing much going on. Veigar and Lilja were perfectly capable of cooking for the boys themselves and carrying the food over to their dormitory. But the thought of spending a second day cooped up in her lonely room was worse than

being busy, so she'd decided not to go back there after breakfast. Her housemates, on the other hand, had seized the
opportunity gratefully and were disgusted with her for not
taking it easy like them. Clearly they thought she was showing
them up as slackers, but then they had been working the
day before while she lay shivering with hangover and anxiety
under her duvet. She had no wish to repeat the experience.

She surveyed the shining linoleum. Once the soapy water
had dried it would look as dull and worn as before, but clean.
This was a good time to mop the floors; she was alone in the
building and there was no risk of anyone coming in and ruining
her handiwork with a trail of muddy footprints. The speed at
which she was getting through her chores made her feel much
better than when she was alone and idle. It was satisfying to
contemplate all she had achieved and compare it to the small
amount that was left. It helped too that the howling of the
wind drowned out any unexplained noises.

Aldís dried her hands on her jeans and opened the door
to the office. She had already cleaned Lilja and Veigar's
upstairs apartment and the classroom and corridor on the
ground floor. All that remained was the office, one lavatory
and the entrance hall. After that she would have to wrap up
warm and brave the elements to sprint over to the main
building, either to help with lunch or to inform the couple
that she had finished for the day. She would decide which
on the way over. She might even look in the cubbyhole at
the end of the corridor, which served as the library, and see
if she could find a book to help her while away a few hours,
though she'd already read all the promising-sounding titles.
Besides, she'd been neglecting her English studies; the textbook was gathering dust on her bedside table, so perhaps it

would make more sense to knuckle down to that after lunch. It seemed the least appealing option, however; housework was actually preferable. The danger was that if she started looking at English grammar, her thoughts would wander and soon she would be thinking about the baby buried in the yard, or her mother, or the mystery surrounding Einar.

She switched on the light in Veigar's office and carried in the half-full bucket. The water was brown with dirt but Aldís didn't care; he didn't deserve any better. She smiled at this paltry act of rebellion. As usual she had to move with care in the cramped room, but it was easier this time as Veigar appeared to have tidied up for once, making it possible to dust. She wiped away a number of rings left by coffee mugs, wondering how on earth he'd found anywhere to put them down. Then, since everything else was looking so nice, she decided to clean the telephone, which was smudged all over with Veigar's large fingerprints. When she'd finished you'd have thought the black Bakelite set had just arrived from the Post and Telephone Company. She paused to admire it.

Before she knew it, the receiver was in her hand. It just happened. There was no need to wonder what was going on in her subconscious; at this moment there was only one person in the world she had reason to call. Aldís took a deep breath and stared at the snow-plastered window. Beyond it, the blizzard was raging unseen. The snow was sliding down the glass, on a downward trajectory like her own life. She could find no foothold, no anchor. Of course she should ring home: that was her anchor. All she had to do was dial the number; she could have done it blindfolded. What was the worst that could happen? Her mother would be at work anyway. But no sooner had she dialled the last digit than she remembered the storm that had paralysed the country from north to south. The bakery where her mother worked would almost certainly be closed.

Yet Aldís did not hang up. She held the heavy receiver to her ear and listened as it rang. The phone on the small hall table at home would be jangling; she could hear its thunderous rings as if she were there. She squeezed her eyes shut to stop the tears spilling over. At the fourth ring the phone was picked up.

'Hello.' Her mother's voice sounded different to how Aldís remembered it – sadder, more mechanical. 'Hello.'

Aldís stood there rigidly, desperately regretting having let her feelings run away with her. This was the woman who had sided with that disgusting creep and accused her own daughter of lying rather than face up to what kind of scum she had dragged into their home.

But this was also the woman who had spent so many evenings bent over her sewing machine, making clothes for her daughter so she would look as nice as the girls who came from wealthier homes; the woman who had tested her on her multiplication tables, put plasters on her cuts after childish escapades, and provided a sympathetic ear for teenage whingeing. The tears were pouring down her cheeks now. Of course she ought to forgive her mother. If the tables were turned, her mother would forgive her.

'Hello. Who is it?' Her mother's voice no longer sounded flat but eager, as if she knew who was on the other end. 'Aldís, is that you? Say something. Anything.' Aldís knew it had cost her mother a great deal to say that; it could have been anyone on the line and she would have betrayed how desperate she was to hear from her daughter. It wasn't like her to advertise her difficulties to the world. Smile, put a good face on things. Don't show that you can't afford the rent rise; that the electricity bill hasn't been paid and is accumulating interest at a terrifying rate. Pretend you don't want to go to the theatre in Reykjavík with your friends who can't talk about anything else; smile and pretend nothing's wrong. It's nobody else's business how you're feeling. 'Aldís?' Her mother sounded on the verge of tears.

Aldís slammed down the receiver. Eyes wide, she stared at the phone, which sat there impassively, as if the conversation had never taken place. She couldn't bring herself to ring again. Not now. Perhaps not ever. Her mother didn't have the answers she needed.

But in that instant the phone started ringing, her resolve melted away and she snatched up the receiver. 'Mum?'

'Hello? Who's that?' It wasn't her mother but some other woman.

'Aldís.' She dried her tears with the sleeve of her shabby jumper, the bobbles scratching her tender eyelids.

'Hello. Was it you I talked to the other day? I was so glad to finally speak to someone that I forgot to write down your name.'

It was Einar's mother. Aldís drew a breath, puffing out her cheeks till they hurt, then slowly exhaled. This just wasn't her day. 'I can't talk to you. I'm not supposed to answer the phone. The person you need to talk to is called Veigar and he's not here right now.'

For a moment there was silence at the other end, then the woman spoke again, sounding even more sombre than in their previous conversation. 'The other day you said I could get in touch. I tried to ring last week at the time you mentioned but no one answered. Is something wrong? Has something changed?'

'No. Nothing,' Aldís answered brusquely. She didn't dare say more for fear of reverting to her friendly old self. She couldn't afford to; she had enough troubles of her own without shouldering other people's.

'Something's wrong. I can hear it in your voice. Has something happened to Einar?'

'There's nothing wrong. I'm not allowed to talk on the phone, that's all.' Aldís wondered if she should hang up, as she had with her mother, but there was a risk the woman might be offended and complain to Veigar. Then he'd find out that Aldís had been answering his calls. 'Really. There's nothing wrong.'

'Are you sure?'

'Yes. I'm sure.' Of course this wasn't entirely true. There was a great deal wrong with Einar, but it wasn't the fault of the care home. 'Can I ask you a question?'

'What?'

'Why's Einar here? What did he do?'

The woman was silent again. Aldís could hear her breathing. 'He slipped up. Badly.'

'This isn't Casualty. What did he do?' Aldís crossed her fingers in the hope that the woman would take the bait.

'I can't discuss it, I'm afraid. I'd tell you if I could.'

'Who's stopping you? Einar?'

'No. Not Einar.' The woman sounded evasive and Aldís thought she might hang up. But what if she did? Why should Aldís want to prolong the conversation? The woman wouldn't tell her anything and it was bound to end up with Aldís having to act as messenger again.

'Why is he here, given his age? Shouldn't he be in prison if he's committed a crime?'

'I can't answer that. I just can't.' The woman's voice had dropped to a whisper. 'Please give Einar my love. Tell him I've seen Eyjalín. She's still very ill. He's actually lucky he's not at home at the moment.' She paused to draw breath, as if to give Aldís a chance to reply, then added: 'I'd be so grateful if you'd do this for me.' Without waiting for an answer, she hung up.

Aldís glanced around in the hope of finding some distraction to take her mind off the phone call. Why hadn't she taken the day off? Moping in bed, alone with her thoughts, could hardly have been any worse than this. She scanned Veigar's shelves hopefully but couldn't see anything of interest. Just a jumble of papers, files and the odd religious ornament. She felt an inclination to smash something.

Then suddenly it dawned on her.

There was no one about, and the storm made it unlikely that Veigar and Lilja would look in. The answers might be right here and she probably wouldn't get another opportunity like this to search for them. Usually she could rely on one or other of the managers to stick their nose in to check up on her. Searching through all the papers would take time and this could be her only chance. Without stopping to consider the consequences, Aldís pulled a thick file off the shelf. Leafing through it, she quickly realised that the contents were of no interest. Receipts and contracts, many of them ancient, nothing to do with the home. The next three files contained the same sort of stuff; she couldn't understand why Veigar held on to such trivial paperwork. All kinds of letters from ministries and a variety of government bodies, all of which seemed to contain standard wording. Judging from what she read, Krókur's existence was necessary but unpopular; people would rather not have to know about it. The fifth file contained final demands and threats of debt-collection measures that would shortly be put into place. Aldís snapped it shut; as long as her wages were paid she didn't care.

She perked up when she saw the sixth file. The spine was labelled with the current and previous year, and when she opened it she saw that Veigar had organised it alphabetically, each divider marked with a boy's initials. She tore it open at EA, for Einar Allen. It contained a single page, which did not appear to be a standard letter. Aldís started to read, oblivious to the shrieking of the wind.

Chapter 21

Ódinn was becoming reconciled to the idea that he was mad. In a way it was a relief; he no longer had to fear the worst because it had already happened. Nanna's explanation that the sounds he was hearing had always been there without his noticing was some comfort, but it wasn't enough. So much else was out of kilter with his idea of reality.

For the last few days, however, his mind had been almost entirely occupied with the question of whether he could conceivably have been involved in Lára's death. The taxi receipt and timing of the accident in the police reports indicated as much; he had been in the area and left the street shortly after Lára fell. Hazy memories of an ambulance and sirens kept coming back to him. Yet, in spite of this, he found it impossible to believe he could have been responsible. He wasn't a violent man; he hadn't even got into fights as a boy. And though he and Lára hadn't exactly seen eye to eye on a lot of things, he'd never once laid a finger on her. Sure, they'd both slammed doors and sworn at each other, but never so much as slapped one another's face, let alone anything worse. The fact that he'd been drunk and in the area at the time of her death didn't alter that fact. So why would he have gone and killed her, so long after their divorce? By far the most likely scenario was that he'd never gone through with the visit, either because he was too tired or because he'd come to his senses by then. His drinking buddy, the guy on his stag do, had left in a taxi, and without him the fun had soon palled.

Another worry at the moment was the way Rún seemed to be going downhill since she'd started seeing the therapist. She had constant nightmares in which her mother chased or lay in wait for her, at school, in the sports hall, the shop, or anywhere else she visited on a daily basis. The only place she could sleep peacefully, undisturbed by bad dreams, was at Baldur and Sigga's house, and she pleaded so hard to be allowed to go and stay that it had become embarrassing.

Nanna had been hesitant about drawing any significant conclusions from this. Rún was probably finally beginning to come to terms with the loss of her mother, and no one said that would be easy. But the more Ódinn thought about it, the more he began to suspect that something much worse lay at the root of her distress, so he phoned Nanna and asked straight out if Rún could conceivably have witnessed her mother's fall and repressed the memory; whether her nightmares could be triggered by the incident returning to the surface as a result of the therapy sessions. Nanna had been disconcerted – repressed memory was a controversial topic in her field – but even so she'd been unwilling to dismiss the possibility.

The urge to just ask Rún straight out was almost more than he could bear. He found himself staring at her as if he could force an answer out of her by telepathy. But he couldn't ask directly because he was afraid he wouldn't be satisfied with a simple no. And that would be disastrous. He was scared of making matters worse, of confusing or destroying her memory. Of course, there was a chance Rún might be able to confirm that he hadn't been in the flat. But what terrified him was the alternative, that she might have witnessed him using violence against her mother.

His personal problems had become so overwhelming that for the first time since he'd started there, Ódinn actively looked forward to going to the office in the mornings. He enjoyed hanging up his coat, filling his coffee mug, sitting down with his headphones, turning on the radio, and opening his files – seeking refuge in the little cubicle that he'd originally found so claustrophobic. There he could forget himself, hearing nothing but the prattling of DJs, interspersed with music; pretend nothing was wrong by immersing himself in his investigation of Krókur. As a result he was making good progress, faster than he would have dared hope, which made him the star of the Monday meeting for the second week in a row.

'I've interviewed four former residents now and they all have a similar tale to tell,' he informed his co-workers. 'Although they don't say so in as many words, it's clear that things were not as they should have been.' Ódinn noticed that his colleagues dodged his gaze when he looked at them, as if they felt responsible for the past operation of the home. 'It's a wonder no one's come forward before now.'

'Is it possible they're getting a kick out of the attention and exaggerating what really went on?' Heimir was sitting in his place at the head of the table and he at least didn't try to avoid Ódinn's gaze, though his lazy eye did its usual sideways dive. 'I'm not sure the testimony of four men is sufficient to remove all doubt.'

'Of course not, but their stories are a strong indication that the state will be liable to pay compensation.'

'Why haven't they spoken out before? Of their own accord?'

'For a number of reasons, I suspect. None of them wanted to become the public face of the home, since admitting they did time there isn't exactly something to be proud of. We mustn't forget that, unlike Breidavík for example, Krókur was a detention centre for young offenders. Three of the old boys I spoke to are now respectable family men and, although they were prepared to talk to me, they wouldn't go to the press. The fourth is a homeless addict who's trying to sort out his life. He didn't follow the Breidavík case in any detail since he was either on the streets or in rehab at the time. He'd heard about it, of course, but it hadn't occurred to him that Krókur might fall into the same category. And even if it had, he probably wouldn't have felt up to coming forward.'

'Right, well, I don't like it but of course I'm pleased you're making such good progress.' Heimir directed a pointed look at the others present, as if to imply that they should pull their socks up. 'Have you spoken to any former staff?' Heimir's lips continued moving after he stopped speaking, as if his volume had been turned down. He was probably trying to work out how old they would be now.

'The manager died about ten years ago, but tomorrow I'm going to see his widow, who ran the home with him. I can't find any proper information about the other staff. Róberta didn't seem to have any records of them.' Ódinn had repeatedly searched through her files. 'The old boys I talked to didn't know the full names of anyone who worked there, so I wanted to ask if you could request a list of them, Heimir. You're right, I need to interview a couple of former employees. They're bound to view the home in a very different light from the woman who ran it.'

Heimir frowned. 'Róberta had a list somewhere, I'm fairly sure of that.'

'Then she must have hidden it well. There's nothing about staff in any of the documents I've found. The odd name crops up here and there, but either the last name's missing or the full name's so common that it's as good as useless. I'd need a date of birth or some other information to narrow the search. I'm guessing you don't want me to ring round everyone with the same name, on the off-chance?'

'Of course not,' said Heimir. 'I'll see what I can do.' He seemed annoyed, and when they spoke after the meeting, Ódinn understood why. It transpired that the office had received a large number of original documents, which he had passed on to Róberta, and he would prefer not to have to inform the ministry that these had been mislaid. However, he promised to look into the matter. Their conversation had the air of a confidential chat, as if they were friends swapping secrets, and Ódinn was on the verge of telling him what Pytti had said about the accident. But the homeless man's story had been so far-fetched that Ódinn didn't like to repeat it in case Heimir thought he was mad. There was no way, thirty-seven years after the event, to find out if Pytti was right. Two of the other old boys he'd spoken to had been at the home before the accident and the third shortly afterwards, so he only knew of it by hearsay, and the rumours he'd heard were even more outlandish than Pytti's account. Ódinn had no idea what to believe.

'Ideally I'd like to get permission to go through Róberta's computer – her e-mail and so on. Maybe I'll find something there. She may have scanned in the documents and not had a chance to save them in the appropriate folders.' Ódinn still hadn't dared tell Heimir about the threatening messages and had almost given up hope of finding a plausible excuse for needing to access her e-mail. Perhaps this was it.

Heimir put on a martyred expression but said he would grant permission.

Instead of returning to his desk and rereading the documents he already knew pretty much by heart, Ódinn decided to check yet again whether he had overlooked something among Róberta's records.

'Why weren't you at the meeting?' Ódinn sat down in Róberta's chair and rolled it over to the filing cabinet under her desk. Staff meetings were obligatory, so he had assumed Diljá was off sick.

'I just couldn't be bothered.' Diljá was on her feet, looking over the partition. 'I know you'll keep your mouth shut but, if he asks, tell him I was waiting for an important phone call. Hopefully he won't ask who from.'

'Tell him it was your gynaecologist. That'll stop him in his tracks.' Ódinn opened one drawer after another, rummaging inside. 'Do you know if Róberta ever took work home with her?'

'Not to my knowledge.'

'You never saw her with files in her bag or anything like that?'

'Well, naturally she carried a bag sometimes. Who doesn't?'

Ódinn raised his eyes from the filing cabinet to Diljá's face and was rewarded with a mocking smile and a heady waft of her perfume. 'I mean, did she ever come in with an empty bag, or box, and take it home full of files?'

'I'm not a security guard, am I? She could have come here with a hundred empty bags in the morning, filled them and taken them home without my noticing. Róberta usually got in before me and left after I'd gone.' Diljá smiled again, more warmly this time. Suddenly her scent smelled nice to Ódinn. She seemed to sense this and fluttered her heavily mascaraed lashes.

Ódinn looked away. 'Shit. What's she done with the stuff? Some of the documents are definitely missing.' He ran his eyes over the pictures on the wall as if hoping to find a safe hidden behind them. Something was niggling at him; something he'd overlooked. That was probably why he kept coming back to Róberta's desk. It certainly wasn't Diljá's flirting that drew him there.

When she spoke again she had dropped the coy act. 'How's your daughter?'

'She's fine, thanks.' Ódinn tried to appear unconcerned but his fingers felt a sudden urge to drum the desktop. He looked back at the wall, and paused at the photo of the boys that Rún had found so unsettling. She was right – there was something about that damn picture.

'You've got a good girl there.'

'Yes, I have.' Ódinn's gaze fell on a key that was hanging from a hook between two pictures. He took it down. It was an ordinary ASSA key, which would fit any type of door. Except here at the office where the locks were all electronic. 'Any idea what this key's for?'

'Yes, it's Róberta's spare house-key. She started keeping it here after she locked herself out twice in a row.'

Ódinn stared at the key in his hand. Could this have been what was niggling at him? Had his subconscious snapped a picture of it and been politely insisting that he find out what it opened? No, that wasn't it. 'Where did she live?'

'On Kleppsvegur. Why do you ask?'

'Oh, no reason. Silly, really. Of course there's nothing there. I expect someone else has moved in by now.'

'No idea. And there's only one way to find out.' Diljá's eyes widened. 'Come on. Let's go and see. God, I'm dying for a change of scenery. We can call it a field trip on our timesheets, and maybe stop off at a café or a bar on the way back.'

It was hard not to be infected by Diljá's enthusiasm. Perhaps it would turn out to be a mistake, like his brainwave of visiting Lára at the crack of dawn with the young guy on his stag do. But this time he wouldn't be left in the lurch; Diljá wouldn't jump in a taxi at the last minute. 'OK, I'm up for it.' The worst-case scenario was that they would walk in on complete strangers, but they could avoid that if they knocked loudly first. It was too late to back out now, anyway; Diljá had her bag on her shoulder and was chivvying him to get a move on. Ódinn gave Róberta's workstation one more glance. It wasn't the key that had been bothering him. It was something else. But what?

Chapter 22

As it was the middle of a weekday, there were plenty of free parking spaces in front of the block of flats on Kleppsvegur. Diljá immediately identified Róberta's mailbox in the lobby by the sheaf of letters sticking out of it like a bunch of flowers. 'Looks as if no one's moved in yet.' She gingerly extracted an envelope, causing several others to fall out. Ignoring them, she examined the one in her hand. 'Pension fund. Probably her end-of-year statement. Who do you suppose'll get the money now?'

'No one.' Ódinn picked up the letters from the tiled floor. Róberta may have been indifferent now to such worldly matters, but he found it disrespectful to leave them to be trampled on by people and dogs. 'She was unmarried and childless. Pension funds are unlikely to pay out in those circumstances.'

Diljá crammed the envelope back into the mailbox, suddenly sober. 'Great. I'm unmarried and childless.' She turned to Ódinn, who was hunting for the right doorbell. 'Now I feel even worse about paying into that bottomless pit. If I get cancer, you can marry me on my deathbed and keep my pension.'

'I imagine you'll have other things on your mind, but thanks all the same.' He sensed she was waiting for him to return the offer, and refrained from pointing out that he had a daughter. Instead, he tapped in the number of Róberta's flat, which he had finally managed to locate. 'I bet there's someone there,' he said, as if he could influence the ringing tone emitted by the intercom. *Answer, answer.*

'Like who?'

'I don't know. A relative or a friend packing up her stuff.'

'Dream on. There'll be nobody there waiting to hand over a box marked "Work-related documents". I went to the funeral and sat in the second pew. The few relatives who turned up were surfing the net on their phones by the first hymn. They'll want the money from the sale of the flat but none of them will bother to go through her stuff. They're that kind of people.'

Ódinn was beginning to regret having brought Diljá along, though it was better than being alone, and, if it had been left to him, he'd never have taken the decision to come in the first place. Now they were here he might as well search the flat. Of course it would have been preferable to have gone through the proper channels, but that would only have complicated matters. He'd be walking around the same flat, examining the same stuff that no one cared about any longer; the only difference would be that he'd be acting under the watchful eyes of an executor or relative instead of Diljá. And if they had to do everything strictly by the book, it was bound to prove tricky to get the documents released.

These arguments had worked fine as justifications until they actually got here. 'Let's just drop the idea.'

'Are you nuts?' Diljá looked disgusted. 'We're here now. What's the worst that could happen? I'll tell you: nothing. So there's no reason to chicken out now.' She took the key from his hand and walked over to the door. 'I'm having second thoughts about marrying you in the hospice.' She tried unsuccessfully to push the key into the lock. 'What the hell?'

'It's probably the key to her flat, not the front door.' Róberta must have assumed she could get in by ringing one of her neighbours' bells. Ódinn was flooded with relief until Diljá went over to the buzzer and picked a number at random. It didn't work, so she tried the next. He watched in silence. What could he do? He couldn't forcibly drag her out into the street. This was a test. If Diljá managed to get them in, he would shut up and follow her. If not, he would feign disappointment and they would return to the office. Which would he prefer, if he had the choice? He didn't know.

'Yes, hello.' Diljá looked so relieved to get an answer, she was almost kissing the pale, plastic grille of the speaker. A tinny 'hello' was heard in reply. 'We're here to fetch some stuff from Róberta's flat. She took home some files from work, which we need to collect.' That was all it required. No need to give their names, specify the workplace or explain how they intended to gain admission to the flat itself. 'Bingo,' said Diljá as the buzzer sounded, and she reached for the door.

The stair-carpet was worn right through to the underlay in places, especially in front of the doors to the flats. On the first floor Róberta had made a rather poignant effort to smarten the place up. A doormat marked *Welcome!* hid the carpet outside her flat. The door itself bore a sign saying *Home Sweet Home*, and on the wall beside it she'd hung a vase containing garishly unconvincing plastic flowers. They were as dusty as the ones in the office and it occurred to Ódinn that she might have been responsible for those as well. 'What do you suppose will happen to this stuff?'

'Probably go to a charity shop. Or the dump. I can't picture her beneficiaries exactly climbing over each other to get this junk.'

'I guess not.' Ódinn thought about the entrance to his own flat, which was as impersonal as the empty apartments on the other floors. No 'Home Sweet Home' for him and Rún. He seemed to recall that Dísa downstairs had a mat in front of her door; perhaps it was the custom for people to mark their homes in some way and he was the odd one out.

'Jesus. No one's been here in a while.' Diljá wrinkled her nose, revealing her prominent front teeth. For a moment she reminded him of a rabbit.

The air glittered with dust and there was a musty smell as if the windows hadn't been opened for a long time. Diljá switched on the light and they went in. The first impression was one of extreme tidiness; the flat was filled with figurines and other ornaments that betrayed rather childish taste, but they were all carefully placed, with no sign of mess. In the rack by the door the shoes had been lined up as if with a ruler. Above, two small evening bags hung from a peg. Ódinn couldn't recall ever seeing Róberta with either. Perhaps she'd brought one to their annual office party, but although he was fairly sure he'd seen her there, Ódinn couldn't for the life of him remember how she'd been dressed, let alone what sort of bag she was carrying. He suspected his colleagues would be similarly blank – the men, anyway. He was about to ask Diljá if she remembered, but she forestalled him. 'Wow. It's like she knew she wasn't coming back. It's so weirdly tidy. She must have sensed she didn't have long to live.'

Ódinn agreed but didn't want to encourage such thoughts, so he said: 'Perhaps she never let it get messy. Some people are born house-proud and insist on keeping everything neat. Let's hope the whole flat's like this, then we'll find the files in no time. Assuming she did actually bring the paperwork home.' He watched Diljá pick up a blue-glazed statue of a plump, smiling child, which was holding up a shell as if it were a treasure. 'Don't break anything. We'd better touch as little as possible.'

Rolling her eyes, Diljá pretended to drop the ornament, then returned it to its place. 'Where on earth does someone buy crap like this, anyway?' She shook her head disapprovingly, as if Róberta had decorated her home with cannabis plants.

'Don't know.' Ódinn didn't want to discuss it. It made him uncomfortable and it was rude. They hadn't come here to pry into Róberta's private possessions or judge her taste. At least, *he* hadn't. 'Let's concentrate on what we came here for – to look for work stuff.' He went into the kitchen where everything was as immaculate as in the hall; even the dust in the air hadn't managed to dull the sheen on the clean, moss-coloured wall tiles. The kitchen windows were dressed with frilly curtains. 'Nothing here, I don't think.' The only objects on the kitchen table were a round, crocheted doily with a teapot on top. There was nothing on the worktop or shelves either. And Róberta would hardly have stuffed the papers in the cutlery drawer or fridge.

'Nonsense.' Diljá squeezed past him. 'Every kitchen has at least one drawer for odds and ends.' She pulled out the drawers, one by one, looking disappointed when they contained nothing but the usual kitchenware and tea towels. 'Perhaps this one is the exception.' She had no sooner spoken than she found what she was after. 'Aha!' She stepped aside so Ódinn could see. 'What did I tell you?'

The drawer contained a number of opened envelopes. Óðinn picked up the bundle, uncovering a heap of pens that were strangely at odds with the general tidiness. Flipping through the envelopes, he saw to his surprise that none were addressed to Róberta. The stamps were oddly faded and although he didn't take an interest in such things, he could tell they were old. 'Look.' He handed one to Diljá and read the address on the next. The name was the same on both, the vaguely familiar-sounding Einar Allen. The address was: The Krókur Care Home. All the letters turned out to be to the same boy. 'Róberta mentioned letters on her timesheet. She must have been referring to these. But why would she have taken them home with her?'

Diljá had removed the letter from its envelope. 'Perhaps she was bored at home. Wanted to read them at her leisure. Didn't get any letters herself. How should I know?' She read in silence. 'This one's from someone called Eyjalín.' She looked at Óðinn. 'Unusual name. I feel like I know it. Could it be the name of a company? Or a cosmetic maybe?' Frowning, Diljá pored over the name at the bottom of the page. 'Have you heard it before?'

Óðinn shook his head. What did the letter-writer's name matter? 'What does it say?'

'Looks like it was written by a girl, not a woman. Check out the handwriting.' She pushed the letter at him. The writing was adolescent, round and cheerful-looking. The accent over the 'í' in Eyjalín's signature was drawn as a heart. 'She's asking why he hasn't answered her letters. She's broken-hearted. Asks if he's stopped loving her; says she hates her father.'

'Isn't that just typical teenage melodrama?' How long would it be before Rún started hating him?

'I don't know. There's something odd about it when you read the rest. She says she doesn't regret anything and that they'll have children later and be happy. Whatever the doctor says. Then she starts asking again why he won't answer.'

'What's so odd about that?'

'I'd guess that Eyjalín wasn't even twenty; between fifteen and seventeen, maybe. You don't tend to give much thought to kids at that age; you're more likely to be waiting for a knight on a white horse. And what's this about a doctor?' Diljá handed him the letter and envelope, apparently expecting him to tidy them away. 'Here. Pass me the others. I'm curious now.'

Of course, he could have refused, but he knew she wouldn't give up until she got what she wanted. Spending time with her felt like ripping off a plaster – it was better to get whatever she suggested over with quickly. 'I'm going to check out the other rooms in the meantime. We'd better not stay too long.' Diljá made no comment, just took the envelopes from him and drew up a chair. Ódinn got on with searching the other rooms while she was absorbed in her reading. He had no desire to watch her rummaging around in all the cupboards, especially not in the bedroom where items of a personal nature were most likely to be found. So he began there. He could search the sitting room with Diljá.

The bedroom was as immaculate as the rest of the flat. The bed was made and Róberta had arranged a row of embroidered cushions on it, which clashed with the rose-patterned throw. Ódinn had never understood the point of throws, let alone cushions. All they did was get in the way when you wanted to go to bed. He wondered what she did with all this clutter at night and guessed she piled it on the upholstered armchair in the corner. There was no room anywhere else. The chest of drawers was almost buried under picture frames and ornaments, while on the bedside table was a large, cumbersome lamp, a book containing a bookmark, and an empty glass. Its drawers were mostly empty, apart from an eye-mask, a bottle of Milk of Magnesia and a pair of tweezers. Ódinn took a quick peek in the chest, closing the drawers immediately when he saw they were full of clothes, apart from the bottom one, which contained knitting needles, balls of wool and a half-completed sleeve.

He closed the drawer and straightened up. To his surprise, he didn't find the flat nearly as creepy as he'd feared, although it felt uncomfortable being in a dead woman's home without permission. He'd been afraid of sensing Róberta behind him or catching a fleeting glimpse of her in a mirror, but nothing like that happened. No gooseflesh or piercing certainty that something was lying in wait for him behind a door or inside a wardrobe. Perhaps the dread that Róberta's relatives would walk in and catch them red-handed had blocked out all other fears. He hoped it was a sign that he was on the mend and would soon return to normal – ordinary, boring old Ódinn. Not a nervous wreck who walked around with a knot in his stomach, seeing and hearing things that weren't there. Perhaps it was the flat itself that had this beneficial effect on him. If so, he'd better get his act together and buy it, preferably with all its contents intact, for fear of ruining the atmosphere. He smiled to himself at the absurdity of the idea, but his smile faded when he heard Diljá approaching.

'That Eyjalín must have been off her trolley in the end.' Diljá stood in the doorway, waving the letters like a fan. 'When you read them in the right order you can tell she's getting angrier and angrier with this Einar. In the last letter it sounds like she's completely deranged. She says he's betrayed her and never loved her, and God knows what else. At the bottom she's written his name and crossed it out over and over again, as if to show how much she hates him. You can hardly make out what it says underneath. I could only read it by turning over the page. Einar must have had a nice homecoming when he finally got out.'

'He died.'

'Oh.' Diljá came into the room. 'Was he one of the boys in the car?' Clearly she had been paying closer attention at the weekly staff meetings than her bored demeanour had suggested.

'Yes.' When Ódinn opened the wardrobe he was met by a cloud of stale perfume. The rail was so weighed down by dresses, jackets and shirts that it bowed in the middle. He stooped to check if there was anything concealed in the bottom of the wardrobe, hoping that he wouldn't find anything. His wish was granted: there was nothing but old pairs of smart shoes, most of them hopelessly out of fashion.

'I saw this woman at the funeral. Sat next to her, in fact.' Diljá was examining the photographs on top of the chest of drawers. 'She behaved pretty oddly.'

Ódinn stood up. 'Define "oddly". Isn't everyone a bit awkward at a funeral? How are they supposed to behave?'

'I don't know. But not like her.'

The photograph had been taken in a studio, but not for any obvious occasion. The woman wasn't dressed as a bride and looked far too old to have recently graduated from college. He'd never been good at working out people's ages but he'd have guessed she was around sixty. Like Róberta.

'Maybe it's her sister.' Half-sister was more likely, given how different they looked. Róberta had been stout, grey-eyed and dowdy; the woman in the picture had brown eyes and high cheekbones. Clearly stunning once, she was still glamorous in late middle age.

'No. The family all sat together on the other side. She was a friend. Or maybe a girlfriend. Whoever she was, she was weird.' Diljá shuddered. 'It was a bit creepy. She sat like a statue throughout the service, staring straight ahead. I swear she didn't blink once.'

'I expect she was just dealing with her grief in her own way. Not everyone can cry in public.' He turned his attention to the shelves at the top of the wardrobe. They contained boxes and bags, all bearing the logo of a supermarket that had long gone out of business. 'There's nothing here.'

After Diljá had peered under the bed and rooted around some more in the cupboards, they went into the sitting room. Neither in there nor in the small adjoining dining room did they find anything connected to work. Ódinn watched as Diljá opened the cupboards in the shelving unit which contained the newish television, then repeated the search in the dining-room sideboard, which emitted a constant clinking of glasses. 'Perhaps she only took the letters we found in the kitchen?' She couldn't hide her disappointment.

'Yes, looks like it.' Ódinn had been leaning on the easy chair in front of the television, which had lace antimacassars protecting the arms and headrest. 'Let's go. We've searched everywhere.'

'Except in the bathroom.'

Ódinn didn't reply, but let Diljá pop in there on the way out. He didn't accompany her, having no wish to see the toiletries and other articles that would probably end up in the dustbin. No one uses soap, cosmetics or perfume left by the dead. While he was waiting by the front door, he happened to notice a key hanging from a small hook. The plastic tag was marked *Garage*. The writing was slightly blurred as if the label had got wet. For the first time since entering the flat he felt a sense of misgiving. So it seemed he was as crazy as ever. He decided to confront it; he'd had enough. If every instinct told him to put the key down and forget its existence, he would do the exact opposite. 'Diljá! There's a garage. Hadn't we better inspect that rather than waste time looking down the toilet?' His voice sounded surprisingly steady.

They went outside and eventually located the right garage. The old hinges squeaked and groaned as Ódinn lifted the heavy wooden door. It was empty apart from an old bicycle and some odds and ends on shelves at the back. 'Where do you suppose her car is?' Diljá walked in and looked around.

'Not here, anyway.' Ódinn felt a deep reluctance to enter. 'It's probably still in town, plastered with parking tickets.' Diljá went over to the bike and picked up a shopping bag from beside it. She glanced at Ódinn, waiting for him to join her. He forced himself to enter the concrete box, feeling the knot tightening in his stomach. He fought an urge to look round and check that the door was still open, as if they were in danger of being locked in for good. Swallowing, he tried to concentrate on what Diljá had in her hand. From the expression in her eyes he could tell he must look ashen. She opened her mouth, then shut it and simply handed him the bag. The handles were tied in a double knot. He undid it and pulled out some papers. Eureka! Documents from work. There was a cardboard box, too, containing still more paperwork relating to Krókur. It was standing by the wall, as if she'd intended to put it in the car but forgot. Perhaps on the very morning she left the garage for the last time.

When Ódinn closed the garage door behind them he felt as if a heavy weight had been lifted from his shoulders, or he had narrowly avoided a car crash. He decided to take the keys to work rather than go back upstairs. They couldn't be sure of being let in the front door anyway. And the longing to get away from here was suddenly more than he could bear.

Chapter 23

February 1974

Tobbi squirmed in his chair, looking as if he wished he could disappear, his freckles all the more pronounced against his deathly pallor. But it didn't occur to Aldís to let him off the hook; she wanted answers, and part of her enjoyed seeing him suffer. It made her feel better, as if she could transfer her own discomfort onto Tobbi. She had cornered him as he left the dining room and forced him into a small sitting room at the back of the house. 'You're lying. You know exactly where they keep the letters.'

'I'm not, I swear. They just take them and I don't know where they put them. I swear it.' His large blue eyes glistened under his shaggy mop of hair. 'I'm telling the truth.'

On balance, Aldís thought he probably was. He was afraid of her and if he could have stopped the barrage of questions by answering differently, he would have done. But she was too desperate for answers to care. 'Why should I believe you?' She wanted to shake him. 'For months you've been helping Lilja and Veigar take what doesn't belong to them; stopping the boys – your friends! – getting post from their parents. They're thieves and you've helped them, and you know what?' The boy shook his head, clearly not wanting to know. 'That makes you no better than them. You're a thief.' Tobbi gnawed at his lower lip, blinking frantically. He looked close to tears and Aldís felt her resolve softening. 'But if you tell me what they did with the letters, you'll be a hundred times better than them. We all make mistakes but we're not often given the chance to make up for them. You're lucky to get a second chance.'

A spark of hope kindled in the boy's eyes, only to fade when he realised that Aldís was still after the same information. 'I swear I don't know what they do with the letters. I wish I did so I could tell you. But I don't.'

Aldís straightened up. She had been leaning menacingly over Tobbi, her hands on the arms of the chair. There was no need for that; he was only a boy and she was an adult, however little she might feel like it. 'Let's say I believe you.' He opened his mouth to mumble something but the words wouldn't come. Instead he nodded, his mouth still open. 'And that you'd tell me if you knew.' Tobbi nodded again, closing his mouth as he swallowed the lump in his throat. 'Then I have a solution.'

His wide eyes narrowed slightly. 'What do you mean?'

'The post van's coming later. Isn't it?'

'Yes. Tuesdays and Fridays. Around three. They send me down at half past, so I needn't hang about in the cold if he's late. I didn't mind when they made me go a bit earlier last summer. Standing down by the road was better than being here. I used to hope he'd be late even though I'd got there earlier.'

'I didn't ask for your life story.' She regretted her words immediately. The little she knew about Tobbi's background was not pretty: his father spent more time in prison than out of it, and when he was home he took out his rage on his son. Aldís had heard rumours that Tobbi had suffered more broken bones than all the other boys put together. She spoke more gently. 'I want you to give Veigar and Lilja all the post, whether it's letters or parcels, then watch them. That way you'll see where they hide them.' She folded her arms. 'Though that doesn't apply to *my* letters. I want all *mine* straight away. Understand?'

'But . . .'

'No buts. I don't care how you do it.' She had searched high and low in Veigar's office and other likely-seeming places, but to no avail. Despondent, she had tried to dismiss the problem from her mind and concentrate on work instead. But this morning she had woken up determined to put the thumbscrews on Tobbi. She had to get hold of the post. Above all, she wanted her own letters so she could find out what had caused that disgusting creep to leave, and whether her mother's regret was sincere. Only then would she be able to decide whether to get in touch.

Then there were Einar's letters. The single sheet she'd found in the file under his initials had been tantalisingly uninformative, though reading it had confirmed her belief that something underhand was going on. The letter was addressed to Veigar from a man called Jóhannes Ólafsson, who styled himself 'Judge'. Instead of writing in an official capacity, however, he seemed to be appealing to Veigar as an old friend or acquaintance. His reason for writing was to ask Veigar to take in a boy who, as it happened, was older than the other residents at the home. Furthermore, this placement was not to go through official channels. There was nothing illegal about it, and the arrangement would be to everyone's benefit. The judge added that he would explain in more detail over the phone, though he did mention that the intention was to administer a well-deserved punishment without the involvement of the criminal justice system. Whereas a court case would be the correct procedure for most crimes committed by individuals of sound mind, in this instance it would only harm the innocent victim, the writer's own daughter. There was no mention of what Einar had done to the girl. It occurred to Aldís that he might have raped her but that was hard to believe. She bent over Tobbi again. 'If you don't, I'll tell the other boys. They won't all be as understanding as Einar. Believe you me.'

Tobbi licked his dry lips. He seemed so small in the big chair; so painfully thin that his knees and elbows looked twice as thick as his limbs. They put Aldís in mind of healed fractures and she almost relented and told him to forget it. But he pre-empted her: 'I'll try. I promise I'll try.' His voice was nothing but a whisper, as thin and fragile as winter's first film of ice. She felt the boy's breath on her face. It smelt of the stew they'd had for lunch.

'Good. Come to me when you've done it. If Lilja and Veigar start ordering you to do other chores, just lie and tell them you've got a stomach ache.'

Tobbi stood up warily, careful not to brush against her, as if he was afraid of receiving an electric shock. He walked away, head drooping, then turned in the doorway. 'What if they catch me? They killed their own baby, and I don't matter to them at all.' Without waiting for an answer he turned and hurried out.

Veigar looked up from his book and stared at Aldís. For once, she stared back. Up to now she had always looked away when he squinted at her from under his heavy brows. 'What's the matter with you today?' His tone was patronising.

Aldís carried on dusting without dropping her gaze. 'Nothing. Why?'

'Well.' He frowned at her again, his eyes narrowing to gleaming black slits. Clearing his throat, he put the book down. 'You seem very distracted.'

Utter bullshit, as they both knew. She was doing everything as quickly and efficiently as ever. In fact, she'd made more of an effort than usual when she discovered that her boss was sitting in there. The room, known as the hall though it was really nothing more than a large living room, was only used for preaching Christian homilies at the boys. The daily assemblies were short affairs, and everyone had to take off their shoes and wash their hands and faces before they went in – as if God wouldn't look at boys with grime under their fingernails – so the room never got particularly dirty. 'I'm taking just as much care as usual.' It felt good to answer back for once, instead of blushing and stammering apologies. 'What exactly do you want me to do differently?'

Veigar rose and came over. Evidently, he didn't know how to react to her insolence, if that was the word for such a trivial act of resistance. He ran a fat finger over the piano lid, examined the tip, then blew away some imaginary dust. 'You've stopped coming to assembly. It wouldn't hurt you to start again. It does us all good to listen to the word of God, whether we are believers or heathens.'

Aldís knew that in his view she belonged to the latter group. 'I'm sure it does.' She hoped her message was clear: no, thanks. 'I've done the usual bits. Anything else you want me to clean?' She was unsmiling and expressionless. He didn't

240

deserve courtesy. She imagined she was addressing the wall behind his head, which, like him, was no longer in its first flush of youth: the wallpaper was faded and had begun to peel at the joins; he had deep furrows between his eyes. 'The lectern, maybe?' Veigar and Lilja referred to it as the altar but it was only an old wooden lectern, placed in front of a sideboard covered with a white cloth, on which stood an incongruously large cross and two mismatched candlesticks. On the wall behind hung a picture of Jesus on the cross. Strange to think that the original probably graced a magnificent cathedral somewhere in Europe. Aldís used to wonder if the Saviour's long-suffering expression owed something to his disbelief at where he had ended up. All he ever heard were Veigar's hypocritical sermons. 'Or is this good enough for you?'

He loomed over her and Aldís wished she had kept her mouth shut and got the hell out of there. She understood now what Tobbi meant. She was of no importance to this man; he was perfectly capable of slapping her, or worse. Who would believe her if it came down to his word against hers? She took a step backwards and the creaking of the floorboard reverberated around the room. The sound said it all: the balance of power had been restored. She cowered. 'Don't get snippy with me, miss,' he growled. His eyes narrowed even more and it struck her how different they were from the eyes of his baby, which had been so uncannily large and dark in the small, deformed head.

'I was only asking.' Her voice sounded gratifyingly composed. She had to get out of here. It crossed her mind to fling in his face that she knew where his child was buried, but she realised immediately that this would be a terrible move. What would she follow it up with? 'So there'? The momentary impulse brought a sudden clarity to her thoughts: how had Tobbi known that the child was born alive? Very few people could have been aware of that. She hadn't mentioned to anyone that she'd seen signs of life, not even when she was drunkenly telling Einar about the baby. All he knew was that Lilja had given birth to a baby that had vanished. A stillborn baby. Not a baby that opened its eyes. She'd left out that detail for fear she'd been mistaken; perhaps people's eyes open after death because the muscles tighten. Better not to make a big deal out of it if there was a perfectly natural explanation or it had simply been a trick of the light. She resolved to interrogate Tobbi again when he brought her the post – if he managed it – and find out exactly what he'd meant.

Veigar's scowl relaxed, to be replaced by a smarmy smile. 'Now, don't let's quarrel – not in front of Our Lord.'

Aldís had no answer to this. Judging by Christ's expression he had more on his mind than their bickering. 'I'm going to start the coffee.' Glancing at her watch, she saw that it was half past two. The watch had been a confirmation gift from her mother and the strap needed replacing. 'I don't want to be late.'

But he blocked her exit, unwilling to let her go so easily. 'Have you been wandering about at night?'

Aldís broke out in a cold sweat. Had she left something behind in the cowshed? Although it was some time ago, the evidence might only just have turned up. Veigar could hardly be referring to anything else, because apart from that one time, she hadn't stirred from her room in the evenings. Einar had dropped hints about repeating the experience but she had prevaricated. She was determined not to have any more contact with him than necessary until she'd found out what he'd done. After reading the judge's letter to Veigar, she could no longer deceive herself that it was all a misunderstanding; that he was innocent, a good person. Now she knew for certain that he'd committed a crime, and one against a young woman, she no longer found Einar as handsome or exciting as she had at first. She wanted to know more, partly out of sheer curiosity but also to get a better sense of his character. As pathetic as it sounded, she thought she could change him, make him into a better person – exactly what her mother had often warned her against: people don't change; you're kidding yourself if you think they do. 'No. I haven't left my room.'

'Quite sure?' She caught a whiff of his aftershave. He splashed it on in the mornings and its potency usually faded during the day, but now it was as strong as when he first applied it, mingled with a sour odour of sweat. Aldís tried in vain to avoid breathing it in. She wished she could blow her nose. 'A few times I've caught glimpses of a girl outside,' he continued, 'and there aren't many of them around here, are there?'

'No.' Aldís leant away, but couldn't escape his body odour. She noticed that his nose was pitted with small, black flecks. She hadn't realised adults got blackheads; she thought they were just a trial inflicted on teenagers. 'I'm usually in my room. When exactly was this?'

'Yesterday evening, for example.'

'No, I didn't go outside then.' Aldís was relieved. Obviously he was confusing her with someone else. But who? None of the boys looked particularly feminine, though perhaps the difference wouldn't be so obvious from a distance?

A flicker of doubt appeared in Veigar's eyes. His facial muscles slackened for a moment, giving the impression that his features were melting. 'Are you sure? Then who can it have been?' He seemed to be muttering to himself, not expecting an answer.

'Not me.' Aldís breathed more easily when Veigar moved away. Now she could no longer see his blackheads or choke on his aftershave. 'Lilja, maybe. Or one of the workmen. Wasn't it dark?'

'It's always dark.'

'Perhaps you were dreaming.' She said it quite kindly, to both their surprise.

'No.' He met her eye, frowned, then picked up his book and walked out without another word.

It was past four o'clock when Tobbi tapped Aldís on the back. He was breathing quickly as if he'd been running, though she hadn't heard him approach. She was relieved to see him; she'd looked for him at coffee time and had begun to fear that he'd been caught spying by Lilja or Veigar. 'I know where they keep it.' He glanced around nervously; his face, so white before, was now red and his freckles hardly showed. They were standing in the drive and she had just crumbled a rusk onto the snow for the bird, which was chirruping agitatedly from the roof, waiting for her to leave. Even feeding it for several months had not been enough to win its trust, and it never swooped on the food until she was a safe distance away, no matter how long she left it between offerings. Ever since the bird had gone missing in the blizzard, it had become even more timid, as if it blamed her for the violence of the wind, but she didn't mind; she was simply glad it had found its way home.

Aldís wiped the crumbs off on her jeans. 'Have you got the post?' The question was redundant; he had nothing in his dirty hands.

'No. I didn't dare take it. There's a whole box of it, and there's no way of carrying it out without being seen.'

'Where do they keep it?'

'In the cellar. I can't go down there. I daren't.' Tobbi licked his lips and shuffled his feet on the gravel. Behind him the sun had begun to sink in the sky and the horizon was on fire. Her mother had told her as a child that a beautiful sunset meant good weather the following day: *Red sky at night, shepherd's delight*. Perhaps it was a sign that soon things would be mended between them. Maybe as soon as tomorrow. Aldís would get hold of the letters and once she'd read them she'd be able to forgive her mother. In spite of the cold she felt warm at the thought.

'I gave the post to Lilja and watched what she did,' Tobbi explained. 'She took it to Veigar in his office and came out empty-handed. So I hid in the room opposite and watched the door through the crack. After an incredibly long time, he came out with the letters. I shadowed him to the main building and saw him go down into the cellar.'

'How do you know he put them in a box?'

'I ran outside and spied through the little window. He nearly saw me but I managed to duck just in time. Hope so, anyway.' His eyes opened wide and his bright red lips turned down. 'Do you think he could have spotted me?'

She shook her head firmly and said: 'No way.' Though how was she to know? 'Whereabouts in the cellar is the box? If I go down to get it, I don't want to have to search the whole place.'

'On the shelf by the stairs.' Tobbi turned, held out his right hand and seemed to be trying to work out which side the shelf was on. 'To the right.' The feverish red spots had faded from his cheeks but his face was glowing. 'Did I do well?'

'Brilliantly.' Aldís smiled at him and curbed an impulse to ruffle his hair. From time to time there were outbreaks of head-lice at the home and, although she had escaped so far, she had no intention of leaving here with her hair cropped like a boy's or she wouldn't even get an interview to be an air hostess. 'Tell me one more thing, Tobbi, then you can go.'

His shoulders drooped and his eyes started darting from side to side. 'I've got to go now. I've got to do my homework and I want to finish before supper.'

Aldís ignored his protests. 'Why did you say Veigar killed their baby?'

Tobbi dug at the frozen gravel with the toe of his scuffed trainers. 'No reason.'

Aldís grabbed the boy's chin and forced him to meet her gaze. In his blue eyes she read a silent prayer: *Go away! I wish you'd never come here!*

'Tell me who told you. I promise it won't go any further. You can trust me.'

'Promise?'

'Promise. Just tell me why you think Veigar killed the child. Then I promise I'll leave you alone.'

'I saw it.' Tobbi tried to wriggle out of Aldís's grasp. His eyes flickered all over the place, frantic to avoid hers. 'I was working in the cowshed with Veigar when they came to tell him Lilja was going to have the baby. I didn't know what to

246

do, but I didn't dare leave. He might've come straight back. I didn't know how long it took babies to come out.'

'Quite a long time, usually.'

'Yes, I know that now. By the time I realised he wasn't coming back it was so dark I didn't dare walk over alone.' Tobbi flushed with shame. The older boys had no doubt bullied him about his fear of the dark. 'So I decided to sleep there, in the hay. But I couldn't get to sleep and when I heard someone outside I went into the coffee room to try and see out of the window. The moon was out and I saw Veigar.' Tobbi gulped.

'What was he doing?'

'He had something wrapped in a white sheet. There was blood on it.' Aldís felt relieved: Tobbi had drawn the wrong conclusion from the blood. 'He had a spade too. He put the bundle down and began to dig a hole by the tree. The ground was hard and he swore a lot.'

'The baby was born dead, Tobbi. The blood was Lilja's. There's a lot of blood when children are born.' Aldís had often thought about what it was like to give birth. She had heard enough of her friends' mothers' grisly accounts of their own experiences to know that she was never going to go through that herself.

'It was alive, Aldís. It cried.'

'Cried?' Now it was her turn to swallow.

'Yes. Even after he put it in the hole. Right up until you couldn't hear any more because of the earth.'

This was even more horrible than she'd imagined. Why did she have to learn this now, at this moment? If only she'd waited. She didn't want the image of the child's face floating before her eyes, the sound of its crying in her ears, when she went down to the cellar tonight. But as she watched Tobbi run away, stumbling twice on the slippery stones, she knew it was inevitable: the dying child had already taken up residence in her mind.

Chapter 24

The old woman smiled gratefully and handed Ódinn a thousand-krona note. 'Thanks for your help.' She had asked him to fix the door of her kitchen cupboard, which was sagging on its hinges. Seeing that he wasn't going to accept the money, she added: 'Give it to your daughter if you won't take it. She's bound to be saving up for something.'

Feeling awkward, Ódinn thanked her and stuck the banknote in his pocket. He closed his toolbox and tried opening and shutting the cupboard door one last time. 'This should hold for a bit. A year, at least.'

'That'll do me.' The woman leant against the kitchen units. She looked much frailer than usual, perhaps because Ódinn wasn't used to seeing her without her thick overcoat. 'I doubt I'll be around that long.'

Ódinn hoped his embarrassment wasn't obvious. 'That's a bit pessimistic, isn't it?' He picked up his toolbox.

'No, really. I've had enough.' She didn't appear particularly sad at the prospect. 'It'll be worse for you two. You'll be alone in the building, but with any luck they'll sell more flats soon. Your daughter could do with some playmates. Perhaps a family with children will move into my flat when I'm gone.'

'I hope Rún won't have to wait that long. I mean, I'm sure

you've got more time left than you think.' Ódinn dithered, keen to go back upstairs but unwilling to be rude.

'No, I sense that my time has come.' She pulled up her jumper at the neck with a surprisingly youthful hand. It was cold in the flat, as it was in the whole building. 'I take after my mother and grandmother in that I'm being given plenty of warning.' She let go of her collar, which fell back again. 'I'm sorry I bothered you and your brother about the racket in the stairwell. I just didn't realise what was happening.'

'I'm afraid you've lost me.' He sighed. His toolbox felt suddenly heavy, though there wasn't much in it.

'That's only to be expected.' She smiled. 'You see, in my family, when your time is up, inexplicable things start happening. You hear and see things that aren't really there. The commotion I heard the other day was part of it. I can't explain it – which is probably just as well – but it'll all become clear in time.'

There was a cold feeling in the pit of Ódinn's stomach. 'I see.' He shifted the toolbox to his other hand. 'Do you hear things, then? Could it be hallucinations caused by some kind of chemical in the building?' Ódinn would never have dreamt that one day he'd actually hope to discover he'd been breathing in toxic fumes.

'Oh no, dear. It's a family trait – a sort of ghost, if you like. It's nothing to do with any chemicals. My grandmother told me it's because you've already got one foot on the other side. As the hour of your death approaches, you connect with what's waiting for you there. She experienced it shortly before she died; my mother too. I didn't really believe them at the time, but now I know it's true.' Her smile was radiant. 'It means you're given a bit of warning to put your affairs in order.'

'Are you sure it's not something in the environment?' Óðinn wanted to shake the shrunken figure into agreement. 'I ask because I've experienced something similar; I keep hearing and seeing things that aren't there.'

The woman's happy expression faded and she looked even older and frailer than before. 'I don't like the sound of that. No, I don't like it at all.'

He was doomed, then. Only now, two hours after he'd come upstairs, could Óðinn smile at the idea. What a load of crap. The smile remained on his face during news footage of a tank crawling along a quiet street. Perhaps the people who lived there had been experiencing the same sensations as him recently. The gun turret swivelled and fired at a building that disappeared in a dark cloud of dust.

'Who's been writing you letters, Daddy?' Rún was holding the plastic bag from Róberta's garage. Óðinn had left the letters in the car when he and Diljá returned to the office, for fear that she'd draw attention to them. He didn't want to have to explain their highly irregular visit to Heimir. When he got home, however, he had worried that the car might be broken into outside the block – he didn't dare leave it in the underground garage – so he'd brought the bag and cardboard box up to the flat. 'There are so many. Are they old?'

Óðinn beckoned her over as he sat trying to focus on the television. It was the news summary now: unrest in the Middle East and conflict in the Icelandic parliament. The news could just as well have been months old. As he took the bag, her fingers brushed against his; soft and cold where his were rough and warm. 'It's to do with work, sweetheart. Nothing important. Not any more.'

'What do old letters have to do with your work? I thought your job was new.'

'They're not letters to us at work. They're connected to a project I'm dealing with. An old case. Nothing interesting.' Reaching for the remote control, he switched off the TV. 'Finished your homework?'

Rún didn't answer. 'I thought you weren't supposed to read other people's letters? Granny told me that.'

'She's right. But sometimes you have to do things like that. I haven't actually read them yet. I might not need to.'

'I've never written a letter.' She didn't sound too concerned. She was wearing a clip to keep her fringe out of her eyes and it reminded him that he'd forgotten to take her to the hairdresser last week. She needed so much doing for her that he could hardly keep up. How did people cope with having more than one child? But the time would come when Rún wouldn't be as dependent on him. 'Well, I haven't written many myself and I'm much older than you. I just send e-mails.' He tied the plastic bag around the letters again and put it down. 'We need to do something about your hair. Remember, we were going to get it cut?'

'It's all right.' She fiddled with the brightly coloured clip. 'Granny rang.'

'Oh?' Ódinn sat up. 'When?'

'At lunchtime. At school.'

'On your mobile?' Rún nodded. Ódinn had assumed he was the only person who called her. He'd asked why her friends from her old school never got in touch and she'd replied that she hadn't had much to do with the kids there either. This had upset him, but he didn't know what to do about it. Lára must have done her best, and if she had failed it was unlikely that his clumsy attempts to improve Rún's popularity would have much success. 'What did she want?'

'To invite me round. But I don't want to go.'

'I'll talk to her. I'll tell her the truth.' Rún's look of terror was so exaggerated it was almost comical. 'I'll tell her you need peace and quiet.' Seeing this hadn't allayed her anxiety, he added: 'I'll just tell her we're keeping ourselves to ourselves for a while and won't be going out to visit anyone.'

Her scared look faded but didn't disappear completely. 'What about Baldur? Can't I go to his house? They were going to invite me for pizza and a video on Friday. Remember?'

His brother had promised as much on her last visit, delighted to be the subject of his niece's hero-worship. 'Your grandmother doesn't need to know exactly what we get up to. Anyway, we'd already decided ages ago that you were going to see them.' He'd rather not teach his daughter that it was all right to stretch the truth on occasion, but her welfare had to take priority.

Rún smiled. 'OK. Can you tell her now? I don't want her to call me again tomorrow.'

There were few phone calls Ódinn dreaded more, but best to get it over with. 'Yes. I'll do that.' He studied Rún: her thin arms protruded from the faded, crumpled Mickey Mouse T-shirt that she'd almost grown out of; bare flesh showed at her midriff, and he had a sudden memory of how squeamish he had felt when he saw Lára disinfecting the black stub of her umbilical cord with a cotton bud when she was a baby. She wouldn't have received such care from him if he'd been a single parent from the beginning. 'Do you miss your mum?'

'Yes. But I try not to think about her much. I feel bad if I do. Nanna told me to try and think about all the fun times I had with her. I'm supposed to hold onto those memories till I'm grown up. Then I'll be pleased I didn't try to forget her. But it's hard. If I think about her too much I get nightmares – even worse than usual.'

'There's no need to be afraid of dreams, Rún. They're only nonsense that the brain invents because it's asleep and muddled. Nanna must have told you that. Don't you dream you're falling sometimes?' Rún nodded uncertainly. 'And that you can fly?' She nodded again and the clip slid down her hair. She unfastened it and pushed it back up. 'There you are then. You're not falling when you dream you are, and you definitely can't fly. It's nonsense, that's all.' Like the idea that people who are about to die can see and hear the dead.

'I know.' But it was one thing to know, quite another to believe. 'Mum's angry in my dreams.'

'She's not angry, Rún. Dead people can't be angry; you know that. After death, all the bad, nasty stuff is forgotten and only the nice things are left.' Ódinn chose each word with care but the result wasn't what he had hoped. Clearly the therapy was beginning to work; until now Rún had retreated into her shell every time he'd tried to discuss her mother or the accident. 'Though you dream she's angry, I can assure you that in heaven no one worries about whether someone's tidied up their bedroom or said something cheeky. All that matters are the things that made you happy.'

'I wish Mum had lived for a bit longer after she fell. She was angry with me when I went to bed.'

Ódinn couldn't concur: he doubted it would have helped Rún to sit by Lára's deathbed. 'I know what you should do.

While I'm talking to your grandmother, you should write your mother a letter.'

'How's she going to read it?' Rún folded her arms, but didn't dismiss the idea out of hand, as Ódinn had feared she would.

'I don't quite know but we'll find a way. Perhaps we can put it on her grave, or burn it so the message rises up to heaven with the smoke, or you can keep it in your room and next time you have a nightmare you can tell your mother to read it. What do you reckon? Give it a try, anyhow.'

Reluctantly, Rún agreed. Ódinn dug out a block of A4 and a pen and sent her to her room, where she could pour out her feelings in private and say goodbye to her mother while he talked to her grandmother. But before she left the sitting room, he asked the question that had been gnawing at him recently. 'Can I ask you something, Rún? You don't have to answer if it makes you uncomfortable.'

'What?' She frowned.

'Is it possible that you woke up the morning your mum died, and heard someone with her? Someone you knew?' She stared at him uncomprehendingly, while the real question he wanted to ask and the answer he wanted to hear echoed in his mind. *Was I there? No, Daddy, of course you weren't.*

'Why are you asking?' Her eyes were full of sadness. *Don't tell me someone hurt Mum. Please, don't. She just fell.*

'No special reason. I just wondered.' What a fool he had been to raise the subject.

'I didn't see anyone. I was asleep and didn't wake up. But there was no one there, I'm sure of it.' She turned on her heel and went into her room, carrying the notepad in front of her like a shield. Ódinn sat there, stunned. He buried his head in his hands and closed his eyes. Rún had lied. He knew her well enough to tell. She had seen or heard something. Of course, that was terrible and might explain why she was finding it so hard to cope with the loss. But why hadn't she said anything? There couldn't be many people she'd want to protect. But he was one of them.

Without giving himself time to think, he rang his former mother-in-law. 'Hello,' he said, leaning back and raising his eyes to the ceiling.

'Who's that?' As if she received many phone calls from men.

'It's me, Ódinn.'

'Oh.' There was no disguising her disappointment. 'Is something wrong?'

'No, no. Not really.' Ódinn sat up so fast he felt dizzy. 'I hear you rang Rún at school.'

'So what if I did?' It was a childish response: if the woman wanted to talk to her grandchild it would have been more natural to ring her after school.

'Well, she's not supposed to use her phone at school.' Ódinn felt their conversation was taking an unfortunate turn – like all their conversations. As if they couldn't speak without falling out. It was the same old story. The woman couldn't forgive him for failing her daughter at the worst possible time and he couldn't stand being reminded of the fact. Would it always be like this? 'I need to say something that I should have said a long time ago.'

'Oh?' The word dripped with suspicion.

'I just want you to know how much I regret what happened with Lára. I'm not saying it was the wrong decision for us to separate but I could have gone about it more graciously, and I could also have treated her and Rún better after I walked out. It's too late to change that now but I wanted you to know that I regret it. More than words can say.'

'I see.' There was a hint of disappointment, as if she'd been hoping for a fight. Perhaps hating him was one of the few things that gave her life meaning. 'I hope you mean it.'

'I do.'

'Did you ring to tell me that?'

'No. I didn't intend to bring it up, though it was long overdue.'

'What did you want, then?'

'I just wanted to let you know that Rún's seeing a counsellor to help her deal with her grief.' He couldn't bring himself to say 'Lára's death' to the woman. 'She's been having a tough time, sleeping badly and feeling a bit low, so I'm hoping this will help.' There was deathly silence at the other end. Óðinn added hastily: 'It's important that she should have as much space as possible, so I hope you understand that she won't be able to visit you for a while.' Again he was met by a stony silence. Óðinn wondered if they'd been cut off. 'Are you still there?'

'Yes.'

'You do realise this has nothing to do with you and that she'll get over it?'

'Rún doesn't need a counsellor. She needs you and me. If you were a proper father you'd understand that. Once a person gets involved with that whole racket they never get free of it. You're condemning her to be in therapy for the rest of her life.'

'It's not a racket. This is an independent child psychologist, a woman. She'd never hang on to Rún for longer than necessary. I've met her, so I'm in a better position to judge than you are.'

'You're a bloody fool.' His mother-in-law slammed down the phone.

No one had hung up on Ódinn for a long time, not since Lára had begun to wise up to her ex-husband's imperfections. As a result, he was too surprised to be angry or offended. He had known all along that their conversation would end badly, but he'd expected her to quarrel with him about Rún visiting, not because he'd sought help for his daughter. Was it possible that the woman suspected, as he did, that Rún had seen or heard more than she let on? Even that he had been involved? She lived in the same street, two doors down, so she could have seen him from her window, weaving his drunken way to Lára's house that fateful morning. Or she might have been loading the washing machine and spotted his arrival, then lied afterwards that she'd brought the laundry round the night before, to avoid having to admit it. If so, it was all too understandable why Rún's grandmother wouldn't want anyone messing with the child's head, since there was no knowing what might emerge. It would be a devastating blow for Rún if it turned out that her father had murdered her mother. The woman's love for Rún was almost certainly stronger than her hatred for him. But perhaps he was letting his imagination run away with him; after all, it wasn't particularly surprising that she should hang up on him.

If only he could remember that morning. Perhaps the memories could be recovered under hypnosis, even though he had been drunk at the time. Scraps of recollection must linger somewhere in his head; the trick was to get hold of them. But the more he thought about it, the more risky the idea seemed – he couldn't be sure that the hypnotherapist would keep quiet if some incriminating fact emerged.

Ódinn stood up. There was no solution. It was clear to him that if he'd played some part in Lára's death, he would rather not know. Indeed, his unconscious may have worked out that it would be best to lock the memories up and throw away the key. Perhaps it was his brain's attempts to drag them into the light that was causing all these strange delusions, rather than the fact that he was doomed. He'd just have to tell himself once and for all that he'd never been anywhere near the incident, then stop brooding over it, and ask the therapist to stop questioning Rún about the morning Lára died. Unless her recovery depended on it.

'Finished.' Rún had come back in, holding out a sheet of folded paper ready to put in an envelope. 'Though I don't know the best way to get Mum to read it.' As she looked at him, he was struck again by her extraordinary resemblance to Lára.

He took the letter, uncomfortably aware of the paper between his fingers. Perhaps it contained something that might shed light on the whole situation. It was this thought that finally convinced him he didn't want to know; anything would be better than having his worst fears confirmed, even if it meant putting up with distorted perceptions for the foreseeable future. 'I reckon I know what we should do.' He forced a smile. 'We'll burn it. Let the smoke carry the contents up to your mother in heaven. Then the nightmares will stop and everything'll be fine. I can feel it.'

Rún smiled back and they went out onto the balcony together. Ódinn opened the barbecue and laid the letter inside, taking care to shelter it from the wind. Then he placed a briquette on top of the white sheet to pin it down, and lit it. They watched in silence as the flames crept across the paper and it shrivelled up. Rún's eyes followed the smoke as it rose to heaven and vanished into the darkness.

'Feel better?'

'Yes. Much.' She grinned, baring the big front teeth she'd grow into one day. 'Much, much. Now Mum won't be angry any more.'

'That's right, sweetheart.' As they went inside out of the cold, she strode along and her whole manner seemed happier. If only he felt the same way. He walked heavily into the sitting room. As the letter crinkled up in the flames he had managed to read part of a line: . . . *you have to forgive Daddy, he really didn't mean to . . .*

Chapter 25

February 1974

The night was as beautiful as the sunset had been. Between the clouds the black sky was studded with twinkling stars and although there was only a half-moon, it lit Aldís's way across the snow. A teacher at school had told them that in the old days people used to believe the sky was a cloth that divided heaven from earth, and that the stars were holes through which the silvery light of paradise spilled out. She had listened, entranced, and put up her hand when the story ended to ask why God hadn't ordered the angels to stop up the holes. Her mother knew how to darn and there were probably lots of mothers in heaven who'd be able to help. Her classmates had sniggered but the teacher smiled kindly and said perhaps the holes were there so that we earth-dwellers would know how bright and beautiful it was in God's house. No one ever came back from heaven, so perhaps this was the only way to show us mortals the glory of paradise. Aldís thought God could have shared a little of this glory with the earth. It wouldn't have hurt.

A white cloud of steam rose from her nose and mouth in the freezing stillness. The snow squeaked underfoot, so she trod carefully in case anyone was lying awake and heard her. Such as Veigar. He might be lurking behind their bedroom curtains, hoping to catch sight of the girl he claimed was prowling around at night. Aldís's eyes were constantly drawn to the couple's window, which seemed to stare at her from the end wall of the house; she couldn't tear her gaze from the white curtains. She pictured him sitting there in the dark, in the heavy chair that was so difficult to move when she was cleaning, his narrow, piggy eyes fixed on her. If she were caught now no one would believe that it hadn't been her those other times. Aldís hugged herself for warmth, though she knew the sudden chill she felt came from within. Instead of looking back at Lilja and Veigar's house, she resolved to face her goal; there was only a short distance left but it felt endless. What was she thinking of embarking on such a mission, alone under the stars? But her yearning for the letters hidden in the dark cellar was too strong to resist.

She ought by rights to have been grateful to Tobbi for telling her where they were kept, but she was still angry with him. Of course, her anger should have been directed at herself, but she'd never been very good at being cross with herself. Because her unhappiness in life had largely been the fault of others, it had become a habit with her to blame all her misfortunes on other people. She kept wishing Tobbi hadn't told her about the baby, but then she herself had forced him to reveal all he knew. The tree loomed large in her mind, though she avoided looking at it, and she thought she could hear rustling from the few withered leaves that still clung to the branches. It sounded like whispering among the farm buildings.

The bird was nowhere to be seen. It would have been a relief to sense its presence. Last time she saw it, the poor

creature had been terribly thin and scraggly, so after supper
she had added a small knob of butter to the breadcrumbs
that had lain untouched since that morning. She hoped there
was nothing the matter with it beyond pining for spring.

She passed Veigar's car. Over the last few days the snow
had drifted around it and the task of digging it out would
fall to the boys. As soon as their shovels got anywhere near
the light-blue paintwork they would be forced to abandon
them and scrape away the last of the snow with their hands.
She had helped them before now to brush the lumps of ice
from their gloves when their own hands were too numb.
Who knows, she might just take a nail and scratch the paintwork the day she left Krókur. It would be a just revenge for
the boys, many of whom developed callused workmen's hands
by the end of their stay. The moon was reflected in the car
window, making Aldís suddenly aware that she couldn't see
inside. This was even worse than looking up at the windows
of the house. At least anyone spying from the buildings
wouldn't be able to creep up behind her, but someone sitting
in the car could open the door and grab her before she realised what was happening. She backed up a few steps, to keep
it in view. Yet the trackless snow indicated that no one had
been near the car for days.

She'd never been so relieved to get to her destination.
Slowly, to prevent the hinges from creaking, she opened the
front door. Clouds had obscured the moon now and she
couldn't see a thing as she drew the candle and matches from
her pocket. There wasn't a sound in the house apart from
the ticking of the grandfather clock that stood in the hall
near the entrance. Until now she'd found the sound
comforting; it reminded her of the carved wooden table-clock

her grandfather had given her mother when he came home from his last trip on the cargo ship. Aldís had never met him because he'd dropped dead the very next day, but she'd always imagined the ticking of the clock was his heartbeat, telling her that although she didn't have a father who loved her, her grandfather was watching over her from heaven. If only she could derive the same sense of security from the ticking of the clock in the hall, but instead of reminding her of a living heart, it sounded as if it were counting down the minutes until some terrifying moment of truth.

Aldís knew every inch of the building, but the darkness was disorientating. She bumped into the doorframe on her way in and almost knocked over a small table in the corridor. The flickering candle flame barely illuminated anything beyond the end of her nose, so she held it out as far in front of her as possible and moved with extreme caution. The familiar surroundings danced in the flame and every step she took towards the cellar felt heavier. When she finally reached the trapdoor at the end of the corridor, her main impulse was to turn and run with her tail between her legs. But she steeled herself and pulled it open, then stood for a moment peering down the wooden steps, listening to her own frantic breathing. The top steps were clearly visible in the candlelight but below that all was black. There was a throat-catching reek of mildew. She bent and groped her way warily down. The thud as she closed the trapdoor behind her echoed through the dark cellar and it was all she could do not to turn back and flee.

She began her search immediately. The longing to get out was so overpowering that she had to work fast. There was the box on the shelf, flanked by light bulbs, washing powder and toilet paper. It was reassuring to see such everyday objects; not even the wavering light could render them alien or menacing. Aldís pulled the box to her, trying to hold the candle at the same time. She'd decided to take her own letters away with her but to pause and read any addressed to Einar on the spot. Reading them wasn't as bad as stealing them.

She removed the other letters and put them down on the steps, noting how few there were, considering the number of boys. Perhaps there was another box of older correspondence hidden away in a corner, or perhaps most of them weren't that sorely missed at home. Some of the letters showed signs of having been originally stuck onto parcels, of which there was no trace. It seemed unbelievable that Lilja and Veigar could have the gall to steal sweets and other little luxuries from their charges.

Every now and then she turned up an envelope bearing her mother's handwriting and her rage boiled over when she saw that they'd all been opened. Cramming them in her anorak pocket, she turned to Einar's letters. She tried as best she could to arrange them in chronological order, though the postmarks had faded. None were dated, as if their contents were timeless.

The first letter was from Einar's mother, and so was the most recent. In the former, the woman wrote nice things about her son and how much she missed him. There was an allusion to '*what you two did*', but no mention of what it was, nor who Einar's accomplice had been. His mother said all would be forgiven in time and he shouldn't brood about it too much or torture himself with guilt. Aldís raised an eyebrow. Einar didn't strike her as a repentant sinner – far from it. If his mistakes tormented him, he kept very quiet about it. Of course, it was possible he lay awake at night on occasion, but appearances suggested that he was good at brushing off any guilt over past misdemeanours. Her curiosity redoubled as she read, but after a quick glance over the woman's most recent letter she was none the wiser. This time his mother said she'd tried to get messages to him but didn't know if they'd been passed on. Aldís's stomach lurched at the thought that Veigar or Lilja must have read this. But the wording was so vague that it could refer to anyone, even some civil servant in town. In spite of this, she read the sentence again and again until she was sure it couldn't be connected to her. The rest contained little of interest, merely a reiteration of how desperately the woman missed her son and how proud she was of him for making this decision. It wasn't specified what the decision was, only that in doing so he had saved his reputation and his future.

Annoyed that the woman hadn't expressed herself more clearly, Aldís picked up the other letters to Einar. They were written in a very different hand. The girlish lettering gave Aldís pause. She ran her finger over the writing, wondering if they were from his sister, though she knew they couldn't be. No sister wrote this assiduously to her brother; there were around ten letters and he'd only been at Krókur a short time. What's more, each envelope was decorated with a heart in one corner. The sender had used light-blue writing paper and matching envelopes. Much more expensive-looking than the other letters in the box. It must have been purchased abroad, in Copenhagen, Paris or London. Aldís was filled with envy.

The letters were all from the same girl, Eyjalín. She signed her name with a heart instead of an accent over the 'i'. It was the name Einar's mother had mentioned on the phone. Aldís felt eaten up with bitterness. 'Eyjalín' sounded so much more glamorous and exotic than 'Aldís'. She remembered the stunning girl in the photo in Einar's wallet and guessed this must be her. The name fitted well with her unusual beauty. No doubt she had a posh surname as well. Aldís sniffed the first letter she took out, but instead of the perfume she'd half expected, she inhaled only the pervading smell of damp in the cellar. Unpleasant as it was, she felt gleeful.

When she started reading the letters, she noticed that the hearts on the envelopes followed a certain code. If the heart had an arrow through it, the writer was madly in love, while a broken arrow meant the girl was heartbroken or seething with rage. The broken arrows increased in number as time went on, until the last four letters were all marked like this.

Aldís forgot everything else as she read. Curiosity, jealousy and incomprehension by turns kept her fear of the dark at bay. At first the girl protested her love at great length, but as time went on she began instead to ask why Einar didn't answer her letters and if he had forgotten her. She mentioned her father a lot too, either saying she hated him or that she was trying to talk him into accepting Einar. If he wouldn't, they'd just have to run away together; up north maybe, or abroad. She seemed keenest on the idea of the States and wrote about a trip she'd taken with her parents to New York several years ago. They could get married and live there without her parents' interference. They wouldn't be able to have children but she didn't want them anyway and neither did he. This was a statement, not a question, and Aldís assumed they must have already discussed their future. In another place, however, she talked of having children with him, so her future plans seemed to change from day to day. She only referred to her mother once, and then only to say that the old bitch still couldn't look her in the eye. Here and there, brief, tantalisingly odd references to her health cropped up, as if they'd slipped in without her knowledge. It wasn't clear whether they referred to an illness or an injury. *'The doctor says I'm lucky. It's still bleeding. I feel so bad. The painkillers make me confused. They want to re-admit me.'*

Worst of all, Eyjalín's letters contained no explanation or even mention of Einar's crime. Aldís replaced the bundle in the box, shuffling them a little so it wouldn't be immediately obvious that someone had gone through the post. She stirred the contents of the box roughly, frustrated not to find the clarification she'd been looking for. But her irritation vanished once she'd closed the box and the rustling of paper had fallen silent. She became aware once more of the eeriness of her surroundings. The candle had begun to smoke; its wick needed trimming. Not that she minded the black smoke as long as the flame kept burning; it was suitably atmospheric. As she was about to scramble to her feet with the box under one arm and the candle in the other hand, she spotted a letter that had slipped out of the bundle and fallen onto the step beside her. The blue envelope was instantly recognisable. The heart on it had been angrily scratched out. Aldís put the box down again and opened the letter.

Who's that slut? I saw you together. I'll never forgive you — I thought you loved me. How could you prefer her to me? She looks like she's dirty and she wears stupid, ugly clothes. And that frumpy

268

blonde ponytail. I bet she's got lice. She doesn't even have a hairband – she uses a shoelace. And I bet that hideous purple jumper's a charity handout. She's nothing but a common slut.

Aldís looked up and stared unseeingly into the darkness beyond the candle flame. She owned a purple jumper that was a bit frayed. But there was no call to suggest it had been a charity handout. She wore her hair in a ponytail. And had once resorted to using a shoelace when she couldn't find her elastic band. Aldís felt tears welling up. Her mother had once told her that those who eavesdrop never hear well of themselves. She wasn't good enough; she knew that. She wasn't trendy either, and no doubt in the eyes of posh girls she was nothing but a common slut. She'd never be an air hostess. Picking up the letter again, she forced herself to read the final lines, but didn't get far:

I'll kill her, Einar, if you ever talk to her again. You owe it to me to love me. Daddy says maybe no one else will want to marry me now. So you'll have to. Or I'll kill her.

A floorboard creaked overhead.

Chapter 26

There was something so grim about visiting geriatric wards and nursing homes, sensing the residents gawping at him in the hope that he'd come to help them while away the time. Óðinn tried to look straight ahead but couldn't help seeing, out of the corner of his eye, the frail heads rising from their pillows as he passed, to check who was there. He thought of the time he had prepared a quote for Baldur for a job that required providing temporary accommodation for workers. The regulations had strictly limited them to one person per room, yet here, from what he could tell, there were as many as four residents to a ward. He overtook an old woman who was inching her way along the corridor on a Zimmer frame. Around her neck hung a handwritten sign with the name of the institution and the phone number.

A busy nurse had directed him to the lounge at the end of the corridor, where Lilja Sævarsdóttir was expecting him. It had been out of the question to interview her in the room she shared, since they would be overheard. The lounge was furnished in typically institutional style: wooden sofas with monochrome, cylindrical cushions, more reminiscent of a waiting room than the sitting room in an ordinary home. On the wall hung a reproduction of a painting by Gunnlaugur Scheving, showing a man in yellow oilskins hauling fish on board a boat. Besides this, there was a large television with a smeary screen, and some bookshelves containing a motley collection of titles, some of which had no doubt been left behind by residents when they were moved within the system or went to meet their Maker. The books lay heaped on the shelves, leaking pages from between their covers. Judging by the state of the residents, Ódinn didn't suppose there was much competition for this reading matter.

A woman was sitting in a wheelchair in the lounge, gazing out of the large window from which the curtain had been partially drawn back. Her attention appeared to be focused on a church spire further down the street. Ódinn had gathered from the files that the couple who ran Krókur were very religious, but that might not still be the case.

The woman's profile provided no clues as to what she had looked like in her youth: age had not been kind to her and her colourless skin hung in heavy folds that blurred the shape of her cheekbones and jaw. Her liver-spotted scalp was visible through the sparse white hair. From the bobbled sleeve of her jumper appeared a hand to match, with mottled skin, bulging veins and twisted fingers. When she turned to him, her eyes were cloudy and watering. 'You people today, you know nothing.'

'No, maybe not.' Ódinn forced a polite smile. 'Are you Lilja?'

Ignoring his question, the woman went on: 'This godforsaken nation's been forced to grovel in the dust.' She regarded him with displeasure.

'I wouldn't say that.' There was a clatter of plates from the corridor. They were clearing away lunch. On his way here, Ódinn had been forced to squeeze past a cumbersome metal trolley on which the staff were loading trays of leftovers. He doubted he would have done any better at finishing the muck on offer. 'My name's Ódinn and I'm working on a report about the management of the care home at Krókur.'

'I know. What happened to the woman?'

'Woman?'

'The woman who came here. She said she was writing a report too. Is everybody at it?'

'It was passed on to me after Róberta died.'

The woman seemed unaffected by the news. Death must seem awfully mundane in a place like this; nothing to make a fuss about. 'I'd rather talk to a man anyway, so it makes no odds. Just don't ask the same questions, will you? It's so boring.'

'I'm afraid there's bound to be some repetition, but please try not to let it get on your nerves.'

The woman snorted. 'What a bunch of amateurs you are. Pathetic.'

Ódinn drew up a heavy chair, part of the institutional three-piece suite, and placed it facing the woman. He didn't dare turn her wheelchair for fear of how she'd react. He sat down and took out his papers. 'I don't know if you followed the discussion in the media at all – about Breidavík and the other care homes?'

'A bloody waste of time.' The woman turned away and gazed out of the window again, her head jerking as if there were a malfunction in her operating system. He assumed she didn't dare meet his eye – due to a guilty conscience perhaps – but revised his opinion when she added acidly: 'It's a disgrace how they dealt with those places, and now anyone can guess what's going to happen: some state lackey's going to earn himself a knighthood by slandering me and Veigar, even though he's no longer here to defend himself. Anyone can see the whole thing's a travesty. And you and your sort will wallow in it at our expense, on the radio and in the press, though it's all rubbish. Well, good luck to you. That's all I say. Just remember that on the Day of Judgement you'll be weighed on the scales of justice and found wanting.'

'But we've no intention of looking for scapegoats,' he told her. 'This is simply part of the general inquiry into the state's treatment of children over a period during which you and your husband were running Krókur. We've no intention of destroying your reputation. I've come here to give you a chance to tell me your side of the story. Naturally, we're all hoping the investigation will demonstrate that everything was above board.' He omitted to add that he very much doubted anything she said would change his mind.

'And just how were homes like that supposed to be run?' She turned back to him, and her head carried on wobbling for a moment or two.

God, she was getting on his nerves. Ódinn felt a strong urge to pitch her off the balcony, then pulled himself together. All he'd been able to think about since yesterday evening was his possible role in Lára's accident. 'I suppose what we're hoping is to find that the children were treated with respect and compassion.'

'Pathetic. All of them.' He didn't know if she meant him and his fellow investigators, or the boys at Krókur. It amounted to the same thing. She was a lone voice in the wilderness; the only person left to answer for the past conduct of herself and her husband, and others in the system. Still, as long as she answered his questions, he didn't care if she got upset.

'I'd like to discuss a few points relating to Krókur. I appreciate that Veigar's no longer here to answer for himself, and I'm not sure how many former staff members we'll be able to interview. I've dug up a few names but not many are still alive; most of them seem to have been a bit older than you and your husband.' The cardboard box he and Diljá had found in Róberta's garage had contained payroll records, but the list of employees Ódinn had managed to scrape together from this information was strangely short, and he suspected there were names missing. A phone call to the National Register had established that only three were still alive. 'I was actually hoping that the list I have would turn out to be incomplete. How many people worked for you during those four years?'

'Can't remember. There was a quick turnover.'

'Ten? Twenty? Thirty?' The list he'd drawn up contained only twelve names.

With an effort the woman held up her hands and counted on her fingers, muttering under her breath. Then she replaced them on the arms of her wheelchair, looking rather pleased with herself. 'Fifteen. Or thereabouts. I haven't lost my memory, you know, though I have a bit of trouble with names.' The index finger she raised to tap her papery brow had swollen joints and a yellowing nail.

'Do you think you'd be able to remember who's missing if I read out the names I have so far?'

'What a stupid question. How on earth can I know in advance? Just read out the names and we'll see.'

Gritting his teeth, Ódinn started reading. The woman put her head on one side. Her lower jaw sagged as he read until finally her mouth hung open as if she had stiffened up on the point of speaking. She closed her eyes and nodded at certain names, but didn't say a word until he'd finished the list. 'I don't know if anyone's missing. And I don't think I've ever heard some of those names. Are you sure they all worked at Krókur?'

Ódinn said they did, as far as he could ascertain.

'There's someone missing.' The elderly face wrinkled in a frown. 'That useless girl.'

'Useless girl?' The list had contained only men's names. 'You don't happen to remember what she was called?'

'No. I told you – I'm getting a bit rusty when it comes to names. She was a dreadful little slut.'

'That doesn't help much.' His attempts to jog Lilja's memory failed and all he got for his pains was further abuse of former staff. He didn't want to give her the satisfaction of asking why she'd called the girl a slut, so in the end he gave up and changed the subject.

He moved on to questions about the boys' treatment: how they had occupied their time, what they had been given to eat and how their other needs had been met. The woman continued to answer sarcastically, though he did manage to extract some basic information. According to her, appropriate punishments had been meted out as necessary, and, after a lot of beating about the bush, he established that the boys had been subjected to both physical and mental punishment, including being locked in dark rooms or made to clean the toilets. By now Ódinn had a bad taste in his mouth. As a boy he'd been guilty of his fair share of misdemeanours and his parents had disciplined him. But, despite being pretty angry at times, they'd never laid a finger on him or his brother, or subjected them to any kind of humiliation. Instead he and Baldur had received countless scoldings and been grounded until they mended their ways. He wouldn't have liked to experience the sort of discipline Lilja was describing. And it would have been harder still to have suffered it at the hands of people who weren't family members; to receive no sympathy, no love or warmth, to have no one to comfort you.

'I gather the business was only just breaking even. Is that why you sold the property?' He phrased it as tactfully as he could. The home seemed to have been on a fast track to bankruptcy, and money worries don't tend to bring out the best in people. Perhaps that explained the couple's harsh behaviour, as described by the old boys.

'What nonsense.' The woman regarded him in disgust. 'Only just breaking even! I've never heard the like.'

'Then why did you close down?'

For the first time since Ódinn had sat down, the woman was flustered. 'Veigar was offered a very good job in town. In the public sector. We sold the property and the buyer wanted to run it as a farm. He didn't want to take on the home, so the boys were transferred. Or sent back to their families.'

'So you weren't closed down?'

'Closed down?' Lilja's head began to wobble again. 'Is that what you thought? That the management wasn't satisfactory and we were forced to close? Quite the opposite. They begged us to carry on but we'd had enough. We wanted to move back to town and we never regretted it.'

'I see. I thought the death of the two boys might have played a part. The authorities must have taken a pretty dim view of it.'

'Good riddance. The older boy, anyway, though the other was a sad little thing – one of the better ones.'

Ódinn busied himself with his papers so the woman wouldn't see the contempt in his eyes. Was she completely devoid of feeling or was it an act – an old woman's defiance towards a system that had turned against her? The four former inmates he had talked to had described the couple as utterly callous, but it was hard to know how much faith to put in their testimony. 'How did it happen? Is there any reason to believe that you or Veigar could have prevented it?'

'You're worse than the woman who came before.'

'Oh?'

'She asked quite different questions.'

'About what?'

'She kept asking about the boy who died, the older one. What was he called again?'

'His name was Einar. Einar Allen.'

'Foreign blood. I'd forgotten that. No doubt that had something to do with it.'

'I see. What did Róberta want to know about him?'

'She asked so many questions. I can't remember exactly what.' Lilja's eyes dropped and her whole body seemed to slump. 'Some people are given everything on a plate but offer nothing but ingratitude in return, and do the unforgivable. Others knuckle down, and pray, but no doors are opened for them and they never receive anything. God tests us in mysterious ways. Sometimes His purpose is impossible to understand.'

Ódinn drew a deep breath. He couldn't make head or tail of this. She could hardly be alluding to Einar. He was the son of a single mother and most unlikely to have received everything on a plate. She couldn't mean Róberta either. 'Do you have e-mail?' The question was absurd in the circumstances but he had to know. Lilja seemed exactly the type to send threatening messages. And she had more to gain than anyone else from having the inquiry shelved. In fact, she was the only person with any interests to protect.

'E-mail? No, mister. I don't have a computer; never have. Why should I get e-mail? I hardly get any letters any more. I don't think I even have a postal address.'

'Then can you think of anyone else who might want this investigation stopped?'

'The instrument of justice.'

'Instrument of justice?'

'Yes. God would want to put a stop to it. And there's me. Can't think of anyone else. Like I said, they're all pathetic.'

Lilja reared up in the wheelchair and one of her feet slid off onto the floor, revealing a thick, dark-brown nylon stocking. Over the years her calf seemed to have sunk down over her ankle. Ódinn looked away. 'No one else?' She didn't respond, so he brought the conversation back to the two boys. 'You didn't answer my question about Einar and Thorbjörn's deaths. Could you go over what happened?'

'One deserved it; the other got mixed up in it by mistake.'

'You mean it wasn't an accident?'

'Nothing happens by accident. God decides everything. And his ways are inscrutable.'

'What happened?' Although no atheist, Ódinn found it uncomfortable to have God casually dropped into the conversation like this. 'Leaving God out of it.'

'They slipped out late one evening. Veigar suspected

someone was wandering around at night but thought it was the girl. The little slut. We didn't realise it was Eyjalín. Her letters were so crazy that we didn't take them seriously. Thought she was disturbed, delusional. Which she was. But she wasn't the only one prowling about at night, as it turned out. Einar and the little boy should have been in their rooms the evening they died.'

'Were the boys free to go out at night? Weren't they monitored?'

'Are you joking? Do you think we were made of money? We used to lock them in but they'd loosened the bars in the window. Veigar discovered that afterwards when he went over the place with the police. They'd propped them up so it wouldn't show. Except maybe when the window was cleaned. But that tramp of a girl didn't report it. She was sacked afterwards anyway.'

'So they broke out. But why? What were they doing in the car and why was the engine running? Where did they get the keys from?'

'I don't have all the answers, if that's what you think. The keys were in the ignition. Veigar always left them there. There were only Icelanders in Iceland in those days. They don't steal other people's cars.' Ódinn opened his mouth to object but stopped himself. The woman was incorrigible. She went on: 'Maybe they were planning to run away, to drive to town. Or just keep warm. No one knows, and anyway it's not important. The snow had drifted over the exhaust pipe so the fumes filled the car. And they suffocated.' She scowled at Ódinn. 'They were discovered lying on the floor in the back. Blue in the face, As if they were asleep.' Ódinn thought this was hardly consistent with the idea that they had intended to drive into town, or they would surely have been found in the front seats.

'I've heard rumours that it wasn't snow that blocked the exhaust pipe but a rag. Is there any truth in that?'

The woman's head trembled more than ever and she had difficulty meeting Ódinn's eye. 'No. No, no and no.'

He didn't believe her. But however hard he tried to coax the story out of her, she flatly denied everything.

He sensed she was growing tired. She was hunched in her chair and her voice had grown hoarse. 'One more thing. Did Róberta ever ask you about this Eyjalín girl that you mentioned? The file contains letters from her, which Róberta may have had a special interest in.'

Lilja was so weak by now that she could hardly speak. 'Some people are given everything but throw it away. Others have to make do with wanting, wanting, wanting.' Ódinn tried unsuccessfully to elicit something more detailed or concrete. Finally, he rose to his feet, said goodbye and told her he'd send a member of staff to fetch her. In the corridor he met the same nurse as before but this time she seemed a little less busy.

'How did it go?' She smiled sympathetically. 'She's not the easiest of people. Snappish in the daytime and spends the nights screaming for a child that no one knows anything about. If we weren't under such pressure to use every bed, we'd give her a room to herself. But it can't be helped.' She walked off down the corridor and Ódinn returned to the land of the living, but just as he reached the entrance the nurse came running after him. 'She wants to tell you something. Do you have a second to pop back and see her?'

Eager as he was to get out into the fresh air, he decided he might as well.

'I remembered her name. That useless girl.' The watery blue eyes were fixed on Ódinn. 'She was called Aldís.'

'Aldís?' Ódinn felt an overpowering need to cough but managed to suppress it. 'You don't happen to remember her second name?'

'Aldís Anna Agnarsdóttir. Three "A"s in a row. That's how I remembered.'

Ódinn nodded and left without saying goodbye. He couldn't speak. He knew Aldís Anna Agnarsdóttir only too well.

Chapter 27

Instinctively Aldís blew out the candle, and everything went black. She had no wish to meet any member of the household at this moment, whoever it was, and for that darkness was her best friend. She perched on the steps, listening to the footfalls approaching overhead. Her heart was thudding, her breathing rapid. Suddenly it dawned on her that if the cellar light were turned on she would be a sitting duck. She fumbled in her pocket for the matches to light her way to a better hiding place, then changed her mind. The person might not be coming down here, and the candle would only give her away. Even the dim light of its smoking flame might be visible in the cracks around the trapdoor. But, on the other hand, if she stumbled around blindly among all the junk, she might knock something over.

As she delved in her pocket her hand encountered a sweet-wrapper and the rustling sounded unbearably loud, as did the hissing of the match a moment later. The candlelight seemed far too bright now. She eased herself to her feet, wondering what to do about the box on the steps. If whoever it was looked down into the cellar and saw it, they might realise there was somebody there. But if she tried to move the box, the noise would be audible upstairs. Deciding to leave it where it was, she made do with closing it with extreme care.

The stench of mildew seemed suddenly stronger. The candle threw flickering shadows around the cellar. Aldís peered round frantically for a hiding place. She could try to duck behind a tyre or box or pile of planks, but would probably be instantly visible to anyone walking past. The hope of finding a refuge faded the further into the cellar she crept, but finally she caught sight of a small door at the very back. The footsteps and creaking overhead indicated that the person was standing directly over the entrance to the cellar now, so she made for the little door without stopping to think what she'd do if it was locked. She bit her lip and tasted blood as she grabbed the handle, but, to her intense relief, the door opened. The iron taste and stinging in her lip revived her and, in spite of her panic, she managed to slip inside and close the door noiselessly behind her. She blew out the candle and closed her eyes. Better to imagine she was surrounded by light than enclosed in a pitch-black cubbyhole, awaiting her fate.

She didn't dare move a muscle since she hadn't given herself time to register the contents of the storeroom before extinguishing the candle. For all she knew, it might be full of jam-jars that would topple over with a crash if she touched them. So she crouched motionless, ears pricked for sounds of the unknown person. Funny how she always felt like praying when she was in a tight corner. Normally she gave little thought to God but it was good to have Him to turn to when all else failed. Though it seemed a bit cheeky to expect the Almighty to wait in readiness for an SOS from her, like a first-aid box that sat gathering dust until there was an accident – at which point it transpired that someone had forgotten to replenish the contents.

Hearing a squeak from the trapdoor, Aldís stopped breathing.

Not until her lungs were bursting did she exhale and take another breath. She fought the urge to back away from the door, as if the darkness would be thicker at the back of the cubbyhole. Staying very still, she concentrated on breathing steadily, and felt slightly calmer. But when she put her ear to the door and heard the wooden steps groaning under the weight of descending feet, she thought her final hour had come. Light appeared under the door and through the keyhole, and she thanked God she'd taken cover. By the unsteady glow, she guessed it was a torch rather than the ceiling light, which suggested that it wasn't Lilja or Veigar but someone who had no more business down here than she did.

The beam of light falling through the keyhole illuminated a small patch of her anorak sleeve. She felt an illogical regret that she hadn't chosen a more brightly coloured one; yellow or red would have been a more cheerful counterpoint to the all-encompassing darkness than dull blue. With infinite care, she knelt down, every nerve taut with fear that she might bump into something. But nothing happened and she was able to put her right eye to the keyhole. Although limited, the view was better than nothing. The rough concrete floor hurt her knees, but the pain was comfortingly mundane, like the stinging of her lip. Even the dank cold felt almost invigorating.

The torch beam appeared to be methodically sweeping the cellar. It passed to and fro across Aldís's field of vision, but the person wielding it remained out of sight. If only she could catch a glimpse of a shoe, some hair, a trouser leg, anything, she might be able to work out who it was. After doing all that laundry she knew the boys' clothes as well as her own. If it was one of them, she wouldn't hesitate to leap out and scare the living daylights out of him, find a release for her pent-up emotions. Unless it was Einar. In that case she hadn't a clue what she'd do. Probably just close her eyes and hope he wouldn't find her.

For the last couple of weeks she had avoided being alone with him, and on the rare occasions when he'd managed to corner her she had pretended nothing was up, claiming to be so busy with her English studies that she couldn't get out in the evenings. The lie about a possible proficiency test and interview for an air-hostess job with Icelandic Airlines had dropped so easily from her lips that she almost believed it herself. But Einar obviously sensed she was avoiding him. It was a good thing he didn't try to test her on her English, as she hadn't actually opened the textbook in weeks.

She could just discern the steps at the far end of the cellar and cursed herself for not having peered through the keyhole sooner. If she had, she'd have seen the person descending – if not their face, then at least their legs and body. At that moment, to her horror, she noticed a pale rectangle by the bottom step, and groped instinctively for her mother's letters. Even as she felt the thick bundle in her pocket, it dawned on her that it was probably the letter to Einar that she had just finished reading when she first heard the footsteps. By some lucky fluke the visitor hadn't spotted it, but Aldís might not be so fortunate when he or she turned round.

The increasing light warned her that the person wielding the torch was drawing near. The bouncing glow showed how difficult it must be to clamber through all the junk. Aldís hoped with all her heart that the person wasn't heading for the little storeroom. So far the torch hadn't been trained directly on the door, but the further inside the cellar the person came, the more likely it was that she'd be discovered.

The silence was shattered by a loud crash as some large object fell over. Aldís almost jumped out of her skin but managed to clamp a hand over her mouth to stifle her scream. Through the keyhole she saw a cloud of dust rising through the torch beam. And for the first time she could hear the mysterious visitor whispering frantically, as if cursing his or her own clumsiness or the clobber on the floor. She couldn't distinguish the words but the voice sounded frightened, as if they were both in the same predicament. The torchlight flashed back and forth, suggesting the person was in a hurry to check that there was nobody in there.

'*Is there someone there? Come out, wherever you are.*' Aldís's heart lurched. The whispering voice was female but there was no way of telling if it was a girl or a woman. '*I know you're in here.*' But there was a slight hesitation, the pauses between words lasted a fraction too long, as if the speaker wasn't sure. Automatically Aldís repeated her prayers, though they did little to boost her courage. '*Come out. I've got something for you.*' The offer didn't sound remotely tempting. '*By the time I've finished with you, everyone'll know what a slut you are. What a bitch.*' Aldís closed her eyes tight. '*Come on. I've got a knife. A sharp little knife. Size isn't everything, you know.*'

Silence fell. A tear trickled down Aldís's cheek and stopped at her hand, which was still clasped over her mouth. She had nothing to defend herself with, but even if the little storeroom had been full of machetes and guns, she wouldn't have dared fumble for them for fear of betraying her hiding place. In a futile attempt to see better, she pressed her face to the keyhole so hard that her eye would probably bear the mark for days. But the pressure of the cold metal and two screws wasn't painful enough to distract her. There was still no sound, and when the torch beam was directed away towards the stairs, she almost laughed with hysterical relief. She bit her lip so hard that it split again and the familiar taste of blood spread over her tongue. The girl was leaving. She'd given up or convinced herself that Aldís wasn't down there. Now all Aldís had to do was sit tight and wait until she heard the trapdoor, then the front door, closing.

Taut with suspense, she focused on the steps and the envelope that was standing on end between the bottom step and the floor. The torch was pointing down, as if to light the visitor's path to the steps and all seemed to be going well. *Up you go, up you go!* Then the light paused on the envelope. Legs appeared in her line of vision, a figure bent and she saw a swirl of long dark hair. A profile appeared and vanished before she could decide if it was the girl from the photo in Einar's wallet. But she was sure it was a girl or a young woman; her movements and the slim legs were not those of an adult. The envelope was picked up off the floor and the torchlight pointed upwards, so Aldís could hardly see a thing. Then it was aimed at the floor again, as if in search of other letters. It stopped at the box and Aldís saw the girl lift the lid and heard the rustling of paper, followed shortly afterwards by a low gasp. Minutes passed. Finally, the box was closed again and Aldís saw the legs retreating up the steps. All went black and Aldís welcomed the darkness, rejoicing at being alone and invisible. She wasn't going to stir an inch until the girl had unquestionably gone.

Aldís was so stiff she could barely move when she woke to find herself lying in the foetal position on the concrete floor of the storeroom. She must have curled up like that in her sleep because the last thing she remembered was her head nodding as she sat propped against the wall. She had decided to spend the night down there, feeling it was safer to wait until other people were awake, then emerge from the cellar as if she had just turned up to work. It was lucky that she'd come out fully dressed last night, instead of merely pulling on her anorak over her pyjamas. No one would notice first thing if her hair was unusually tousled or her teeth hadn't been brushed. She could always nip over to her room later on for a quick tidy-up.

There was no way of guessing the time in the pitch-dark cellar, but she had the feeling it must be morning. She didn't dare open the trapdoor, though, until she heard the sound of ordinary activity upstairs. Before long, footsteps crossed the floor in at least two different places and the faint echo of voices reached her. She could have wept with relief. Nevertheless, she opened the door of the storeroom warily, still not quite believing she was safe.

Her toes ached with the cold and she could hardly feel the fingers of one hand but her eyesight was sharp after long hours in the dark. Stiffly, she rose to her feet, joints clicking. She emerged from the cubbyhole, impervious now to the smell of mould; she probably smelt the same herself. That gave her pause; she hoped no one would notice or question her about it. At the top of the steps, she waited until she was sure no one was near, then swiftly climbed out of the cellar. The light and warmth were so wonderful that she wanted to fall to her knees in gratitude, but instead she closed the trapdoor and dusted herself down.

There was a tap on her shoulder. 'Where did you spring

from?' Turning, she saw Einar gaping at her in astonishment. 'What's happened?'

Aldís ran a hand over her tangled hair and tried to appear nonchalant. Meeting his gaze, she determinedly ignored the thick dark lashes and chiselled cheekbones. 'Nothing, I just overslept and didn't have time to get myself ready.'

Einar looked sceptical but asked no further questions. 'I miss you. We never seem to see each other.'

'I told you, I've been busy studying.' Aldís's voice was as hoarse and dusty as if it had just been unearthed from a box in the cellar. She coughed. 'I don't want to be stuck here for the rest of my life.'

When he smiled, she remembered why she'd fallen for him. It had nothing to do with their situation. He was simply so much better looking than anyone else at Krókur – but then he would stand out anywhere. 'Me neither.' Gently he pushed back a lock of hair that had fallen over her cheek and tucked it behind her ear, then dropped his hand. 'What about taking a little break this evening? Just for an hour or so. We could hole up in the cowshed and chat for a bit. This place is doing my head in.' There was no doubting what he really wanted.

'Maybe. I don't know.'

'When do you think you will know? I'm not going to risk sneaking out if you're not coming. Veigar's got it into his head that there's someone creeping around at night and he's all jumpy about it. He gave us a bollocking yesterday, as if it was one of us.'

Aldís couldn't bring herself to smile or respond. She was still too overwrought, and besides, she wasn't sure she wanted to reveal what she knew about the girl. Not unless she could use it to drag his story out of him. 'I'll let you know at coffee time.'

She hurried out without saying goodbye. The sky was overcast; the morning unrelentingly dark. Aldís almost ran to the little house. She wanted to wash her face and brush her teeth. And throw up. Suddenly she felt horribly sick.

Chapter 28

'I worked out where I knew the name from.' Diljá was standing over Ódinn, hand on hip. As always, she was a little too dolled up.

'What name?' Ódinn gaped at her, aware of how dopey he must look. Since coming back from the geriatric ward he had been staring unproductively at his screen, perplexed by the endless stream of questions running through his mind. For the first time he felt grateful for the dullness of his workplace: no one had disturbed him or asked why he was sitting as if he had turned to stone in his chair. Until Diljá appeared.

'Eyjalín. I had the feeling I knew the name, remember? Now I know where from.' Diljá held out a sheet of paper, still warm from the printer. 'She wrote an obituary for Róberta.'

Ódinn tried to focus on the text. It was brief and gave no reason to suppose that the women had been related or particularly close. Apparently Róberta had lent Eyjalín a helping hand when others had turned their backs on her, and for that she would be eternally grateful to the dead woman. 'This doesn't really tell us anything.'

Diljá looked miffed. She snatched the paper back, the sudden movement causing a jingling among the tangle of necklaces that hung down to her waist. 'What did you expect?'

She frowned. 'Are you all right, by the way? I was told you were behaving a bit oddly – just sitting in front of your computer.'

'I'm all right. I was just thinking.'

'Then put your mind to this.' She waved the page at him. 'How about ringing this woman and asking her about her relationship with Róberta?' She shook her head in exasperation, causing her necklaces to rattle loudly again. 'Or do you want me to do it?'

Ódinn didn't know what he wanted. He was finding it impossible to get his head round the two different aspects to this case, particularly when one affected him so personally. 'Yes, please.' He tried and failed to smile. 'Since when have you been so interested in this case, anyway? I thought you believed it would bring bad luck or some crap like that.'

'I'm bored. Simple as that. And it looks to me like you could use some help. You're in a bit of a mess, aren't you?'

'I'm afraid you're right.' Ódinn chucked a pencil at the pen jar on his desk, but missed. 'If you wouldn't mind ringing her, that'd be great.'

'OK.' Diljá seemed on the point of adding something, then spun on her heel with one last jingle and returned to her desk. Just before she disappeared round the corner, she glanced back, their eyes met and he thought he detected pity in hers. He bristled; he couldn't stand it when people felt sorry for him. They were welcome to like or dislike him, but pity him, never. His anger brought him to his senses. What was he thinking of to let this shake him so badly? If he found it odd that Rún's grandmother hadn't said a word about the fact she'd worked at Krókur, he should go ahead and ring her and demand to know why. Staring blankly at his screen wouldn't solve anything. There might be a perfectly natural explanation for her silence. In fact, that might be why she'd been behaving so oddly towards him lately: she'd missed the opportunity to tell him about the connection when it first came up and afterwards had been unable to find the right moment. She must have twigged when Róberta introduced herself, since she knew the name of his office. Perhaps there was a reason why she hadn't mentioned it then, but he couldn't understand why she hadn't admitted it last time he took Rún round to see her and the subject of his new assignment came up. Was she ashamed of being linked to the place or afraid that her connection would disqualify him from the task? The more he thought about it, the more likely this seemed; in these times of austerity his ex-mother-in-law might well have been afraid he'd lose his job, with repercussions for her grand-daughter. A rather dramatic reaction, maybe – but not inconceivable.

Ódinn's colleagues looked up as he headed to the small meeting room for some privacy. It was freezing in there and he closed the window before selecting his mother-in-law's number. While waiting for her to answer, he inspected a framed poster that had not been on the wall the last time he'd used the room, and wondered if it had been put up as a joke or if Heimir misunderstood its meaning. It depicted a magnificent eagle soaring through the sky, with the caption: *Leaders are like eagles: you won't find either here*. Ódinn's gaze moved to the whiteboard which someone had finally got round to cleaning. Even the faint shadows of the writing that had been left there undisturbed for so long had now vanished – before he'd had a chance to work out the significance of the dates.

'Hello.' Rún's grandmother sounded as if she'd been taking an afternoon nap. She sighed as he introduced himself. He derived a certain amount of pleasure from finally being able to turn the tables; this time she was in the wrong. He got straight to the point.

'Why didn't you tell me you used to work at Krókur?' There was no response. 'Wouldn't it have been logical to let me know, under the circumstances?'

He waited, giving her a chance to recover her composure. When at last she spoke, her voice was higher, her tone less abrasive than usual. 'Would it have mattered? I worked there as a cleaner for a few months. I wasn't responsible for the boys.'

'But you knew what went on there?'

'So did lots of other people.'

'Most of the people who worked there are dead. You were probably the youngest member of staff.'

'How was I supposed to know that, Ódinn? After I left, I never gave the place another thought. I know nothing about the people who worked there before or after me.'

'You should have told me anyway. Now I'll have to report that I'm related by marriage to a former employee of the home and explain why I didn't reveal the fact straight away. If you'd only told me at the beginning it might not have been a problem, but now it'll look suspicious. Or at least very odd.' This wasn't strictly true: Heimir would have removed the case from him immediately if the connection had been established at the outset. Despite the fact that, as an engineer, he could be trusted to take a rational approach, as Heimir had put it.

'How did you find out?' Her tone was accusing, as if someone had betrayed her trust.

'Never mind.' Ódinn had no intention of sharing any confidential details, even if she was his former mother-in-law. Another person would have to take over the report now and he didn't want to compromise it for them. If there was any justice, it would land on Diljá's desk. She'd have her hands full dealing with this prickly woman. 'Since it's out in the open now, would you be prepared to tell me when you were there?'

'Can't you find out for yourself?'

Ódinn now bitterly regretted having apologised to her for his shortcomings; the woman didn't deserve it. 'Yes, I could, but I thought you might want to spare me the effort. If it's not too much to ask.'

There was a short pause at the other end. 'I started there in September '73 and stayed until February or March '74.'

'So you were there when the accident happened?'

'Accident?' She knew perfectly well what he meant; this was a transparent attempt to buy herself time. Perhaps she'd grown so used to lying to him that she now did it automatically.

'You know the one I mean. The accident that resulted in the deaths of two boys, Einar Allen and Thorbjörn, whose second name I can't remember.'

'Jónasson. Tobbi Jónasson.' She said it so quietly that Ódinn had to strain his ears.

'So you do remember?'

'Yes. Will it be in the report?'

'Among other things. But someone else will interview you about it.' He longed to give her the third degree but knew she would only hang up on him. 'Did Róberta contact you?'

'No.' She was lying. If Róberta hadn't been in touch, Aldís would presumably have asked who he was talking about.

'I see.'

'No. You don't see anything.' And with that their conversation was over.

'Don't go. We're expecting a visitor and this is as good a place as any to entertain guests.' Diljá's manner reminded Ódinn of his old cat when it used to bring home a bird or a mouse. 'Unless you wouldn't mind putting on the coffee and fetching the cups. We'll have to be nice if we're going to get anywhere.'

'What do you mean?' Ódinn had been on his way out of the meeting room. He had tried three times to call Aldís back before giving up.

'Eyjalín wants to meet us, so I asked her to drop by. She must have a lot on her mind because she said she'd come straight over.'

'Diljá, I'm not sure I should be present. Something's come up that alters my position and I assume I'll be transferred to another case.'

'Another case? There aren't any other cases.' Diljá poked him with a long, green fingernail. 'What's going on? Are you cracking up?'

'Yes, actually.' He told her what had emerged from his interview with Lilja. 'It would be wrong of me to have any further involvement in the inquiry. I hope you believe me when I assure you that I was completely unaware of this connection until just now.'

'Oh, for God's sake, stop whining.' She made a disgusted face. 'Since when did family connections matter in Iceland? Are you nuts? Everyone's related to everyone else. I'm not talking to this woman alone – I don't know enough about the case, so you can just get off your moral high horse and wallow in corruption like the rest of us.' She ushered him out. 'Fetch some cups. I'll see to the coffee.'

Not long afterwards the receptionist announced Eyjalín. They rose to their feet and, after she had removed her leather gloves, shook hands. To Ódinn her hand felt unusually hot, slender and elegant. He was careful not to squeeze too hard for fear of crushing the delicate bones. 'How do you do?' This was the woman in the photo that Diljá had waved in his face in Róberta's bedroom. Clearly he wasn't the only one with a link to people involved in this case.

The woman must have been around sixty, like his mother-in-law, but looked ten years younger. Maybe it was because she was so well turned out, in a coat with what appeared to be a genuine fur collar, under which she was wearing dark-brown trousers and a light-coloured cable-knit jumper that must have cost a packet. Around her neck she was wearing two gold chains that were worlds apart from Diljá's costume jewellery. There was no grey to be seen in her shoulder-length dark hair, which was as thick as that of a much younger woman. Perhaps it was a wig. Her features were aristocratic: high cheekbones, large eyes and full lips. The only visible sign of ageing was the fine lines around her eyes. Almost everything else about her looked as if it were tailor-made. 'How do you do?' She smiled awkwardly, surveying the room. 'This is cosy.'

Diljá made a face behind her back, then offered her a seat and some coffee, both of which she accepted. She sipped from the clunky canteen crockery as if it were the finest bone china. 'Nice and hot.' Then she replaced the cup on its saucer and stared blankly into space. Ódinn was beginning to suspect that Eyjalín was a bit unbalanced, and feared she would break down in tears or display some other even more disconcerting behaviour. It was lucky Diljá was here; she'd know how to handle the situation.

'We'd like to begin by thanking you for agreeing to meet us at such short notice. It's only right you should know that Ódinn took over the case from Róberta and I'm only helping him out. As you're aware, Róberta died very suddenly, so we're rather at sea – we don't know exactly what she did or didn't discuss with you. So I'm afraid this may seem a bit repetitive.' Diljá turned from the woman to Ódinn, and now they were both staring at him; Diljá as if she had succeeded in checkmating him; Eyjalín more innocently, eyes wide, as if she expected him to provide her with vital answers that she had long been waiting for.

'Eyjalín,' he began. The woman nodded as if to confirm who she was. 'We'd be grateful if you could briefly outline your dealings with Róberta and explain how you met.'

'She rang me.' The woman gazed into her coffee cup as if she could read the answers there. 'She'd found my letters among the papers from Krókur and the name's not very common – except in my family, of course. Though since I was born no one's wanted to use it. People might think the child was named after me.'

'Oh,' Diljá blurted out, then clamped her lips together.

'Originally she wanted to know if I had any idea why the boys' post had ended up in the home's archives – whether it meant they'd never actually received the letters from their family and friends.' She cleared her throat and sat up straighter. 'And lovers.'

Ódinn straightened his shoulders in an attempt to mirror the woman's dignified posture. He had the feeling she'd be more cooperative if she thought he came from a similar background. 'And were you able to enlighten her?'

'Yes. The boys never received their post. There was no end to the vindictiveness of the couple who ran the home. As you can imagine, the people who sent the letters couldn't understand why they never got an answer. Some of them are still coming to terms with it.'

Out of the corner of his eye, Ódinn saw Diljá raise an eyebrow. He hoped Eyjalín hadn't noticed. 'We've seen the letters – let me assure you that we haven't read them in detail but we have read enough to know that you wrote to Einar Allen, the boy who died during his time at Krókur.' Eyjalín nodded without comment, so Ódinn continued: 'It was treated as an accident, and no doubt it was, but I've heard rumours – completely unsubstantiated – that this wasn't the case. Do you have anything to say about that?'

'Yes.' Again the woman sat up; she seemed to shrink whenever Ódinn spoke, then inflate when it was her turn to answer. 'Einar and Thorbjörn were murdered. I'm convinced of it, and if it hadn't been for my father, the incident would have been investigated properly at the time and the truth would have come out.'

'Your father?' Diljá leant over the table, her necklaces clinking. Eyjalín eyed the costume jewellery and Ódinn thought he detected a faint look of contempt. 'How was he connected to the inquiry?'

'My father was a judge. I can go through my ancestry if you like, but it would be extremely tedious for you. Let's just say that members of my family have long held high positions in society and been considered . . .' She searched for the right word: '. . . superior.'

'But that doesn't explain why your father put a stop to the investigation. I'd have thought his type would have wanted everything done by the book?'

'He thought I'd killed them.' Eyjalín took a sip of coffee. 'Is this made from freshly ground beans?'

Neither of them knew how to respond. Diljá was the first to break the silence. 'Why did he think that?'

'I was in rather a bad way at the time and had gone out there secretly several times to visit Einar. Or try to. I only wanted to see him. I was there that night, but I wasn't involved in their deaths. I'd never have hurt a hair on his head. I loved him and he loved me.' She gave a sad smile but there was a deranged glint in her eyes. 'We were so in love.' She put down her cup and patted her mouth with her fingers. 'I'd written to him over and over again without getting an answer. You can understand how I felt, can't you?' Ódinn nodded fervently, trying to fake sincerity, and could see Diljá doing the same. 'If those horrible people hadn't withheld his post everything would have turned out differently. He'd have replied to my letters and I'd have been able to rest and recuperate as the doctor ordered.'

Ódinn didn't dare ask about her illness. The woman was such a bizarre mixture of formality and candour. Who knows what details might be volunteered? He let her talk. 'Róberta was the first person who believed me. Everyone else thinks I'm crazy. If I so much as mention it, they start talking about having me put away, so I've learnt to keep quiet.' She smiled. 'It can be useful to know how to keep one's mouth shut.

But when I met Róberta I was allowed to talk at last. We became great friends and she understood me, and, what mattered more, she believed me. Losing her was terribly hard. She'd promised to do everything in her power to expose the truth.'

'Do you know who was responsible – if it wasn't an accident?' Ódinn regretted having closed the window. It was hot and stuffy in the meeting room.

'I'm not sure – but I have my suspicions.'

'Would you be prepared to share them with us?' Diljá enunciated the words embarrassingly clearly, as if addressing a simpleton.

'I'm convinced Veigar was to blame. There was a rag blocking the exhaust pipe, but someone removed it and shovelled snow over the pipe instead. The most absurd part of the whole thing is that Daddy was so desperate to prevent suspicion falling on me that he made a deal with Veigar – the actual murderer – without realising what he was doing. He always thought I'd done it. So he wangled Veigar a good job and a cheap flat in town, and found a buyer for the farm. Everybody happy.' She screwed up her face. 'Except me.'

'Your father must have acted fast.' Ódinn wasn't sure he fully understood the sequence of events. 'Who found the rag and how did your father ensure it didn't fall into the hands of the police? They must have been summoned immediately.'

'Veigar found the rag. Or he and Daddy together. And me.' Seeing that they didn't follow, she elaborated: 'Just before it happened, Veigar had caught me behind the buildings. I'd given up trying to see Einar and was on my way back to the road where I'd hidden Mummy's car. I used to sneak over there at night sometimes. No one at home knew; they couldn't understand why I slept so much during the day and attributed it to my illness. Anyway, Veigar caught me, hauled me into his office and demanded to know what I was doing there. When he realised who I was, he rang Daddy and asked him to fetch me. That's why he was there when the whole thing was discovered.'

'So your father and Veigar were the first on the scene?' A light was beginning to dawn on Ódinn.

Eyjalín nodded. 'I was with them too. Daddy actually dragged me to the car. When he saw Einar and the other boy he tried to push me away but it was no good. I saw them. It was horrible.'

'And you say that Veigar noticed the rag?'

'Yes. I think I've remembered that right.' Eyjalín closed her eyes and remained like that for a moment. Then she opened them wide. 'Yes, that's what happened. Veigar found it.'

'But why would he have drawn attention to the rag if he'd put it in the exhaust himself? Surely he'd have taken you both inside, then disposed of it when nobody was looking? The police must have taken a while to arrive, so he'd have had plenty of time.' The look of complacency faded from the woman's face.

'I hadn't thought of that.' She ran her tongue over her lips, and her fingers, laden with gold rings, tapped out a nervous rhythm on the table. Her shoulders shivered as if she felt a sudden chill, but it couldn't be with cold as the heat in the meeting room seemed to grow more oppressive by the minute. 'Then it must have been her,' she hissed from between clenched teeth.

'Her?' Diljá was mystified.

'Her. The whore.' Eyjalín placed a trembling hand on her heart. 'Aldís. Of course.'

Chapter 29

March 1974

At last it seemed the end of winter was in sight. The faint promise of spring in the air was enough to lighten Aldís's step as she hurried from the little house over to the dining room. It was still an hour until sunrise but the darkness didn't feel as impenetrable as it had lately; it was as if it had been diluted. The air wasn't as cold in the lungs either, and didn't sting her cheeks or fingers. The bird fluttered overhead, apparently aware of the same subtle shift. It had rallied recently, as if it believed the worst was over and winter wouldn't last forever.

In honour of the occasion she had dressed in her least scruffy clothes and left her hair loose. She had put on mascara too and for once felt satisfied with her reflection. She was looking good and so was the weather. But that wasn't the only reason. If she'd been feeling as low as she had lately, she'd have dragged on her usual old rags and failed to notice the change in the weather and the light. But now the pain had lifted, and that was largely thanks to her mother's letters. She'd read every word of them, in the right order, at least ten times. Her eyes kept misting over with tears. She missed her mother so badly that there was no more room for resentment. And she wept for the injustice of the fate that had driven them apart.

In hindsight, it was as if neither had been in control of their reactions, as if inexplicable forces had been at work. The letters were a good example. If Aldís had been allowed to see her mother's repeated pleas for forgiveness and expressions of unbearable sorrow and loss, her rage would have evaporated instead of intensifying. Admittedly, it still wasn't clear why she'd thrown out that disgusting man, but at least she'd got rid of him almost as soon as Aldís left, which suggested that she had believed her and recognised what a creep he was.

Today Aldís was going to hand in her notice. Today she was going to march into Veigar's office, though she wasn't due to clean it until tomorrow, and make that call to her mother. She wasn't exactly looking forward to the conversation, but at the same time she couldn't wait to be free of the last traces of anger.

The bird whistled overhead, overshadowing Aldís's satisfaction at her decision to leave. What would happen to the poor creature when she was gone? She dreaded breaking the news to Veigar and Lilja as well. She couldn't decide which of them was likely to take it better, or if it would make more sense to face both at once. Now that she had finally made up her mind, she didn't want to spend another day here.

She'd have liked to pack this evening and leave Krókur first thing tomorrow, but that was wishful thinking. There was no one waiting to take her place and it was highly unlikely that Lilja would offer to take over her chores so she could get away sooner. Aldís was afraid they would force her to work out her notice; she wasn't even sure how long that was. A week? Two weeks? A month? Or even until her successor could start? What if they couldn't find anyone?

Would she be stuck here forever? No. Aldís made a detour round a large snowdrift and resolved that if that were the case, she would simply walk out.

The smell of coffee greeted her in the kitchen. That was unusual. Hákon was sitting nursing a steaming cup, the kitchen worktop was awash with water, and he appeared to have strewn the contents of the coffee packet over the table. She fetched a cloth from the sink, determined not to let this ruin her day. 'You're up early.'

'Yes.' He took a mouthful of coffee, staring into space. Once she was back up north or living in Reykjavík she would no longer have to be around people who barely noticed her.

'Any particular reason?' Aldís swept the water towards the sink with the cloth.

'Haven't been to bed yet. Just about to go.' Despite this announcement, he took another gulp of caffeine. 'Veigar ordered me to watch the place. He still thinks there's someone prowling round here at night.' Hákon drank some more, watching her over the rim of his cup. 'He thinks it's you.'

Feeling the blood rush to her cheeks, Aldís turned away to wring out the cloth. 'I wasn't outside last night, if that's what you're implying.' Thank goodness she'd refused Einar's request to meet up. She had to admit to herself that she was longing to be alone with him again: what held her back was the need to know more about him. Since she'd made no progress in finding out for herself, she'd probably have to ask him straight out. Perhaps she'd do it when they said goodbye. 'What on earth makes him think I'm wandering around at night? Not that there's any reason why I shouldn't – there's no reason for him to keep watch.'

'I think he's more worried it might *not* be you.'

'Did you see anyone?'

'Not a soul. Unless you count the man in the moon.' Hákon put down his cup and brought out a snuff horn from the pocket of his shabby anorak. He shook out a thick line onto the back of his left hand. Before sniffing it up his nose, he locked eyes with Aldís. 'You know that boy's not for you, Aldís.'

'What boy?' She knew perfectly well who he meant.

'I'm only telling you this in case you're sneaking out at night to meet him. You're too good for him.' Crumbs of black snuff clung to his septum.

'Well, I'm not.' Her protest was feeble. 'Why are you so sure he's wrong for me, anyway?' Her daydreams of a new life, far from this place, had sometimes included Einar, sometimes not. When she pictured a reunion with the girls from her class, he was part of the story, since most of them were now shacked up with boys from their school, uninspiring specimens though they were. Einar also had a bit part in the version where she was an air hostess, but he didn't feature at all in her imagined meeting with her mother. Daydreams didn't have to be realistic.

'Like that, is it?' A dark dribble of snuff oozed from one of Hákon's nostrils, heading for his upper lip, and Aldís felt her stomach churn. She averted her eyes, gripped the sink with both hands and retched violently, bringing up nothing but slimy saliva. Behind her she heard Hákon repeat: 'I said, like that, is it?'

A cold sweat had broken out on Aldís's forehead and she knew her face was chalk-white. The heaving had brought tears to her eyes and her mascara was probably smudged. 'I'm ill.'

'No. You're *sick*.' Hákon stood up, went over to the sink and put down his empty cup beside her. 'And it's morning.'

Aldís spat out more saliva and stared at him uncomprehendingly. 'What do you mean?'

'You'll work it out.' He left the room, his spindly legs hardly making any impression in his loose trousers.

Aldís turned back to the sink and retched again. This time she brought up a powerful gush of brown bile.

The phone call was postponed. All pleasure at having made the decision to quit her job and ring her mother had evaporated, leaving nothing but the despondency that had paralysed her for the last few weeks. This was the first time she'd actually vomited, though she'd felt queasy now and then in the mornings: all it took was a boy with a snotty nose, leftover porridge in a bowl, a drainy smell in the toilet. Of course it was possible she had a stomach bug and would wake up tomorrow feeling as optimistic and happy as she had this morning. But she knew that was wishful thinking. Her breasts were tender and she was late, too. No further proof was necessary. She'd cast her mind back with an effort to her last period and calculated that she was at least two weeks overdue. It was a sign of the monotony of life at Krókur that she hadn't noticed sooner. Every day was the same; they piled up behind her with nothing to distinguish them.

But she mustn't go to pieces. She would get through the washing up after supper, just as she had managed to keep up a front this morning, at lunchtime and all afternoon. Work drove her on, providing her with a lifeline so she wouldn't collapse in tears.

'I'm going home soon.' When she turned round, Tobbi was standing behind her, smiling enigmatically. He held out his plate as if it were a special gift. He had come in late for supper because he'd been handing up tools to Veigar who was patching the cowshed roof.

'Just put it on the table.' Aldís studied the boy with his too-long hair, his cheeks still bright red from coming in out of the cold. 'Congratulations. Are you looking forward to it?' She wasn't sure what he wanted her to say and felt too dispirited to think of anything else.

Tobbi shuffled his feet. 'Yes, sure.' He scratched his head. 'Mum's ill. That's why they're letting me go.'

'She'll get better,' said Aldís, though she guessed the prognosis was unlikely to be good. Boys weren't allowed to leave just because their parents had flu. 'When are you off?'

'Tomorrow morning.' The big toes of both feet were sticking through his socks. His trousers were too short and Aldís realised he had grown since last autumn when she arrived at Krókur. He hadn't put on any weight, though; his worn clothes were as baggy now as the first time she had met him. 'I don't know if I'll see you again, so I just wanted to say goodbye.'

'I expect you'll see me at breakfast.' It came out brusquer than she'd intended. The boy's gesture of friendship had touched her more deeply than she could bear at that moment. It took so little to make her cry these days and she couldn't let him see her tears. 'Thanks, Tobbi, love. I'll miss you.' She forced a smile. 'I'm going to leave soon too, so perhaps I'll bump into you in town.'

'When? Are you moving to Reykjavík?' The eagerness in his face was heartbreaking. A boy of his age shouldn't be

309

that excited at the possibility of bumping into a woman he barely knew. 'Maybe I could visit you.'

'Yes, you do that.' Aldís turned back to the last bits of washing up.

Tobbi made no sign of leaving. She could hear him breathing behind her. 'Can I tell Einar?'

Aldís's hands stopped moving in the dirty water. A small air-bubble rose from the rubber glove with the hole in it. 'Sure, why not?' She heard Tobbi dash out, clearly excited to have something to tell. Another air-bubble escaped the glove. Aldís carried on washing up. A couple of glasses crashed together and one broke in half. Aldís fished out the pieces and threw them in the bin. She didn't bother to hide them under the other rubbish as she would normally have done, no longer afraid of a scolding from Veigar or Lilja. She had other things on her mind. Tobbi was bound to mention her imminent departure to Veigar in the car tomorrow. She would have to hand in her notice before then. She took the last glass out of the scummy water and laid it on top of the drying rack, not caring that it was cloudy and still had a crust of milk in the bottom.

Aldís knew the couple had gone over to the hall as usual after supper to pray – or so they claimed – but Aldís suspected it was a ploy to avoid helping with the clearing up. Perhaps they sat there reading or relaxing after the day's work.

She turned off the light and went out into the corridor. The door to the hall was closed but she could hear a muttering that could well be praying. Taking a deep breath, she ran a hand over her hair, then knocked before her courage could desert her. It reminded her of swimming lessons at school;

sometimes it was better to dive straight in than lower oneself into the water inch by inch. She opened the door without waiting for an invitation. The couple were sitting on the front bench, faces turned to see who had the audacity to burst in on them like that. Lilja's hands were still clasped together.

'What's going on?' Veigar seemed more surprised than angry. Anxious, even. Perhaps he was expecting bad news about the cowshed roof.

'I'm leaving. I just wanted to let you know.' It was all she had prepared. A silence fell that no one seemed willing to break. 'When can I go?'

'Leaving?' Lilja appeared hurt.

Veigar kept his calm, though it was obvious he thought she was being unreasonable. 'You can't just leave.'

'I'm handing in my notice. When can I go?' Aldís was aware that her face was scarlet. She wished this were over, yet felt proud of herself for speaking out at last. 'I know I have to work out my notice. How long is it?'

Veigar spluttered. Aldís couldn't remember seeing him at a loss before. 'Won't you think again, Aldís, dear? We were just saying it's time to review the wages and so on. There's no need to rush into anything.'

'I'm pregnant. I can't stay here any longer. When can I go?' The words poured out like this morning's vomit. She had a hunch that once she'd said this, there would be no turning back. The part of her that longed to get away had taken over and intended to make sure that she wouldn't be swayed by any fair-sounding offers.

The couple sat there, stunned. Veigar put his arm round Lilja who looked away and fixed her eyes on Jesus. 'Did you say pregnant?' Veigar licked his lips. He avoided Aldís's eye.

'Yes. I think so. Or, rather, I know I am. I've got to leave.' Aldís gripped the door jamb as if to stop herself running away.

'Who's the father? Is it someone from here?'

'That's none of your business.' She blushed even deeper red and tightened her grip on the doorframe.

'Are you going to keep the baby?' Lilja's gaze was still fixed on Jesus, as if the question was addressed to him.

'Yes. Well, we'll see.' All of a sudden Aldís found the situation absurd. She wasn't even sure she was going to have a baby, and certainly hadn't decided what would happen to it or to herself. Her despair had been so great – it simply mustn't be true. But if it was, she would just have to deal with it. Perhaps Einar would shoulder his responsibility. It would undeniably be easier to cope with his help; she knew from personal experience what it was like being brought up by a single mother. And, however much she loved her, she couldn't bear to end up like her own mother. She and Einar would just have to work it out together. That would be best for the child and for her. For him, too. But first they needed to get a few things straight.

It was as if Veigar read her mind. 'If the father's who I think he is, he might be able to help if you decide to get rid of it.' He stood up.

Aldís didn't understand this but sensed that it wasn't kindly meant. Her anger over the letters and the couple's intolerable behaviour suddenly flared up, as if she'd received a physical blow. 'You're wrong. Anyway, at least my child won't end up buried in a hole in a farmyard.' She let her fury get the upper hand. 'Buried *alive*.' Without waiting for his reaction she fled into the corridor and didn't draw breath until she was outside the building. Behind her, she heard Lilja give a scream of anguish that pierced her to the marrow. She put her hands over her ears. Revived by the fresh air, she grinned bitterly. There was no way they would force her to work out her notice after this.

The moon still hung in the sky and the stars lay scattered over the heavens as on any other evening. Nature seemed oblivious to the transformation in Aldís's life. She sat on the bench behind the little house, gazing into the darkness. She heard the snow crunching but didn't look round. Whoever it was would either walk past or stop and speak to her. What did it matter?

'Tobbi told me you're leaving.' Einar sat down beside her, hands in his anorak pockets.

'Yes. I've got to get away from here.' The puff of steam forming in front of her face made Aldís long for a cigarette. But there would be no more smoking from now on. Perhaps she could have one to celebrate if it turned out she wasn't pregnant after all.

Einar heaved a sigh. 'I was hoping it wasn't true.'

Together they stared out into the black void beyond the farm. 'Veigar made a comment about you, Einar, that I need you to explain.' Without looking at him, she continued: 'It's terribly important for me to know what you did and why you're here. I can't tell you why just now, but hopefully there'll be a chance later.' She could hear him breathing heavily and out of the corner of her eye she saw him bow his head. 'I have to know, Einar. You have to let me in on the secret.'

And just as Aldís thought things couldn't get any worse, the impossible happened. But it wasn't until she came across the bird, lying dead in the snow by the door to the little house, that her tears finally began to flow.

Chapter 30

Diljá came and perched on the corner of the desk in Róberta's cubicle, where Ódinn had taken refuge after their meeting with Eyjalín. He couldn't face returning to his own desk and having to speak to his colleagues or resume work on the report that it was now clear he would never finish. His immediate impulse had been to rush out of the building but he hadn't known where to go. Diljá put her warm hand on his shoulder. 'I told you. Iceland is a small country. You can't turn a corner without bumping into an old friend or a relative, or an ex. Almost everyone's connected somehow.'

Ódinn gave a hollow laugh. 'Whatever.'

'This is bullshit. I really don't see why you should give up the case.' Diljá folded her arms, pushing up her shapely bosom, and for an instant Ódinn forgot his troubles, then he looked away, ashamed. 'Seriously. Who needs to know? Heimir wouldn't find out if you tattooed it on your forehead in big letters.'

'I have to declare it. I don't care who knows about my connection to Aldís. I can't go on with it for my own reasons.' There was no way he could sit down at the computer and bash out this new information for the report. It was hard enough trying to write objectively when you knew the people involved, let alone when your former mother-in-law, the grandmother of your child, was accused of causing the death

315

of two boys forty years ago. It didn't matter that the person who'd made this claim was a fruitcake. 'I'm finding it hard enough to keep my head straight, and I find I keep having to manipulate the facts, however clearly I try to set out Eyjalín's accusations.'

'Are you close to Aldís?'

'God, no. She can't stand the sight of me, and it's mutual.' Ódinn exhaled. 'I'm thinking of Rún. My daughter's got real problems. It would be terrible for her to witness the media frenzy if it emerged that her father had mishandled this investigation and that her grandmother was a murder suspect.'

'Oh, please. I don't believe Eyjalín knows a thing. So what if your former mother-in-law fancied this Einar, as Eyjalín claims? Last time I checked, young girls didn't go around killing the boys they were crazy about. And come to think of it, how can Eyjalín still be in love with someone who died so long ago?' Diljá rose to her feet. 'She's off her rocker – I hope you realise that.' Ódinn shrugged. In the circumstances he probably wasn't the best judge of who was or wasn't sane. 'But she must have been absolutely delighted to meet Róberta, and I bet the feeling was mutual.'

'How do you mean?'

'Róberta was lonely and didn't have many friends, then suddenly this posh woman turns up, thinking she's her saviour and treating her like a confidante. It must have worked like a drug on the poor woman. I bet that's why she took that stuff home – to earn brownie points with Eyjalín by returning the letters to her or making sure they wouldn't be referred to in the investigation. Unless she was planning to look into the matter herself. At the very least Eyjalín must have been the reason why Róberta started taking a personal interest. You saw the photo. Who on earth gives someone they barely know a framed photograph of themselves? And what kind of person would put the picture up in their bedroom? They were both a bit nuts. You should have seen Eyjalín at the funeral. You'd have thought she was mourning her twin sister.'

'That doesn't alter my decision. I can't work on this.' Ódinn rubbed his eyes. The lids felt like sandpaper. 'You'll sort it out, Diljá. The case will be in much better hands with you and your lack of compromising connections.' Ódinn stared at the photo of the boys on the wall and they stared back, forever frozen in 1974, the year the picture must have been taken. He was about to do some mental arithmetic to work out how old they would have been today when it suddenly dawned on him. The dates on the whiteboard; Einar had been eighteen when he died, much older than the other boys. And what's more . . . 'Jesus!' He took the photograph down from the wall.

'What?' Diljá leant in to scrutinise the picture. 'It's not as if you haven't seen it before.'

'Yes, but I've only just realised what it shows.' The photo of Einar and Thorbjörn must have been taken at Krókur early in 1974, at some point before their death on 5 March. Lára had been born in November 1974. The resemblance was unmistakable in the still-boyish features. Ódinn groaned. It also explained Eyjalín's hatred of Aldís, whose relationship with Einar had evidently been more intimate than the woman had cared to admit. She'd claimed that Aldís's feelings had been unrequited. No doubt that was why, once her theory about Veigar was shown to be untenable, she had shifted the blame for the boys' death to Aldís.

He tried to remember what Lára had said about her father.

Ódinn had taken little interest in her family and the subject had rarely come up, but he did remember that her father was supposed to have died before she was born, and that her parents hadn't been living together. He also had a vague memory of hearing that her father's family lived in America, though he could be wrong. Lára's patronymic was the generic Karlsdóttir, a second name often used in the old days when paternity was uncertain or the mother wanted to conceal the father's identity. But there could be no doubt: Einar was Lára's father and Rún's grandfather. 'I'm calling it a day. I can't take any more.'

Ódinn leafed distractedly through yet another magazine in the waiting room. He didn't know why he was doing this, only that it seemed to help fractionally to look at pictures of a bunch of carefree foreigners. Perhaps the solution would be for him and Rún to begin a new life abroad, far from Lára's grave and everything connected to her; far from Aldís and her messy past. He put down the magazine. Going abroad wasn't the answer: he and Rún would never be like the beautiful, happy people in the pictures. Besides, for all he knew the father and daughter in the golfing magazine might be coping with the same sort of traumas as them. Perhaps the father was afraid he'd murdered the mother of his child and that his mother-in-law had killed the little girl's grandfather. And the moment they put down their clubs they'd be overwhelmed by the horror of it all. Yeah, right.

He suspected Nanna and her colleague at the practice had deliberately avoided putting a clock in the waiting room in case the ticking triggered anxiety in their patients. Although he had nothing better to do than to wait for Rún, it was incredibly tempting to fish out his phone and watch the time pass. Without warning, the door opened and Nanna appeared with a flushed-looking Rún. He looked up from his phone. There were still ten minutes left. 'Could I have a word?' Nanna smiled warmly at Rún. 'You can wait out here in the meantime. There are some Disney comics on the shelf.'

Rún walked silently past Ódinn and sat down, head drooping. It hurt Ódinn to abandon her like this but he felt obliged to do as Nanna asked. As she closed the door behind them Rún looked up and their eyes met for a second before the door shut. 'Do sit down. I won't keep you long.'

'That'd be good. We've got to be somewhere else shortly.' It was a lie but he wanted to get back to his daughter as soon as possible.

'Right.' Nanna looked as if she'd been asked to break the news of a death. 'I just wanted a word with you about the condition you insisted on the other day – that I shouldn't talk to Rún about her mother's death.'

'Yes. I'd rather you didn't.' Ódinn didn't know what to say if she demanded to know why.

'I don't know what your objection is, but I have to say it seems very unwise. Of course, I'll respect your wishes, but I wanted to ask you to reconsider.'

'I can't. Not at the moment.'

She looked surprised, then narrowed her eyes when she began to speak. 'You asked if your daughter could come to me for counselling. It's very much against her own wishes – like most children, she'd rather do almost anything than talk to me. She's not here on her doctor's advice or because she was ordered to undergo treatment, so I assume you'll stop bringing her if I say I can't continue without addressing her mother's death. Am I right?'

'Yes. You're right.' He longed to confide in her about his worries, to let the floodgates open. But there was no way he could do that. Nanna would have to notify the authorities if it emerged that he thought he'd pushed Lára out of the window. 'It might be all right to discuss it later, but not now.'

'Then I'm afraid there's not much I can do for her.' Nanna seemed genuinely disappointed. She steepled her hands and Ódinn noticed how small and slender her fingers were. 'The accident's a great weight on your daughter's mind. It's not the only thing that's troubling her, but it's the most serious.'

'Not the only thing?' Ódinn sat up. 'What do you mean?'

'Well, for example, her relationship with her grandmother is more problematic than I realised at first. Rún's terrified of her. She also has various unresolved issues in relation to her mother, which have nothing to do with her death. Rún's life hasn't been easy, you know. And you have some responsibility for that, as I'm sure you're aware.'

Ódinn wanted to put his hands over his ears. It didn't bother him to hear that Lára and Aldís had failed Rún, but it hurt to have it flung in his face that he had too, though he knew he was guilty. 'I am aware of the fact. I'm trying to make up for the past. Unfortunately, it can't be undone.'

'Just saying that isn't enough. As a weekend father you could do the fun bits and ignore the rest. But now you have to deal with the difficult, boring, everyday grind. And you mustn't fail her. Don't forget that you're all she's got.'

'I do realise that.'

Nanna expelled air so loudly that it sounded like a sigh.

'Though I'm unhappy with your decision, I won't stop seeing Rún.' She put her head on one side. 'Do you realise what an unusual demand this is? Parents never normally interfere with their children's therapy. I can't actually remember a single example.'

'I wouldn't know,' Ódinn muttered. He didn't care; he had to think of Rún. And himself.

'No. Naturally you wouldn't.' Nanna licked her lips thoughtfully. 'Leaving aside her mother's death, I can talk to Rún about her life in general, her relationship with you and hopefully with her grandmother. Usually it does children good to spend time with their grandparents, but being a grandparent doesn't automatically make one a better person, so it may be that she's not the best company for Rún. If it's considered undesirable that she should be alone with her, you'll need to ensure that they only meet under supervision, and preferably not too often.' She studied Ódinn to gauge his reaction. 'How does that strike you? Is there any reason to be concerned about the woman's effect on Rún? What kind of a person is she?'

'I really don't know. We're not particularly close.'

Rún kept her eyes down and mumbled as they said goodbye to Nanna. They drove home through the slush in silence. As Ódinn wove his way through the traffic, he noticed that all the occupants of the other cars were staring straight ahead except for Rún, whose face was turned aside. People must think she was sulking: a spoilt brat who hadn't got her own way.

There was unusual activity outside their block. Ódinn nudged Rún. 'Look. Flashing lights. At our house.'

Rún turned and craned her neck to see. 'An ambulance.'

In the circumstances it seemed inappropriate to roar into the car park, so Ódinn took his foot off the accelerator. He wondered if he ought to turn round and pretend he'd forgotten to go to the shop, or offer to buy Rún an ice-cream. Last time she'd seen an ambulance close up it had been taking her mother's body away. But the damage was already done and Rún was bound to see through his ruse. So he pulled slowly into their parking space and got out, disconcertingly close to the flashing lights. The ambulance doors slammed and two uniformed men appeared on either side. 'Good evening.' Ódinn grabbed the driver's arm. 'What happened?' Seeing that the driver was about to reel off some routine questions, he added: 'There are only three people living in that building – us two and an older lady. Has something happened to her?'

The man darted a glance at Rún, then nodded, his face grim. He climbed into the ambulance, turned off the flashing lights and drove away. Rún looked at her father. 'Why did he turn off the lights?'

'Maybe they were broken.' He squeezed her small hand.

They were the only ones left in the building. Rún and him. The old lady had been right; she had been doomed. And that didn't bode well for him.

Ódinn didn't want to go inside. He lowered his eyes to Rún, who had her face turned up to his. In the yellow light her resemblance to her grandfather Einar was unmistakable. Stooping, he kissed her lightly on the head. 'Tell me something, Rún.'

She frowned warily. 'What?'

'I know you don't like talking about it but it's terribly important to me that you do now. Then I promise never to mention it again. Ever.' He kissed the top of her head again, smelling the faint fragrance of her shampoo that he wasn't allowed to pinch. He understood: it smelt too good to be wasted on him. 'Why don't you want to talk to your grandmother? Is she mean to you? Does she hurt you or do something you don't want her to?'

Rún shook her head. 'No. Promise never to talk about it again?'

'Yes.' Ódinn held up both hands. 'Scout's honour.' Rún seemed to accept this. 'She keeps asking me questions. She holds me tight and won't let me go. I don't want to answer.'

'What does she ask about?'

'The morning Mummy died.'

Ódinn hesitated. 'About whether you were awake?'

Rún dropped her gaze to the ground. The hot-water pipes had melted the snow, revealing wet grey paving stones, and Ódinn hoped she wasn't picturing the pavement her mother had fallen onto. Her voice was high and thin when she answered: 'Yes.'

Ódinn decided to go for it. He wouldn't get another chance. 'Does she want to know if you heard or saw me in the flat?'

Rún jerked and looked up at him in surprise. 'You? No. She asks about herself. If I was awake when she arrived.'

Ódinn was speechless, astonished at himself for not having thought of it before. He hadn't gone anywhere near the flat; it was Aldís who had been involved somehow. Now that his eyes had been opened, it was easy to visualise: she'd turned up with the laundry and dropped in to see her daughter on the way, perhaps for a coffee. But instead she must have quarrelled with Lára, lost her temper and pushed her to her death as she was sitting smoking on the windowsill. Either deliberately or accidentally.

Ódinn felt drunk with relief. It was as if he'd been reborn, not as a new person but as himself, as he had been before all this started. He hadn't committed any crime. He might not be proud of his past failings but, in comparison to Aldís, he had nothing to reproach himself for.

He no longer felt cold. Suddenly he was filled with a sense of courage and optimism that he'd forgotten he was capable of. How could he have failed to work this out earlier? All the weird things he'd been seeing and hearing recently must have been his subconscious trying to wake him up, trying to alert him to the fact that all was not as it should be – and nothing to do with the dead trying to contact him. He wasn't doomed! Now his life could begin again.

There was no point hanging around; he was going to sort everything out. 'You know what, Rún? Today is a new beginning for you and me. Tomorrow I'm going to talk to your grandmother and from now on she'll leave you in peace. This time we're going to handle things right.' He looked to the east, as if anticipating a premature sunrise in their honour, but there was nothing to see but the dark evening sky, preparing for night. 'A new life, Rún. Starting today.'

She regarded his wide grin dubiously, but eventually returned it. Ódinn shoved his hand in his anorak pocket in search of the house keys but pulled out Róberta's key instead. The key to her garage that he'd forgotten to return. An inexplicable chill ran down his spine and he put it back in his pocket. He'd return it tomorrow. On the first day of their new life.

Chapter 31

March 1974

Her tongue felt like an old flannel, but Aldís couldn't drag herself to the bathroom to quench her thirst. She lay face down on top of the colourful bedspread. She had no tears left. Her life lay in ruins and she had no future. But she'd known that, even before she spoke to Einar and asked him the one question that really mattered. She had confided in him that she'd read his letters and believed she'd had an encounter with Eyjalín, who was completely insane. When he didn't contradict this, her fears about what the girl might be capable of redoubled. But that hadn't been the worst part of their conversation.

What a terrible fool she'd been. But at least she'd done one thing right: she hadn't told Einar she was pregnant. By the time he'd finished talking it had been unthinkable. She had stood up, grey in the face, and taken herself back to her room, stopping only to bury the bird's corpse in the snow. Only then had she allowed the tears to flow, overwhelmed with grief for the poor creature, but far more for her own stupidity and shattered dreams of a future in which she and Einar brought the child up together, happy ever after.

Einar had done his best to play down his part in what he and Eyjalín had done, hinting that she had been responsible.

But his eyes were evasive and Aldís was suddenly old and wise enough to see through him. No one would let himself be tricked into going along with such an act.

Aldís burst into painful sobs and rolled over onto her back. Her breasts felt sore from lying on her front. Her thoughts went out to Eyjalín, wondering if she'd suffered like this after Einar got *her* pregnant. She must have done, though for different reasons. Aldís was miserable because she didn't know where her life was heading; all she knew was that the outlook was bleak. Eyjalín had suffered because she had a tyrannical father who'd been implacably opposed to her relationship with Einar and, even more, to her having his child. Aldís had grown up without a father, so she couldn't really put herself in the other girl's shoes. And even if she'd had a father, she was sure she would never have resorted to that method of ending her pregnancy.

Einar had seemed detached as he told her the details, as if he'd merely been a bystander. Aldís closed her eyes and clutched her belly at the thought of the wire coat-hanger and his comment that the method was widely used around the world. She had involuntarily crossed her legs on the bench, as if afraid he would produce one there and then, and invite her to try it.

Einar had noticed and fallen silent until she asked him to go on. Yet she couldn't bear to listen to the end. She wiped her eyes. Why was she feeling sorry for herself? Compared to Eyjalín she had no reason to complain. The procedure had been both a success and a failure: a success in that they'd destroyed the foetus, but in their clumsiness they'd caused her to haemorrhage. Eyjalín had hidden her condition from her parents, concealing the fact that she was growing weaker and weaker. They hadn't noticed anything until forty-eight hours later, when she collapsed unconscious from blood loss. She was lucky to survive. To make matters worse, she developed an infection and was informed, after a long stay in hospital, that she would never be able to have children.

According to Einar, Eyjalín had incurred brain damage from the blood loss: she wasn't the same person after her illness. Aldís had refrained from pointing out to him that it wasn't an illness as such. It was futile trying to get him to see the facts.

His story explained so much. Eyjalín's father had arranged for Einar to be sent to Krókur rather than to prison, despite his age. That way the matter could be hushed up, he would receive his punishment, and Eyjalín's reputation would be saved. There was no court case that might have leaked out. And men who owed her father a favour had disposed of the health records. Meanwhile, Einar's mother had been persuaded to convince her son that this was the best solution: abortions were illegal unless the mother's life was in danger or the foetus was damaged, so his prospects were not good if the case went to court. It didn't help that they had performed the operation in a shark-fisherman's shed and disposed of the foetus in the sea.

If they hadn't done that, Einar would never have come to Krókur, and by now Aldís would have rung her mother and would be considering where to go next, to Reykjavík to pursue her dream of becoming an air hostess, or back up north to her childhood home. But now all doors were closed to her, and all she wanted was to go to sleep and never wake up. Perhaps the bird would be waiting for her on the other side, plump and happy in the land of eternal summer. Yet there would be no justice if she took her own life because of what Einar and Eyjalín had done. Someone always gets punished when a crime is committed, but not always the guilty party.

As Aldís lay and wept over her fate, she realised she had at least made one sensible decision. She hadn't told Einar about his unborn child and now she never would. She wanted nothing more to do with him and would simply have to solve the problem of the baby's patronymic at a later date. She wouldn't bat an eyelid if they met in the street, even if he had a girl on his arm and she was alone. And of course she would be alone. Men didn't want other men's children; at least her mother had never married and the only man who had wanted her hadn't loved her enough to leave her daughter alone. She'd probably end up working at a bakery like her mother, and the high point of her week would be when the French waffles didn't sell out and she was allowed to take the leftovers home.

Aldís leapt to her feet and was rewarded with a headache and dizziness. It was time to snap out of her self-pity. The thought of cold water from the tap galvanised her, and although her head was still splitting, the dizziness receded. She picked up her anorak from the floor where she had flung it and regarded the tight garment anxiously. She'd never be able to zip it up over a baby bump. Would she have to spend all her savings on maternity clothes that she'd never need again? No, she'd rather put up with having a cold stomach.

Oddly enough, she no longer had the slightest doubt that she was pregnant. This morning she had allowed herself to hope that there was some other explanation, but now that seemed laughably childish. She should have cottoned on some time in the last two weeks, but she'd pushed the thought away, and if it hadn't been for Hákon's remark in the kitchen, she would have carried on ignoring the obvious.

There was a tap on the door. It made a hollow sound and Aldís's heart beat faster as she called out, 'Who's there?' What would she do if it was Einar? She felt sick remembering what he'd said at the end of his story: he was planning to dig up Lilja and Veigar's dead baby and threaten to expose them if they didn't let him leave. This had been the final straw. There was something wrong with him, some inner coldness that she'd failed to notice before. For an instant she considered climbing out of the window and letting herself fall to the ground.

'It's Hákon,' came the reply.

Curious to know what he wanted, Aldís opened the door a crack without giving a thought to her appearance. None of the workmen had ever knocked on her door before. And she hadn't minded; it was good to be left in peace in her room without having to worry about visits at all hours. 'Hello.' Her voice was husky.

Hákon surveyed her dishevelled appearance in surprise. 'Sorry to disturb you.' The man was barefoot and his pyjama trousers bulged over the waistband of his jeans. 'I don't know what's going on, Aldís, but Lilja was here just now. She wanted to talk to you but she was in such a state I wouldn't let her in.'

'Oh?' Aldís felt her knees buckling and clung to the door. She couldn't face a scene with Lilja on top of everything else. Besides, she was perfectly capable of berating herself; she didn't need Lilja to do it. 'What did she want?'

'I don't know how to say this but she wants you out of here.' Hákon ran a hand through his untidy hair. His stubble was grey, his cheeks covered in a network of broken veins. 'This evening.'

'This evening?' Aldís gasped. She tried to remember if she had any clothes on the washing line and mentally reviewed her wardrobe. When she came here one battered old suitcase had been enough, though it was falling apart. She'd added next to nothing to her possessions since then. 'Where am I meant to go?' Of course he wouldn't know, but who else could she ask?

'Don't you have any friends or family in town?'

Aldís shook her head. She felt like a child.

'Do you want me to talk to Lilja? They'd have to allow you time to make arrangements.'

'No.' Aldís bit her lip and it split in the same place as it had that night in the cellar. The taste of blood did nothing to distract her from her predicament. 'I'll go anyway. I'm not staying here a minute longer.' Petulantly, she thought to herself that Lilja would regret this: Aldís would die of exposure, alone on foot with her suitcase on a winter's night, and everyone would blame the couple.

'You're not going anywhere unless you have somewhere to stay. You can't seriously be planning to spend the night outside?'

'I'll work something out.' Her knees were about to give way.

'What's going on?' Hákon put his hands in his pockets and only then realised that his pyjamas were sticking out. Embarrassed, he tried clumsily to tuck them under his waistband. 'Lilja was in such a state I thought she was going to

330

explode. She was calling you such ugly names I had to tell her to shut up – I was shocked.'

'She's a stupid old bitch. I want to leave. If she comes back you can tell her that. I'm packing and then I'm going.' There was a lump in her throat but she didn't let the tears spill over.

'You're not leaving on foot. Are you mad? Lilja said Veigar would drive you to town. You're to go and sit in the car when you're done. She said Veigar'd be ready in about twenty minutes. Can you pack that fast?'

'Yes.' If she told him how few possessions she had, the tears would overflow.

'Make him drive you to the Central Bus Station. They'll let you rest in the waiting room till morning. You should be able to take the bus back up north tomorrow.' Hákon held out his hand. 'It was nice knowing you, Aldís. Best of luck. Remember things are never as black as they seem.'

Aldís could feel the rough skin of the man's palm. 'Thank you. Good luck to you, too.' She closed the door, threw her suitcase on the bed and began cramming clothes into it. Next she emptied the dressing table and chest of drawers, and chucked the English textbook in on top. A few minutes later, having taken a moment to quench her thirst and splash her face with icy water, she added her toiletries from the bathroom and shut the case.

She sat down on the bed in her anorak and shoes, looking around for the last time. She wouldn't miss any of it. Then she went over to the window and looked out. The engine was running, though it could hardly be to warm the car up for her. She saw a short figure cross the drive, glancing around nervously. Tobbi spotted her, waved, then broke into a run and came to a panting standstill below her window. He signalled to her to open it. 'I just wanted to say goodbye. I heard Lilja say she was sending you away this evening.'

Aldís wished she could pull the boy up to her. 'Thanks, Tobbi. I'm sure we'll meet again. I'm probably going up north. Maybe you'll pass through some time.'

The boy peered round, then looked back up at her. 'Sorry I didn't tell the truth about that horrible girl in the dining room. I was so scared of her. She was lying in wait for me when I went to fetch the post and forced me to tell her which room was Einar's. Then she made me meet her and threatened to hurt me if I didn't help her see him. Then you turned up. She was horrible. She smelt of blood.' He was breathing quickly. 'Is that why Lilja's sacking you?'

'No. It's not because of that. It's not your fault – it's mine.' She was about to say more when she was distracted by a figure appearing round the corner. She recognised him by his gait, the way he ducked his head against the wind. She wanted to say a hurried goodbye to Tobbi and shut the window. If Einar had heard about her dismissal, he'd want to know the reason and she couldn't explain. Though at least discussing it through the window would be preferable to having him in her room.

'You're both here. Just the people I wanted to see.' Like Tobbi, Einar kept his voice down. He snatched off the smaller boy's hood and ruffled his hair, making it even more of a mop than usual. Then he looked up. 'I just wanted to warn you. She's here. I caught a glimpse of her just now behind the buildings. You'd better lie low.' He had no need to explain: Tobbi pulled up his hood and peered around fearfully. To Aldís's relief, Einar didn't seem to have heard that she'd been dismissed. Now she'd never see him again and could concentrate on sorting out her life. Seeming to sense this, he stared at her as if he wanted to memorise every detail of her tear-swollen face. Only then did he register the state she was in. 'Are you ill?' She shook her head, wiping her face as if to make it smooth again. Einar looked as if he was about to ask more questions, so she said a quick goodbye, closed the window and watched them cross the drive together.

A movement by the corner of the main building brought a knot of fear to Aldís's stomach. A slash of bright green cut through the gloomy surroundings. She opened her curtain a fraction wider in the hope of seeing the movement again and thought she could hear some sort of commotion and shouting. Einar and Tobbi seemed to have heard the noise too because they stood frozen to the spot beside the car. Two figures appeared round the corner and the boys immediately ducked. The figures headed towards the yard, apparently startling the boys because Einar opened the car door cautiously and he and Tobbi slipped into the back seat. The larger figure was having difficulty dragging the smaller one along. Not until they drew near could Aldís see who they were.

Dropping the curtain, she backed away from the window. The hairs rose on her arms and she hastily turned off the lights so no one could see in. What if Eyjalín evaded Veigar's clutches? She might still have the knife she had threatened to use that night in the cellar. Curiosity drove Aldís back to the window. She saw that Veigar was trying to march Eyjalín, with a great deal of kicking and screaming on her part, over to his office. He was probably planning to lock her in the little storeroom, where troublemakers were sometimes left to cool their heels, while he waited for the police. The thought of Eyjalín shut up in the dark pleased Aldís no end.

The girl kicked and struck out, and apparently managed to claw Veigar in the face as he opened the door. At that he lost control and slapped her. Eyjalín slumped down and Veigar dragged her inside. The door closed; everything returned to normal: Aldís might almost have dreamt it. Then the lights went on in the house.

Aldís turned her gaze back to the car. There was no movement visible; neither boy stuck his head out to check if the coast was clear. Perhaps they had got away while she was preoccupied watching Veigar and Eyjalín. That must be it. There was a strange air of stillness about the car; she couldn't quite work out what it meant.

Aldís sat down on her bed and stared at the suitcase by the door. On the way south the bus driver had tied up the handle with string for her. Perhaps it would be the same driver on the way home. She had nowhere else to turn. Her savings wouldn't stretch far in Reykjavík and who would want to employ a feckless girl who'd gone and got herself pregnant? Worst of all, she hadn't rung her mother. She'd have preferred to hide behind the telephone receiver while delivering her news. She remembered reading somewhere that you could never really go home once you'd grown up; the chick couldn't crawl back into the egg. Nothing would be the same.

Well, she would just have to deal with that problem later. Presumably she'd be able to phone from the bus station. What to do in the immediate future was her most pressing concern now. She had no desire to sit out in the car and wait while Veigar dealt with Eyjalín; it might take half the night. Perhaps, given what had happened, they wouldn't leave until tomorrow morning after all. Aldís flopped back on the bed. She closed her eyes and tried to block out all thoughts. Now she just needed peace to exist.

She was jolted awake from a fitful doze by the sound of a car, and stumbled to her feet, convinced that Veigar must have set off for town with Eyjalín. But his car hadn't moved. Another vehicle had parked in the yard and out stepped a man she didn't recognise, wearing an overcoat. He glanced around, apparently unsure about where to go, then Veigar appeared and beckoned him over.

For a while nothing happened. But Aldís couldn't tear herself from the window, so she witnessed the moment when Veigar, Eyjalín and the stranger finally emerged.

Eyjalín kept her head down and allowed herself to be propelled along by the stranger who had his arm round her shoulders. As they passed Veigar's car, he opened the driver's door as if to switch off the engine, only to reel back, clamping a hand over his nose and mouth. He made a second attempt and this time managed to turn off the engine, then shouted to the stranger who went over to join him. Eyjalín tore herself free and peered inside, in spite of the man's ineffectual attempts to stop her.

The silence was shattered by the girl's piercing scream. The three of them were standing there at a loss when Hákon came running out in his pyjamas. He shoved Eyjalín aside, looked in the window, then tore open the rear door.

Aldís clapped her hand over her mouth when she saw him pull a body out of the car and lay it on the snow. It was Einar. Next he pulled out Tobbi.

They lay in the snow, deathly still. Like the bird.

Standing there at the window, watching through her tears as Veigar snatched something that looked like a black cloth out of the exhaust pipe, she realised that it should have been her in the back seat; her, lying there staring with glazed eyes at the night sky. Not poor little Tobbi. Someone always gets punished when a crime is committed, but not always the guilty party.

Chapter 32

'I couldn't care less if you believe me, Ódinn. I long ago gave up worrying what other people think of me. If it weren't for Lára and then Rún, I'd have got in touch with the authorities years ago. For the first few years after I left Krókur, I was convinced no one would listen to me; no one would take a young single mother seriously, and if I'd tried to alert people to what had happened I'd have been lucky not to be locked up in the loony bin.' Aldís wrapped her arms round her thin body and leant back on the sofa. She was surrounded by embroidered cushions, decorated with lurid designs of stags and colourful flowers in wine-red and moss-green shades. Ódinn and Lára had received two of these cushions as a housewarming gift, and on the rare occasions that he'd visited their old flat after the divorce, they seemed to have proliferated. What had become of those kitsch, badly stuffed cushions? Perhaps one had been placed under Lára's head in the coffin. 'In any case, access to information was very limited in those days. Just because I didn't see any news about the investigation, that didn't mean it wasn't happening. But when I still hadn't seen a word about it in the papers two years later, I began to despair that nothing would ever happen.'

'Well, it has nothing to do with me any more. You'll have to discuss your version of events with my successor. And presumably the police too.' Ódinn was longing for a coffee but Aldís hadn't offered him any refreshment.

'It's not *my version* – I was a witness. I'm telling you what I saw and what I know.'

'You'll still have to discuss it with someone else. We'll find out later this week who's going to take over the report – there's no time to lose if they want to meet the deadline.'

'You think this all boils down to some *report*?'

'No. I realise it doesn't.' Ódinn held his temper. Their conversations always descended into sniping. 'But the report will give you a chance to bring this to the public's attention. If that's what you want. I don't suppose you gave Róberta too easy a time.'

'She was such a mug. I don't know what her intentions were but she seemed to be snooping into my affairs on Eyjalín's behalf. You can imagine how I felt about helping her.'

It seemed obvious now that Aldís had sent Róberta those threatening e-mails, getting decades of repressed rage out of her system. His theory was lent support by the presence of an old computer with a cumbersome monitor in the room opening off the dining room. 'Did you threaten her?'

Aldís hugged herself tighter. 'She wouldn't listen when I said I didn't want to talk to her. I'd had enough of her endless phone calls, here and on my mobile and at work. It's not as if I'm indispensable – I'm sixty and competing with immigrants who make no demands. No one wants to employ an old woman who's always on the phone. It's still six years till I can claim my pension, and the dole only lasts two years. A man with your education should be able to work out the shortfall. I can't survive on thin air.' Aldís loosened her arms and took a deep breath. 'Yes, I sent her some messages. What else could I do?'

'I don't know.' Óðinn shifted and his chair protested. It must have been a long time since a man last sat on it. 'I didn't come here to judge you for what happened in the past, Aldís.' The past no longer mattered apart from a few details he'd come here to straighten out in order for him and Rún to start living a normal life. 'If Lilja intended to murder you by stuffing the rag in the exhaust pipe, she should be charged, but I wouldn't get your hopes up. Even if she was the only person who knew you were supposed to wait in the car, it'll take more than your unsupported testimony to stir the prosecution service into action after all these years. Especially as Eyjalín will do everything in her power to convince them that you were guilty. I'm no lawyer but I assume they would examine the possible motives. People don't just go around killing for no reason. If the woman had no clear motive for wanting you dead, no one will listen to you.'

'Do you think I haven't thought about why she did it?' Aldís went on to tell him about the deformed baby that Veigar had taken from Lilja's bed and buried at the foot of a tree. She described how she had blurted out to the couple that she knew what had become of their child, and guessed from Lilja's reaction that she hadn't known the whole story until that moment. The realisation that her baby had been born alive after all and that her husband had killed it must have tipped Lilja over the edge.

Her madness had found an outlet in attempting to silence Aldís – the 'Whore of Babylon', in Lilja's eyes. When all else fails, it often helps to kill the messenger.

'I thought about it as I was travelling back up north on

the bus, and every evening for years. I didn't exactly have many distractions, living with my mother, bringing up Lára alone. Otherwise I might have forgotten all about it. In fact, I'd given up brooding on it long before Róberta got in touch.'

Aldís hugged a cushion to her, stroking it as though it was a cat. She seemed exhausted, like a counsel for the defence who has presented her summing up, but knows it's not enough.

'I'm not here about that, Aldís.' Ódinn shot a glance at the cushion and she put it down. 'I need to talk to you about your relationship with Lára. And Rún.'

'In that case you'd better tread carefully.' Anger brought colour to his ex-mother-in-law's cheeks and for the first time Ódinn could picture what she'd looked like as a young woman. Pretty, but not too beautiful; just what most men like.

'What do you mean?' Ódinn's voice conveyed his weariness with this endless hostility.

'I know what's behind this. You're going to accuse me of something that you, of all people, have no right to.' She snorted. 'I brought Lára up so she wouldn't suffer the same fate as me and my mother. You can imagine how I felt when you walked out on her and history repeated itself, in spite of all I'd done to try and prevent it.' She met Ódinn's gaze with such contempt that he felt his cheeks burn. 'You ruined my relationship with her. She misunderstood everything I did to try and build her up, and took everything I said as criticism. No doubt you'll experience that for yourself. Though I hope not – I'm too fond of Rún.'

'I reckon I know what happened that morning.' If he didn't come straight out with it, he would only have to sit here and endure more abuse. 'There's nothing "behind this" – I just don't want you to see Rún any more, that's all. She has to look forward now, not back. If she remembers anything, I want her to forget it. I don't care about justice. I just want to take care of Rún and do what's best for her. It's up to you what you do but I haven't discussed it with anyone, so you needn't worry that I'll shop you.'

The contempt vanished from Aldís's face, to be replaced not by fear but by astonishment. 'What on earth are you talking about?'

'Lára. I know you pushed her. It doesn't matter whether it was an accident or not because it can't be undone. I won't go to the police. In return I just want you to leave me and Rún alone.'

'You're such an idiot.' Her voice was warm and full of pity, quite the opposite of what Óðinn had expected. He thought he saw tears glistening in her eyes, but perhaps it was only the gleam from the wonky standard lamp beside the sofa. She raised her eyes to the ceiling and gave a low groan. Then, turning to face him, she told him the whole story. He sat in silence, listening until he couldn't bear it any more, then left without saying goodbye, the key to Róberta's garage still in his parka pocket.

The pencil travelled back and forth across the blank top page of the A4 pad. It left behind a steel-grey sheen, interspersed with paler shadows showing the imprint of what had been written on the page above, the page Óðinn had burnt for Rún out on the balcony. He had meant to rub the pencil over the whole page first, then read her letter from the beginning, but he couldn't help seeing the odd word and

phrase as he worked. All desire to read it had deserted him
by the time he finished, but he forced himself. There must
be no misunderstanding; too much was at stake. What he
read left him crushed, and afterwards he tore the page from
the pad and scrunched it up. He couldn't face reading it
again; didn't even want to see it. He sat in the kitchen with
the crumpled ball of paper in his hand, considering his
options: what would happen now and how could he make
the best of the situation, save what could be salvaged? But
whatever alternatives he came up with, however he approached
the problem, he could see no way out. It didn't matter what
action he took; he would never be able to accept the outcome.
Was he prepared to walk through fire to save himself? Emerge
badly burnt and reconcile himself to the kind of life and
suffering that would await him when it was over? No. Was
he prepared to put Rún through all that? No.

He ripped the paper to shreds, went out on the balcony
and let the wind blow the pieces away. Then he paced back
and forth in the sitting room, thinking until his head ached.
He rubbed his forehead, slapped his cheeks lightly, then
called to his daughter. 'Rún. Let's go round and see Baldur.'
He put on his shoes, dialled his brother's number and
announced their visit, then hung up and watched as Rún put
on her anorak. She smiled at him, excited about this unexpected treat, and he smiled back.

It was this smile that stayed with him as he slipped the
sleeping pills, which he had been prescribed after Lára's
death, into her Coke at the hamburger joint. Her smile, and
her carefree laughter during their brief visit to Baldur and
Sigga. Again and again he recalled the happy sound of her
childish voice as she said goodbye to them, promising to

come back at the weekend. And he remembered the moment in the car when he'd said she could give up handball, and suggested getting supper at the Hamburger Factory, for which he was rewarded with a kiss. Just like any normal father and daughter. No one would have guessed that shortly after this he would send them both to their eternal rest.

A passer-by, if they'd happened to glance into the car as the drug took effect and Rún's head began to nod, might have been taken aback. Especially if they'd seen the tears pouring down her father's cheeks as she went out like a light. But no one tried to stop him. And no one did anything to prevent him from driving into Róberta's garage with the sleeping child in the front seat and closing the door behind them, though he thought he'd seen a curtain twitch in one of the flats when he opened it.

Ódinn had switched off the engine while he was closing the garage door, and was sitting now beside his sleeping daughter, making up his mind for the last time. Once he switched on the ignition again, there would be no turning back.

The terrible letter flickered like a film behind his eyelids.

Darling Mummy, sorry I pushed you. You shouldn't be cross with me because it was your own fault. I was trying to sweep up the broken glass like you told me and if you'd stopped telling me off I wouldn't have pushed you with the broom. I wasn't strong enough to hold onto it and pull you up when you grabbed it. But it was your fault I broke the bowl as well. I was just so angry with you. You said I was making it up. But I wasn't lying that I'd seen Daddy out of my window. He was there and he was probably coming to collect me like I said. I just got so angry when you said he was stupid and couldn't wake up that early, not to collect me anyway. You shouldn't have said so many nasty things about Daddy all the time. Perhaps he didn't like being told off either and that's why he left us. So you must forgive Daddy, he didn't really mean to. He loves me. Now I've said I'm sorry, Mummy, will you stop coming into my dreams? I love you - a big kiss, your Rún.

It had confirmed Aldís's story.

That morning, when she'd opened the door to the flat with trembling hands, she'd found Rún awake and in a state of shock. Misinterpreting the situation and assuming that the child had witnessed Lára falling out of the window, Aldís had panicked and shooed her into her room. When the police arrived, Aldís had been sitting stunned on the edge of Rún's bed, having just heard the girl admit that she'd pushed her mother but that it hadn't been her fault. Out of her mind with terror, Aldís had lied to the police that she'd just woken the girl, so they hadn't tried to interview Rún on the spot. Afterwards, when they were alone together, Aldís had told Rún to say she'd been asleep, but the girl had stared at her and said she had no idea what she was talking about: she *had* been asleep, so there was no need to tell her to say so. Bewildered by this, Aldís had started to believe that she must have been mistaken. Yet she knew deep down that this wasn't the case, and took every opportunity to try and force Rún to tell her what had happened, but in vain. Out of concern for her grandchild she hadn't mentioned it to anyone, let alone reported it to the police.

It was that same concern that now made Ódinn turn the key in the ignition and roll down the windows. If news of this got out, Rún's life would be ruined. She would be commited to an adolescent psychiatric ward, then sent away to an institution until she had grown up, whereupon the next institution would take over. Adults served their sentences and were pardoned after a set number of years, but it was different for kids. He was afraid there was some defect in Rún. An inner coldness that meant, whatever he did to help her, she would always repeat the act in the end: push the class bully in front of a car; drown the child Baldur and Sigga adopted in the bathtub. Or something equally terrible. Even if he managed to cover up how Lára had died, he was unlikely to pull it off a second time – and for Rún it was even less likely.

Ódinn took her little hand in his. The small fingers twitched slightly and he gently tightened his hold. The air was becoming thick and grey, as if they were trapped in a mist. He no longer felt bad. He was feeling good. He smiled and took a deep breath. In no time at all he was feeling so happy that he'd forgotten the whole thing, forgotten why he was sitting here with his daughter in a strange garage, in poisonous grey air.

A smile split his face from ear to ear; he felt blissfully happy with his daughter there beside him. His eyelids grew heavy and he let them droop. Just before they closed he thought he saw Lára, walking past the windscreen, her face furious. With an effort he managed to open his eyes again but there was nobody there. Again a smile crept across his lips. Here they were, he and Rún, the two of them together. He couldn't remember why; all he knew was that it was good. It didn't get any better than this.

Epilogue

The newsreader concluded the report on the police investigation into Ódinn's death. 'Turn that bloody thing off.' Baldur was sitting in his dressing gown at the kitchen island, watching Sigga make coffee. In front of him were the weekend papers; he tutted testily over them every time he came to another spread containing a feature or brief item about his brother's case or the Krókur care home. 'We ought to cancel these bloody rags. They're a disgrace.'

'It'll pass.' Sigga yawned and popped a grape in her mouth. 'Something else'll happen soon to distract the media's attention. It's a slow news month.'

'You'd have thought they might at least consider the family before destroying someone's reputation.'

Sigga swallowed the grape and fetched a couple of cups. 'I bet you've read a million news stories that have hurt other people, without giving them a second thought. No one cares about strangers. We certainly don't.' She stationed herself in front of the coffee machine, as if to hurry it up. 'Just chuck them out. I don't want Rún to see them and I can't face reading any more myself.'

In spite of his declared intention, Baldur carried on reading. 'Now some bright spark has come up with the idea that the couple didn't kill their baby at Krókur – the bones the police found buried in the yard show that the child didn't have a brain, so it didn't actually count as human. It was more like killing a bodily organ, and there's no law in this country against killing your liver, for example. I hope that cheers up the woman who gave birth to it – she won't get any sympathy from anywhere else.' He snorted in disgust. 'And here's one comparing the composition of exhaust fumes now with those in 1974. According to what it says here, Óðinn was unlucky to die. It required much less exposure in the seventies because exhaust fumes were so much more toxic back then.' He looked up. 'How dare they write stuff like this? What difference does it make?'

Sigga refrained from pointing out yet again that he should just stop reading and flick past the coverage of the incident in the garage and Óðinn's investigation of Krókur. They never wrote about one case without mentioning the other.

'I'll refuse the free papers and cancel my subscription to the others tomorrow. I've had it up to here.' Baldur folded up the paper and stuffed it in the bin. 'I should've done that the moment they first rang us.' He pulled his dressing gown tighter around him. It was cold in the house; the clear night sky had left the land exposed to frost and the central heating was slow to react. 'What sort of person blabs to the media at a time like this?'

'Well, the woman who saw Óðinn going into her dead neighbour's garage and called the police, for one. And Diljá who worked with him on that bloody report. And Rún's grandmother, and no doubt several others I've missed. Perhaps the journalist was only trying to get in touch with you to get a clearer picture of what happened. It's what I'd have done in his place.' The coffee had finally filtered through, and although the funnel was still dripping, Sigga pulled out the jug and filled their cups. The delicious aroma made her feel properly awake at last. 'They weren't to know that you were as much in the dark as everyone else.'

Baldur accepted the cup in silence and swirled it round to blend in the milk. 'Do you think I could've prevented it?' He took a sip and closed his eyes while waiting for the caffeine to take effect. 'I keep wondering if he said something or dropped a hint when they came by, anything that should have rung alarm bells.'

'We've been over this, Baldur. He didn't say or do anything different from usual.'

'I just don't understand it.'

'No. Nobody does.' Sigga sipped her coffee again, warming her hands on the hot cup. 'Oh, by the way, I forgot to tell you. Rún's grandmother called again yesterday. She's still desperate to talk to you.' Baldur had the memory of an elephant when it came to people he believed had wronged him. When Aldís went to the papers about the Krókur case, he had stopped talking to her for good, so now the woman had resorted to trying to reach him through Sigga.

'Didn't you tell her the matter's closed?'

'Yes, I said you didn't want to talk to her and that she should stop calling.'

'How did she react?'

'I think she finally got the message. But she asked me to tell you that she only went to the media because the police refused to listen. She felt she had no alternative.'

'Yeah, right.' Baldur gestured to the bin where the papers now resided. 'She could have waited a bit longer after Ódinn's death. Then we'd have avoided all this publicity. Would it have killed her? She puts off going to the police for decades, then suddenly it's a matter of urgency. Stupid bitch.'

'She claimed it was vital for her to pre-empt someone called Eyjalín.' Sigga held up her hand when she saw that Baldur was about to explode. 'Don't blame me. I'm just telling you what the woman said. Anyway, I don't suppose she'll ring again any time soon.'

Baldur's shoulders relaxed and his face grew calmer. 'Good. I'm glad.'

'Well, let's hope so. She promised to stop trying to get in touch but claimed she had information that you'd regret refusing to listen to. All very odd.' Sigga ate another grape.

'Why didn't she ask you to take a message if it's that important?'

'Apparently she can only tell a relative – I can't be trusted because we might get divorced one day.' Sigga smiled at Baldur. 'Poor woman, she's not quite right in the head.'

'Who?' The child's voice emanating from the kitchen doorway was not at all sleepy. Sigga and Baldur were both equally embarrassed. They would have to get used to the fact that they weren't alone in the house any more. They hadn't a clue how long Rún had been standing there and neither was experienced enough with children to know how to discover in a roundabout way what she might have heard.

'Good morning, little lady.' Baldur held out his arms. 'How did you sleep?'

'Fine.' Rún clambered up onto the barstool beside him. She was wearing the new pyjamas Sigga had bought her after she was discharged from hospital. Baldur had refused to take anything from Óðinn's flat into their house; he wanted to stress that Rún was cutting all ties with the past. They had hastily redecorated a room to appeal to an eleven-year-old girl and filled the wardrobe with clothes. She was embarking on a new life and the old one was to be swept under the carpet. Sigga had her doubts about this uncompromising approach, but made no comment. How were they to know the best way to respond to such a series of calamities? No one could answer that except the professionals, and Baldur was adamant that they weren't to be allowed anywhere near Rún. The doctors had recommended counselling once she had recovered, but he pooh-poohed the suggestion. Sigga had her doubts about it too, especially when they discovered that Ódinn himself had sought help. Therapy certainly hadn't managed to save her brother-in-law.

'I dreamt about Daddy.'

The couple exchanged glances. Before the silence became too prolonged and awkward, Sigga said quickly: 'You know what, Rún, I dreamt about him too. It's not surprising when we're all thinking about him so much.' She wasn't lying; she had dreamt about Ódinn, and although she couldn't remember the details, her dream had left a lingering sensation of unease.

'He wasn't happy.' Rún put her elbows on the table and rested her chin in her hands.

'What?' Baldur gave her a friendly pat on the shoulder. 'Don't be silly. Of course he's happy. He's in heaven. Everyone has a whale of a time up there. Let's not think about him now. Let's talk about something nice. Like, I was wondering if you and I should go and see a film while Sigga's at the gym?'

Rún squeezed out a smile from between her fingers, then raised her chin from her hands and nodded. Shivering slightly, she said she would go and get dressed. 'I'm freezing.'

In the doorway she turned. Her pink pyjamas were a little too loose and the trousers were about to fall down. She looked so waif-like, somehow. Sigga felt a pang and cursed herself silently for not having paid more attention to the size, but consoled herself with the thought that Rún would soon grow and in no time she'd be having to buy her new clothes. She winked at the girl, who responded with a subdued smile, then vanished into the hallway.

'Everything's going to be fine.' Sigga leant over the table and took Baldur's hands. The chill from the granite worktop penetrated her dressing gown, giving her goose bumps. 'Everything's going to be *just* fine.' She tried to shake off the remnants of last night's dream and repeated her words as if to give herself courage. '*Just* fine.'

Baldur kissed the back of her hand, leaving a coffee-brown mark. 'Of course. Why wouldn't it be?' He didn't sound as convincing as she'd have liked.

Rún inclined her head as she stood outside the kitchen door, hoping to hear more. She sighed, unsure if it was from happiness or fear. She was happy here. Uncle Baldur loved her; Sigga too. Really, it was much better than living with Daddy, and much, much better than living with Mummy. Such a pity Mummy and Daddy couldn't understand that. If they'd loved her as much as they said, they'd be pleased for her and leave her alone.

Warily, she opened the door to her room and peered in. The bedside light was on. She hadn't turned on the main light because she'd been in such a hurry to go and find Baldur and Sigga. It was so much better than being alone with the shadows in this pretty room. She reached for the light switch.

The shadows fled, making everything much better. Rún breathed easier and went in. It would be fine, as Sigga had said. She was kind of dreading the time when Baldur went back to work because he was always away so much. Daddy had said that. She felt the hairs prickle on the back of her neck; she only had to think of the word, *Daddy*, to feel bad. *Don't think about him. Don't think about him*. Better to think that everything's going to be fine. Of course. Why wouldn't it be?

She dressed hurriedly. The wardrobe was full of clothes in every colour of the rainbow, but she always wore the same pair of jeans and the jumper with the big cross on the front. She felt comfortable in these clothes and didn't want to wear anything else. God would see the cross and think she was good and look after her. Perhaps she should ask Sigga to take her shopping to buy a crucifix to wear round her neck. Then God really would believe she was a good girl. Everything would be fine.

Rún hurried out again, closing the door behind her but leaving the light on. She walked quickly down the hallway but stopped herself from breaking into a run so Baldur and Sigga wouldn't ask what the rush was. She didn't want to have to tell them what she thought was after her. In spite of her resolve, she burst into the kitchen.

'You're in a hurry.' Baldur raised his eyebrows and smiled, pleased to see her. There was no question that he loved her. Suddenly she felt all warm. Now she had everything she could wish for. Then the warm feeling faded and a slight chill crawled down her spine. Everything would be perfect if it was just her and Baldur. If Sigga wasn't there, he'd have to look after her; he'd stay at home instead of going out to work. And they could be together all the time.

Rún beamed at Baldur. He returned her smile.

Everything was going to be just fine.

I REMEMBER YOU
YRSA SIGURDARDOTTIR

This horrifying thriller, from an international bestseller,
is partly based on a true story.

Don't go. Don't go yet. I'm not finished.

In an isolated village in the Icelandic Westfjords, three friends set to
work renovating a derelict house. But soon they realise they are not alone
there — something wants them to leave, and it's making its presence felt.

Meanwhile, in a town across the fjord, a young doctor investigating
the suicide of an elderly woman discovers that she was obsessed
with his vanished son.

When the two stories collide the terrifying truth is uncovered . . .

HODDER

Have you read Yrsa's crime novels?

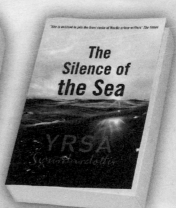

Out now

HODDER